STATE OF UNION

Book Two of The God Head Trilogy

Sven Michael Davison

BEDOUIN
PRESS

State of Union

For information about this title or to order other books and/or electronic media, contact the publisher:
Bedouin Press
P.O Box 570169
Tarzana CA, 91357-0169
www.bedouinpress.com

Library of Congress Control Number: 2012912820
ISBN: 978-0-9855528-5-5

Printed in the United States of America

Cover by Derrick Abrencia
Interior design by 1106 Design

Publisher's Catalog-In-Publication Data
Davison, Sven Michael.
State of union / written by Sven Michael Davison. — 1st ed.
p. cm. — (The god head trilogy ; bk. 2)
LCCN 2012912820
ISBN 978-0-9855528-5-5
ISBN 978-0-9855528-4-8

1. Nanotechnology—Fiction. 2. Terrorism—Fiction. 3. Science fiction. 4. Suspense fiction. I. Title. II. Series: Davison, Sven Michael. God head trilogy ; bk. 2.

PS3554.A96S73 2012 813'.54
QBI12-600156

FOR

Jeannine, Isaac, Abby, and Jake

Acknowledgements

I would like to thank the following with all my heart: Jeannine, for your continued love and support. Isaac, I can't help but love you more every day. Abby and Jake for your companionship. Ashley Pawlisz for your feedback on nano-technology. Steve Lekowicz for your skilled critiques. Marcy Natkin for your expert editorial skills. Mom, for your constructive criticism and support. Dad for your unconditional love. Mark for your sage advice. Roger DaSilva for your first-hand knowledge of Brazil for this book and *State of Mind.* For feedback, support, and help: Erin, Karl, Arjuna, Lucina, Derrick Abrenica, Rick Blackhawk, Steve Cantos, Peter Coggan, Devon Downs, Tomy Drissi, Perry Grundman, Don Jefferies, Danny Kaye, Van Ling, Andy Nelson, Jessie Parker-Campbell, Scott Preston, Bryan Reesman, Steven Rowley, Summer Simons, Bhanu Srikanth, Gina and Adam Vadnais, Nancy Van Iderstein, Peter Ventrella, and Ann Zald.

State of Union
Table of Contents

1. Quarry ... 1
2. Solipsism ... 10
3. Wake ... 17
4. Pandemic ... 24
5. Apostle ... 30
6. Maxwell ... 41
7. Immortality ... 47
8. Lenticular ... 54
9. Slide ... 67
10. Sommelier ... 70
11. Shelter ... 78
12. Missing ... 82
13. Max2 ... 91
14. Sword of Damocles ... 98

15. Sardines....103
16. Terra Nova....110
17. Beartracker....117
18. Homecoming....125
19. Promise....132
20. Travissi....139
21. Conquistador....147
22. Immunization....156
23. Rust....162
24. Garbage....167
25. Broken Council....171
26. Invasion....177
27. Kamikaze....186
28. Cargo....197
29. Foot Soldiers....201
30. Abort....210
31. Messenger....217
32. Tomb....220
33. Tsang....229
34. Terminus....235
35. Misdirection....243
36. Strains....249
37. Terrorists....256
38. Dope....260
39. Dream Spun....268
40. Regret....274
41. Punjab....278
42. Trigger....284
43. Mannequin....295
44. Regicide....298
45. Circle....305
46. Baboon....313
47. Hunted....322

48. Obsession 328
49. Children of Parks 332
50. Descent 341
51. Monkey Business 346
52. Pariah Express 352
53. Brain Freeze 359
54. Massacre 366
55. Conversion 370
56. Bells 378
57. Hope 382

Chapter 1
Quarry

A heavy beat vibrated the air. The music was a disjointed blend of Samba, Reggae, and Techno. Thick smoke, dancing strobes, and gyrating patrons made it difficult to identify the figures seated against the back wall on the opposite side of the dance floor. Jake pushed through the sweating population of the Ubatuba Surfclub. He had spent the past few months tracking down Roberto Pacheco and the trail had ended at this Brazilian bar.

Two years ago, Jake led an invasion force into Roberto's house. He had been running a child pornography studio in a Beverly Hills home. During the arrest, Jake lost his temper and severely beat Pacheco. His actions set Pacheco free and Jake was dismissed from the force. The only way back in was to volunteer for a Chip implant… and that had not gone well.

As he drew closer, he noticed Roberto seated on a long, low padded bench, leaning against a wicker-paneled wall, surrounded by an entourage of tween boys and girls. Some of them hadn't bothered to conceal their weapons. To his surprise, Roberto stood up and smiled right at him. Roberto wore a button-down pink silk shirt. The shirt was open and flapped like a pair of wings, revealing curly gray chest hair. His hairline had receded considerably in two years. He showed no signs of the beating he had received at Jake's hands. The man's smile was perfect white.

"Jake, my friend! Sit down! Sit down!"

As Roberto gestured, the grim-faced tween entourage made room around their master. Jake was nervous. Kids this age were far more likely to put a bullet in his head, just to impress their leader.

Jake thought of the Kill Switch concealed within the wallet, which was stuffed inside the pocket of his Bermuda shorts, and felt encouraged. Wallets were going the way of the wagon wheel in the majority of countries. People used their thumbs, retinas, Omnis and Chips for identification and monetary transactions. Since currency was simply numbers floating from one ledger to another, why use cash? But currency had not vanished. Thankfully, Brazil was one country that appreciated printed bills and an old-fashioned plastic ID.

The Kill Switch had cost Jake thirty percent of Sanchez's bank account. The device was a hand-made black-market piece of hardware and he had set it to hack every P-Chip security code up to five feet away. With three million out of over eight billion of the world's population chipped, he wondered if he should have extended the range. He hoped that the information he had obtained regarding Roberto Pacheco was accurate. Otherwise, this operation was futile in addition to being extremely dangerous.

He took a seat. The kids shot him malicious looks. Many had not reached puberty yet. Roberto leaned back and took a sip of a big fruity drink with an umbrella floating in the ice. Even though he was a foot away, Roberto had to yell to be heard over the music. "I'm very impressed with your timing. It was exactly two years ago today that you broke into my home and tried to beat me to death."

Jake's delivery was emotionless, flat. "What a coincidence."

"Aren't you a little out of your jurisdiction?"

"I'm on sabbatical." Jake turned to the waitress who had rushed over the moment he had taken a seat at Roberto's table. He ordered in Portuguese. "Jack. Perfeito."

"You speak like a native." Roberto continued to smile. "Must have been the Chip."

"Must have." He had learned to speak Portuguese after cutting The Chip from his head.

Roberto leaned back and handed his drink to the boy sitting next to him: a human coaster. "What do you hope to accomplish here?"

"Not sure." Jake waited for the Omni on his wrist to vibrate. Then he'd know the Kill Switch was ready to strike.

Roberto laughed. "Really? I thought you had a plan for everything." He lunged and grabbed Jake's hair. He jerked Jake's head forward. A gun was pressed into Jake's back. He assumed the gun was in the hands of the girl sitting to his right; she looked no older than thirteen. Roberto spoke into his ear. His breath reeked of Cachaca, the beverage made from fermented sugarcane that so many people drank in this country. "Hold still, my friend. I want to be sure you're not chipped again or have any other listening device."

He tried to remain calm. He hoped that the warm scanner pressed to the back of his neck would not penetrate the synthetic wallet and detect the Switch. The material was created to throw scanner detection off. A small hand checked his person. As his lackey probed, Roberto used his free hand to pull the HK V2 from the holster under Jake's arm.

"I follow the news on Sanchez. You pulled quite a number on him."

Sanchez had run the Enhanced Unit program for National Police Departments from Washington DC. He had been the Director of Homeland Security and leader of the God Head team that hacked every cop with a Chip. Hacked people were known as Pin Heads. When Jake blew Sanchez's plot out of the water, Jake chased him down to Rio and had him arrested. But Jake managed to keep Sanchez's hidden bank account all to himself. The money was helping him finance this little stunt, among other things. He was a rogue and had no affiliation with anything beyond his own conscience.

"Luckily I'm not wanted anywhere so I know you don't have backup." Roberto released Jake's hair and sat against the wall.

Jake leaned back. *That's what you think.* He glanced at the skinny girl next to him. She smirked as she shoved the scanner into her sequined bag. He felt sorry for her as he turned back to Roberto. "How do you know I don't have an army of pissed off parents waiting in the alley?"

Roberto ignored the question. He set Jake's gun on the table and took back his drink. "After the trial, I spent months dreaming of getting my revenge against you. But my mother put it best. Not only did I survive your beating, it allowed me to walk free. I should be thanking you!" He polished off the glass and slid the umbrella above his right ear. It hung in the greasy strands of long black hair that clung to the sides and back of his balding head.

Jake wondered why this man was not growing new follicles if he was chipped. He grew nervous about the intelligence he had gathered on Roberto.

"Now the great Jackhammer comes to me after losing his life twice. And he wants what? Justice? Justice for whom?"

"The children you forced into child pornography." He turned and looked Roberto squarely in the eyes with calm, cold anger. "For all the lives you've wrecked."

Roberto shook his head. "No. All my children were either sold to me or abandoned. I have given them a home. And if what I did was a crime, why do so many people put money in my bank accounts for my art?" He placed a cigarette in his mouth and the human coaster lit it. "I'll tell you why you are here." Roberto blew smoke toward the ceiling and pointed his lit cigarette at Jake. "This has always been about Lalo."

Jake froze. How did this scumbag know about the boy who died next door when he was twelve?

Roberto smiled and nodded to the girl next to him. She pulled out a folded piece of paper from her bag and handed it to Jake. He unfolded the heavy stock. It had been over a decade since he had held an actual photograph. It was an image of a dead man. The body was a few days old and had been lying in a hot place judging by the bloating. The eyes stared through puffed slits. He did not recognize the corpse.

"Nice to hold paper, huh?" Roberto took a puff off his cigarette. "Kids down here still read newsprint, unlike those back in the States. The only constant is change, yes?" He flashed his white teeth.

Jake held up the photo. “Who is he?”

Roberto laughed. “I was certain you would have used your Chip to find him. You cut it out too soon.” Roberto gestured at the picture of the dead man with his cigarette. “That photo was taken this past January. Before you were implanted.”

He ignored the photo and continued staring at Roberto. “I wasn’t in full control of my person the last time I worked for the LAPD.”

Roberto shrugged. “Same lame excuse you used at my trial... You lost control... something like that?”

Jake handed the photo back to the girl. He wondered what was taking the Switch so long to make a lock onto Roberto’s Chip. Maybe he wasn’t chipped. The girl placed the photo on the table next to Jake’s gun. He had the strong urge to lunge for it, but half the kids around him were already fingering their triggers.

Roberto frowned. “Alonso Florez.”

Jake recognized the last name. Fidel Lalo Florez was the boy’s full name, but everyone had called him Lalo. Lalo had never shown up to Jake’s twelfth birthday party because Lalo’s father had killed him. Jake knew the father had disappeared south of the border shortly after the murder, but he could no longer remember the face. Take away the bloating and that face could be Lalo’s dad.

Jake’s drink came and he took a sip. The whiskey burned the back of his throat. Pain often made him feel like he was tied to reality. Pain was what saved him from the P-Chip back in LA. He felt the back of his neck for good measure. The surgery on his scar had almost erased any evidence that he had been enhanced. He dug into the area with his fingers. It all felt natural. He wondered if his Omni would ever vibrate. He tilted his head toward Roberto and pointed at the photograph. “Did you kill him?”

Roberto watched Jake’s actions with fascination. He exhaled a spout of smoke into the air. “No, he did it all by himself. My defense lawyers came across him when they researched your life. He o.d.’d in a Splice house somewhere in Oaxaca Mexico.” Roberto pointed to the picture. “That’s from his file at the coroner’s office there.”

Jake couldn't hide his smile. The news was deeply satisfying. But then it occurred to him that Roberto might be lying, trying to shake him off his current purpose. He hated doubt and had rarely felt it before being chipped. After The Chip, he continued to doubt the reality of everything. It was why he had surrounded himself with the unfamiliar. It was also why he was tying up loose ends with Roberto. He wanted to feel alive again. And yet the more he lingered down here searching for this man, the more he felt like he was under the influence of a God Head, or Skull Fucker as they were referred to on the Brazilian street.

Roberto dropped his middle finger in Jake's drink then applied the liquid to his lips as if he were putting on lipstick. "What was it like? Having someone lock you away in your own head and use your body to commit crimes?"

The question knocked him back into the moment. Roberto acted like he had a Chip implant. His use of vocabulary was far better than Jake remembered. Plus the bio Roberto had on him was too detailed. But he needed to be sure. "Why don't you get an implant and find out?"

Roberto turned and lifted his oily hair to expose his neck. Jake saw the telltale scar. Roberto was chipped. At that moment his Omni tingled against his wrist. The Kill Switch made a lock. Anxiety eased into confidence.

Roberto turned back to him. "I guess I'm just not interesting enough to be hacked."

"Yet." Jake winked and placed his right hand over the Omni on his left wrist. All he needed to do was touch the face of the Omni and the device would send the command.

Roberto smiled. "I do know what it's like to be a Skull Fucker." He turned to his entourage. "Every one of my children is chipped and they are the best actors I've ever had. You really have to see my holo-porns. The production value would give Mother Teresa a boner."

Two of the boys across the table wore tank tops, exposing their tattooed shoulders. An image they shared was a bald head with the shaft of a penis half buried into The Chip implantation scar. Jake glanced at the girl next to him. Her exposed shoulder displayed the same tattoo. Roberto smiled and presented his shoulder. His tattoo was of an erect penis hanging above a bowed bald head. Roberto was their Over Lord, God Head, Skull Fucker.

Jake felt sick to his stomach. *Jesus, what if I'm locked onto one of these kids?* "You're disgusting."

"And you're naïve. You claim to have a sense of right and wrong, a code of honor? Bullshit. Do you think there is a higher power that judges us? Do you believe in God? Karma? If so, then why am I free and you're still playing policeman long after the establishment that you loyally served rejected you twice?"

Jake nodded to the photograph. "Why is Alonso Florez dead?" He took a sip of whiskey to show he didn't care that Roberto had put his finger in the glass. His mind reeled with how to circumnavigate this new dilemma of the children being chipped too.

"Florez partied for twenty years after killing his son. He died from a Splice overdose. I'd say he died happy. Will you be as lucky?" Roberto took a drag on his cigarette. "Fate does not subscribe to humankind's sense of right and wrong. Life is as random. Luck does not favor the good or the bad. Luck just is. From my point of view, you aided and abetted me in my escape from America's draconian justice system. I ask you, are you an agent of good or evil, Jake?"

"You've become quite the philosopher." Jake smiled. "Must be The Chip talking."

"Answer the question." Roberto's breath soured inside of Jake's nose.

Jake stalled for time, waiting for the right moment. "There is a bit of both in everyone. But the majority of us try to do as much good as we can and fight the demons when they try to drag society down." Jake's wrist tingled again. Another Chip was compromised. He tried to keep his composure while calculating a plan B.

Roberto blew smoke in Jake's face. "A child's point of view." Roberto leaned back and put his arm around his human coaster. "Okay, Justice Jake, what's it going to be? Pistols at dawn? You going to take on me and my family right here in this bar, or are you going to go through with that date you made earlier today on the beach? What was that hot Asian girl's name? Tomoko?"

Jake's eye twitched. How long had Roberto been watching him?

Roberto tapped his head. "I love this thing." He gestured to his entourage. "Their eyes and ears are my eyes and ears. My kids infest Ubatuba, not to mention many other parts of Brazil. You even paid one of my children in Rio for information on me. That was a couple months ago." Roberto scratched his head pretending to be thinking. He turned and pointed his cigarette at Jake. "About the same time you nailed Sanchez." Roberto picked up the HK V2 and aimed it at Jake's face. Several children pulled out pistols and pointed them at table level toward him. He felt a barrel pressing into his back as well. His wrist tingled twice. Four Chips were linked to the Kill Switch.

Roberto leaned into Jake's face until they were almost kissing. "Let's make this simple. I will dispense the same justice for your crimes as you would have for mine." Roberto ejected the gun clip but caught it before it left the grip.

The music continued to rage. The Surfclub patrons were engrossed in their own eddies of life, oblivious to his dilemma. He was out of options. He allowed his mind to drift to the woman he had met on the beach that day. Her name was Tomoko. She was attractive with her wet hair tied back, long board under her arm and a shorty hugging her lithe frame. Tomoko had been very loving to Lakshmi. His Husky had taken to her in an instant. Lakshmi was Jake's litmus test for everyone. It seemed a lifetime had passed since he had met someone who could make him feel comfortable being himself. Yet, he barely knew her. Roberto's eyes and ears were not entirely accurate; Tomoko was Peruvian of Japanese descent.

Roberto closed his eyes as he slowly slipped the clip back into Jake's HK V2. "What did you bring to our little gun fight? Is your clip filled with yellow darts, blue darts, purple darts?" Darts had been the standard of law enforcement worldwide for over six years. Yellow knocked a person out, blue woke them up, purple was filled with Splice—an interrogation drug. Roberto opened his eyes. "Oh, might there be bullets in this dainty?" He shuddered with pleasure. "Hollow points?" He pushed hard and the clip locked into place. "Pump enough into a victim and any one on the list will kill." Roberto aimed the gun at Jake's chest. "But I will fire one shot. Let fate decide and you will see she is morally agnostic." Roberto leaned in close and spoke into

Jake's ear. Roberto's hot breath pushed at the strands of Jake's hair. "Before I inseminate you, I need a promise."

Jake grit his teeth. Lakshmi was back in the hotel room and he could not bear the idea of letting her down because of a stupid miscalculation. "What." He replied.

"If you survive this, you'll dedicate your life to a higher purpose. Morality does not condone the act of revenge. And in your case, revenge is clouding your judgment."

Roberto pulled the trigger.

Chapter 2
Solipsism

Jake stood in the doorway of the apartment. Flies buzzed around the sweat on his temples, searching for a drink. It was 110 degrees in the sun, 100 in the shade cast by the balcony above. The world was quiet. He took a step inside the doorway into a large living room. A floorboard creaked. It was too dark to make out anything within so he waited a moment to allow his eyes to adjust to the low light. A wallet-sized cockroach skittered out of the room. He saw three shapes seated on a low couch before him. He took another step and realized this room was the same configuration as his old apartment back in Westwood. The smell of death was stifling. A fly landed on his cheek and he crushed it.

He shuffled forward. The shadows on the couch began to take shape. He recognized all three corpses. The first was Fidel Florez, aka Lalo, a small boy around twelve years of age. The second was Garth Klawans, the college graduate who had died with Bobby Collins and others during a raid led by Jake. Jake had been chipped then, and taken offline—placed in a coma so his body could be used like a marionette by the God Head, Cameron Greene. Jake had thrown Garth out a second story window. The third corpse was Doctor Regina "Gene" Chilcot. Koren had murdered her while Jake stood a few feet away, his consciousness offline.

Lalo was broken and bruised. His jaw was knocked out of place and hung to the left. He was swollen and bloated like the image of his father's corpse. A maggot crawled out of his right tear duct and slithered down his face. Lalo's mouth creaked when he talked. "Why did you let my father go?"

"I didn't mean to, but—" Jake felt terribly guilty for making any excuse. "I was busy with criminals in LA."

"Do you think he has more children?" The boy asked. A Fly buzzed into his broken mouth.

Shame crept into Jake's chest. "I don't know. I hope not."

"I think he did. I think he killed them, too." Lalo shrieked. "You were supposed to stop him!"

Garth laughed, forcing a shower of yellow pus to exit the bullet wound in his forehead. "Grow up, Lalo. This asshole threw me out a window and then watched his partner pump this hole into my face. You think Jake *The Jackhammer* Travissi would lift a finger to help you?"

Regina spoke with a crackling voice, as if wax paper were stretched across her throat. Bits of old black plastic garbage bag hung out of her mouth. "Jake watched the same partner do this to me and he did nothing."

"I tried…" A surge of grief was injected into Jake's being. "I was offline—"

"We've heard enough excuses, *Commander*." Lalo uttered Jake's old title with disdain and flicked a cockroach at his face. The insects darted in and out of every facial orifice.

Regina's crackling voice cut in. "You let Sanchez go. You let Roberto go. You let this boy's father go. Are you an agent of good or evil?"

Jake jerked his head back and plowed the side of his face into sand. The sound of surf surged in his ears. He was soaked in sweat. He rolled over on his back to study his surroundings. It was night and he was lying on a beach by a low stretch of bungalows. His chest ached from the impact of the yellow dart. He checked his Omni, a holo-message waited to be played. It was 2:00AM.

He had been unconscious for roughly an hour. He got to his feet and felt his pockets. Roberto and his gang had taken the key to his 2010 Alpha 159 and the wallet containing the device. But he still had his room pass. They had dumped him behind the bungalow he had rented at a rundown resort.

A jolt of fear coursed through him and he sprinted for his room. He reached the front door and touched the room pass to the handle and the door clicked. He threw the door open and a sliver of moonlight fell on the sleepy face of his dog. She stood up and wagged her tail.

"Come here, girl!" She wiggled with delight. He closed his eyes and let her kiss his face repeatedly. "Daddy is getting slow in his old age."

His Omni tingled. He sighed and sat back in the doorway, letting the sound of the surf and the unconditional love from his Husky wash away the anxiety. He touched his Omni so its nano-skin structure would transform from a watch into a tablet. Then he opened the app for the Kill Switch. It was still hacking, which meant it remained within five feet of a potential victim. But the victim could be anyone if one of Roberto's kids tossed it in a gutter.

The app for the device showed five acquired targets. The targets formed four points of a square with one target located in the center on one side. He thought about the configuration and realized the targets were riding in a car.

His Omni emitted a ding. The message was still waiting. He navigated to the message menu. The identity of the sender was blocked. He smiled.

Lakshmi barked, sensing his rising hope. Her tail banged against him.

He scratched his best friend with his left hand and hovered his right index finger over the play button. He sucked in a deep breath and pressed play.

The three-dimensional head of Roberto Pacheco floated above the Omni. "Yellow darts?" The face screwed itself into an expression of extreme disappointment. "The Jackhammer would have brought bullets. He would have carried out justice to fit his moral code." Roberto sighed.

He shrank Roberto's floating head and opened up the Kill Switch's tracking window on the Omni. He could cherry pick among the five dots. He studied the background of Roberto's projection for any clues of his location among the targets.

Roberto prattled on. "This can only mean one of three things."

Jake glimpsed a shoulder to Roberto's left. He could be in the right front or right rear passenger seat, or the center. Jake deactivated both dots on the left hand side of the car.

"You've reached a higher understanding that all life is sacred—even mine, you've lost your balls, or you've lost your marbles. I'm guessing the latter because this device in my head has been working overtime updating information on you. In fact, I know more about you than you do!"

Jake's finger hovered back and forth over each of the three target dots.

Roberto's holographic hand appeared clutching a cigarette, he took a drag and his hand disappeared again. "So do me a favor. Let's table this for a later date." His head disappeared in a cloud of smoke. Roberto's hand appeared again to waive the cloud away. "Why don't you go travel for a bit. Find yourself again. In the meantime… GET LAID! Jesus, that alone will clear your head."

Jake heard the faint hum of an internal combustion engine. Given that he saw only electric cars at the bar, he felt it was a safe bet that Roberto was in the Alpha. He gritted his teeth with frustration, and continued searching all around Roberto's image for any clue of his location. The obvious choice was the front seat as it had the most legroom when set all the way back on its track.

Roberto rolled his eyes. "It certainly helps me!" He took a drag. "Or you can download any of my holo-porns for free. I gave you a friends and family access code." Roberto looked concerned and serious. "Come back when you are you again, and we can pick this up where we left off. But know this. For my part, I have moved on." Roberto put the cigarette back into his mouth. "Oh, and mull this over. Are you ready?" Roberto leaned into the camera, which enlarged the hologram image into one big face. "Solipsism." He smiled. "Only guess which one of us is the dreamer!" The head dropped out of view but the audio continued. "God I love this Chip! I'm like… a god!"

Then Jake saw it, a shoulder on the right side of the empty frame! The message stopped. He deactivated all targets except the one in the center. Then he jammed his thumb into the small oval at the base of the display: The Kill Switch. The screen flashed and went dark. He held his breath waiting for the green confirmation screen he had seen in the simulation. Nothing. He tried to re-engage. Nothing.

"Fuck." He closed the app and dialed the Ubatuba police department. He spoke Portuguese to a young policeman on duty. He explained he had been darted at the Surfclub and his Alpha was stolen.

"Given the year of the car I doubt we'll find it. That's a collector's item in Brazil," the tired officer replied in Portuguese. "But we'll let you know if anything comes up."

The holograph disappeared and he sat in the entryway listening to the surge of the surf with Lakshmi. *Did it work?* The device either crapped out, or did its job, but he was no longer in contact. He'd simply have to wait a few days to see if Roberto's body surfaced in the news. *That's what you get for buying black market product.*

He opened Roberto's message and played it again, listening to every word. When the message played out, he sat in the dark with his beloved Lakshmi. Roberto was certainly different than he had been in court or on the months of surveillance recordings Jake had watched before the bust in December 2028. Roberto had access to all information whenever he wanted it and it had noticeably changed him. The Chip helped evolve Roberto into a supercomputer. Unfortunately, the implant did not improve him in the department of sociopath and sexual deviant.

He wondered why he had blown three months chasing down this old ghost. *You're trying to get a foothold in reality. Everything that made you an individual was ripped away by the God Heads. The recurring nightmares you've been having are related to the anxiety you feel about being chipped.* He distrusted his internal dialogue as he was never quite sure if his thoughts were really his own.

He reflected on his recent nightmare—one of many he'd been having over the past few months. Lalo was always among the dead in those particular dreams. In a way, Roberto had done him a favor by handing him a coroner's photo of Alonso Florez. Lalo's death had been the catalyst for Jake's life in law enforcement and that case had finally reached closure. Or had it? Did the device work? Was Roberto lying about the photo?

His anxiety returned and he closed his eyes. Roberto's voice echoed in his head. *Are you an agent of good or evil, Jake?*

From Koren's point of view, my methods make me evil. Jake had been in the room when Gene had been killed earlier this year. True, he had resisted his God Head's commands to kill Gene, but he witnessed his best friend's murder and the murder of others while he had been chipped.

Maybe it was time to retire The Jackhammer and start embracing a new direction in life. He stared up at the sliver of the December moon and saw manmade scars.

The more he contemplated his recent life the more he realized he was just a vigilante, working outside the law. He chuckled. *I've made a career out of bending rules.*

Is that all I have ever been, an agent of revenge? He did not like the answer. Doubt was a legacy of the P-Chip and the God Heads who had controlled him.

He archived Roberto's message and looked up solipsism. He found a few definitions but was willing to bet Roberto was referring to metaphysical solipsism. The only reality was the self and everything else was an extension of the self. Basically, everyone was part of one person's dream. "So you think it's your world and we just live in it, Mr. Pacheco?" He stared at the application menu on his Omni. The Kill Switch app was still there. "Well, tonight you may be right."

What if a God Head continues to manipulate my mind? Then the God Head is the dreamer, and I am just a part of that dream. Having been hacked, that was pretty much the truth of it.

He sighed and rubbed Lakshmi's belly. He was tired of the circuitous argument. "Come on, girl, let's get some sleep." He rose. "We've got a date with a Peruvian surfer girl in about twelve hours."

He closed the door to his bungalow and stepped into the center of the room. The holo-vision snapped on. It was standard procedure for the night shift, who turned down a room, to activate the motion triggers on the holo-vision. He was immediately accosted by an ad for the P-Chip, spoken in Brazilian Portuguese.

A kind-faced man in a khaki suit addressed the room. "Optimism is when you feel good about yourself, your family, and the world around you."

Jake searched for the remote to turn off the device. Images of people smiling in sunshine dissolved into one another. The man continued. "What would the world be like if everyone was optimistic?" Scenes of tranquil mountains, jungles, and oceans flashed on the screen. "The world would look brighter, more promising, more peaceful." Images of two brain scans popped up on the screen. One contained bright spots glowing throughout. The other showed dark areas. "These are scans of the human mind. The brighter one belongs to a person who is naturally optimistic. Things come easier to him. He always sees the positive side to any situation. The dark scan is of a person who is chronically depressed. She feels terrible all the time; her mood affects those around her. She is lonely. She does not get promoted, her life is bleak and without much hope."

The image of a small chip floated into the dark mind. Tiny filaments filled the head. "What if we give her optimism." Once the filaments filled the dark brain, it changed color to match the optimistic mind. The new brain dissolved into the head of a woman smiling at a beautiful sunrise. The man spoke. "Ahhh, experience a rebirth! Now imagine optimism coupled with intelligence! What would the world be like if everyone were optimistic and intelligent? Dare I say Utopia?" The image changed to a city that resembled ancient Greece. People in togas were engaged in painting, talking, and living a life of leisure. "Change is possible in our own lifetime. And change starts with a Third Eye."

Third Eye? Was that how they were marketing the P-Chip? Jake figured out the holo-vision was controlled with his key card linked through his Omni. He pulled up the menu to switch off the holographic images. The host smiled. "Consult your physician today."

A CryLyte logo popped up on screen and a deep voiced narrator spoke. "CryLyte means enlightenment."

Jake hit the off switch. Lakshmi whined. He shook his head and wondered if escaping the damn P-Chip was even possible.

Chapter 3
Wake

Rush hour, and yet there was relatively no sound in the massive city. Electric cars whooshed by. An orderly river of people flowed north and south on either side of the road. No one spoke. Only the murmur of shoes and the light hiss of fabric filled Jake's ears. The sensation was unsettling. His skin crawled. He dug his fingers into his neck, just under the base of his skull. No Chip… as far as he could tell.

He gazed down the corridors of skyscrapers. Cristo o Redentor, the massive statue of Jesus gazed down from his mountaintop, yet the buildings weren't right for Rio. He weaved his way through the pedestrians. They moved in unison, as if they were soldiers in the world's largest parade. He came to a long climb of steps. It reminded him of Rome. *Yes, these are the Spanish steps.* He turned and looked south. He was in a courtyard and beyond that he saw a bay. *Is that Manhattan's George Washington Bridge in the distance?*

He singled out a man in the pedestrian ocean. "Excuse me, can you tell me what street I'm on?"

The man did not miss a step. He continued to stare into the back of the person ahead of him and marched on. Jake singled out a woman and spoke in Portuguese. "Excuse me, Miss. I'm lost. Can you tell me what street I'm on?"

He was answered with an identical reaction.

He grabbed a man coming from the opposite direction. "Sir, I need your help."

The man ripped away and continued as if he had lost his balance for a moment.

Jake stepped into the stream and raised both arms to block three rows of traffic. "Listen to me!"

All streams halted. Thousands of eyes stared straight ahead, lacking the spark of life.

He swallowed hard as he realized he was the only person moving in a world painted in still life. Then every eye refocused on him. The crowd surged, surrounding him. Arms slowly rose in unison. Thousands of fingers pointed at him from every direction as far as he could see. Every mouth opened. One massive and shrill scream issued forth, assailing his ears.

He fell back. Bony fingers dug into his body.

He jerked into a sitting position. The side of his face struck the nano-skin tent surrounding him and he opened his eyes to see orange fabric glowing under the sun, buffeting from an Antarctic wind. There was always light this far south of the circle, but the sun was slightly higher indicating morning. Cold air trickled into his doublewide sleeping bag. The shrill screams from his dream continued but he identified them as the King Penguin colony.

He wiped the sweat off his face and checked his Omni: DECEMBER 23, 2035, 7:00AM. He was happy that his Omni simply told the time. All Omnis were configured to display the day's headlines, weather, and of course advertising before they were shipped to each consumer. He had made a pact to block all such signals while they were on their worldwide trip.

He straightened his legs and bent toward his knees. The pain in his hamstrings felt good. He automatically checked the back of his neck for the presence of a Chip. It was all part of his morning routine, just as the nightmares were part of his nocturnal experience. Only now, with years gone by, the dreams had been occurring less frequently.

The corpse dreams had stopped five years ago. The day that he had awoken on Brazil's Ubatuba beach with a dart bruise on his chest, three things had happened. The first was a news report of Roberto's body being found in a ditch on the north side of town. The second was a call from the police stating they had recovered his car by the Surfclub. The third was his call to the Oaxaca police department in Mexico confirming Alonso Florez was indeed dead.

When Jake had met Tomoko for their first date a few hours later, he had been practically walking on air.

Hard to believe it all happened five years ago. *Where did the time go?* He kept Roberto's holo-message and played it from time to time. The message was saved in the same file as the news of Roberto's body turning up. Cause of death: catastrophic brain aneurysm.

Jake began his routine push-ups followed by sit-ups. When they were at sea, he always swam a mile or two around the boat when they had no wind. His body was almost as fit as it had been before The Chip.

Lakshmi barked outside the tent. He smiled and shouted, "I hear ya, girl!"

The tent zipper hummed as it opened. "That's good because you're missing a gorgeous day." Tomoko poked her head in and grinned at him. Her face glowed red from windburn.

Fresh cold air struck his sweating body. "Smells like the wind is in our favor."

"Onshore breeze. Bird stink is inland."

He kissed her as she bent toward him. "You should have woken me."

"If your body wants to sleep, let it."

He shrugged.

She frowned. "Body Snatchers?"

He pulled a package from his pack with a massive logo blazing across it: CleanRinse Towellete. He wiped his sweat off. "Yup. In the City."

She held his head. "I'm so sorry, honey. Maybe it's time we revisited civilization? Prove that the world has not succumbed to Third Eyes."

He pushed her back. "You've been gunning to see people for weeks now. It won't help."

She raised her eyebrows in a compassionate almost pleading way. "It's called therapy, Jake, and it's been around for over a hundred years."

Lakshmi poked her head in and plopped down between them.

"Lazy hacks," he scoffed. "These days all therapists are prescribing Chips. Nobody does any real work anymore."

"You sound like Sanchez and those other clowns you helped put away." She gazed into his eyes. They were kind, brown and beautiful. Most of all, they were filled with love. "Plenty of people on this planet value their autonomy and freedom."

He sighed, eager to move off the subject of his psychology. "Thanks for taking the trip with me." He smiled as he pulled a microfiber temperature control shirt over his torso.

"Thanks for asking… Happy five year anniversary." She handed him a piece of scrimshaw about the size of a quarter. It was a perfect rendition of their boat, the *Pachacuteq.*

"When did you have time to carve this?"

"When you're at the wheel, or when you're sleeping." She smiled as she flashed a hand signal for Lakshmi to go outside the tent. "The bone is from our Easter Island trip last year."

"This is amazing, I don't know what to say…"

"That's good because you need to see the King chicks before the cruise ships come in. My Omni shows two scheduled for today." She shoved him back down onto the sleeping bag. Her icy fingers dove below his navel.

"I'm crazy about you."

"Show me." She smiled and bit his lip.

Lakshmi poked her head in and fired off a happy bark.

Jake shouted. "Guard the house, Lakshmi!"

Lakshmi whined and pulled the zipper down with her teeth. As he and Tomoko made love, he could hear Lakshmi happily banging her tail against the tent's orange nano-skin. He thought about how much he loved both of them.

An hour later, they wandered amongst the King penguins and their chicks. Farther north, many chicks were almost the size of their parents and beginning to molt. These were still very small and covered in brown fluffy down. The sky was deep blue, the ground almost black, which was a high contrast to the blue and white ice that gripped the mountains inland. Jake had seen photos of this area taken fifteen years ago. The shoreline had been a mile farther out to sea and everything was either black ocean, or white-blue ice.

Lakshmi heeled closely to his leg. One of the laws that stuck after the Antarctic treaty dissolved was the banning of any non-indigenous plant or animal outside Antarctic city limits. He agreed with the law but he was breaking it anyway. He had personally trained Lakshmi and she had been given a command to stick close. She would not even pee unless it was in their port-o-potty or onboard their sailboat. He was not interested in disturbing the natural beauty. They were visiting to witness only, not to touch. The chicks though, were so curious they tended to approach for a quick nibble on a boot or snow pants. The chick's curious behavior made Tomoko laugh and her joy was infectious.

On all their shore landings, there were fewer penguins compared to the You Tube videos shot at the turn of the millennium. Ocean temperatures had been rising which stopped the upwelling of nutrients in the Antarctic waters. The lack of nutrients was killing off the krill population and the krill fed everything including the fish, seals, penguins, and whales. The oceans were turning into a vast interconnected desert. He laughed when Tomoko said her Japanese cousins were still lobbying to harvest whales. Her cousins had cited the fact that water levels were returning to normal and Mother Nature was finding ways to compensate for change. Whales were returning.

Oceans had been steadily rising since the turn of the millennium, threatening island resorts like Hawaii and the Maldives, but seventy nations with borders on the sea had brought levels back down to mid twentieth century marks through desalination. Beaches around the world were saved, but the new threat was exposed shorelines as oceans continued to recede.

There was no way for nature to compensate for the radical changes in the ocean's food chain because technology had made it possible to overfish every drop of the sea. The rate of oceanic extinctions was now equal, if not greater, than terrestrial populations dying off in the last remaining rainforests.

He shook off his depressing train of thought. He wanted to respect and enjoy what was here, not what was lost. He wondered if he couldn't be doing more to help the situation. From the tiny glimpses he and Tomoko saw when they visited civilization, the world was rocketing downhill fast. In fact, he didn't even have to visit civilization to see it all around him in places like this nature reserve.

He put his hand in his jacket pocket and felt the soft feather. It was time. "I was going to give this to you earlier, but I wanted to savor your anniversary gift a little longer."

She turned and he presented her with a long slender blue feather; it was reminiscent of a pipe cleaner.

"Where?"

"Papua New Guinea, during our hike in the rain forest. Looks like a blue bird of paradise, but hard to say since it was not attached to its owner. Happy anniversary."

She kissed him. "I love you."

"I love you, too."

A loud horn echoed across the bay. They gazed out toward the water and saw a massive cruise ship beyond their small forty-foot sailboat. It was time to go. They made their way back to the observation platform to pack up their gear. Within ten minutes, they were on the electric Zodiac powering back to the sailboat.

"I love the penguins, seals, ice and whaling station ruins, but I don't want us to spend Christmas alone again this year." She held on to Lakshmi. The water was getting choppy. Weather could change on a dime down here.

His stomach churned and anxiety crawled into his throat. He hated being in big cities during the holidays, especially the ones in Antarctica, as they represented everything he felt was wrong with society. They had been down here for a couple of weeks. He hoped Antarctica's natural beauty would trump her desire to return to civilization, but he began to feel the desolate beauty exacerbated it.

"It's been six months since we've visited a major port. If we set sail now, we could be in McMurdo tomorrow afternoon. We could ski Mount Erebus and have dinner at Shackleton's."

He released a massive sigh.

She punched him in the shoulder. "You always adapt just fine when we return to civilization."

"Yeah, but Mac Town? It's the worst of all Antarctic cities. It's like Vegas on ice."

They reached their sailboat, *Pachacuteq*, and Tomoko grabbed the ship's stern and began to tie off their Zodiac. He switched off the motor and tied off the rear of the Zodiac to the ship's stern as well.

Tomoko talked over her shoulder. "With our mode of transportation, I don't see any alternative."

"The ski runs are plastered with half-mile-long ads," he grumbled. "They have geosynchronous orbital holo-banners that screw up the Aurora Astralis..."

"Just shut out the holo-ads and try to enjoy the surrounding beauty. I want to be with people, Jake. I never thought I'd say this but I miss civilization."

His heart sank. She had been saying this repeatedly and in shorter intervals for the past six months. He had vetoed her request too many times. He owed her. "Ok." His heart sank even more with his concession. He bent down and received a kiss from Lakshmi. "Come on, girl." He lifted her up and put her in the sailboat. When he turned, Tomoko was there smiling at him.

"Thank you." She gave him a passionate kiss.

A Cruise ship's horn roared. His Omni shouted, "*Pachacuteq*, this is the *Klabanov*. Over?"

He spoke into his Omni. "*Pachacuteq,* go ahead." He helped Tomoko up onto their forty-foot sailboat and the waves began to buffet harder.

"Just want to apologize for our wake. Over."

He slammed down onto the floor of the Zodiac as he saw Tomoko tumble over the rail onto the sailboat above. "Gee *thanks, Klabanov*. Over."

Chapter 4
Pandemic

The scene as they docked in McMurdo was an assault on Jake's very humanity. The bay, which once sheltered a scientific station with a summer population of twenty-five-hundred was now home to a glass and concrete city with a year-round population of seven thousand and a tourist population peak of an additional twenty thousand. Holo-banners coated all surfaces and hovered above every structure. Everything from coffee to hemorrhoid cream was advertised with a seasonal holiday spin. The ski trails of Mt. Erebus rippled with every color in the rainbow. Sponsors impregnated the snow with nanites, which worked as a group to display massive video ads. Even if skiers disrupted the positioning of the nanites, the nanite matrix allowed them to compensate in a millisecond so the half-mile long video ads remained intact.

He used one of his aliases, Chance Mandrake, to pay for their $3,000 a night slip. After making a few calls from her Omni, Tomoko found a room at the pet-friendly Amundsen resort. Apparently Mac Town was all booked up for the holiday so it was a lucky find. Jake wondered why everyone they passed wore surgical masks around their face. Some modeled them over a scarf or balaclava. He checked pollution levels, but they were fairly low in this part of the world.

They boarded a tram headed in the direction of the Amundsen Resort. A small holo-ad flashed under his seat for the Robert Falcon Scott Museum. It preserved the Kiwi station as it had looked at the turn of the millennium. It had been abandoned once the Antarctic treaty died and the world powers began to divide up the last continent.

He noted the temperature was a warm seven degrees Celsius, yet Mac Town's chamber of commerce made sure fake snow vomited forth every hour from tall pipes located all over the city. The snow was filled with computer-controlled nanites that changed color according to a city program. Thankfully, the faux snow was kept classic white today so the attempt at a winter-wonderland illusion was not a total loss.

"That's a beautiful dog." A woman seated across from them smiled. She wore a fake fur and a small fortune in jewelry. "What's his name?"

He stroked Lakshmi's head. "Her name is Lakshmi."

"Such a happy girl. Six?"

"Eight." He noticed the woman, and her husband seated next to her, had thin pale skin. They had both undergone a few cosmetic surgeries. It was typical for anyone over fifty these days. They were also part of the minority not wearing masks.

"What's with all the masks?" Tomoko asked.

The woman chuckled. "Where have you been, dear?"

"Under a rock." Tomoko answered. "My boyfriend and I have been traveling the lesser known parts of the world."

The husband, sporting expensive designer winter gear, leaned in. "MaxWell flu. Worse than the Spanish epidemic in the last century."

"We came here to escape." The woman grabbed her husband's hand and gazed at him with relief. "It's airborne and every continent is infected save this one." She smiled and nuzzled into her husband. "I'm surprised you managed to get here. Most flights have been quarantined."

"We sailed." Tomoko smiled.

The woman turned to her husband and patted his hand. "Why didn't we think of that?"

"You hate boats, dear."

"I liked our Disney cruise."

"That was a horizontal skyscraper with wave stabilizers."

"Then we should look into getting our own boat." She winked at Tomoko and Jake.

Jake cleared his throat. "So why aren't you wearing masks?"

"We've been immunized," the wife said with a smile.

"Flu shot?" Jake asked.

"No, no, no. This is a nano-virus. Only a Third Eye can protect you."

Jake gripped Tomoko's hand. His heart skipped a beat and his neck began to sweat. The human race was faced with an epidemic and The Chip was the only cure? Inoculation and immunization were euphemisms for implantation.

Tomoko turned her head to him. "Are you okay, Jake?"

The husband's face lit up. "Of course, that's who you are! Jake Travissi, from Los Angeles. You were all over the news a few years back." He turned to his wife. "This is Jake Travissi, Loretta. I'm accessing the old clips now."

Loretta smiled at them with renewed interest. "Oh my, Newman, yes! I remember watching that fiasco when we were living in Red Deer!"

"Red Deer?" Tomoko asked.

Loretta patted Tomoko on the knee. "North Alberta… Canada. You two really need a Third Eye if you want to keep up with the times."

"Didn't you tell the driver you were getting off at the Amundsen Resort?" Newman grabbed his bags from the overhead shelf.

Tomoko stared out the windows. The bus had stopped next to a massive hotel. "Yes, this is our stop." She stood up and smiled.

"Merry Christmas." Loretta leaned over to Tomoko. "You might want to check on Jake. He doesn't look well."

Jake didn't notice they were stopped in front of a massive structure built to look like Neuschwanstein Castle in Germany—only this version was jet black with holo-banners floating above the spires. His mind was still reeling from the information. He touched Newman's arm. "Was this immunization voluntary or compulsory?"

"Voluntary, but Parliament is pushing to mandate immunization. I hear your government will follow suit. Millions have died world-wide."

"Did you say *millions*?" The number rocked Jake to his core.

Newman's face fell. "It was chaos for the first month. Riots around the world. People stopped going to work, no one could travel, it was anarchy." He brightened up. "Then they found the cure. It was all pretty much back to normal by Thanksgiving—that's Canadian Thanksgiving in October." He winked and followed his wife off the bus.

"Please exit the bus." The bus' navigation computer spoke with a female voice.

They all disembarked and he turned to Tomoko as the bus rode on. "Did you hear what Newman said?"

Lakshmi rubbed against his leg.

"I can't believe they were so nonchalant about it."

"A million is just too big of a number for some. It's much easier to wrap your head around an individual, a dozen at most."

She shook her head. "I don't care. With that number there must be death all over the news."

He exhaled sharply and gazed up at the hotel's massive structure towering above them. "Looks like something Satan and Sleeping Beauty might have sired."

She yanked him toward the entrance. "Come on, Jackhammer. You'll feel better once you've had a hot shower."

He smiled. She always used his old LAPD handle when he was acting like a curmudgeon.

"Hey look! They have an actual human doorman." Her enthusiasm sounded forced. He could tell the news was weighing heavily on her. He wondered if they would be skiing this afternoon or watching holovision into Christmas Eve.

"Merry Christmas. Can I get your bags?" The doorman was dressed like a nineteenth century Antarctic explorer complete with a fake sealskin coat and boots. Sweat collected in his eyebrows.

"And you're a bellhop! Cool!" She smiled trying to get into the spirit.

Jake gripped his pack. "We've got it under control." They had one backpack each and he was starting to count every dollar in their account. It had taken five years for them to run through Sanchez's funds. He would need a job soon.

"Sorry, sport." Tomoko patted the doorman on the arm.

Jake swung around behind the doorman and checked the man's neck. The collar was too high to see if he was chipped.

The doorman nervously glanced back. "Is there something wrong, sir?"

Tomoko shot Jake a withering look.

He gazed coolly back at the doorman. "Maybe."

She grimaced. "Forgive him. He's LAPD…" She put her hand up to block her comments from Jake's eyes. He heard her anyway. "Suspects everyone. Curse of the job."

The doorman smiled.

"And he suffers from post traumatic stress." With that, she dragged her reluctant boyfriend inside.

Jake was impressed by the cavernous lobby, which was supported by whole tree trunk timbers on the walls and ceiling. He tapped a timber to see if it was real. He frowned. Concrete.

She shook her head. "You promised to give that up."

"Give what up? Checking for wood? Loving Lakshmi?" He knelt down to rub his Husky's head.

Tomoko rolled her eyes. "Checking people's necks for implantation scars."

He stood up and proceeded under the massive timbers toward the grand nineteenth century check-in desk. "You heard what Newman said. Implantation isn't compulsory… *yet*. Jesus, there's pandemic and the only way to combat it is to get implanted? This is some scary shit." He froze. One of the lobby holovision projectors displayed the image of a man he had once known. The image changed to a holographic scene of protesters in the streets of New York, Los Angeles, London, Berlin, Moscow, New Delhi, Beijing, and several others. He touched Tomoko's arm while keeping his eyes locked on the holo-display. "Uhm, can you check us in?" He ran over to the main sitting area of the lobby.

"Jake!" She shouted after him. Lakshmi plopped down next to her, as Jake gave his Husky the hand signal to sit.

He picked up the narration as he drew near. "Disciples of Paul protests against compulsory immunization drew over ten million supporters in thirty cities worldwide."

There was a constant stream of animated advertising and interactive prompts in the lower third of the image, but he was used to tuning it out.

The camera cut to a handsome metro-sexual Chinese man named Jin Chen. Jin was seated on an architectural, yet painful-looking chair. His thirty-foot-high image filled a small portion of the lobby. There were five other projectors like it, displaying other programs. Mainly sports.

Jin spoke. "With me tonight is the Reverend J. Parks, spiritual leader of The Disciples of Paul, CEO of Cobalt Industries, and the architect behind these demonstrations."

Jake felt a wave of excitement, guilt, and sadness when Joaquin Parks' image appeared in the lobby. Parks' black hair was slicked back and much longer than it used to be. He wore a small diamond crucifix in his left ear and his teeth looked like beacons of holy light. His white suit and scarf shimmered with a heavenly glow. Most likely nano-cloth that reflected light in any color of the wearer's choosing. Expensive stuff. *So this is what became of the immature tactical officer I met almost six years ago.*

Chapter 5
Apostle

Jake glanced at the other four displays. Three showed sports. The fourth was some Hollywood gossip channel about Holo-star Alyssa Tasker's Splice addiction and subsequent rehab.

He focused his attention back on the towering images of Jin and Parks. "Hello, Jin-o!" Parks slapped Jin on the leg. Advertisements danced and wiggled around his holographic feet, like ants trying to upstage the scene. Parks twisted in his seat. "What's with these chairs? Water-boarding would be far less painful if you have interrogation in mind."

Jin held his serious composure. "I see why they call you the Mirthful Minister."

"Don't forget the ever popular Ass-postle, or the Irreverend!" Parks guffawed.

"You don't object to your media nicknames?"

"Not at all. Nothing should be taken too seriously. If you can't poke fun at a situation, then you're holding on too tightly. Laughter is a universal language. I believe the Good Lord has a fantastic sense of humor. Why else would he have allowed someone to make these chairs?" Parks patted the seat beneath him.

Tomoko settled into a comfy couch close to Jake. "I checked us in on the Omni. Sure you don't want to watch this in our room?"

Jake shook his head dumbfounded as he continued to stand. Lakshmi nuzzled the palm of his hand. He scratched her head as he watched.

Jin cleared his throat. "Millions have suffered and died from the MaxWell epidemic, why have you orchestrated these world-wide demonstrations against the only cure available?"

"That's a serious question, Jin-sing, and deserves a serious answer." Parks leaned in toward the camera so his head was enlarged. His expression grew deadly serious. "I mourn for every one of those souls who has perished. This plague is not the work of God, but of the Devil working through the instrument of Man. We have reached The End of Days. Morality is on the endangered list, the human race is so self-absorbed that it has lost all sense of community. Cyber-space has fostered a world where people living a few feet from each other no longer interact in person. This immunization, or chipping of every individual on this planet, is the final step leading to Judgment Day. The Disciples of Paul protest for all of God's children. All of humankind have become lambs being led to the slaughter."

Jin appeared incredulous. "What does this have to do with fighting a virulent disease?"

Parks leaned back. "Listen closely, Jin-o-cide." He turned and faced the camera once again. "Third Eyes, P-Chips, Head Jacks—whatever you want to call them—are an abomination. They do not enhance humanity. They usurp the human mind and convert it into a computer server. Third Eyes steal individuality and make it possible for a single person or entity to change the hearts and minds of the masses with a flick of a switch." He snapped his fingers with a loud crack. "Third Eyes are chains forged in the fires of hell by Satan himself."

"I see." The camera angle changed. Jin was now facing the lobby. "So you subscribe to the conspiracy theory that the MaxWell nano-virus was released deliberately to speed the complete adoption of Third Eyes worldwide?"

"Read your Bible, Jin-e-o. The signs are all around us." Parks raised his arms and gestured in all directions. "We're way past theoretical."

"I'm a Buddhist and I believe we should move on now."

Parks half stood. "You mean I can get out of this torture contraption?"

Jin maintained his composure. "If you'd prefer to stand, I'm sure we can accommodate."

"Oh no. When in Rome." Parks sat back down with a grimace. His nano-suit changed color. His shoulders were now blood red and the fabric had faded to pink near the lower coat pockets.

"The Disciples of Paul have their roots in the Sons of Christ, or S.O.C., isn't that correct?"

Parks smiled. "If by roots, you mean some of my flock and even some of the chapters used to follow The Sons of Christ, then yes."

Jin opened his mouth but Parks railroaded on through.

"If your question implies that I'm the leader of a terrorist organization, then I'll call you a liar. Do the Disciples of Paul agitate? Yes. Are we fearful of what is going on around us but not afraid to take action? Absolutely."

Jin's gaze narrowed. "So you are not a terrorist?"

"No, Jin. I swear on the Holy Bible I am not."

"The bombing of an Indonesian mosque in 2033 had nothing to do with you or your church?" Footage of bloody and screaming people exiting a broken and burning building filled the space where Jin had been.

"No, Mr. Chen." The hologram switched back to Parks. "As the Lord is my witness, neither myself nor my flock had anything to do with that tragedy. I believe I cleared the DOP of that incident in 2033, 34 and 35."

The image of Jin towered above Jake once again. "Yet three members of your flock were involved with the S.O.C. when they were blowing up mosques under Reverend Blake. One of them was involved with the Jihad Brotherhood when that group blew up the Santa Monica Pier in 2028."

The mention of that incident made Jake wince. The Santa Monica Pier bombing had been the core image for hacking into his mind when he had been chipped himself.

"Circumstantial." Parks waved his hand. "None of the members of my flock were responsible for those heinous acts. Just because you belong to the Cub Scouts doesn't mean you're actively working on every merit badge."

Jin laughed. "I'd hardly call either organization the Cub Scouts."

"All I'm saying is that no members of the DOP are terrorists and if one of my children sought shelter from a previous association with a terrorist organization, it was because they woke up and realized they were not walking The Lord's path." His suit turned black at the shoulders but faded to gray toward his legs.

"What about the pact you made with the Clerics of the Jihad Brotherhood to jointly harass The Immortality Project?"

Parks laughed. "For the JB and the DOP, conflicts are as old as the faiths we represent. But we do agree on a few fundamentals. The Immortality Project, like Third Eyes, is an idea that affronts The Lord and the doctrines he has given to humanity. I wouldn't say we made a pact, but we have agreed not to harass each other in Los Angeles where this *Doctor* Eberstark runs his immortality experiments."

Jin interlaced his fingers. "So you're not part of a joint plot to murder and destroy Eberstark and his work?"

Parks shook his head and sighed. "The Spanish Inquisition was disbanded in 1834. Are you sure you're not trying to channel them right now? Who's supposed to be the crackpot in this conversation?"

Jin sat back and an image of Parks in full dress police uniform popped up on screen behind him. Jake recognized it as circa 2030, when they were both members of Homeland Security's Enhanced Unit. "There was a time when you were a poster boy for Third Eyes. What happened?"

"I was hacked and afterward realized I did some terrible things under the influence of others. I saw my partner kill himself and I spent a long time soul searching after that. A few months later I joined the Progressive Church and found Jesus Christ."

"That's where you met The Church's number one patron, trillionaire Max Whitney?"

Parks smiled. "Mega Max. That's right."

"He not only took you under his wing, you both co-founded the DOP with his fortune?"

Parks chuckled. "People called us the Dopes and Mega Max fired back by saying we were the oldest dope on the street. One shot of The Lord and you were hooked forever. He turned the criticism on its head."

Jin stroked his jaw and pointed to Parks. "The common perception is you influenced that line."

Parks shrugged and became very somber. "I'm not really sure who said it first. It's not important. Max was like a second father to me." His suit was back to blinding white.

Jin nodded. "He left you everything?"

"He left The Church everything. I'm just a simple shepherd."

"Your position as the CEO of Cobalt Industries has afforded you a lavish lifestyle complete with mansions, limousines, and expensive clothes. You even have a fleet of nuclear HJs that fly you to anywhere in the world without refueling. What do you call them?"

Parks smiled. "The Four Horsemen of the Apocalypse."

"An allusion to your End of Days theory?"

"That's right, Jin-opolis."

Jin checked his Omni. "Artificial Intelligence will speak to the press for the first time on New Year's Day. Will the DOP be there to protest?"

Parks winked. "Is that Chinese New Year, or calendar New Year, Jin-o-tonic?"

Jin looked pained to be treated in such a cavalier manner. Before he could respond, Parks laughed.

"I'm just pulling your string, Jin-e-bop. I believe some of the members of our Beijing chapter will be demonstrating on New Year's Day, yes."

Jin composed himself. "What do you have against Artificial Intelligence?"

"AI is the creation of an alien life by humanity, a domain that only the Good Lord is wise enough to administer. The human race is simply too immature to be siring new life forms. The dangers of something going wrong are too great. These scientists are out of their depth. Haven't you seen those old Terminator or Matrix movies? Put simply, AI is Satan's work. You'll see."

"Muslims will be protesting, too. Do you see a conflict between your two groups?"

"Not at all, Jin-zilla, it shows they have more sense than usual."

"With all this money and power, do you feel entitled to sow discontent? Do you enjoy fighting governments that are simply trying to help their citizens who would otherwise perish? Were you vaccinated against polio?"

"I feel it is my responsibility and duty to be a voice of reason in these chaotic and dangerous times. I preach the gospels and they have served humanity since time began." Parks shifted in his seat. "To answer your last question, yes, as an infant I was vaccinated for polio. But polio vaccines can't be hacked by God Heads to force victims to carry out their will." His suit turned red/pink again.

"So what preventative measures do you suggest we take against this evasive airborne nano-virus?"

"I believe in prayer and the Nemp. That and my filter which I rarely take off." Parks held up a white surgical mask with a poker-chip-sized disc affixed to the base. Jake wondered what function the disc served.

Jin continued his interview. "As you recall, society was in a state of panic. The world economy was on the brink of total collapse before Third Eyes were found to have 100 percent effectiveness against the nano-virus."

"Nemps worked, too, but it meant giving up our 21st century society for a 19th century one."

"So you don't subscribe to the American Congress' idea, and the world's majority of citizens, that Third Eyes should be mandatory for every individual in order to stop the spread of the MaxWell contagion?"

"Majority?" Parks laughed. "You should see the turnouts to my protest rallies. I say the majority want their freedom from having computers stuffed in their skulls. Enhancing one's body with machinery is an abomination of God's greatest work."

"If you look at the numbers showing up to your protest rallies, you'll see you're definitely in the minority," Jin corrected.

Parks laughed and slapped his leg. "Spin it 'till you win it, Jin-bo-lin!" His suit was black and gray.

Jin waited for Parks to compose himself. "What about pacemakers, or surgical nanites that cure many cancers and other nuisances from our lives? Are you against those technological advances in medicine?"

Parks placed his hands together in a prayer pose. "If a machine serves one purpose with no potential for enhanced intelligence or the ability to compromise the mind, then it's fine. Nanites and Third Eyes are miles outside that category."

"You share a lot with Islam with that sentiment."

Parks smiled. "Even Satan was a member of heaven until he was cast out."

Jin raised his eyebrow.

Parks patted the man's leg. "Come on, Jin-on-the-rocks. I'm pulling your leg. I do not condemn all Muslims, just those who are fundamentalist, militant Jihadists."

Jin leaned in. "The DOP have chapters all over the world and many governments have ousted them, claiming they harbor and promote terrorists."

Parks yawned. His glowing teeth made it seem like he was radiating spiritual energy. "We've come full circle, Jin-Beam. But I'll walk with ya." He leaned forward and twisted in his seat. "Pakistan and Iran have banned the DOP but that's the extent of it. Besides, religious persecution is older than the gospel."

Jin checked his Omni tablet. "I show that most of the Middle East and much of Africa have banned the DOP but then those are all Muslim countries. I'm surprised you were able to establish a truce with the Jihad Brotherhood so easily. Is there more to this truce than meets the eye?"

Parks winked. "Never underestimate the power of The Lord." His suit was back to glowing white.

"Is there a significance to why your suit keeps changing color?"

"Indeed there is, Jin-er-ator. The nanites have been configured to represent every individual on this planet. When the suit turns red, that's in recognition of those who have died from MaxWell. When it turns black, it represents those who have been chipped or immunized. The suit constantly downloads statistics so whenever it changes color there is a real-time update. For those who can't afford a nano-suit, we're selling these nano-pins." He fished a small pin with a head the size of a penny from his pocket. "You can get them in red, black, or both and all donations go to charity. Celebrities and politicians are following suit—pun intended."

"How noble of you." Jin crossed his legs. "You're famous for stating you have no regrets. Does that include your participation in the murder of many innocents back in 2030?"

Parks sighed and shook his head. "I deeply regret my part in those deaths. If it wasn't for the forgiveness of Jesus Christ, I might have killed myself in the same fashion as my partner. But sin does not forgive sin. I was implanted with a Third Eye and it is a documented fact that I was hacked during every murder committed by the LAPD's Enhanced Unit and myself. You should show footage of that hearing to refresh your viewers' memories.

"There are many who believe Pin Heads should be held accountable even when they're offline. The argument is that a truly good person should be able to resist a God Head when faced with commands to commit murder."

Jake noticed a few people had gathered around him. Two women silently communicated in a rapid-style sign language. He realized they were both chipped. The physical hand gestures meant they were speaking in real time instead of cognitive time as he had been trained to do at the Mayo Clinic when he had been implanted back in 2030. Real time was pretty inefficient. Then again, most people these days didn't get training after implantation. Why pay for a class when you could download a tutorial?

He refocused on Parks.

"Luckily, the United States Supreme Court does not agree with countries like China in this regard." Parks winked. "But, you're talking about the Travissi Paradox. The official argument is that his chip was flawed which kept him from being completely controlled. But as a preacher I hear what's on the street, and most believe Jake's indomitable spirit kept him from pulling the trigger when hacked. But let's be clear that he was in the room when murders were taking place. He didn't physically kill anyone but he didn't prevent murder either. Based on your argument does that make him innocent?"

Jin rubbed his jaw again. "So you do not feel responsible for those you killed in cold blood?"

Parks leaned forward. "I do not. I am a man of clear conscience and a servant of The Lord."

"So no regrets? About anything?"

Parks leaned back and chewed his cheek. "I do have one regret." He smiled as if he were about to crack one of his jokes. "I regret not treating my first hero with more respect."

Jin was genuinely curious. "Who was that?"

"Commander Jake Travissi."

An advertisement for sailing Antarctica popped on. Jake checked the audience around him.

An Indian man nodded at him. Jake saw two scars under his nose; he must have been born with a double cleft pallet. Jake was surprised because modern surgery could erase all evidence of it. The man was an inch taller than Jake, broad, but a bit soft under the skin. His short uneven black hair was streaked with white. He was dressed for subzero temperatures but the sweat on his face told that he had not prepared for this mild day.

A small Indian woman stood between them with her index fingers plugged into her ears. She had the wild-eyed look of a feral cat. She was very petite and shorter than Tomoko. Though her hair was tied back in a ponytail, scores of single strands waved about like sea grass. None of her clothes matched and she wore a large pendant on her chest of the god Ganesha.

When she noticed him looking in her direction, she took three steps forward and addressed him rapidly in perfect American English. She nodded at the holo-display. "Like watching monkeys throwing feces at each other in a zoo. Baboons tend to throw more feces in a given time frame than any other primate. But that data has never been correlated with contemporary broadcasts." The woman gave him a forced smile. "I hypothesize the volume Homo sapiens throw to be exponentially higher."

Jake turned back to the holo-display, not sure he wanted to engage this odd person. She moved closer, fingers remaining in her ears.

"It's fascinating to watch human behavior. As a policeman, wouldn't you agree?" the woman asked.

He turned back to her. "Do I know you?" He noticed both Tomoko and Lakshmi studying her. Tomoko smiled at the fingers in the ears.

The woman stared right through Jake. "Why would you know me?"

The urge to spin the woman around and check her neck pulsed through him.

The Indian man stepped forward with a smile. "Forgive my wife." His Indian accent was faint. Jake could not place the dialect. "The art of conversation has always eluded her." He shrugged. "Scientist." He extended his hand. "I'm Sumit."

Jake took Sumit's hand. "Jake Travissi. This is Tomoko."

Tomoko nodded back.

Jake nodded to his Husky. "And Lakshmi."

The Indian woman flopped down on the ground like a kid. "Oh what a beautiful Hindu name!" She began stroking Lakshmi with great affection. Her legs were spread out, as if she were a five-year-old playing jacks at school.

Sumit's face glowed red and he smiled sheepishly. "This is Anjali."

Jake paused for a moment. During his first few weeks in Rio back in 2030, he had been reunited with Lakshmi. Gordon King was the man who had cared for his dog while he was chipped. King was also the leader of a group called The Order of Erasmus. King asked Jake to join and Jake had refused, but King gave him a contact name should he change his mind. "My day is filling up with coincidences. Do you know Erasmus?"

"Gordy was right." Sumit smiled. "You are sharp."

Jake stared down at Anjali. She giggled as Lakshmi licked her face.

Jake cleared his throat. "My answer is still no."

Sumit was a tad flustered. "We're not here to sell you on the cause. We just thought you might want some company. It is Christmas Eve after all."

Jake fired back quickly. "We're planning on hitting the slopes." He continued to glance at Anjali who remained sitting and giggling. Tomoko tried twice to engage her in conversation, but Sumit's wife was razor focused on Lakshmi.

Sumit shook his head. "I'm sorry, we're getting off on the wrong foot. Anjali and I were already here on business. We happened to be looking at the visitor's manifest when we spotted your name."

"So much for my alias," Jake grimaced.

A sneeze rang out in the room. Everyone jerked their head in the direction of the sound. He was shocked to see people backing away in terror from a man seated in a chair wiping his nose.

A loud hum vibrated the room.

Lakshmi barked.

Anjali jumped up in anger, clapping her hands over her ears. "I hate Nemps!"

The holo-displays flickered out and the lobby suddenly went dark.

A woman screamed.

A soothing voice shouted out over the dimly lit room. "Everyone please remain calm while we exercise decontamination protocol. This will only take a minute. We apologize for any inconvenience. Thank you for your patience and understanding."

Subdued light poured in from the windows overlooking the main street. Jake's eyes started to adjust. Two security guards wearing facemasks approached the man who had sneezed and escorted him to a side door.

The old man gazed at one of his captors. His voice shook. "It's just a cold."

"I'm sure it is, sir."

"Please let me go!" The man pleaded and struggled. "You're hurting me!"

The door closed behind them.

Everyone stood, staring at the space where the man had exited.

Jake heard only the sound of his own breathing.

Chapter 6
Maxwell

The lights snapped back on revealing a distraught man walking in circles and a woman crying. A resort manager pushed her way to the center of the vast hall. When she spoke, her voice was amplified by speakers hidden all over the room. Jake saw no microphone and realized she was chipped.

"I wish to thank each and every one of you for your patience during the Nemp. Please note that the gentlemen who sneezed has been taken to our Amundsen Clinic where the doctor on staff is testing him for MaxWell. We have full confidence the test will be negative and that Antarctica's status as a MaxWell-free continent will remain intact. Please note that our doctor is the finest in Mac Town so if anything ails you, feel free to give her a visit."

Anyone who wasn't wearing one before now, put on a mask. Only he, Tomoko, Sumit, Anjali and the manager were mask free.

Tomoko addressed the three of them. "What was that business with the light?"

Anjali answered dryly, "MaxWell can be weakened or killed with a N-N-E-M-P."

Tomoko pressed further. "How does a massive surge in electrical conductivity stop a virus?"

"I said N-N-E-M-P, not E-M-P." Anjali sounded annoyed. "E-M-P would mean detonating a nuke. We've found that a low level N-N-E-M-P—or Nemp, non-nuclear electromagnetic pulse kills the nano-virus but leaves low-shielded electronic devices intact, although electrical currents and spectral waves are blocked while the pulse is active. The MaxWell contagion was designed in a laboratory. It is a nano-virus, meaning it has a programmable DNA structure. Six months ago MaxWell jumped from its secure environment and no natural immune system can stop it. If caught early, Nemps can kill it, but the only current cure is a Third Eye."

"MaxWell?" Jake asked.

Anjali turned toward Jake and jumped a bit, as if he had just popped into the room.

Sumit put a loving arm around Anjali and answered Jake. "It's the name of an EU pharmaceutical company. They were working on the ultimate flu vaccine using nano-virus technology. After the virus escaped, fifty international lawsuits were filed and the MaxWell Corporation declared bankruptcy."

Tomoko laughed nervously. "I bet the conspiracy theorists are having a field day with this one."

Anjali responded with a loud and exaggerated laugh. When she saw the surprise on Tomoko and Jake's faces, her mouth twisted shut and she appeared embarrassed. Then she blurted out, "We do not believe they are theories. We believe—"

Sumit stroked her hair and kissed the top of her head. It had a calming effect. "This is not the best place to converse. These two just arrived and are probably eager to get to their room—here we go." He pointed to the giant holo-display.

Anjali rolled her eyes dramatically. "Holograms."

Jake turned and saw a giant holo-display of a woman in a lab coat. He instantly thought actress because she looked like a model wearing a costume.

Plus she wore regular glasses—not an Omni configuration—and real people rarely wore them anymore. She appeared very concerned. "MaxWell is deadly serious."

He turned to see Anjali with her back to the image and her fingers stuffed into her ears. He addressed Sumit. "Okay, first I see a broadcast of Joaquin Parks, then an ad for sailing, and now we're seeing a public service announcement on MaxWell?"

Sumit opened his mouth but Anjali jumped in before he could get a word out. Her fingers remained in her ears. "Everyone on the planet can be tracked through the clothes they wear, the credit accounts they use, Omnis, Chips, finger prints, retina patterns—look around the lobby."

Jake scanned the room as Anjali continued, "There are dozens of sensors tracking everyone's identity." Many shaken people milled about. On the ceilings he did notice tiny devices tucked in the shadows of the massive beams. "The holo-displays are tied in with the system. They display programming that fits each profile that enters this room. Since the Nemp incident, everyone is probably thinking about MaxWell. Since the sensors cater to chipped profiles first, I bet all the displays are showing nano-virus information."

He took a look and there were graphics and models of how the virus worked on every display. "On the nose."

Anjali continued to rattle on with her fingers in her ears, staring directly at Jake. "For non-chipped people like us, computers track our Omni use. For example, any time you use yours at sea, your location is pinpointed by a satellite network and a myriad of databases. The sheer number of people on this planet makes most individuals relatively safe from cybercrime. They simply aren't worth the effort. However, everyone is tracked by advertising and marketing computers so they are given multiple opportunities to be sold goods and services on a minute-by-minute basis. Anyone watching this program with their Omni or linked with their Chip can buy the clothing they see, cars, ships, vacation packages, or simply interact with other viewers."

That information had been the same when he lived in LA, he just chose to block it on his Omni or ignore it, but he found her delivery highly fascinating. "Thanks for the detailed explanation." He noticed the display showed a twelve-foot double helix of the MaxWell nano-virus DNA with engineered nucleotides that were programmable and adaptable. Its design made it impervious to all conventional methods of treatment and it had originally been constructed to attack multiple strains of flu virus, not the vital functions of a host.

The actress continued her narration. "But there is a disadvantage to the engineered configuration, it is susceptible to a mild non-nuclear electromagnetic pulse, or Nemp." The woman popped back on screen. "But in our society that relies so heavily on electricity and complex circuits, even low impact Nemps are impractical. Small-targeted bursts can stave off the nanovirus, but as I said before, this virus is airborne. So what do we have in our arsenal against it?" She held up her finger. The screen crash zoomed in on a tiny Chip clinging to the pores in her skin. "A Third Eye guarantees full recovery and immunity."

Jake saw a familiar simulation of a Chip implanting into an androgynous figure. The woman continued to narrate. "A Third Eye can adjust a body's chemistry, help to regenerate damaged tissues, and continuously enhance the body's immune system to match the fluctuating properties of the MaxWell nano-virus. Using its own matrix, it can help the body manufacture a hundred variations of an antibody per hour. Tied in with the medical information broadcast over the Cyber-Wire, it can create targeted antibodies that can match the mutation rate of MaxWell and wipe it out." The actress popped back on screen. "In other words, it fights on the same playing field as MaxWell. Any other treatment would be like fighting a nuclear missile strike with a sling shot." She smiled. "So why risk yourself or your loved ones any longer? There is a cure! It's simple and less painful that getting a shot."

The camera cut to a small child crying as a doctor stuck him with a needle and syringe. The image cut again to a smiling family waiting in line outside an electric van with the familiar Nanotechnologies Incorporated—NTI—logo stenciled on the side. INNOCULATION was stenciled under the logo.

"Immunization takes less than five minutes and is now subsidized by the national healthcare plan. So there's no excuse!"

The scene cut to a crane shot revealing bulldozers pushing bodies into a mass grave. "Stop MaxWell before it kills your family and whole communities like it did last summer. Immunize today."

The NTI logo towered over Jake. A man's voice boomed out. "This has been a public health announcement from your friends and neighbors at NTI. NTI, reaching beyond potential."

He turned to Anjali who continued to stare at him with her fingers in her ears. "You should buy a pair of earplugs."

"I keep a pair in every pocket and have jars of them at home. However, this ensemble came back from the cleaners this morning with the pockets emptied."

He fought his urge to smile, as she seemed deadly serious and a bit upset by the situation.

Sumit pulled his wife in for a hug. Her face was buried in his chest but she did not pull her fingers out of her ears. "How about we treat you to Christmas Eve dinner at Shackleton's? It's one of the best in Mac Town and it's right here in the resort." Sumit upped the stakes. "They have real meat and fish on their menu."

Tomoko's mouth trembled as she stared at Jake with big pleading eyes. Dreams of real food had been the topic of conversation for over a month now. Finding fish at the end of their lines had become miracle work and in their land travels, meat was a luxury they could not afford. They were always eating substitutes that were in the shape of meat but were not the same in taste or texture.

Jake's stomach growled.

Anjali pulled away from her husband and backed up until she was looking at both Sumit and Jake.

Sumit threw in the deal closer. "We're buying."

"Ok," Jake replied and Tomoko squeezed his hand with excitement. These two gave him an uneasy feeling, but then again, he rarely trusted strangers. "But I'm ordering a filet to go for my girl here." He nodded to his Husky. Lakshmi's tongue flopped out in a half smile as she gazed at the four of them with friendly blue eyes.

Anjali shouted with enthusiasm. "I say we order the menu for her!"

Sumit nodded with satisfaction. "Then it's a date. Shall we say twenty-hundred?"

"Eight is fine." Jake smiled.

Sumit steered his wife toward the lobby doors. She turned and waved sadly to Lakshmi.

Jake followed the couple for a few feet so he could study their necks. Sumit's was only half exposed given his short thick black hair. Anjali's ponytail blocked everything.

Tomoko elbowed him when he returned. "You're almost as nutty as she is."

Chapter 7
Immortality

Sumit did not have much of an appetite lately and Anjali had forgotten about dinner plans the moment they left the lobby. *If only I could go back to being a simple scientist again.* He felt glum these days and did everything to put on a happy face. Anjali was busy working on formulas with her Omni. She once had a Third Eye, but that had not gone well.

He missed being a scientist, but in the modern world everything was tied to celebrity. Eighty percent of the world's brick-and-mortar universities had closed in the past ten years due to the Cyber-Wire. The most charismatic professors had millions of students that took their courses via Cyber-Universities. Scientists were the same. They had to seek the spotlight to gain followers so that projects could be funded.

He hated the system, but he had no choice but to follow its rules. While Anjali researched, he worked to ensure they had the funds to keep their research plane airborne. Sumit had been petitioning his government hard for the Ashoka Chakra, India's highest honor. He was told if he and Anjali could come up with an alternate cure for MaxWell soon, their probability of receiving it would be high. A medal like that would not only solidify funding for life, it would guarantee their names in the history books. But just in case, he had other irons in the fire.

For the past few weeks, pressure had been put on him to work even more political and social angles for the organization. He preferred to be behind the scenes and deal with research. In that he had much in common with his wife. However, Anjali was too much of a robot to understand his politicking. She thought he was slacking in his scientific duties. She didn't understand he was pedaling to keep their rickshaw on track. He had contributed quite a bit to Anjali's trials for the cure to MaxWell; it was what had led him to this moment. There was so much to do concerning Jake, Parks, The Order of Erasmus, and The Consortium. Thinking of all the tasks before him was overwhelming and his heart rate increased.

He tried to take his mind off the future by working nano-viral case studies with Anjali, but he found he was unable to concentrate. So he resorted to what all the troglodytes did for distraction: turning on holo-vision.

Most hotels did not bother having holo-screens in their rooms since Omnis had holo-vision accounts that traveled with each individual user. The Amundsen Resort was an exception. Since Sumit had checked in as a virologist, he found the default channel was the American version of India's Scientific News.

A familiar face hovered over the mini-bar. He recognized it as a stock hologram of celebrity scientist Roald Eberstark, the American who had half of Hollywood and Bollywood pouring money into his research. Sumit felt a twinge of jealousy. Since the late twentieth century, Roald had preached the law of exponential returns; the idea that scientific achievement, especially in technology, advanced by an exponential degree every one to two years. In this respect, the scientific community generally accepted Eberstark's theory. Most everyone in Sumit's generation remembered their first cell phone, smart phone, tablet, Omni, and finally their Third Eye, all technological revolutions which had happened within the past thirty years.

Eberstark also predicted the mapping of the cognitive and emotional aspects of the human mind by 2030. He further predicted a fully developed, self-aware, and sentient AI that would match human intellect and behavior by 2040. In the latter case, he overshot by five years. Third eyes linked to human minds had revolutionized scientific discoveries. Everything was taking less time to create. There were currently three AI projects going on in the world, the most advanced of which was in Beijing.

Eberstark had a theory that humans would be able to upload their consciousness into the Cyber-Wire and attain immortality there. His work was based on God Head technology. If a hacker could invade a person's mind and trap the consciousness inside the brain, couldn't a person's consciousness go the other direction? Jake Travissi's counter-hacks during 2030 had shown this was possible on a limited scale. Eberstark was working hard to upload the entire mind, consciousness, emotions, personality, and all, into Cyber-land.

Hollywood types, business executives, and anyone who feared death, showered Eberstark with money. He had his benefactors convinced that he was close to realizing his theory. The Cyber-Wire was vast, practically infinite with plenty of space to hold humanity's consciousnesses. He called his foundation The Immortality Project, or IP.

Eberstark's progress instilled panic into the anti-technology/religious fundamentalists like Parks' DOP and the Jihad Brotherhood. These groups heard "soul," instead of "consciousness" and thought Eberstark was playing God. The fundamentalists felt they had already lost ground with the marriage of humanity with computer chips. They drew the line on Eberstark's endeavors.

Sumit shook himself out of his mental diatribe and focused on the news at hand. Eberstark's California lab was a smoking ruin. The word LIVE circled above the three-dimensional footage. He turned on the volume and glanced at Anjali. She was engrossed in her world of case study models. He envied her.

The footage switched to bodies under sheets being carried out of the smoking ruin. "Once again, it has been confirmed that Doctor Roald Eberstark, the founder of The Immortality Project, has been killed. His lab has been destroyed and the entire scientific staff working on the Immortality Project may have perished as well. Four suicide bombers were involved. Authorities are trying to ascertain their identity and if they are indeed connected to the Disciples of Paul and The Jihad Brotherhood."

Sumit sat up on the edge of the bed, horrified. What right did these throwbacks to the Middle Ages have to impede science? He did not agree with many of Eberstark's fringe beliefs, but the man did not deserve to die for his actions. He was harmless. Sumit's disdain for men like Parks and the Jihad Brotherhood steeled him in his mission. Men like these needed to be removed from society. They had no business in the 21st century. Their rigid ways steeped in ancient ritual and misdirected morality were good for humanity when it was in its infancy and the chances of dying while hunting to feed a family were quite high. But in a world of education and the scientific method, their belief systems were archaic. No, not archaic—insane.

He was raised as a Hindu but he had given up religion as a teen. He showed up to religious rituals when required by family and friends, but he simply saw the events as curious windows into a superstitious past. A past ruled by men like Parks and the Clerics who ran the Jihad Brotherhood.

In a surge of exasperation and disgust, he changed the channel. His jaw dropped when he saw two people battling each other before a live studio audience. One combatant was a middle-aged Caucasian man dressed only in a pink tutu. His arms were bound to his sides by a gold rope that dug into his paunch and flabby breasts. His opponent was a young woman dressed in a standard issue NATO military uniform. Her arms were tied down with gold rope as well. Each wore a large two-foot floppy balloon strapped to the tops of their heads.

It took Sumit a moment to realize the balloons were oversized dildos. The balloons were filled with a purple jelly. The combatants sword fought, trying to strike a blow with a dildo. They trudged around a giant glazed donut. The studio audience chanted: "Splooge! Splooge! Splooge!" The woman lunged then twisted her back so the purple dildo smashed into the man's face and exploded. Purple goo shot all over his flesh and the crowd went wild.

The announcer, a model in a string bikini, flashed a million dollar smile. "Sergeant Mercolino is our winner!" The announcer's face filled the frame.

Sumit saw nothing but perfect gleaming rows of teeth. "Stay tuned for the Sergeant's final trial, Splooge Brats!"

The image switched to a preview of things to come. The Sergeant, now wearing a chartreuse-electric nano-bikini, walked like a sumo-wrestler on a thirty-foot-long pink dildo. Her opponent was a man in a dog collar and nothing else. He looked unsteady standing on a thirty-foot purple dildo, adjacent to the pink one. Both wore spiked cleats and were trying to scrape the opponent's dildo and slice it open with their shoes.

Sumit's jaw dropped. *We've bred away all intelligence. With subsequent generations seeing less disease and the idea that every human life is sacred, humanity's story has become a survival of the dumbest.* He changed the channel.

A grim reaper towered over the mini-bar. Its scythe flashed out toward Sumit's face. Reflexes caused him to lean back to avoid the hologram. A photograph of a smiling white family was sliced in two by the blade. A narrator spoke as the image cut to the grim reaper slashing hundreds of family photos and laughing. "MaxWell kills. Get immunized before you lose everything that is important to you."

Sumit blinked. *Subtlety is a lost art.*

He thought back on his childhood. He had not grown up with a lot of money like Anjali had. However, his father was a well-known physicist and his mother a respected university professor. His parents had gone into debt to have his double cleft palate fixed soon after his birth, but they did not have the money to have it erased forever with follow-up surgery. Sumit had been teased about his appearance as a child. It forced him to withdraw and find confidence in solitary academic pursuits. Tests did not have a face on them when graded. Tests had right or wrong answers. Like physics, there were black and white solutions to every problem. Physics did not have an emotional component. He found it easier to exist in a world like that.

He regarded Anjali again. She was lost in her work. Her numbers were her friends and family, there was little left inside her for humanity. He loved her deeply when they first met. He even loved her during their first years of marriage when they found out she was unable to have children. It took a few years before he realized she could never love him the way he wanted to be loved. At first he blamed her cold heart on his appearance, but in Anjali's case, it was her affliction that kept her emotions retracted. He respected her scientific mind, but he had not loved her in many years.

After failing to have his emotional needs met through his wife, Sumit turned to questions of humanity and what it would take to build a better world. Doctor Morris, the father of the Third Eye, had recruited him into The Order of Erasmus when Third Eyes were in beta testing. Morris had believed in building a scientific community that transcended politics and existed to advance humankind. Sumit enjoyed discourse with like minds and began to feel as if he was part of a larger family.

In a way, Sumit continued to believe in Morris' original mantra. But so much had changed since then. Morris and Veloso—the chip's co-inventor—had died violently within months of each other. Humanity was teetering on a precipice. Now he was in Antarctica, facing the biggest challenge of his life.

A male newscaster's face popped up over the mini-bar and a map of China and India stood behind him. "India's claims that China has stolen many of its bio-technology secrets places the ceasefire between those two countries at risk. Meanwhile, Korea continues to dispute Japan's fishing rights in the Japan Sea."

Anger washed over him. He remembered the Bachelor Wars. They got their name because both China and India had roughly fifty million men between them who could never find brides. It was a condition created by years of aborting girls, or genetically selecting males. Males took care of families. Girls simply represented dowries, or in other words, a massive loss of income. The decades long practice had created a generation without women. With all the testosterone surging in both countries, crime increased, so war seemed to be the best solution. Border disputes over Kashmir and other parts of the two Asian nations were the public reasons for fighting, but the real reason was both nations had a surplus of disposable life. Karma created by the deaths of all those would-be baby girls.

China invaded Kashmir. His older brother Paavak ran a processing plant outside Pathankot. Chinese drones bombed the city and the plant. Paavak, his wife, son, and daughter were all killed. Two years and millions of dead later, there was a ceasefire and borders returned to their pre-war status. Sumit had lost his favorite brother because of some ludicrous political grandstanding. He swore he would never be a victim of political circumstance. He would play politics and ensure his seat on the other side of the crosshairs.

A woman newscaster appeared and Sumit was appalled to see a recording of a Splooge match playing behind her. Her suit changed color in solidarity for MaxWell deaths. An increasing number of people were copying Parks' symbolic display over the past week. "It's official, the game show *Splooge* is rated number one in America and the EU, defeating the six year reigning champ, *Making It with Eddie*." She turned to her co-host. "Seems everyone is in need of some mindless distraction."

The co-host nodded. "I hear you, Lewis. Our next story dissects the borders of America. Despite decades of security measures against terrorism, is American security merely an illusion?"

Sumit knew of a small group of very wealthy and powerful individuals who had built homes in remote areas of the world. Their plan had been to wait out this wave of craziness, and then come back after the carnage. Only this time, the world was about to be consumed by Shiva's wrath. There would be no place to hide. Technology had shrunk the earth into a village. The untouchable few, who thought they could ride out the storm, were now choosing sides: The Order of Erasmus or The Consortium. Neither organization was in the news, but both were behind everything truly newsworthy.

He turned off the holoprojector. Maybe Parks was right. Maybe it really was The End of Days. The very idea of Parks made him shudder. Parks was additional proof that the average IQ had dropped by forty points in the past five years.

Sumit was pleased. He had watched a total of six minutes worth of holovision. It made him feel far more comfortable about his next task.

Chapter 8
Lenticular

Skiing on Mount Erebus was beautiful. The views of Mac Town, the shoreline, and the vast expanse of ocean were stunning. The temperature had dropped to thirty-one degrees Fahrenheit, cold enough to keep the artificial snow in Mac Town intact. From this distance Jake could appreciate McMurdo. The city was reminiscent of a calm picture of the past.

The mood was shattered as soon as he looked down at the trail. The snow was covered in patches of advertising that followed each skier as she or he rocketed downward. There were more snow boarders than skiers out today but that was fairly typical. Tomoko had opted to stay in the room and watch news with Lakshmi. She had made the wiser choice.

This year would be his last hurrah. Sanchez's money was just about spent. Jake and Tomoko had done a good job stretching it out. He thought about working here as a cop, but the idea of going back into any type of peacekeeping work held little appeal. *Too bad forklift drivers have been replaced by robots.*

It was all a silly notion anyway. He was not interested in living in this city. Some other spot in Antarctica might work, but not this one.

His Omni beeped, heralding a new message as he ascended on his second chairlift ride: The Amundsen Resort confirms the guest who sneezed in the lobby had a common cold and NOT MaxWell. Management would like to offer all lobby guests who witnessed the event 50% off an additional night's stay at the Amundsen.

After skiing three runs, he returned to the room and took Lakshmi for a jog while Tomoko stayed glued to the news. After months traveling with a self-imposed blackout on their Omnis, she was starved for information. He knew she was traveling under extreme conditions out of love for him. He also knew she had been ready to go home for some time now. He felt a bit selfish holding her back. He knew what she wanted, he was just afraid to make any changes. But with the money running out, and this crazy epidemic, change was coming regardless.

He took Lakshmi to the Scott museum. Facing east, the base held the illusion of being isolated on the edge of the great white continent, a place relatively untouched by humankind. They walked around the buildings and saw several Weddell seals lying on shore. The seals snorted and barked when they noticed Lakshmi. He used hand signals to tell her to stay close. Lakshmi sat with head cocked as she observed the mammals. They had seen several species of seal in their travels, but always in low numbers. The strangest was the leopard seal. The animal was more a cross between a serpent and a fish.

He gazed out over the black Antarctic Sea. The Ross Ice Shelf had melted away for good about eight years ago. He checked out Mount Erebus towering over everything. It had been dormant for fifteen years, but geologists continued to predict it could erupt at any time. It was still an active volcano under its peaceful surface. Much of its geothermal activity was being harvested to power cities like America's Mac Town and Italy's Terra Nova.

He spotted a white cross on an outcropping of volcanic rock. He fixed his Omni on it and identified the object as the Vince Cross. He read the history and was taken back to the times of the early Antarctic explorers. They had dangers of a different kind, but life was certainly simpler, and humanity had not achieved a stranglehold on Mother Nature.

His attempt to distract himself at the museum was unsuccessful. The image of Parks continued to pop into his head. Ever since the broadcast, he noticed everyone on the hotel staff and some guests were wearing his red color-changing pins. Jake decided to do a little research on his Omni. What he found was appalling. Many DOP members had been tied to terrorist acts over the past three years. Parks himself was spending more time and money in court to separate his church from the incidents. Jake saw the breaking news that Parks was being tied to the death of a Doctor Eberstark. Jake couldn't believe the immature kid with a decent heart could change so much in five years.

Jake took pleasure in the fact that the grounds around the museum were deserted. He and Lakshmi explored farther and farther away from McMurdo, enjoying the barren country beyond. This time of year there was no night, just a long sunset and sunrise between 10:00PM and 2:00AM. He checked his Omni and cursed. It was almost 7:00PM and he was miles from the resort. Lakshmi was overjoyed at their heart-pounding run back to the room. Along the way, there were several places where he was forced to slow down because massive patches of black ice were forming as the city cooled. He wondered why the sidewalk heaters weren't running.

They entered their room panting and found Tomoko decked out in a gorgeous evening gown. The blue feather he had given her was woven into her hair.

"Sorry we're late," He wheezed.

Tomoko checked the time in the mirror as she made the final touches on her makeup. "I wasn't worried. Not even MaxWell could make me miss this meal."

He planted a big kiss on her mouth and she pushed him back. "You have until I finish redoing my lips if you want to join me." She smiled and went to work. "Oh, our hosts provided this gown and rented a suit for you."

He went to the closet and found a crisp black suit hanging all by itself. "Reminds me of riot trooper armor."

"Put it on and I promise to attack you after dinner."

"I'd better take a quick shower."

Jake and Tomoko stood in awe when they entered Shackleton's Lounge. The establishment sat under a massive transparent dome that framed Mount Erebus. The volcano's gigantic bulk dominated the room. The sky was filled with orange and red lenticular clouds. They reminded him of melted ice cream pools frozen in the sky.

He whistled. "Now that's awe inspiring."

"It's like the surface of Jupiter up there," she marveled.

It took them several minutes before they could tear their eyes away from the view. When they did, Sumit stood up and waved from a table near the outer ring supporting the dome.

"We noticed you minutes ago, but you were in a daze." He laughed when Jake and Tomoko joined them. Sumit wore a black tux and Anjali was wrapped in a gorgeous orange and red Indian Sari.

Jake couldn't stop gawking. "I still am."

Anjali glanced at the view behind her. She spoke matter-of-factly. "Stable moist air flows over the mountain. The crest of the wave reaches dew point. The combination creates the lens or lenticular shape."

Sumit poured an Argentinean Malbec into Jake and Tomoko's glasses. "Anjali is not much of a romantic."

"I'm emotional!" she snapped. "It's just all this racket makes it hard for me to concentrate."

Tomoko leaned over to Anjali. "I love your dress."

Anjali gazed at her for an instant, as if searching for a response. "Thanks. I like yours too." She began pulling balls of butter from a silver dish and lining them up on her plate.

Jake wondered if Anjali had some form of autism. There was chatter in the room, but it was not as loud as the volume on the lobby holo-displays. "So what business were you conducting down here, Sumit?"

"There's a biogenic lab in town. They're working on an alternate cure for MaxWell. Anjali and I are in trial stages. We were down to compare data."

Tomoko interjected, "Couldn't you do that over the Cyber-Wire?"

Sumit grew serious. "For security purposes, no. The Consortium has tapped every information stream and has been injecting false data everywhere to stall our efforts."

"Consortium?" Jake asked.

Anjali cut in. "Remember Senator Crennon and Director Sanchez?"

Tomoko compassionately gripped Jake's hand under the table. "He's been trying to forget."

Sumit nodded sympathetically, but Anjali plowed on through. "They were part of an international network, or at least we know Sanchez was. The members call themselves The Consortium. They are powerful people who share a common interest in using The Chip to govern society and consolidate power under one united body."

Tomoko shook her head. "A global state of union. Sounds nice until you dig down to the underbelly."

Anjali shifted her concentration to the basket of hot dinner rolls, which had just been placed on the table. "Technology is moving so fast that everything is reaching a state of union. Machines with humanity, viruses with mechanics, animals with people, lines are blurring everywhere..."

"To your point, Tomoko," Sumit added, "Power and control are good motivators to unite those who crave it."

"I suspect if they get what they want, they'll start to turn on each other," Jake commented.

Sumit pursed his lips. "We're told they have a body of laws to deter anyone from getting too powerful and turning against the rest. They also have a rudimentary version of AI, which will be a part of their overall plan. There won't be enough of them to govern the billions of chipped citizens."

Jake remembered his conversation with Sanchez back in Rio, before he handed his tormentor over to Homeland Security. "They want to control the masses through The Chip. So MaxWell—"

"Did not escape by accident," Sumit nodded.

Anjali split open a dinner roll and began spreading a massive amount of butter on it.

"Was MaxWell engineered to motivate mass immunization with Third Eyes?" Jake asked.

"Yes and no," Sumit answered. "We think it started much like the Personal Chip. It was an invention to better humanity. MaxWell was going to be a cure against all flu viruses. But somewhere along the line The Consortium got involved and it was engineered as an agent to force those who are against The Chip to be implanted."

"Can I take your orders?"

Everyone swung around to see a waiter dressed in some odd nineteenth century garb that looked like a hybrid of Imperial Russian and French military uniforms.

Jake noticed the waiter staring at Anjali. She was carefully carving some mathematical equations into the buttered surface of her roll using her knife.

"Come back later." Sumit smiled. "We haven't had a chance to look over the menu yet."

The waiter broke his stare and gave a courteous smile. "Please take your time."

"I watched the news for hours today and the media pooh-poohs the conspiracy idea. Why is that?" Tomoko asked. Jake could see the alarm on her face.

Anjali photographed her calculations with her Omni, and then took a bite out of the bread. "The media is trying to control fear. Plus no one outside of Bollywood would truly believe a group of people are capable of an act that would kill millions wholesale."

Sumit continued. "The information we've gathered is secondary. We don't have evidence like Jake did when he exposed the initial Chip conspiracy."

Tomoko shook her head. "With millions dead, I would think everyone would be looking to hang someone for MaxWell."

"Ten million and the number is growing." Anjali took another bite from her roll.

Jake had a hard time buying Anjali's lack of concern, even with autism.

"Ten million... I heard it several times today and I still can't fathom that many faces." Tomoko turned to look out the window, a tear in her eye.

Jake noticed Anjali studying Tomoko's reaction with extreme interest.

Sumit observed his wife.

Jake turned to share Tomoko's view. The majestic volcano retained its otherworldly lenticular cap. Murder on that scale was horrifying. How could it be justified? It made him want to weep with Tomoko. He fought back his sorrow and concentrated on the view. He wished he could take their sailboat and glide on that wondrous vapor trail in the sky.

Sumit broke Jake's train of thought. "You were right."

Jake turned to face Sumit.

"We do need you."

Jake sat back and sighed. Tomoko's eyes conveyed concern for him. He loved her for that. He craved compassion after the horrors of being hacked and imprisoned in his own mind. He was convinced that residual memory implants were a key to his nightmares. He had been at a loss on how to address his nightmares, except through escape and the passage of time. But Tomoko proved to be a great source of strength and peace for him.

He turned to Anjali and Sumit. "What could I possibly do? I'm a cop. I'm not a hacker. I'm not a virologist."

Anjali laughed. "That's for sure."

Sumit quickly cut in. "Jake has advantages in many areas you don't, my dear."

Anjali bit her lip. "I'm sorry. I find social intercourse to be incredibly fatiguing." With that she opened her leather bound menu and hid behind it. It had been years since Jake had seen anything but a digital menu.

Sumit continued. "We want you to go after Joaquin Parks."

Jake coughed. "As in… what?"

Sumit smoothed the tablecloth. He opened his mouth then closed it.

"You mean kill him?" Jake pressed.

Sumit's eyes went wide. "No! We want you to talk to him. See if you can get him to join us."

"Why me?"

Anjali clapped her menu shut. "Christmas Prix Fixe! Can't wait."

Flustered by his wife's interruption, Sumit stuttered. "Y-you s-saw the broadcast. He still holds a torch for you."

Anjali quickly interjected. "He *idolizes* you. You're his one regret."

Jake laughed. "You arranged to have that interview displayed in the lobby. It was a setup."

Anjali smiled proudly. "Yes I did! It took me ten minutes to compromise the lobby computer and force it to run that week-old upload when you entered the hotel!"

Jake glared at Anjali in anger.

Anjali turned red and disappeared behind her menu. "I can't decide on dessert."

Jake turned his anger to Sumit. "Why me? Haven't you approached Parks?"

Sumit fidgeted. "We have, but we can't get a single response out of him or the DOP."

Tomoko took the words out of Jake's mouth. "Why are you interested in Parks?"

Sumit relaxed a bit. "He runs Cobalt, the world's largest heavy weapons manufacturer. His church has been hitting God Head sites on all sides. Because of his religious status, he plays by a different set of laws than the rest of us. He's able to travel to many quarantined countries and we have reason to believe his four HJs are really mobile God Head facilities. Lately he seems to be striking scientific institutions, especially around the development of AI. Then again, it's hard to tell if he's to blame, as the Jihad Brotherhood has been busy in that area as well. We need to know where his allegiance lies. If we're to win this war, we need him on our side. If he chooses The Consortium, then he needs to be eliminated."

Jake couldn't believe what he was hearing. "That kid is the key to your fight against The Consortium?"

"That kid will be thirty next year," Anjali's voice rose from behind the menu.

Jake shook his head. "Thirty is still a kid in my book."

Anjali continued. "Whitney's Cobalt Industries made trillions selling heavy weapons and vehicles to both sides during the Bachelor Wars. Now Parks has that money, and legacy."

Sumit rubbed his wife's arm. She withdrew and hid behind her menu again. Sumit's face flushed from her reaction. "Cobalt Industries makes all sorts of war machines. They specialize in Military Hover-Jets. Parks has access to nuclear powered aircraft that never need to refuel and are not affected by EMPs."

Jake did not quite trust Sumit. He was trying too hard to sell the anti-Parks initiative. "What are *your* feelings on Parks, Sumit?"

Sumit jerked a bit. He looked as if he were slipping off a cliff. "What do you mean?"

"I mean, you just spat out your mission, but how do you personally feel about Parks?"

Sumit's eyes flashed with what Jake read as hate. "I think Joaquin Parks is a menace. I just found out today that he was behind the death of Roald Eberstark."

Jake shook his head. "He's a suspect. I saw the same upload."

Tomoko cut in. "I saw it, too. Eberstark was working on transferring the human consciousness into the Cyber-Wire."

Jake winced. "Living forever in cyberspace sounds a bit dark and lonely. I have first-hand experience."

Anjali interjected from behind the menu again. "You could set up any environment in cyberspace. It would be like a holo-deck from that old TV series Star Trek."

"According to Eberstark's plan, AI would assist in building robot bodies for each consciousness so humanity could return to the physical world after the body dies," Sumit added.

Jake shook his head. "Why do all recent advances in technology fail to appeal to me?"

Tomoko gently touched his hand and smiled in agreement.

He returned to Sumit. "So if it were your call, you would have me assassinate Parks?"

Sumit's jaw dropped. He appeared painfully uncomfortable. "Yes."

"I appreciate the honest answer." Jake felt disgusted that this man would think of him as some hired thug.

Sumit quickly interjected, "But I am not in charge and hardly in the majority." He laughed nervously. "Erasmus believes Parks is more of a con-artist and given the right incentives, could be persuaded to join our cause. Adding Cobalt's firepower and the Disciples Of Paul would bolster our power a thousand fold."

Jake gazed at Mount Erebus again. Perhaps this really was all just a crazy world dreamed up by some God Head. Was there a term when you were trapped in another person's dream? Solipsism didn't quite fit the definition.

Sumit continued, "And you would not believe the security Parks has around him. Since last year, he travels with four or five children from his flock. He says he wants to give kids in the church a chance to see the world. But the real reason is they are a deterrent against any assassination attempt."

Tomoko was appalled. "That's horrible."

Jake could not believe Parks was using children as a human shield. If it were true, there might be merit to Sumit's story. *Are you an agent of good or evil, Jake?* Jake released a long sigh and picked up his menu. "Let me think about it. I want to order before I lose my appetite."

Everyone ordered from the Christmas Prix Fixe menu. By the time dessert and Lakshmi's filet mignon arrived, the mood was lighter.

Sumit laughed as he finished his story. "Can you imagine? Digging a crater in the Antarctic ice cap at the pole so there are 360 degrees of ski runs leading down to a winter village?"

Tomoko shook her head. "I can't believe people in the United States were close to approving the idea." She punched Jake's arm. "What's wrong with your people?"

"Hey the decision was blocked, right?" Jake finished off the third bottle of wine by distributing it in all four glasses. "At least *my* people didn't carve up the face of the moon." He threw the comment at Sumit.

Spotting the empty bottle, the sommelier came by but Sumit shook his head no. Sumit held his glass up to Jake. "Touché."

Anjali parroted her husband. Jake felt sympathy for her. She had been trying very hard to be social since they had ordered dinner.

Jake took in the view. It was 10:00PM and the sky was filled with reds, blues and purples. A band of golden sun sat on the edge of the horizon, a midsummer's night in Antarctica. As he marveled, he saw the area around the Scott Museum shimmer as if heat were rising all around it. Black ice sheets covered all the streets and sidewalks of Mac Town from the day's melt and the night's freeze. He rubbed his eyes to get rid of the shimmer. *Must be the wine.*

The ski runs on Mount Erebus flashed with electric light: MERRY CHRISTMAS and HAPPY HOLIDAYS exploded in a myriad of languages.

"Excuse me, I have to use the WC." Sumit stood up and left the table. A little fear crept into Anjali's eyes as she watched her security blanket leave.

Jake took the extra filet and wrapped it in the synthetic bag the waiter had given him. He stuffed it in the pocket of his rented suit. He touched the scrimshaw quarter Tomoko had carved for him and he smiled.

Tomoko turned to Anjali. "How did you two meet?"

Anjali played music with the rim of her wine glass as she stared at Tomoko. "It was an arranged marriage. Our parents were friends and we were both bright in the sciences. It was difficult at first but Sumit has been wonderfully understanding. Any other man would have left me at the altar."

"I'm sure that's not true. You're a lovely woman."

Anjali forced a smile. "Thank you." Then she looked out the window.

Tomoko stood up. "I think I need to use the powder room myself."

He watched Tomoko leave as Anjali turned and commented, "I've spent my whole life wishing I could be someone like her."

He turned back to Anjali. "Autism?"

Anjali turned red. "Asperger's. Only ten percent of all cases are women. I'm in a very small and elite group. I prefer equations over people… but I desperately wish I could be included in the party of life."

He nodded sympathetically. "Must be hard."

She laughed. "Especially in an Indian household. I was ten when I was diagnosed. My parents were relieved to find out there was a reason for my odd behavior, but the boy I was supposed to marry withdrew his offer. My parents spent two years locating a family who would say yes to the union. My mother and father were ready to give up when Sumit's family came along. We were both considered socially challenged. A perfect match."

"He's very kind to you." Jake smiled.

She blushed. "How about you? Getting married?"

It was his turn to blush. "Thinking about it."

"Does she love you?"

He was about to say *isn't it obvious* but reminded himself whom he was talking to. "Yes. She loves me very much. I love her too."

"How can you tell?"

"The way she looks at me, treats me, talks to me. It's in every expression she makes toward me." He smiled. "Plus she says it often."

Anjali shook her head. "Too abstract. I have read about identifying love but never see the empirical evidence."

"Must be hard."

She nodded. "Why have you been at sea for five years?"

Jake opened his mouth, about to give a superficial answer, but something stopped him. "I've been running from my past." He smiled. "But no matter how far I go, I always seem to bring it with me."

She cocked her head. "I have the same problem. My lab is my ship and my work is my ocean. But inevitably I always find myself having to pull into port." She folded her napkin. "Is Tomoko running too?"

"At first… but now she does only because I do."

They regarded each other in complete understanding.

A loud sneeze rang out in the restaurant. All conversation died and the power went out. Anjali covered her ears. "Nemp!"

The holiday light show on the face of Mount Erebus continued to dazzle.

A Maître d' walked to the center of the room. "Ladies and Gentlemen, please remain seated and calm until the Nemp passes. I ask that the person who sneezed please follow me to the infirmary."

Everyone looked around but no one was taking accountability.

"I'll just view the footage from our cameras then." The Maître d' unfolded his Omni and frowned. "When the Nemp passes."

Jake saw the couple from the bus. The wife was whispering something to her husband when she suddenly sat upright, twisted her face, and released a tremendous sneeze. Her eyes went wide with shock. Within a second ten others followed suit. There was a domino effect of mass sneezing around the room.

People began to stand in horror. The Maître d' appeared nervous. The lights snapped back on. The Maître d' raised his Omni to his lips. Jake guessed he was ordering the Nemp to be switched back on and to get the room quarantined. Then the Maître d' sneezed and looked like he was about to piss his pants.

Jake spotted Sumit entering the dining room with an expression of alarm. He rushed toward their table.

Just then, Jake sensed movement from behind. He spun around as a section in the base of the dome shattered. Cold wind howled in. A soldier in nano-skin camouflage leapt through the opening with machine gun blazing.

Chapter 9
Slide

Jake crouched and wheeled around to look for Tomoko. He realized that the shimmering effect around the Scott Museum had been from camouflage ponchos worn by an invasion force.

Bullets whizzed over his head. Screams were everywhere. Tomoko was not in the room. Good. She was smart. She'd get Lakshmi and get the hell out.

He spun around just in time to see Sumit get shot in the neck as he tried to pull a confused Anjali out of the line of fire. A split second after Sumit went down, Anjali was hit in the thigh with a bullet. Jake dove under a table and saw the camouflaged boots of a commando just a few yards away, making his way around the edge of the dome. Jake's years of tactical and combat training took over. He grabbed two steak knives off the floor and rolled under the table towards the soldier. Jake threw. The knife sunk into the man's camouflage poncho in the groin area. Instead of a scream or any sign of pain the man swung his weapon down toward Jake.

Bullets tore through the tabletop above as he dove for the table next to the commando. There were three dead bodies on the floor. Jake grabbed a body and swung it out behind the soldier. His attacker spun around. Bullets slammed into the corpse. In that instant Jake jumped out from under the table, grabbed the soldier's head, and slammed his remaining blade into the soldier's neck between the jaw line and the armored collar.

They both went down, the soldier struggled, his Third Eye in full survival mode. Jake jerked the blade into the soldier's spinal column. The man went limp. Jake pushed the body off of him and grabbed the man's gun. It was a T-37. A military issue he had seen a lot of in South America during his travels. This one supported a grenade launcher fixed under the barrel. Lying on his back at the edge of the dome, he cocked the launcher and fired a small black bomb toward the troops coming through the hole in the glass. The area exploded and three commandos went flying.

Jake dove and rolled over broken china, glassware, and bodies, always keeping his head below the tables. Bullets whistled and chewed into everything around him. He fired another grenade in the direction of the thickest gunfire. It was followed by an explosion mixed with screams.

Jesus, Jake you're killing innocent people! You've got to get out of here. You're no match for Chipped commandos.

He noticed a pair of winter camo boots through a tunnel created by several dining tables. He stood up and shot the owner of the boots. The soldier staggered and went down. More shimmers could be seen beyond the restaurant entrance inside the hotel. He had been lucky so far. But any more troops in this room would be zeroing in on him fast. He dove back to the spot where the Malik couple had dropped. Sumit gripped his neck, trying to stop the blood flow. His clothes and the carpet around him were soaked in blood. Anjali was motionless. Bullets hammered into the wooden shield above them.

Jake checked on Sumit first. "I've got to get you out of here."

Sumit gagged on his own blood. "Anjali knocked her head on the table. She's fine."

The bullets were beginning to destroy the integrity of the table; it would not be protective much longer. "Can you travel?"

Sumit shook his head. “Leave me. Save Anjali.” Tears welled in his eyes.

Jake understood all too well the mad desire to save one you loved. He was worried sick about Tomoko and Lakshmi, but there were far too many chipped soldiers between him and the main hotel.

Jake used his body to cover Anjali, and then he aimed his grenade launcher at a nearby section of the dome. He fired while turning his head. A split second later the explosion covered them in Plexiglas. He wasted no time hanging the weapon over his shoulder and lifting Anjali. He dove for the new opening just as he heard a grenade launcher pop behind him.

They flew from the dome just as the opening exploded behind. The concussion hurled them down onto the ice and they began sliding and tumbling wildly down a hill toward the hotel’s east wing. He was certain Sumit had been killed by the last explosion.

Jake desperately dug his fingers into the ice in an attempt to slow their progress, but they were traveling too fast. He felt woozy and his vision began to fog. He felt the throb of a head wound. On his mad toboggan-less ride, he managed to grab hold of Anjali’s arm. He pulled her in and hugged her with what little strength he had left.

Moments of the attack flashed in his head. The commando he had killed wore the insignia of the Argentinean army. Every soldier had been silent and the knife wound to the soldier’s groin had no effect. Jake was certain the unit was Chipped.

Why are the Argentineans provoking a war with the US?

They slammed into the east wing and began spinning. A nearby explosion sprayed glass all over them. Some cut into his face. He tried to pull the gun off his shoulder but it meant losing his grip on Anjali. The effort made him dizzier.

He was still spinning when blackness overtook him.

When he awoke from his fog with the sensation of hot breath against his neck, he felt himself slide at a slower pace. There was a large weight on his chest. “Tomoko,” he whispered as he gripped the body tighter. No, the person on his chest was not Tomoko.

Blackness.

Chapter 10

Sommelier

Tomoko wore a smile on her face as she reflected on the romantic view from the Shackelton Lounge. The food was superb and their hosts were highly engaging. Anjali was trying so hard but seemed horribly inept at socializing. Yet, Tomoko liked her and was looking forward to getting to know the eccentric virologist better.

Tomoko was not keen on the topic of MaxWell and Chips, but her wine buzz killed any deeper emotions she might have felt about the depressing world events.

She was about to enter the ladies room when the sound of the explosion erupted behind her. She ran back toward the dining room. The sound of machine gun fire slowed her steps and the sight of the panicked sommelier running out of the room struck fear into her heart.

"Run!" The man collided into her at a four-way junction. They both hit the carpet. Gunfire and screams filled their ears from the direction of the hotel lobby.

The sommelier tried to scramble away but she grabbed his shoulders. "Is there another way out?"

The man struggled like a petrified animal. He was trying to flee toward the lobby.

Years of Jake's tactical training on the sailboat kicked in for Tomoko. She could hear him now: *Be calm, always look for the advantage. Chaos gives you time.* She slapped the sommelier. "They're coming from both sides. Where does that hallway lead?" She nodded to the fourth and only option.

The man snapped out of his panic mode. "That's the kitchen!"

More gunfire and screams echoed from the dining room and lobby. She heard a sneeze, which was hard to believe under the circumstances. A loud explosion sent flaming debris toward them from the direction of the dome. "Is there an exit from the kitchen?"

"Yes!"

She pulled on him. "Let's go!"

They ran side-by-side into the kitchen. The massive stainless steel room was empty. The staff had already escaped. The sommelier led her through a maze of steam, burning meat, and bubbling caldrons. She noticed a rack of chef coats and grabbed several. The cold was going to be just as deadly as this mystery invader.

The sommelier crashed through the emergency exit and she followed him under an electric red, orange, and deep blue sky. Mount Erebus towered over them; its snow-encased peak reflected the red light of the Antarctic night. Explosions reverberated all around the city. Plumes of black smoke trickled into the sky from various areas including one of the hotel turrets.

The sommelier's feet shot out from underneath him and he crashed onto a sheet of black ice. The entire area around the hotel was covered in it. The man cried out and began to panic again. The more he flailed the more he slid about like a capsized June bug.

"Shhh!" Tomoko hissed as she tried to make her way over to him without falling down herself.

He had a Caribbean accent. "You think they can hear me with all these explosions and gunfire?"

"I have no idea, but why draw attention to ourselves?"

The man laughed then began to cry out in rage as he crashed onto his face. "Fucking Christmas ice! They engineer it to freeze like this to better reflect the lights of the city and Mount Erebus."

"I smell a lawsuit… if anyone survives this night." She heard a roar behind her. She turned to see a streak of flame fly out of one of the hotel turrets and lick a block of rooms below. The attackers were going out of their way to burn the city down. They were on the west side of the dome. She heard more explosions and gunfire from the eastern side. Or maybe it was the other way around depending on the orientation of the map. She found direction at the South Pole confusing.

"Hold still!" She barked as she held on to a drainpipe and extended her hand to the flopping sommelier.

He calmed down and reached out for her. Their fingers almost touched when his arm broke between the elbow and shoulder. Blood sprayed everywhere as he screamed. She lunged at him. Her inertia shot them a hundred yards across the ice toward a low steel structure painted to match the resort. Bullets chewed the ice behind them. She had no idea where the sniper was hidden or if it was a sniper. Jake told her most militaries worldwide were Chipped. A Chip could make a blind man a marksman in any army. *Then why not aim for the head?*

She used her elbow to dig into the ice and pivot them until they hit the building feet first. She launched them into a small alley created by the hotel and the steel structure so they'd have some cover. The sommelier would not stop screaming so she shoved the sleeve of one of the chef's coats into his mouth.

A drone flew overhead, firing bullets into the night. It had zeroed in on them before she managed to push them into this alleyway. They slid to a stop in front of a garage door with a glowing access pad. "What is this place?"

The sommelier moaned.

"We need shelter so I can tie off that wound. Otherwise, you'll bleed to death." She grabbed his face. "Can you get us in there?"

The man snapped out of his pain ride long enough to glance at the door and glowing pad. He pulled the white cloth out of his mouth with his good hand. "The snowplow shed. Low security. I might have access."

She helped the sommelier to his feet.

He cried out in pain. "Fucking took out my left arm! I'm fucking left handed!"

Sweat ran down Tomoko's face from trying to hold up the sommelier and keep her balance on the ice. "What's your name, sommelier!"

"Trevor," the man replied.

Tomoko channeled Jake. "Okay, Trevor. Concentrate on that pad. Use your right hand and get us in there. In there is shelter. In there we can hide from this firefight. In there I can save your life."

The man nodded and carefully entered his code. "You get one chance before it locks up and sends out the alarm." He hit enter and the door rolled up, revealing robot snowplows tucked into charging stations. There was no room to maneuver inside. She guided Trevor over the bulky vehicles to one of the largest versions parked in the room. Its solar cell grid was big enough for Trevor to lie comfortably flat.

She helped him up. "How do I close the door?"

"Hit the close button on this side."

She found it and sealed them in. She then attended to Trevor's wound. His shirt was soaked in blood and his arm hung limply from the top of the bicep down. The bone had been sheared in two by a large caliber bullet. She found the entry and exit holes in his sleeve. She tore an arm from one of the chef coats and made a tourniquet to cut off his circulation between the bicep and shoulder. It was the best she could do.

With Trevor taken care of, she put on the remaining two coats. They did not do much in the way of keeping her warm but she felt less exposed. She ripped the rest of the coat she had used for Trevor's wound to create wraps for her feet. She had been wearing heels when she was on her way to the bathroom, but had lost track of them after that. Her feet were freezing. Trevor wore a tux, but he would need warmth soon. She searched the garage for something to make a fire with, but all she found was fiberglass and steel.

They spent the next two hours listening to the sounds of destruction. Considering the actual purpose of their shelter, there were no windows to watch the progress through. She kept her mind off of Jake and Lakshmi's safety by trying different methods of coaxing her Omni to life. It had been smashed sometime during the escape. Trevor's had been lost during their escape.

"I'm surprised you're not chipped," she commented when she finally gave up on her Omni.

"I've never been the early adopter type. Plus the idea of having any device in my body scares the crap out of me. But my father passed from MaxWell and my mother and two brothers were immunized back in DR. They are fine."

"DR?"

"Dominican Republic."

"You're a long way from the tropics, Trevor."

"Call me Pink. The boss calls me Trevor."

"You're a long way from home, Pink."

"Where I come from, you go where the money is."

She took off her chef coats. It had been growing steadily warmer for the past hour.

"It's getting hot in here," Trevor commented.

Glowing progress bars on the charging stations illuminated the room. Small rivulets of condensation ran down the sides of the snowplows. She stood up from her perch on the machine next to Trevor and made her way to the front door. She felt the steel surface with her hand and it was warm. She made her way to the side closest to the hotel and felt again. It was very hot. "We have to leave. Now."

"I am not going anywhere."

"You don't have a choice." She stumbled back to Trevor.

"I am not moving."

She stared at him. "When I open that door, we could be facing a wall of fire. You won't have time to get off this vehicle and run from the building."

"I'm not moving."

She stood staring at the stubborn idiot, wondering how to motivate him. Her concentration was broken by a loud crack emanating from the wall she had touched earlier. A bright glow appeared and smoke began to pour into the room. "I'm opening that door. Follow me or die here!"

She stumbled around the parked machinery and the charging stations. When she reached the door she saw Trevor grunting his way toward her. She went back and helped him make his way to the panel.

"Do I need a code?" she asked.

"We're inside. Open should do the trick."

She hit the button and the door slid up. Fire roared in from the top of the doorframe. They scurried out into the alley leading to the main street. Flames raged all around them. Melted snow evaporated quickly from the pavement.

When they reached the main street, Trevor ran toward the center of town. Tomoko spotted a drone performing a kamikaze run into the town hall. The building exploded.

She shouted after him. "No! Head for the water!"

"The hospital and police are this way!"

She glanced at the harbor observation deck across the street. The harbor reflected the gold, red, blues and blacks of the sky as well as dozens of fires in the city. The observation deck was untouched. If the fire jumped to it, they could dive into water. There were plenty of flames to keep them warm.

Trevor either did not hear her, or did not care to listen. He continued running toward the city where there were gaps in the hungry blaze. She walked slowly toward the harbor observation deck, thinking he would come to his senses soon. She glanced back in his direction and saw he was roughly four hundred yards away, holding onto his bad arm to keep it from swinging like a bag of wet spaghetti. When she glanced again she saw him fall to the ground. The echo of the bullet came a second later.

Tomoko ran for the observation platform. She found a small beam under the main superstructure that she could sit on. It would be cold laying above the harbor waters, but better to be out of sight. If she needed to warm up, she could attempt to catch some heat topside. The fires would eventually be high enough to hide her from the soldier's eyes. The drones were another matter, but she'd just have to take a chance if it came to that.

"Stupid." She did not realize she had been repeating that same word for the past ten minutes until she secured a place where she felt safe and hidden. She thanked Jake for all the tactical and first aid training he had given her.

Performing combat maneuvers on a sailboat's slippery slanted surface made most of this easy. Plus, it made the time on the water quickly pass.

She watched the city burn in the glassy reflection of the water. She hoped Jake and Lakshmi were somewhere safe. Her thoughts drifted to her family back in Lima. Her parents were the grandchildren of Japanese immigrants who had left Japan at the end of World War II. She was born on July 10, 2001. Her father had built a successful shipping company and was disappointed his firstborn was not a son. She had been largely ignored by her father her whole life, especially when her younger brother had been born in 2005. All her mother's talents were tied into being a skilled socialite. She had no interest in being a mother or housewife. Tomoko spent most of her childhood interacting with a string of nannies and the DVDs in her father's den.

As she grew older, she discovered surfing, pottery, and carving. Her brother played sports, got good grades in all the right subjects, and had been groomed to take over the family business. She was encouraged to disappear with her surfing friends. Nobody in the family understood her artistic desire to work with clay. She was always the oddball and had never felt welcome. Money was used to keep her occupied outside of the house.

Since she was not welcome at home, she had searched for acceptance outside Lima. When she graduated college, she ran to Paris to study art at the Sorbonne University. After Paris, she spent time studying under European and Japanese pottery masters between extended surf vacations. The money always came, but any invitations to spend time with the family were conveniently overlooked. Her mother would say, "We simply never know where you're going to be."

"I'd fly home anytime if you made me feel welcome."

"Tomoko," her mother would cluck, "you're always welcome."

But whenever Tomoko arrived at the family home, she found that everyone was busy and she was not invited to come along.

She never married, and after she turned twenty-one her father began saying; "I hope you find a good husband so I can stop the payments. You're too old to be taking money from me, Tomoko."

She would have gladly traded her father's money for his love. She took what she could get.

She met Jake when she was twenty-nine. Jake reminded her of a wounded bird, and like her, Jake was broken and in need of nurturing back to health. He was kind and he understood feelings of anxiety and rejection. He wanted to travel the world as a carefree vagabond and she was in love with the idea. Lakshmi had sealed the deal.

After a few years at sea, she grew weary of avoiding society, but she tried to accommodate Jake's healing process. Now the world was collapsing and she wanted family. She wanted to go back to Lima and confront her parents. She wanted to reconcile. She hoped that Jake would be by her side. The MaxWell news had been the final wakeup call. She was not the type of person who could run forever. Neither was Jake, or so she hoped.

Trevor Pink had a family. Now he was dead. It was time to take charge of the time they had left. But first things first, she had to survive this attack.

Chapter 11
Shelter

Jake awoke with the greasy texture of burning plastic in his nose and mouth. He rolled to one side and felt aches and pains hit him from head to toe. He felt a warm tongue on his face and smiled.

"Hey, girl." He opened his eyes and saw his trusty Husky smiling over him. He felt a great weight on his chest and for a moment he was delighted with the idea that he had woken up with Tomoko in their sleeping bag. Then reality flooded back. He hadn't let go of Anjali since the fall from the Shackleton Lounge. He gently pushed her to the floor and stood up. He was inside an entryway. Glass from the double doors had blown inward from some explosion. An icy breath danced through the jagged hole framing black clouds of smoke beyond. The hotel and much of Mac Town was ablaze.

He slipped his hand into his pants pocket and felt the steak and the quarter-sized scrimshaw. Holding the carved object in his fingers felt like touching Tomoko. It gave him comfort.

He patted himself down and found blood on his left pant leg. There was a pool of it on the floor but he did not have a wound. It had to be Anjali's blood. His gun was gone. Must have come off in his descent from the hotel. He turned and examined Anjali's unconscious form. He felt for a pulse. She was alive, but he needed to stop the bleeding. She had a nasty bump on her head. He lifted her up and observed Lakshmi.

"Where's Tomoko?"

Lakshmi barked and whined as she ran back and forth by the door.

"I want to look for her, too." He observed the unconscious Anjali in his arms. "But we can't." It frustrated him to admit it.

Lakshmi whined and rubbed up against his leg. Lakshmi had somehow escaped the hotel. She not only located Jake in the snow, but she had dragged them here over the icy streets. "I've got a steak for you, girl but first we have to fix up Anjali."

After studying his surroundings, Jake realized he was in the lobby to the Scott Museum. This was the old Kiwi base they had visited earlier in the day. "Smart dog! You remembered!" Shuttle holo-ads had shown bunks, science stations, and an infirmary.

Carrying the unconscious Anjali, he made his way back into the museum. The orange and yellow glow from the Antarctic night filtered through thick glass. He passed a heavy steel pressure door complete with wheel lock. He made a mental note to come back and shut it once he tended to Anjali.

He found the infirmary and laid her on the table. Most of the boxes behind the steel cabinet doors were empty, facades for tourists. He found some old coats and cold weather gear and pulled sizes for both of them. It was not freezing in the building yet, but the power was off and heat was escaping through the broken entryway.

After searching the cabinets, Jake found a bottle of hydrogen peroxide inside a sparse first aid kit. He pulled Anjali's saree apart around her thigh wound and noticed the wound had bled a little. He poured the liquid in and around it. The hole bubbled and fizzed. He made a bandage out of his shirt—the cleanest cloth he could find—and wrapped it around her thigh. He bundled her up, tore a pad off one of the gurneys, and placed her on the floor in a corner. He figured if the explosions came this way this was the best area for cover.

He put his hand in his suit pocket and found the synthetic bag wrapped steak. He knew Lakshmi had smelled it but she was faithful to her training. He smiled at her with immense pride. "You earned this and a hundred more, pretty girl." He unwrapped the steak and handed it to her. She gingerly took it in her mouth and lay down to savor it. "Guard Anjali."

Lakshmi barked in reply and he left the room to work on power, heat, and security. *What about Tomoko?* He pulled out the scrimshaw and stared at it. He had spent years training her aboard the *Pachacuteq*. She'd find a hiding place and wait this thing out. A person could survive the summer night, especially with Mac Town engulfed in a conflagration. He needed to sit tight and work out a plan. He laughed at himself. He was in the most remote, hostile place on earth with an army decimating the only shelter within miles. The plan was basically wait and be captured. At least Anjali would get medical attention once the enemy secured their position. Where were the Americans? Surely this attack tripped a slew of alarms across the satellite grid.

He found a map of the museum in the lobby. There were two corridors off the main entrance. Both of them had all-weather pressurized doors that could be sealed and locked. He stepped through the hole in the front door. Fires raged in the west and an orange and yellow sky hung over the black ocean to the north and east. The mighty Mount Erebus stared down at him from the south. They were surrounded.

He stepped back into the museum. He closed the storm doors in the back of the lobby and sealed off the main heat leak. He found the old generator room. Even though Antarctica was now powered with geothermal, wind, ocean waves, and radio waves, every building had to have a gas generator in case of an emergency.

He checked the generator's fuel. It was still good. Nice to know the curator was keeping up on maintenance. Jake placed his finger on the switch and hoped there was no Nemp radiating about. His vision faded a bit and he felt dizzy. He blinked and concentrated. He hit the switch and the motor whined and chugged to life. He found the thermostat and cranked up the infirmary to seventy degrees.

He walked back to the infirmary and stumbled. The dizziness was worse now. He checked himself in the mirror and noticed his face was covered in blood. There was a laceration on his head, which was still oozing. He found some old suture and needle, circa 1998. "Jesus, this stuff is almost as old as I am." He grit his teeth and began to sew himself up using the mirror as a guide. It was an incredibly slow and painful process. He took time out every minute or so to douse his wound with peroxide. He was exhausted by the time he was done.

He turned to Lakshmi who sat in front of the closed door to the infirmary. "Good girl."

He collapsed.

Blackness.

Chapter 12
Missing

Sunlight beat down on Jake's torso through the window in the hall outside the infirmary. He opened his eyes and checked his Omni, 5:07AM.

Lakshmi gave a whine from her position by the door. He staggered to his feet and let her out to relieve herself. He checked on Anjali. Her bandage was dry. Despite her pale complexion, her pulse was stable and her temperature was normal. Time to find food and water. A museum should have both in quantity, but he could always melt snow if need be.

He wandered about the corrugated halls of the New Zealand base. His hand wandered to the scrimshaw in his pocket. He pictured Tomoko at the wheel, enjoying the hum of the wind in the sails and the hiss of the keel cutting through water. Her smile warmed his heart no matter what the weather was like. She knew him better than anyone. She was his best friend. *She's fine. She's a survivor.* He continued to reassure himself.

You should have asked her to marry you.

I was afraid she'd be taken away, or worse yet, I'd wake up and find out she was an illusion. He felt her absence. He realized they had not spent a night apart since December 21, 2030. He had no interest in being apart again.

He found a snack shop and discovered processed food wrapped in microwave bags behind a counter: hamburgers, hotdogs, and Ahi tuna sandwiches. He chuckled when he read the ingredients. THIS PRODUCT MAY OR MAY NOT CONTAIN FISH, POULTRY, BEEF, PORK, EXOSKELETAL MATTER, OR EQUIVALENT PROTEIN SUPPLEMENT. THIS PRODUCT IS NOT KOSHER. He smiled at "exoskeletal;" it was the marketing term for bugs. More and more the world was turning to insects for protein. CHUM-CHUM IS NOT RESPONSIBLE FOR ANY ALLERGIC REACTION YOU MAY HAVE TO THE CONTENTS OF THIS PRODUCT. CHUM-CHUM ASSUMES NO LIABILITY... The list of disclaimers and lawsuit-dodging verbiage from the Chum-Chum Corporation was four times longer than the ingredients. He savored the memory of last night's steak. It would be a long time before he'd be eating the real McCoy again.

He shoved two burgers and two tuna sandwiches in the microwave and walked to an observation window to check on the world outside. Black smoke enshrouded McMurdo, and most everything in the surrounding area. Mount Erebus was hidden by a curtain of smoke. *Why haven't they attacked this base? Surely they can see the power signature and the heat this place gives off.*

He had not heard any explosions since waking up. He half hoped to hear the sound of shells as it might herald the coming of the Cavalry. No dice. He checked his Omni. There was a pile of information on the invasion. He was surprised the Argentines were allowing signals to come through. One of the reasons might be the drone he saw last night. They needed secure airwaves so their remote pilots could control them from safe distances. Receiving a signal was one thing, sending was another. A transmission would be the easiest way to pinpoint anyone in hiding. There were probably hundreds of Omnis receiving signals that were attached to dead bodies. It would be a waste of time to track an Omni that way. Although accessing information was still a transmission. The Argentine troops would be using coded signals. His transmission would be naked. He decided to risk a cyber-wire link, but not a call as that would certainly draw attention. He checked the Brazilian streams first to get the Latin American perspective.

He watched shaky footage of troops running through the streets of Mac Town. There wasn't much to see other than smoke grenades and a bit of gunfire. A drone flew over the city. Then the footage looped again. A polished Brazilian news anchor floated above his Omni.

He switched off the Omni's translator, thinking he might as well keep up his language skills. "Argentine troops landed in Antarctica at the US city of McMurdo this morning. Argentina's President Maite Ospina stated that this was a pre-emptive strike citing evidence of a viral weapon engineering lab located there."

The scene cut to Argentine President Maite Ospina standing behind a podium. A satellite image of McMurdo glowed behind her. "This is the site—" She turned and one of the buildings farther inland glowed red. "—where the Americans not only weaponized the MaxWell nano-virus but are hiding the antidote as well."

He whistled. *That's one hell of an accusation.*

Lakshmi let out a bark and he turned his attention to the doorway. She danced back and forth, wanting him to follow. "Okay, girl. I'm coming." He quickly folded his Omni into fourths and shoved it in his pocket. He grabbed a gift shop bag, stuffing into it sandwiches, some bottled water, and some nano-skin cans of Coke.

"Let's go."

She led him back to the infirmary where he found Anjali sitting up on her makeshift bed, leaning against some green steel drawers. She was redressing her wound.

"How are you feeling?" he asked as he approached.

"The dressing is pretty slipshod, but looks like someone did their best."

"Someone did."

She looked up and smiled. "I–I'm sorry. I'm grateful you saved my life."

He presented his haul. "Thirsty?" He dropped his bag on the old asbestos tiled floor and lined up the goods in front of her. She reached for a can of Coke and took the faux Ahi tuna sandwich.

She guzzled half the soda before she released a deep satisfying belch.

He broke out laughing. "Nice one!"

She turned red. "I sometimes forget about the social nuances. I was thirsty, that's all that was on my mind." She pointed to her thigh. "So where did you learn your trade?"

"Considering your glowing appraisal…" He smiled.

"Sarcasm, I like that." She touched her bandages gingerly. "The dressing isn't bad. I was just surprised to feel the bullet still in there."

"Best to leave it in until we get real help. I have the feeling we'll be captured before the day is out."

She nodded with no emotion, simple acceptance of facts. "We're the only ones here?"

He opened a bottle of water and took a swig. "Yup."

"The museum was a good place to bring me, but we're pretty much trapped by the topography and McMurdo."

He guzzled. "Mmmm Hmmm."

"You didn't answer my question. Where did you learn to dress a wound?"

"Part of my advanced tactical training with the LAPD."

"They teach you to kill and heal?" she smiled.

"Emphasis was on kill. But we had to know how to patch each other up, too."

"Sumit?"

Jake swallowed hard. He had been purposely avoiding the subject. "Do you remember him rushing to the table?"

She thought for a moment. "I remember the explosion and the bullets." She looked up at him. "He ran back to me."

Jake nodded. "He was hit first. In the neck."

Her face contorted. It was the first time he had seen deep emotion in her other than embarrassment.

"I went to him first." Jake felt a twinge of shame so he turned his head. "He insisted I rescue you."

They sat in silence, with the occasional gun fire or explosion muffled beyond the museum.

"When I pulled us out of the dome, there was an explosion. I don't see how he could have survived." He forced himself to look at her. Tears rolled down her cheeks. He automatically reached out to comfort, but she shied way.

"Thank you again for saving my life."

He gestured to Lakshmi who sat patiently by his side, eyeing the food on the floor. "Thank her. She's the one who brought us here. I held on to you, she held on to me." He bent down and grabbed the only sandwiches left: faux tuna burger or faux beef. He held them up. "Which one, girl?"

Lakshmi barked at the tuna sandwich.

Anjali turned to the Husky. "Thank you, Lakshmi."

The sandwich disappeared in three bites.

Anjali wiped off her cheeks. "I'm not hungry." She pulled bits of her fish burger off and hand fed them to Lakshmi. "I absolutely love animals. Their emotions are unfiltered. Their love is unconditional. There are no hidden meanings, or agendas with them. They are easy for me to read." She turned to him. "I wish I could relate to people like I do with animals, but it takes monumental effort. I find it much easier to relate to equations. My work relaxes. Socializing stresses, it is one of the hardest jobs on the planet."

"I'd say you related to your husband fairly well."

She gave a small laugh and wiped another tear away. "I couldn't give him what he needed. But I loved him as best I could. I still do."

They both stroked Lakshmi.

"What's going on out there?" She sounded desperate to change the subject.

"Mac Town is burning to the ground." He unfolded his Omni and handed it to Anjali. "Argentines say they were justified because the Americans have a genetic lab here to weaponize the MaxWell virus… You wouldn't happen to know anything about that would you?"

She laughed. "They'd say anything to justify taking this area back again. They're still smarting after the US beat them in the war of 2017." She pushed away his hand holding the Omni. "I can't watch any kind of hologram. The editing and shot choices throw me off. I prefer to read all communication." She picked up her own Omni lying by the side of her mattress. "Mine is set to display all news in text form."

He saw the text on the face of her Omni. Two transmissions the enemy might find… or the cavalry. It was obvious she had been reading up on things while he had been foraging for food. "So what *is* going on?"

"We were at the McMurdo lab on the twenty-third. They are working on a cure for MaxWell, but Sumit and I saw no signs of weaponizing. Although, we had our suspicions before we came down. It's possible they hid it from us." She turned and offered the rest of her fish sandwich to Lakshmi. The Husky gingerly took bites from her hand.

He leaned against the cabinet next to Anjali. "Let's see what the Yanks have to say."

She put greasy fish-substitute-coated fingers in her ears.

He turned red with embarrassment. "Ah, I forgot."

"It's okay. I know I'm weird."

"I don't think you're weird."

She shrugged. "Animals are honest, too."

He opened his mouth then thought better of it. He stood up and searched for a bowl to pour a bottle of water in for Lakshmi. He found an old mortar and pestle and used the mortar for a dish. After he gave Lakshmi the bowl, he placed his Omni on a countertop and found the American Presidential address on YouTube. President Ortiz, a fairly attractive woman in her late fifties with Nicaraguan roots, appeared on screen. She had been elected in 2032, when he and Tomoko had been sailing to ports in Vietnam, after he had stopped paying attention to American politics.

The stern President spoke to the cameras. "The United States denies all accusations by the Argentine Government and sees this recent aggression as an act of war. As I make this statement, steps have been taken to strike back and strike hard. I will have more to say to my fellow Americans and the citizens of the world when I take the floor at the emergency meeting of NATO later today."

He whistled. "Sounds bad… like world war bad."

Anjali smiled. "International relations have grown exponentially worse since the outbreak of the virus. Now that MaxWell Pharmaceuticals is bankrupt and its corporate officers have testified and claimed the leaks in their containment systems as pure accident, people want someone new to blame. Conspiracy theories are rampant, but not many relate mass Chip implantation as a cause for MaxWell's release, except a few fundamentalist groups, and no one takes them seriously beyond their own members. Despite all the show of force, we won't have a third world war. We've advanced beyond that possibility."

He slumped down and grabbed a burger. After one bite he realized he should have nuked another Ahi tuna sandwich. "We'll just be a Chipped society and Sanchez will have the oligarchy he outlined to me five years ago."

"I can see the appeal." She rubbed her temples. "The majority can be irrational. The Chip is the best solution I've ever seen to bringing world order. There's simplistic beauty to it."

He almost choked. He pointed to the meat paste with white lettuce and sweaty bun as the culprit, but she was on his "watch carefully" list. Her sympathetic words mirrored The Consortium's agenda and raised his internal alarm.

She turned to him. "You miss The Chip?"

He scoffed. "Not at all."

"Even at times like this?"

He thought about it. Right now he'd be tied into all the news networks of the world. The Chip would be translating every language and he'd have a detailed understanding of all sides within seconds. He could even spy on the progress of troop movements by satellite if he still had his old clearance codes. But as a member of the only species on the earth to be cognizant of free will, he cherished his independent mind. He answered, "Nope."

"You had to think about it before you spoke."

"There were advantages." He took another bite and opened a second bottle of water. "But the price was too high."

She nodded. "You were hacked for four months?"

"I was a Pin Head from the day of my implant, March 17th, 2030 until I cut it out on June 30th of the same year. It was like being buried alive."

"My experience as a Pin Head felt like being trapped under a waterfall, spinning in an eddy, not knowing up from down, wanting to drown and yet somehow being kept on life support. It was worse than a prison cell because I could no longer control my physical or mental self."

He turned to find her gazing into space with fear in her eyes. "You were chipped?"

"You seem surprised. Most people in my profession embraced The Chip. With Asperger's, The Chip was a chance to be normal for the first time in my life." She turned her back toward him with a grunt of pain and pulled up her hair. He saw the scar at the nape of her neck.

He winced. "When?"

"I was chipped from November,2033 to May 2035. For the first year, my Third Eye was a dream come true. The Chip took all the work out of socializing. It gave me correct responses to questions and menus to start normal conversations. It filtered out the noise and distractions I experienced when watching holovision, or during conversations in public places. Having a Chip was like being reborn with a best friend I never had inside my head."

She leaned back against a locker. "I also benefited from the usual advantages all scientists have. I could go longer without sleep, my memory expanded exponentially; I built databases in my mind of all my calculations for future reference. I was able to construct case study models in my head and save them. I could extract knowledge from a world database of research with one thought."

She observed him once again. "The scientific community generally acknowledges that The Chip has increased the human mind's abilities a hundred fold. Scientists in all fields have been making advances in the past five years that would have taken them fifty under normal conditions. AI is the child of a union between humanity and machine; of that there is no doubt." She sighed and leaned her head back once again. "I miss The Chip terribly. Sometimes I think my fear is irrational."

She turned back to him. "I had a rotating encryption code on my Chip security. There were fifty digits and the digits cycled randomly every second. My Chip was impossible to hack and yet someone made it through. With my line of work I was a high profile target; but Sumit and I came up with the algorithms and programmed them into my Chip. Only someone in our lab could have hacked me. After my Chip was removed, Sumit and I moved out of the lab in New Delhi and started again in Tianjin. That was just six weeks before the first reports came in of the MaxWell outbreak."

Jake felt his gut knot up and his throat constrict. The conversation was spinning him into memories he preferred to repress. His nightmares were bound to be more intense tonight. Jake swallowed hard. "Why not take your Chip offline? Disconnect from the Cyber-wire?"

"You know better than that. If you want to stay connected with knowledge, you must be joined to The Wire. Even the troops outside are linked to a central command. New models don't even have an off switch except the 8S."

He nodded.

"Between 2032 and 2034 there was a group of God Heads who called themselves the Free Thinkers. They embodied the true spirit of hacking. They were anti-establishment, pro-revolution, and claimed to promote freedom and equality. For a time, they seemed to be hacking to promote just that. I wish that they had been the ones to compromise my codes. I might have done something heroic."

"What happened to them?"

"They were wiped out by hacked agents in the span of a month. Agents like your Enhanced Unit back at the LAPD." She turned to him. "Erasmus is positive The Consortium was behind it."

There was a loud bang down the hall. Jake shot up and Lakshmi bounded off, ferociously barking. A deep voice shouted in Spanish.

The cavalry that President Ortiz had spoken of would be too late.

Chapter 13
Max2

He ran to the sealed environmental door. Lakshmi paced in front of it. Her bark turned to a whine. The lobby was on the other side. A series of faint booms, like wrecking balls hitting the city, shook the museum then silence. The world seemed peaceful. Lakshmi whined.

"What's the matter, girl?" He patted her as he put his ear to the steel barrier and listened. Only the ringing in his ears could be heard. He stood with his hand on the wheel lock. *Wait for the breach or surrender now?* A breach might mean explosives and an increased risk of harm or even death. He checked his Omni. No Signal. They were jamming now. He gritted his teeth. "Lakshmi. Guard Anjali."

The Husky bowed her head with a whimper and padded back down the hall with her tail between her legs. With Lakshmi out of harm's way, he turned the wheel. The locking bolts slid out of the steel frame with a loud *Whunk.* He pulled. The door swung back with ease, revealing two dead Argentine commandos slumped at the foot of the door. Another dead soldier lay by the reception desk.

He bent down and slid his fingers between the body armor and neck of the nearest body. The skin was warm but there was no pulse. He stepped over the figure and checked the next soldier. Same. He pulled a machine gun from the fingers of one of the commandos and hugged the corrugated wall. He walked cautiously into the lobby.

Wind whispered through the broken glass of the lobby door. As he breathed, lonely wraiths of condensation appeared around his mouth before disappearing on the air. The sweat on his back cooled, causing him to shiver.

He kicked at the dead soldier by the desk and checked the man's pulse. No heartbeat, and the skin was cool. He approached the main entrance with caution, gun at-the-ready, and peered outside. More dead Argentines lay among the rocks and snow leading to the smoking ruin of Mac Town. He spotted the tail of a drone amid the bodies. Nothing was flying. Nothing was moving. Everything was dead.

He slung his weapon onto his shoulder and jogged back to the environmental door. He closed it then ran back to the infirmary.

When he reached the room, he found Anjali rubbing Lakshmi's neck.

"Can you move?" he asked.

"What's wrong?"

"They're all dead, every one of them and I didn't see a single wound." He flashed his Omni. "They're jamming, which explains why the drones are down. I'm thinking nano-virus, gas, or P-Chip hit the soldiers. Virus scares me most."

"If it's gas, it's too late for us, or it dissipated. If it's MaxWell, then it's undergone an exponential mutation to kill everyone simultaneously." She reached up to the countertop behind her and tried to pull herself up. She winced with pain. He rushed over and pulled her arm over his shoulder. "I'm too short for that!" she protested.

"Fine." He scooped her up in his arms. "You're what, ninety-four?"

"Pounds?" She was insulted.

"Look, I need to know your weight so I know how far I can carry you. I'm guessing a mile tops, if your ninety-four."

"I'm not insulted that you're guessing my weight, I'm insulted that you still use pounds as a unit of measurement. I'm forty-two kilos."

"Ninety-two pounds, that's what I said." He carried her to the lobby with Lakshmi at his heel.

"Set me down there." She nodded to the chair behind the reception desk. "And place one of the bodies up on the desk."

He followed her instructions and hauled the lightest of the three corpses up on the large reception desk so she could examine it.

She pulled away the armor and voiced her observations. "No perspiration, no sunken eyes, and the lymph glands…" She felt with her fingers and her face grew puzzled. "Are not swollen… This isn't right." She rose to her feet with some difficulty and began to strip the corpse. Jake came over and helped her. Once the man was in his briefs, she felt around under his armpits, inner thighs and feet. She slumped back in the chair when she was done, visibly fatigued.

"Well, doc?"

"I'm beginning to think MaxWell has mutated. It's just…"

"What?"

"They are all wearing Nemp transmitters on their Omnis." She picked up a device from the pile they had made from the corpse's belongings. "MaxWell is a nano-virus that attacks a host's lymphatic, respiratory and nervous system. A patient can die from failure in one or more of those areas. It acts faster than any human body, or biological countermeasure can handle. However, MaxWell can be weakened or killed by a Nemp and can be eradicated by The Chip working in unison with a host's immune system…"

He watched her eyes fill with worry as she gazed over the dead soldier. He continued her sentence. "The host's immune system?"

She continued staring until he snapped his fingers in front of her face. She jumped and looked at him with bewilderment.

"You were about to finish your thought about this soldier's cause of death…"

She patted the cold skin of the corpse. "He has the symptoms we saw in some of the early stages of the counter-virus we have been working on."

"Counter-virus? What happened to cure?"

"Often we inoculate with a weaker form of the original pathogen. It gives the body a chance to form antibodies so when the full strength version arrives, the body is prepared." She felt the back of the soldier's neck. "But our work is not so simple because the MaxWell nano-virus has cybernetic—intelligent—properties and attacks multiple systems at lightning speeds." She puzzled for a moment. "This… this looks like the counter-agent we and the Americans down here are developing. Our cure is a nano-virus, like MaxWell. However, it is smarter. It is designed to attack all nano-viruses other than itself, and it can override *any* Chip and give base commands to the body to increase recovery rates. Our nano-cure can also attach itself to a Chip and compromise it. Once attached, our nano-cure can receive basic commands through a host's Chip to help it adapt and attack any nano-virus other than itself. The downside is our nano-cure can also receive basic commands like stopping a heart rate, creating a brain aneurysm, or being told to mimic another type of infection so it is misdiagnossed."

So far, he was trying to figure out the benefits of her cure. He was familiar with the built-in security of Chips. The device he had used to kill Roberto Pacheco would not have worked with the Gen 4.5 and beyond. Five years ago Gen 3 was the latest model worldwide. Jake's 4.2 had been in the experimental stages and not for mass consumption. Now NTI and CryLyte were selling Gen 7—civilian—and 8—military. The new models were an absolute bitch to hack. For Anjali to say this nano-*cure* could override any Chip was one hell of a claim.

She continued. "When our nano-cure multiplies inside a host and reaches critical mass, the nano-mass can gather at the brainstem. Then they combine themselves to form a Personal Chip in a non-chipped host. Once they have combined, they can perform the functions of a Gen 7 Chip. We finished the nano-cure, but had not fully worked out a Nemp resistant strain…"

His jaw went slack. His scalp began to itch from the rage that was welling up within him. The room began to dim and he could no longer contain his outrage. "What the hell is wrong with you people? Don't you ever think about the consequences when you create something this powerful? These guys might be infected with some sort of Nemp resistant Chip in viral form?"

She shook her head. "No, our nano-cure is only resistant to low level Nemps, like the one that affects MaxWell. If a stronger wave is introduced, or a real nuclear generated EMP, our version will die, as well as fry every circuit in the wave area."

"You're not getting it! I'm saying that MaxWell wasn't getting people chipped fast enough so you decided to make Chips viral! You want to infect humanity with Third Eyes!" He shook with rage. The news couldn't be worse. "After everything that has happened to the world, to me, to YOU! You've been developing this?" He grabbed the soldier's Omni and hurled it at the wall. He began pacing around the lobby.

Lakshmi whined and backed into a corner. He had not felt this level of rage since finding Lalo's body next door to his apartment so many years ago, and just before he started to beat Roberto Pacheco during his arrest.

Anajali nervously shook her head. "Jake, when our nano-cure enters a host, it fights MaxWell, and when it encounters a Chip, it attacks that Chip and prevents all signals outside the brain from entering the mind. It returns an implanted or infected person back to normal. It resets life back to the days before The Chip."

"And replaces it with a nano-virus Chip!" He laughed. "If a human mind can think of it, another human can hack it and give a kill command. Or worse yet, lock them in the type of prison you and I escaped from. You're fooling yourself, Anjali!"

"Jake, this was the only way to fix the problem. MaxWell is the twenty-first century's version of the atom bomb. The only way to fight it is with a hydrogen version. It's an arms race."

He spun around and locked eyes with her. "Bullshit! Don't even try to go there. Where is your sense of morality? Of humanity? Is the prerequisite to becoming a scientist to be emotionally dead? Morris didn't look at the ramifications of his P-Chip invention until his partner was murdered by a Pin Head. Oppenheimer didn't realize sharing secrets on the Manhattan Project with the Russians might be a bad thing until the FBI followed him for being a communist. And now your little elite club of scientists—which by your own admission is Chipped!—has been creating cybernetic virus hybrids that can kill, or worse yet, imprison someone in their own mind!" He pulled on his hair with bewildered rage. "It's like loading a gun, then handing it to a three-year-old and expecting them to know how to respect it. What the fuck, Anjali? I thought The Order of Erasmus stood for the individual over the collective?"

"We do. But current projections of MaxWell show anyone not chipped will be dead within the next six months. Our nano-cure will not only block MaxWell, but phase out The Chip as well."

He shook his head. "Leaving a nano-virus—not a cure—in its place." Jake grit his teeth. "You're handing The Consortium the human race on a platter."

Anjali sighed. She looked tired, drained and weak from her wound. "We've been working on our solution since the outbreak in June. Even so, we're not sure if we can implement it in time." She stared at the corpse under her fingers.

"Something tells me you missed your taxi."

"We don't know yet. I'm just speculating." She cleared her throat. "I'd love to hear your solution to MaxWell. Criticism by itself is easy and, quite frankly, naive."

Roberto Pacheco had called him naïve and it pissed Jake off. "Reprogram it. You say the nucleotides can be programmed and the nano-virus is smart. Reprogram it."

She shook her head. "The matrix is formed in a lab, once it is combined with a biological virus, it takes on life of its own. It can mutate, or receive signals and act on those commands, but it can't be reprogrammed, just like people can't be reprogrammed."

He slammed his fist against a wall. "Don't buy it! If people can be programmed, so can a fucking human-made virus!"

She lifted the soldier's head and stared at his neck. "We've tried it. We can get to a solution faster using another nano-virus."

He kicked the desk with frustration and rage. She had the emotional intelligence of an electric toothbrush. The image of Tomoko entered his mind and he longed to find her. They needed to get back on the boat and sail as far away from here as possible. Anjali stumped him for now. He swallowed his anger and calmed down. "I need more time to think about this."

Anjali nodded.

"So that building the Argentine President showed is a biogenic lab?"

She wiped her hands off with a napkin. "It is and there are hundreds around the world. The MaxWell lab in Antwerp was the one that released the nano-virus that caused the pandemic. Were the Americans responsible for the faulty storage containment system in the Antwerp lab? Did they introduce the mutating version of MaxWell? I don't know. We suspect The Consortium was behind it all and MaxWell could have been created elsewhere before it was released in Antwerp."

He reflected on the facts. "Ten million dead and the non-chipped survivors are looking at six months to live..."

She stared at him. "One thing is for sure. The last remaining continent is now infected with some form of virus, maybe a Max2. There are no more safe harbors, Jake. You cannot run."

Chapter 14
Sword of Damocles

The idea of a Chip in viral form continued to enrage Jake as he turned to look out the lobby doors. Through dissipating smoke, he noticed soldiers in winter camouflage approaching the museum. They stopped occasionally to check on deceased commandos. He gripped his gun tightly. He could not tell if they were Argentine reinforcements or someone else.

"What is it?" Anjali asked from behind the desk.

He ignored her and raised his weapon to look through the scope. They were American. He placed the gun on the ground. "The cavalry." He flashed a hand signal to his Husky. She whined and lay down by the desk.

He stepped out of the smashed front door and approached the troops with his hands in the air. "Hello! I'm an American! I've got a wounded woman and my dog inside the museum!"

The soldiers walked steadily forward, faces hidden by balaclavas. Their guns remained with barrels pointed at the ground. One of them broke from the group and marched briskly over. He pulled his balaclava down revealing a smile.

"Commander Jake Travissi. Pleasure." The man extended a hand. "Lieutenant Mark Howard, United States Marines."

Jake shook it. "You have me at a disadvantage, Lieutenant."

"Standard Issue Chip sees all. We have you on file as coming into port yesterday. We ID'd you when you checked us out with your scope from that doorway." The lieutenant nodded toward the museum.

Jake turned to see sunlight blazing off the corrugated structure. He could see nothing beyond the dark maw created by broken glass.

"Merry Christmas, Mr. Travissi. This is what I call a winter wonderland. Hoorah!"

Jake gazed out at the smoking ruins beyond the Marines. "How many dead, lieutenant?"

The man sobered up quickly. "Numbers are preliminary but based on satellite and first wave intel we're looking at seventy to eighty percent casualties to the civilian population."

Jake's throat closed and he forced a cough to get his words out. "You find a Tomoko Sakai among them?"

The man smiled. "She's alive and well aboard the *Southern Star*."

Relief flooded through Jake. He wanted to give the eager lieutenant a big bear hug. "And my boat?"

The lieutenant stared at him blankly for a moment then shook his head. "I'm sorry, Commander, but there's nothing left of the harbor. These fucks—Argentines did a number on us. On Christmas to boot—and they claim to be Catholic."

Jake felt as if a bomb just detonated over his head. "Gone?" The forty-foot *Pachacuteq* had been their home for five years. They had sailed the entire Pacific Rim, Mediterranean, Atlantic, China Sea, and Antarctica Ocean. There were a lot of memories at the bottom of McMurdo Sound. At least he still had Tomoko and Lakshmi. He wondered how many could say the same about their loved ones on this black Christmas morning.

A sudden urge to go home and introduce Tomoko to his mom swept over him. He'd ask her about the father who had left him when he was two. He was sick of dodging the past.

The lieutenant interrupted Jake's reverie. "You can check the harbor out yourself if you don't believe me."

"No… that won't be necessary." He shook himself back into focus. "So how do I get to the *Southern Star*?"

"We've got RHIBs that will taxi you. *The Star* is a US cruise ship we commandeered for the rescue mission. All the civilians will be stationed there." Two PFCs arrived on the scene carrying a stretcher. They stopped and saluted the lieutenant. The lieutenant addressed Jake. "You mentioned a wounded woman inside?"

Jake nodded. "Anjali Malik—"

The Lieutenant quickly interrupted. "Is she the wife of Sumit Malik?"

Jake was taken off guard. It was eerie to think he used to silently communicate, in the blink of an eye, just like this Lieutenant was doing with his troops. "She is. Is he alive?"

The PFCs carried the stretcher to the museum. Jake shouted after them. "She took a bullet to the thigh. She's stable but having trouble walking." The men waved as they continued toward the museum. "And watch for my dog!" He turned back to the Lieutenant. "Sumit?"

The Lieutenant nodded. "Found him an hour ago near the hotel. Had a nasty neck wound and some third degree burns. He was one of the first ones in surgery. He's got a new artery and skin regenerators. He's going to be fine." The Lieutenant paused for a second to process more information. "In fact, he's being transferred off our ship to the *Southern Star* to make room for more triage patents."

Jake clapped the Lieutenant on the arm. "That's great news!"

"Is Mrs. Malik a personal friend?"

Jake opened his mouth but paused as he thought about his response.

The Lieutenant helped him. "Will you want to accompany her aboard the *Southern Star*?"

"Yes." Jake felt he owed her that much and figured he'd break the good news, too. He pointed to an Argentine corpse. "What happened, Lieutenant?"

"Not sure."

"My Omni went down when the drones crashed. You did something."

"Oh, that. Yes. We jammed every frequency and dropped a Nemp burst for five minutes before we made the first beach landing. None of that would have affected these commandos."

"So what happened?"

The Lieutenant shook his head. "Don't know. Press is saying the Sword of Damocles."

"Sword of Damocles?"

"In chipped warfare there's a text book strategy to hack into the TC—Tactical Command of the enemy and give one order to all enhanced troops. Usually the command is *sleep*—to conform to the New Geneva Convention, but in this case, it would seem the command was for the heart to stop."

Jake's skin went cold. A Max2 virus could attach itself to a Chip and receive a kill command. But Anjali said it was experimental... He swallowed hard. "What's your best guess, lieutenant?" Over five years off the force and he still fell into investigation mode.

The soldier spat in disgust. "One of the terrorist factions did this. More of the fuck-nut groups seem to spring up every day. The going strategy is to commit some atrocity, frame an enemy for doing the deed, then sit back and watch all your enemies tear themselves apart." The lieutenant gazed at the corpses and the crashed drone. "I know for a fact we didn't have the TC hacked when the Sword hit. I was in the first wave, and these fucks were dead when my feet hit the beach. No Marine fired a shot, cyber or otherwise."

"If this type of strategy is common, aren't most people skeptical of what they see?"

"Everyone is afraid. Between July and August, MaxWell put the world in a state of near anarchy. It was a living hell just keeping order within the border." He appeared somber and distant as he recalled that time. Then he blinked and assumed a professional demeanor. "The world is back on her feet. Now, people just want to feel safe. Shoot first, ask questions later."

Jake whistled as Lakshmi came bounding out of the museum with a big smile on her face. She leapt up into his arms and began licking his face.

"That's quite a pup you've got there," the lieutenant commented.

"Hoorah! This pup is seven years old."

"Got the energy of a teenager."

The two PFCs came out carrying Anjali on a stretcher.

"How's my patient?" Jake shouted as he put Lakshmi down.

Anjali gave a thumbs up.

Chapter 15
Sardines

Jake rode with Anjali, four other survivors, two PFCs and Lakshmi on a rubber RHIB out to the *Southern Star*. He held the piece of scrimshaw tightly the whole way. He had broken the news about Sumit before they had even boarded. He accompanied her all the way to the infirmary and was surprised to see Sumit on his feet. He had bandages on his face, arms and hands, but he was willing and able to be by Anjali as they prepped her for surgery. It warmed Jake's heart to see such a dedicated husband.

The moment he left the Maliks, he told Lakshmi to find Tomoko. She happily took on the task but maintained a patient gait as they made their way through the ship. The Lieutenant's death toll estimates ran through his mind. *Seventy to eighty percent casualties… that has to be close to ten thousand people.*

As they walked down a berthing corridor, a man stepped out of his cabin. When he saw Lakshmi and Jake, he spoke over his shoulder to his unseen cabin mate. "Goddamn Navy pulls us off our vacation route to rescue dogs? We'd better get our refund. Stupid Mac Town snobs!" The door slammed shut.

Jake marched up and pounded on the door. No answer. "Hey, asshole! Ten thousand people died while you were enjoying your Christmas Eve dinner in the galley last night. Think about that when they ask you to share your berth with the survivors!" He kicked the door. "I hope they make you sleep topside, prick!"

He turned to see Tomoko smiling at him from a perpendicular hallway. "Making friends with the locals?"

He ran and scooped her into his arms. "Oh, Jesus did I miss you." He kissed her passionately and slammed his hand against the wall to keep them from falling on the floor. He glanced backward to see the man he had chastised leering at him from his doorway. Jake barked. "Step back into your room, sir, before I plant my foot in your ass!"

The man cursed under his breath and slammed his door.

Tomoko laughed and Jake grabbed her face with both hands. "Guess what?"

Her smile dropped as she touched the stitches on his forehead. "What happened?"

"No idea." He flashed a smile. "Guess what?"

"What?"

"I love you." He kissed her again and they fell on the floor.

She pushed him off. "I'm sorry about the *Pachacuteq*…"

"It's just a boat." He went in for another passionate kiss.

She pushed him off again. "Just a boat?"

"Okay, no. It was our life. But I don't want to think about it right now." He kissed her again.

She broke away, smiling. He loved it when she played hard to get. "Uhm, shouldn't we be helping with the rescue? The majority of the passengers are. I came aboard for a medical exam and to get a room assignment."

"We have a room?"

Twenty minutes later he got a better look at their private suite from their leaky air mattress. The place was a storage locker for all-weather gear. They held each other in a naked embrace; their clothes were strewn about. The room was so tight that rolling a foot in any direction meant bumping into steel shelves lined with supplies. He craned his neck to see Lakshmi pressed against the closed door, watching them with interest.

He picked up one of several boots that had shaken loose and pummeled them during their passionate reunion.

She smiled. "Steward told me there are a few more rooms like this one. Ship can hold 580 passengers but she sailed half full. There aren't many vacationing because of MaxWell. Everyone must be immunized before they can board."

He shook his head. "We were lucky to be in backwater ports over the past six months."

"Agreed." She played with his navel. "How are the Maliks?"

"They both got hit. Sumit worse than Anjali—"

"Oh no!"

"But they'll both be fine." He stroked her hair and noticed the bird of paradise feather had melted.

She nuzzled his chest. "I'm glad. They're both sweet."

He touched the burned patch in her hair. "What happened after you left our table?"

She moved to his left side. "I was with Trevor, the sommelier."

"I remember him. Is he onboard?"

She grew silent for a moment, and then she mustered up the strength to tell her story. He held her close as she spoke. As she reached the end she stared up at the supply shelves, tears flowing down her cheeks. "I kept thinking they were tracking us with heat-seeking visors and the flames around that observation deck could only help. I repeated the mantra: 'Remain calm. Keep alert. Stay low.'"

He kissed her and wiped a tear from her eye. "See all that training rubbed off. You're a good student."

"Please." She slapped his six pack "It's called good genes and common sense." She laughed and wiped her nose.

He laughed with her.

"I'm so happy you and Lakshmi are safe."

He thought of the dead army lying on the nearby shore and the possibility of Max2. He would never let Tomoko out of his sight again. He held her close. "I'm happy, too."

Another twenty minutes later and they were both getting dressed. Lakshmi opened her eyes and rolled on her back with her paws limply hanging in the air.

Tomoko laughed and bent down to rub the Husky's tummy. "Yes, yes, pretty girl. You get some lovin' too."

After exiting the cabin, he approached a young and intimidating Private Lussa about going ashore and helping find survivors.

"My orders are to make sure everyone stays aboard, sir," Lussa responded.

"Can I speak to your superior officer?"

"You are speaking to her."

"Yes, of course I am." Jake turned to Tomoko. "Let's go to the bridge and see if we can get any movement there."

Jake, Tomoko, and Lakshmi made their way up through the decks and growing crowds to find the bridge. When they reached the gangway to the wheelhouse, they found a Private Hernandez stationed at the door.

Jake stood in front of the Private. "I'd like to speak to the person in charge."

Private Hernandez stoically stared ahead. The door opened. "At ease, Private." Captain Shibley was easy to identify with her double bars and name badge sewn to her winter camouflage fatigues. Hernandez stepped aside so the captain could address Jake. "What can I do for you, Mr. Travissi?"

"We'd like to help with finding survivors. I have a dog."

"I listened to your request via Private Lussa on C deck." She tapped her head. "I am in full communication with my platoon twenty-four-seven."

"So we can go?"

"You may not. The military has sensor equipment far superior to any dog, Mr. Travissi. You should know that. I have orders to keep every civilian safe and that's what I will do. I have orders to sail once we have twelve hundred aboard. Search and Rescue will continue without us."

"Where are we going?"

"The Italian port of Terra Nova. You'll be able to catch a flight to anywhere in the world you like courtesy of Air Italia. A formal announcement will be made for those who are not chipped once all are aboard. Now if you don't mind." The captain closed the door.

Defeated, they made their way back to the main deck. The ship began to feel claustrophobic with all the Mac Town survivors pouring in. RHIBs arrived every five minutes with a dozen civilians in each. Every individual had been instantly cataloged and accounted for the moment they were seen by a Marine. They were checked into the ship's database as well as international personnel lists and immediately assigned a berth. Some were packed in with existing passengers or placed in common rooms such as the gym, dining hall, or observation lounges. Jake and Tomoko had been very lucky to get a private suite.

On the bow, a PFC passed out water and field rations to a growing crowd of dirty and disheveled survivors. Lakshmi was cursed a few times as she tried to weave through the legs of tightly packed civilians. Jake picked her up and pushed his way back to the stern so she wouldn't get stepped on. As he forged a path down a glass-covered portside corridor, Sumit rose from a stairwell.

"My god!" Tomoko hit Jake for downplaying the injuries.

Sumit smiled from under his bandages. "It looks worse than it is."

"Why aren't you in the infirmary?" Jake asked.

"I needed some air. How are you two holding up?"

Jake helped make a path for them to get to the aft deck. "Fine. More importantly, how's Anjali?"

"They removed the bullet. She lost a lot of blood and has a chipped femur, but she'll be fine. Thank you for saving her life. She wouldn't have made it without you."

Jake opened the door to the aft deck and stepped through. "I'm just sorry I wasn't able to get you both out."

"It all worked out in the end."

The four of them side-stepped along the wall away from the busy doorway. The aft was almost as bad as the foredeck.

Sumit shook his head as he studied the black cloud hanging over McMurdo. "What a horrible tragedy. If they hadn't started the fires, there would be a lot more people alive right now."

Shell-shocked survivors milled about like zombies. Two marines handed out military rations.

Sumit turned to Jake. "We could use all the help we can get."

Jake shook his head. "I'm not sure I can convince Parks to join Erasmus. He's always enjoyed a unique flair." He looked Sumit in the eye. "I'm not sure I could kill him either."

Sumit nodded. "Anjali told me you were upset about the direction of our work. You have to trust me when I say we looked at all the options."

What bothered Jake the most was Anjali's sympathetic comment about a chipped society. That's exactly what would happen once Max2 ran amuck. "How did those Argentine troops die?"

"Inconclusive, but it doesn't look good for you Yanks, breaking Geneva II and all."

Jake scoffed. "I'd say this Christmas invasion doesn't look good for Argentina."

Sumit shrugged "Most see you Yanks as swaggering football players who refuse to accept their place as a second rate economy. The UN will condemn Argentina for the invasion, but it's much scarier to know America is willing to throw a kill switch rather than immobilize troops with a sleep command."

Jake was surprised at Sumit's attitude when taking into account what the man had just gone through. Why was he so harsh on his rescuers?

Marines hoisted wounded civilians over the stern in stretchers. The one in the lead shouted, "Make a hole, people! Make a hole." Soldiers and stretchers passed.

Sumit shook his head in sorrow. He turned to Jake. "If you don't choose sides soon, you're just another Pin Head in waiting." He followed the Marines through the open door offering to help.

"He's got a point," Tomoko added.

"Yeah..." But Jake had a hard time throwing in with a team that supported Max2. Before he could say yes to any more missions, he focused on finding the best moment to propose to Tomoko.

Chapter 16
Terra Nova

They cruised into port around 10:00AM on December twenty-sixth. Jake was lucky enough to find a spot at the rail to view the Italian base-turned-tourist-destination. The town reminded him of photos he had seen of Antarctic bases before the treaty expired. It had the rustic feel of a place where research was conducted and did not have any of the tacky commercial touches of the now destroyed McMurdo.

The Maliks did not appear again. Tomoko had tried to visit them in the infirmary, but it was off limits to non-family members.

The Italians were very welcoming and handed out subzero parkas to each survivor as they walked off the pier. A low front had moved in and the sky was gray. Temperature was –2 degrees Celsius. Jake observed his old millennium coat. It was safety yellow with stripes of silver reflective plastic. It reeked of mothballs. He discovered an old plastic safety whistle attached to a ring and a crusty lanyard inside one of the pockets.

Volunteers split them into groups of forty and led them onto shuttles. They were couriered to the airport where two hangars had been set up as temporary shelters.

Captain Shibley was not quite correct in her information regarding transportation off Antarctica. Air Italia offered free flights to one major city in six different countries where survivors could pick up other flights home. There were still plenty of commercial flights out, which one could purchase for discounted rates.

The view of Terra Nova aboard the *Southern Star* had been deceiving. As soon as the bus took them through town, Jake noticed plenty of restaurants, apartments, and hotels. The streets were just as crowded as Mac Town. However, the Italians had built more conservative architecture that blended into the environment—whites, grays, and blacks.

"What a drab place," one of the survivors standing next to him commented.

When they stepped off the bus, an Air Italia *Scramjet* screeched into the gray mist. *Scramjets* could be anywhere in the world within two hours. Regular jet flights back to the States could take half a day or more.

Jake and Tomoko grabbed cots in the corner of the hangar. There were a thousand beds in the open space. The din of hundreds of voices reverberated off the corrugated roof. The place was in chaos as there were too few Italians fielding questions from an overwhelming and demanding majority.

One Italian shouted out, "If any of you have third eyes, please access the Terra Nova inforrmation center on the Cyber-Wire. You will find all the information you need there!"

Jake sat on a cot. He pulled off his Omni watch and pressed the button so it would unfold into a tablet. He searched for flights as he opened a window to his bank account. The number floating in the upper corner made his heart sink: Less than two thousand dollars. "Party's over," he mumbled.

Tomoko climbed up behind him and wrapped her legs around his waist. "Let's go back to Lima and work in a little café together."

He turned to her "You want to see your parents?"

She nodded. "The past twenty-four hours have been pretty sobering." She kissed him on the neck. "Plus, my dad might be willing to help us out."

He shook his head. "I'm fine with visiting Lima but we're not hitting your dad up for cash. Besides, I was thinking of heading to the States."

Her eyes went wide. "LA?"

Lakshmi hopped up on the foot of the cot. The composite frame groaned. He turned to his Husky. "I'm not sleeping on concrete, folks. Someone has to get off."

Tomoko gave the hand signal and Lakshmi's smile disappeared as she hopped back down to the cold concrete floor. Tomoko rolled her eyes and pointed to the cot next to Jake's. Lakshmi smiled again as she made herself at home on the bed.

"LA it is," Tomoko prodded.

"What about Lima?"

"My past isn't keeping me from getting married." She leaned over and kissed him.

"Hold that thought." He dragged his Italian jacket out from under his cot and pulled out the old plastic whistle. He threaded the whistle and the lanyard off the metal ring. He got down on his knees with Tomoko facing him on the cot.

He took both of her hands into his and slid the band onto her ring finger. It was ridiculously large. "I love you, Tomoko Sakai. Last night was the first night I spent without you in five years. I don't ever want to experience being apart again. Will you marry me?"

She jumped up and squealed. She turned around twice before sitting back down hard on the cot. The cot toppled backward and she crashed into the concrete. He leapt over the cot in horror, hoping she had not cracked her head. The din around them was so loud that no one heard or noticed. She gazed up at him with tears in her eyes. He dropped to his knees and caressed her face as he gingerly felt around the back of her head with his other hand. Lakshmi was on the other side, giving her tender licks.

"Are you hurt?"

She reached up with both hands. She rubbed Lakshmi's jaw with one, and took his hand in the other. "I'm fine."

"You're crying."

"Because I'm ecstatic."

He gathered her in his arms and they kissed. The din of a thousand voices faded out and all he could feel was her nestled in his arms. *If only I could freeze this moment.*

Tomoko broke for air. "I never thought I'd miss the supply closet."

At that moment, Jake's eyes fell upon a face he thought was familiar. The African American man hadn't aged a day in over five years. Lakshmi approached him with her tail wagging. A military winter camouflage parka was draped over his shoulders but it was obvious he was a civilian. Jake had met this man over five years ago in Rio when he had delivered Lakshmi back to Jake. His name was Gordon King, aka Erasmus.

The man approached. "Hello, Jake." He wore thick rimmed glasses, which meant his Omni was configured into a heads-up-display like the web-connected glasses Google made a few decades back before scores of people complained of eye strain. Jake never liked configuring his Omni into glasses because the experience of looking through them felt like the Chip interfaces he used to have.

Sarcasm laced Jake's voice. "What a *coincidence* meeting you here, Erasmus."

"Please, call me Gordy. Considering what happened to Sumit and Anjali, not really. I take care of my own."

Jake sobered up. "How are they?"

"Surprisingly well. Modern medicine gets better by the second. There's an upside to chipping doctors after all." Gordon King kneeled down and gave Lakshmi a treat. "I see you've been taking good care of my dog."

Tomoko rose to study Gordy.

Jake stood up, shaking his head. "You had her on loan while I was in prison." They shook hands. "You look great."

Gordy smiled. "Ever hear the old saying, black don't crack?" He rubbed his bald head. "The haircut hides the receding gray."

Jake chuckled and noticed an old man standing a few feet away. The stranger's arms were tightly crossed as he stared at his cowboy boots. He was about as tall as Jake, with white hair tied in a ponytail, and brown watery eyes. He appeared nervous. There was also something familiar about him. He was dressed in jeans and a black leather jacket under the same style military parka that Gordy wore. A turquoise bolo hung around the man's neck, probably from the American Southwest.

Tomoko approached Gordy. "You're The Order of Erasmus?" She held out her hand. "I've never met an Order before."

Gordy took her hand. "I've never been called an organization before..." He finished shaking. "I have the feeling I came at a bad time."

Jake pulled the cot upright and tossed the bedding underneath. "Not at all. Please, have a seat." He pulled up Tomoko's cot. All the rest were now taken. Some were occupied. Most people conversed, wandered, or complained—there was a whirlwind of activity.

"Is your friend going to join us?" Jake nodded toward the stranger with the bolo. He blocked traffic, like a tree planted on the middle of an expressway. People muttered as they navigated around him.

Gordon replied, "When he's ready."

Tomoko stood up, annoyed. "You don't just leave an old man standing in traffic like that!"

The old man stiffened up when he saw Tomoko coming. He looked younger and more commanding when he wasn't slouched. He held up his hand to prevent Tomoko from getting closer. The gesture almost knocked a pedestrian over.

"The way he's making friends, it might be wise to invite him now." Jake watched as the old man joined the stream of traffic and disappeared.

"He'll be back." Gordy sat down with a groan. He rubbed his lower back. "Much better."

Jake gestured to Gordy's coat. "You military now?"

Gordy opened his jacket to show off a nano-mesh shirt. It displayed a plaid pattern. "Civilian! I work at NTI. We're field testing a lot of our S&R equipment."

Tomoko sat next to Jake. "I thought you came down to check on the Maliks? Which story is your cover?"

Gordy flashed a smile and leaned forward. "The Argentine invasion was ballsy. The sudden death of their entire force is extremely alarming. I've found no evidence the US hacked into Argentina's strategic command, and I have the security clearance to know."

Jake raised an eyebrow. "Sumit hinted it was the Americans."

Gordy shook his head. "We're in the same cell and share the same sources. Considering what he went through, I'm not surprised if some of his deductions are a bit emotional right now."

"I came to the same conclusion." Jake noticed the old man watching them from a few bunks away. "I'm not joining."

"I'm not asking you to. I'd just like your two cents." Gordy took a breath. "The Order of Erasmus is dying. Literally. We've lost a dozen cells over the past year. Each time a cell goes dark, we investigate. Usually we find no trace of the cell, or we find bodies. I'm not sure how long the organization can keep going. I could use any help I can get, even if it's an idea."

Tomoko stood up and Jake assumed she was going back to the old man. He addressed Gordy. "Advice on how to bring the good Reverend Parks to your side? Or to stop creating a viral Chip?"

Gordon threw up his hands. "I know. Crazy." He looked Jake in the eye. "But if The Consortium beat us to it, we're in deep shit."

"Jake?" Tomoko tugged on his sleeve. She stood next to them with the stranger behind her. "This gentleman would like to speak to you."

Gordy rose. "I sent my contact details to your Omni. Any communication with me will be coded and bounced around several places before I receive it. But I will receive it."

"Aren't you two together?" Jake pointed to the old man.

"Not exactly." Information streamed around the rims of Gordy's glasses. "Consider him a gesture of goodwill. Nice to see you again."

Jake shook Gordy's hand. "Will he be able to find his way home?"

"Yes." Gordy scratched Lakshmi's ears one more time before he disappeared into the crowd.

The old man took Gordon's seat.

"What can I do for you, sir?" Jake asked. The old man appeared tired and weary, as if he were carrying a great weight. "You're not as good at hiding it as Gordy."

The man's eyebrow went up.

Jake added. "The pressure you're all experiencing fighting this conspiracy."

The man smiled. Gold bridgework was rare in this day and age. His voice was deep, strong, and steady. "You have no idea, Jake."

Jake hoped this would be over soon. He wanted his moment with Tomoko back. "Ah, you have a Chip, too?"

The old man wrung his hands. "No. I've been tracking you for some years now."

Jake sighed. "You saw my broadcasts back in 2030 and decided to join The Order to help in the good fight?"

The man stared into Jake's eyes. "Hmmm. No, I was tracking you before that."

Jake could not shake the feeling that this man was somehow familiar to him. "You a cop?"

"No, Jake. I'm your father."

Chapter 17
Beartracker

Jake's belly laugh lasted a good sixty seconds. Tomoko sat by his side and rubbed his back. She was curious and puzzled. The old man persisted. "No joke. I'm Jon Travissi, your father."

Jake felt the back of his neck to confirm he was not chipped. Satisfied, he stood up. "I don't know what game Gordy is playing at but this is too much." He studied the white haired old man. His piercing brown eyes were dead serious. "Oh, what the hell. I'm broke and probably stuck in this shelter for a while. Let's play this out." He pointed to his own eyes. "Let's start with genetics. I've got blue eyes. Yours are brown and judging by your complexion there are few folks, if any, with blue eyes in your ancestry."

The man nodded. "I'm half First Nation. My mother was a blonde-haired blue-eyed Parisian by the name of Helen Moget. Your mother, Abigail Gustafson, is also blue eyed so you inherited the recessive gene from both sides."

They shared similar bone structure but, it was all so incredibly absurd. Jake sat down next to Tomoko. "So the day after Argentina invades US soil, you get a call from Gordon King and he says, 'Hey, I need to fly down to Antarctica and by the way, your son Jake is there! You guys want to be reunited after you ditched him and his mother thirty-five years ago?'

Jon shook his head. "I wanted to reach out to you long ago, but shame kept me from doing it. When you were on trial for beating Roberto Pacheco, I called you a few times but hung up when you answered."

"I got a lot of that in those days, as well as reporters, death threats, whacko fans—*If* you are my father, that would have been a good time to talk. A better time would have been right after my second birthday, when you walked out."

"So you believe me?"

Jake threw his head back and laughed again. "You need reassurance from me? I said I'd play this out, remember? So we're playing it out. Go on, my Native American friend."

"Hmmm." The man nervously turned to Tomoko who stared back at him with disdain and skepticism. He licked his lips. "I reached out to you when you were on national news with Homeland Security. But you said I was a liar and hung up. Now I believe it was The Chip, or a God Head talking."

Jake had spent many hours aboard the *Pachacuteq* pondering how The Chip had fucked up his life. One aspect was that the God Heads had played him like a puppet. His body was interacting with friends, relatives, and colleagues on a daily basis, but his own persona was not at home. He had been taken offline as they say. He had no details of what happened during those three and half months he had been chipped. He had witnessed the death of his best friend, Regina Chilcot, and it only registered through latent memory leaks and vague nightmares.

He sent pre-recorded messages to his mother on her birthday and Mother's Day, because he didn't want to open up the wounds and experience the pain again. The emotional and physical rape he experienced at the hands of the God Heads was a place he did not want to return to. So he pretended like everything was fine. He pretended he still had relationships back in LA.

A wave of anger flooded through him. Sanchez and this bullshit Consortium had robbed him of his life, and the lives of those who were close to him. And now this asshole was sitting before him. If Jon was truly his father, he was just as evil as Sanchez. He had walked out on a struggling mother and a two-year-old son. He had erased his tracks so Jake's mother could never find him again. Jake was lucky that his grandpa Gustafson was there for him until Jake was ten. He had been a father figure until his death.

"You're good, old man. Using The Chip to confuse me is good."

"Your mother can confirm who I am. Gordy says you barely speak to her now. From what I gather you used to be very close. After The Chip, you ran. You're still running. Just like I did."

Jake jumped up, cocked his fist and slammed it directly into the old man's face. He felt the cheekbone crack under his knuckles. Several witnesses screamed.

The fantasy lasted a split second. Jake grit his teeth and sucked in a deep breath. No need to repeat the Roberto Pacheco mistake. He unsnapped his Omni and tossed it on the cot. Even without a Chip, it was far too easy to invade people's privacy in this day and age. "Goddamn thing is worse than a jail bracelet."

"That's why we don't allow them, or Chips, on the reservation."

"Would you stop it!" Jake felt a twinge of hope that Jon really was his father and that scared him.

"Call your mother. What do you have to lose?"

"For one thing, I think she'd be mighty upset."

"Hmmm. That you didn't call her for Christmas or that she'll be the last to know you got engaged?"

Jake wheeled on him.

Jon smiled. "Saw it with my own eyes. You were both lost in the moment. As it should be."

Jake fantasized about decking him again. He sat back down with Tomoko in order to calm down. A DNA test wouldn't be too hard to get and they'd have results within an hour. Calling his mother would be even faster. Jake picked up his Omni. Tomoko and Lakshmi were riveted to his every action.

He scrolled through a few menus and hit the link to his mother's Omni. Within a minute her head floated above the stiff sheet of nano-skin. He lay the Omni with his mother's image floating above down on the cot. Her blonde hair was pulled back and showed streaks of gray. Her ice blue eyes were full of energy even though her face was that of someone on the cusp of sixty. Her skin was still creamy, but there were crows feet around the eyes and mouth. He could tell she was stressed as her face looked a little gaunt. She gave her signature warm, loving smile.

"Jake! It's so good to see you! Merry Christmas! How's Tomoko and Lakshmi? Fill me in on your latest travels!"

"Merry Christmas, Mom." A massive wave of guilt surged through him. He had been a heel of a son the past five years, only calling her directly once.

Tomoko put her head into the camera field. "Merry Christmas, Abigail." She smiled and she dragged Lakshmi into view.

"It's pretty noisy. Are you in port somewhere?"

"Yes," Tomoko answered. Jake could tell she was biting her tongue, allowing him to command the conversation.

"You both look so healthy and happy. I can't tell you how good it is to see you. I've missed you so much." A tear welled up in her eye.

"What's wrong, Mom?"

"I've been dismissed from work. Congress passed an emergency law in September. All healthcare professionals must be Chipped—'immunized'—in order to work around patients. I was the only nurse at Cedars who refused the implant. All the doctors, nurses, residents… even the cleaning crew, all but the robots of course—"

Jake leaned in close. "How are you holding up?"

"I'm okay, but Nancy, Consuela, Linda—all my friends at the hospital aren't talking to me. They think I'm being paranoid. Who would want to hack a healthcare provider?" Abigail laughed. "I do sound paranoid, don't I? They're busy and that's why they don't return my calls. Plus it's the holidays, so everyone has family priorities."

Jake felt terrible. This was the wrong time to call. It was always the wrong time to call. He knew his mother had talked to him when he was hacked. He had no memory of the events as his God Heads wanted to steer him clear of any family while they were busy trying to kill him. The cold dead responses he had given while hacked had torn up his mother. "I'm so sorry, Mom. I agree with your decision a hundred percent. How can they pass a law like that?"

"It's the worst health crisis anyone has ever seen."

He glanced at Jon stoically sitting on the cot across from him. He wearily stared at the back of Abigail's holograph. One of the wrinkles between his nose and mouth glistened. He had shed a tear. *Opportunity seldom comes at moments of our choosing,* Jake thought to himself, *but it takes wisdom to know when acting on it will cause regret.* "Mom…"

She gazed at him with a motherly smile.

"There's a man with me who has made a considerable claim and I was hoping you could clear up his story."

"Anything for you, son."

He turned the Omni 180 degrees so his mother faced the old man. Jake walked with the Omni toward Jon and sat next to him to witness his mother's reaction.

Jon bent down so that Abigail could get a better view of his face. "Hello, Abigail."

She squinted and scrutinized him.

Jon smiled. "I haven't aged very well."

Her face went slack and tears rolled down her cheeks. She whispered. "Jonathan…"

"Abigail." Jon sounded embarrassed.

"Where—" Anger brewed under her sadness.

"Arizona." Jon grew nervous. "Sorting things out."

She grit her teeth. "Dad tried to track you down. It didn't take long before we found out Jonathan Travissi was an alias. He traced your name change back to Thor Plass, a child who had died in 1992. Dad found nothing after that."

Jon bowed his head. "When my past caught up with me, I ran rather than drag you and Jake into it. I thought I was protecting you, but I was just being selfish. That was who I was then."

Abigail gazed at Jon. "So… who are you now?"

"Perhaps it would be best to come to you." Jon Travissi looked at his son. "There's much to discuss."

Jake sat frozen next to… his father. The word had been attached to a fantasy for so long he could not believe this physical manifestation. Jon was a coward and a liar, no less. The irony made him want to laugh. Of all the images he had, anything resembling this man had never crossed his mind. "What's your real name?"

"I have two birth certificates, Jon Beartracker and Alfred Moget… I prefer Jon Beartracker. Beartracker was my father's name."

A tear ran down Abigail's stiff face. "Your Italian orphan story was always light in the details…"

Jake was pissed that this man had made his mother cry. "We're done here."

Abigail raised her hand. "No. I want to talk."

Jake sighed and sat on the concrete floor.

She wiped her eye. "People do foolish things when they're twenty-one and in love, Jake. I thought it was romantic that Jon was a screenwriter—a storyteller." Her eyes locked on Jon. "When you left, I realized even your job had been a lie."

Jon nodded with shame. "I survived by creating multiple identities. I was proud of my knack for making up characters. I thought it would be easy to be a Hollywood writer. But it was harder than getting away with credit card fraud."

Jake scoffed. "You had a name like Jon Beartracker and you chose Travissi as your pen name? I would think a First Nation screenwriter back in the 1990s would have cleaned up in Tinseltown."

"Jake." The small projection of his mother's head appeared disappointed.

He threw up his hands. "Why are you taking his side after all his bullshit?"

"Because I like the idea of you coming home, and I have a lot of questions." She glared at Jon.

Jake could relate. Under his anger he was curious, but once his questions were answered, he wasn't sure whether or not he'd deck the bastard.

Jon turned to Jake. "You like movies?"

Tomoko jumped in to ease the tension. "He loves them, and books."

Jon nodded. "A reader under fifty, I can respect that. Seems the only new literature coming out these days is presented in 140 characters or less. A legacy of the digital age."

Lakshmi put her head in Jake's lap, eager to be part of the party. Tomoko sat on the floor on the other side of Jake so his mother could view everyone. Jake grimaced. "What's in this for Erasmus?"

Jon raised an eyebrow. "Nothing. Gordy wants to earn your trust."

"That's it? You two have no other agenda than to reunite the Travissi—excuse me the Beartracker clan? Where's Joaquin Parks these days?"

"The preacher? I have no idea. I spent the first half of my life earning a living as a liar. I'm good at weeding them out. Gordy has no ulterior motives in bringing us together."

Jake stood up. "Why should I trust you?"

"Because you're a good cop. You can read people as well as I can," Jon smiled.

Jake shook his head. "LA isn't on the list of approved cities we can fly to. Maybe we do this in a few months."

"Gordy is footing the bill for the *Scramjet*. The LAX flight leaves every day at 10:00AM. We can have a night on the town and then leave in the morning. I have a hotel room you two can stay in if you want some privacy."

Tomoko's hopeful gaze caught Jake's eye. The idea of privacy appealed to him too.

"Wait, where are you?" His mother asked.

Jake ignored his mother. He felt uneasy about the situation. He wasn't ready to become chummy with this man and there must be an angle. "Seems too neat."

"The Order of Erasmus has been helping my people because we've been fighting MaxWell immunization. Gordy discovered I was tracking your Omni transmissions on the Cyber-Wire and I confessed that you were my son. He didn't believe me either so he had my DNA tested against yours." Jon blushed a bit. "The Mayo Clinic still has your DNA from when you were chipped—Gordy now knows I was telling the truth. When he discovered you were in Antarctica, he invited me down."

"Wait! Antarctica?" His mother was visibly upset. "You'd better not be anywhere near McMurdo."

"We're in Terra Nova, Mom."

Tomoko touched the whistle ring on her finger. He put his hand over hers. He wanted to tell his mother in person. He'd be pinching himself every hour to be sure he was experiencing reality, but it was time to go home and face all the demons. They'd hash it out with Beartracker, get him out of the picture, and move on with their lives. Given the financial situation, it was hard to turn down the offer.

"We'll be on tomorrow's flight." He looked around the crowded hangar. "Unless the flight is already booked."

Chapter 18
Homecoming

Jake walked the streets of downtown LA. His ascendancy from rookie to commander had taken place in record time and set historical precedence within the LAPD. Critics said his success was due to a perfect storm. The LAPD was short on recruits, as were police forces in general, before they opened up careers to immigrants as a way to gain citizenship. This meant guys who had joined before the implementation of the citizenship policy got to jump a few rungs in hierarchy to ensure new recruits would be on a slower track. The LAPD had suffered from bad publicity and Jake was a successful officer, an inspiration to both citizens and the cops whose morale had needed a boost. Within the department, he bent rules, but most of his superiors turned a blind eye because he got results. All that changed on December 7, 2028 during the raid on Roberto Pacheco's child pornography studio in Beverly Hills.

Jake paused his career retrospective. Something was not right. He made a slow three-hundred-sixty-degree turn. The streets were empty. He closed his eyes. No sound but a slight rustling. He opened his eyes to see a crumpled piece of paper blowing down the street. That was odd. There were hardly any paper products imported or produced in the US these days.

He turned and was intrigued by a large warehouse ahead. It was the building that once housed Club Euphoria. The barbed wire gate that once held back crowds for bouncers to approve or deny entrance onto the exclusive scene looked out of place. Like a hair hanging from the corner of someone's mouth. It was high noon, so an empty and silent club made sense. But the streets in the area should have vehicles, pedestrians, and food carts. Only the sound of his shoes crunching on asphalt gave a hint of human activity.

The door to Club Euphoria was open. A breath of cool air with the light scent of drying alcohol wafted over him. He stepped inside the abyss. He groped his way forward, waiting for his pupils to dilate so he could see something. His eyes adjusted and he found himself inside a large circular room made of massive stone blocks. He gazed up and saw that he was in a silo. There wasn't a ceiling; the walls simply disappeared into blackness dozens of stories above.

The sound of human footfalls grew around him. He noticed a spiral ramp cut into the side of the silo, like grooves inside a gun barrel. People marched upward in single file, just inches away from each other. They numbered in the thousands, ascending into the black hole above. He checked the area where the silo met the stone ground. He realized he was on a floating disc of rock and the silo extended into blackness dozens of stories below. The room was reminiscent of an Escher design.

"Hello! Can anyone point the way out of here?" he shouted.

The people marching up the spiral cut were all ghostly pale and stared straight ahead. Each displayed the same vacant expression on their face.

He spied a strip of rock leading from his island of stone to the ramp. He deftly leapt and jogged up to the ramp. There was no room to squeeze his arm in between the automatons much less get his body onto the ramp. "Excuse me." No one seemed to be aware of him. He rammed his body in between two people. He was immediately caught in the upwardly marching mass. It was hard to breathe. He was forced ahead, keeping a steady gait. A cold stone wall stood a few inches to his right and the open abyss was just an inch or two to his left.

He thrust his right shoulder into the inside wall. He pushed forward, trying to make his way up the inside of the column of automatons. People precariously leaned to the left, their bodies hanging out into the open air to let him pass. They continued their mindless ascent, despite his rapid movement up the inside track.

"Wake up!" he yelled.

Every automaton simultaneously halted.

Jake slowed down and stopped. Individuals turned to face him. He saw the glazed look of Pin Heads in everyone's eyes.

A twinge of terror crawled up his neck. His survival instincts took hold. He gripped the nearest ashen-faced man and shook him. "Fight them. You're in there somewhere!"

Hands snatched from all sides. Jake struggled. His feet were lifted from the ground and he rocked on a wave of groping hostile hands. There were four times as many automatons around him than was physically possible given the narrow corridor.

He was flung into the abyss. For a split second he saw the cold emotionless faces of those who had ejected him. Gravity tugged. The automatons broke into laughter. He freefell into the darkness below and passed thousands of laughing Pin Heads. Their faces blurred as he picked up speed. The laughter grew in intensity. He felt the impact of cold stone.

Jake's eyes flew open. The earth filled the space overhead. He could see all of South America fixed to the curve of the earth. He was comfortably seated in his Six-G seat onboard an Air Italia *Scramjet* bound for LAX. He had never passed out during a G-force takeoff before, but then again, it had been a while since he had been aboard any aircraft.

He was seated in the view portion of the cabin. Holo-projectors covered every surface displaying real-time footage of the universe beyond the hull of the aircraft. It was like floating inside one of those mid-twentieth century planetariums with HD footage of the solar system flying by. For many passengers, this type of travel was unnerving, especially upon reentry, so the back half of the craft remained opaque with small holo-screens fixed to the back of the seats in case a passenger was curious as to what was going on outside. If he were in the aisle seat he could lean out and see all the way forward to infinity, as if there were no cockpit blocking the view.

Tomoko reached out from her seat cradle and touched his hand. They were in the fifteen-minute orbital freefall before the ship would descend as a fireball toward LAX. Every aspect of the *Scramjet* flight was exciting, but definitely not for the faint of heart. He was impressed that Jon had the proper medical releases on his ID to prove he was fit enough to fly aboard a low orbit transport.

"Another nightmare?" She squeezed his hand.

"Yeah." He nodded, although she could not see him because of the bulky seats. They were made to cradle the body during high g-force takeoff and landings. "I'm pretty nervous about this trip." He chuckled. "No turning back now, I'm literally strapped in for the ride."

"You'll be fine. Focus on me whenever you have doubts. I'm no illusion."

He squeezed her hand. He felt lucky to have her in his life. "Hard to believe that every hour hundreds, if not thousands, of people take commercial flights like this that are basically what Yuri Gagarin and Alan Sheppard made history with back in the sixties."

"Ladies and gentlemen," the pilot's voice buzzed from the seat speakers, "for those who are interested, take a look at your personal holo-screens for a nose view. We're currently freefalling toward North America and will be entering into Earth's lower atmosphere in five minutes. Mexico and California are prominently displayed."

Jake's holo-vision was activated on the seatback in front of him, but he soaked in the planetarium above. The world swung down toward the front of the ship as the craft maneuvered into a nosedive toward North America. The seats in front blocked most of his view of the earth, so he focused on his holo-screen. California and the Baja Peninsula grew in size. A fiery glow began to envelop the entire cabin as the nose sliced into the atmosphere.

A woman in her mid fifties occupied the hull seat next to him. She stared up at the fiery glow enveloping the cabin with a broad grin. He could see her reflection on the faux glass wall next to her.

He waved his hand so she could see him. "You've done this a few times?"

"I hate flying, but these crazy seats were all that were left. I've got my Third Eye generating enough natural relaxants that I could be skewered by a Pamplona bull and I wouldn't care. I love my Chip."

They entered the atmosphere and generated a sonic boom. There was a steep, rapid descent toward the Pacific Ocean a hundred miles off the coast of LA. Then the ship leveled out and used engines to fly over the city, turn a hundred and eighty degrees, and approach the tower at LAX. He was exhilarated to see clouds race above his head and to watch the city fly past the woman seated next to him.

They landed on December 29th, 2035. There had been a massive backlog of people trying to fly home. Tomoko and Jake explored Terra Nova while waiting for a flight. They had missed out on donated clothes and prices were astronomically high so they wore their rented rags, but they splurged for clean underwear. Jon loaned Jake a shirt, since Jake's had been used to dress Anjali's wound. There had been two-hour long waits for showers at the shelter so Jon had let them use the one in his hotel room. Jake and Tomoko wound up crashing on his floor for a couple of nights. The hotel management had been charitable to them considering the circumstances, but Jake could tell they were not happy about Lakshmi.

They picked up his dog at baggage claim. She had been administered a blue dart in order to fly and was a bit shaky. He was pissed that they shot her, but figured a complaint would be wasted on a chipped employee. They placed her on a luggage cart and met up with Jon. The four of them lined up for decontamination.

Travelers walked into Nemp chambers, ten at a time for a ten-minute blast. Jake couldn't help thinking about the Argentine soldiers and if they had died of Max2, this procedure might be useless. But as far as he knew, only The Order of Erasmus, The Consortium and he were aware of Max2's existence. Afterward, they were scanned for bombs, drugs, and any other contraband. Finally, they were allowed to line up for customs. Tomoko was directed into a separate line for international travelers while Jake and Jon were funneled into the citizen line.

Jake was first up to the immigration counter. The chipped employee sat inside a hermetically sealed booth. A speaker below her window crackled to life. "I saw that you were on the flight manifest, Commander. Welcome home. Any chance you'll be going back to work? MaxWell has created a shortage of cops."

He grinned back at her like an idiot. He did not like all these chipped folks instantly accessing his information and getting familiar with him.

"Place your hand on the scanner, Commander," she directed, "and look into the red light." He found a smudged black piece of plastic with a retinal scanner below her window. He stooped to put his hand on the plastic and line his eyes up with the light. "Perfect."

He saw a brief red flash.

She smiled. "I hope this isn't too forward of me, but I wanted to thank you for making Third Eyes safe for the rest of us."

"Made it—" He couldn't believe the PR spin. Then again, NTI had the rights to his likeness in any promotions of The Chip. Apparently they had used it liberally after he had given them a PR heart attack in 2030. "Talk about turning lemons into lemonade."

"Excuse me?"

"Nothing." He winked.

"Your citizenship has green bars all across. True patriot."

"Glad to hear it."

He met Tomoko and Jon on the other side of the booth. They were now free to take a subway to The Valley. Jake felt like springing for a cab.

"Jon," he didn't think he'd ever call this man Dad, "I've got a stop I want to make. Mind if we meet you at Mom's in an hour or so?"

"See you soon." He smiled and walked over to the tram stop that would take him to the LAX train station. Cars hummed, and pedestrians milled about the terminal buildings.

Jake got in line for one of the cab kiosks and sighed.

"What is it?" Tomoko asked.

"I'm relieved. I was half expecting everyone to be a hacked zombie around here." He listened for other languages. Some travelers spoke Spanish to the kiosks. One man spoke Japanese, but there was a distinct absence of multiple languages. MaxWell continued to have a ripple effect.

Their turn came up and he spoke to the computer dispatcher. "I need a cab for two adults and one Husky."

A female voice spoke back to him. "Please place your luggage on the scale."

He noticed a large rubber pad by the kiosk. "It's at the bottom of the ocean."

"Please place your luggage on the scale."

"We don't have any."

"Please give your destination or full trip description for an accurate quote."

Tomoko shook her head. "We have human dispatchers back in Lima."

The computer dispatcher spoke. "Please give your destination or full trip description for an accurate quote."

He turned to the Kiosk. "Hollywood Forever Cemetery, wait for twenty to thirty minutes then take me to 18605 Hatteras Street in Tarzana."

"That will be five hundred and thirty four dollars even."

He sighed. "Good lord, inflation has gotten bad since I left. Wouldn't have been more than four hundred back in 2030." He placed his thumb against the scan plate.

"Eye at the light, please," said the voice in the black-and-yellow-striped box.

He bent down so his eye could be scanned along with his thumb. "Since when did all the retina scans come into vogue?"

"Retinal scans are required for non-chipped citizens as a primary form of identification since the Credit Fraud Act of 2032," replied the computer.

"Did you hear that, dear?" He winked to Tomoko. "We're second class now." An electric cab hummed up to the curbside and electric doors disappeared under the car. There were two rows of seats but no dashboard and no driver.

"Jeez. No emergency steering wheel?" he commented. "I'm surprised legislation allowed that to pass." They lay Lakshmi in the back seat. She was more alert now but still a bit groggy. Jake and Tomoko settled into the front for a better view. They buckled into the five point harnesses before the car sealed itself and took off for the cemetery.

Chapter 19
Promise

As the taxi hummed along, holo-billboards triggered audio inside the cab to blast non-stop advertising.

"Mute!" Jake shouted but the audio continued to blare at deafening levels. Lakshmi howled. The ad they passed showed a plump white haired gentleman with a receding hairline and thick black-rimmed glasses.

"I'm Doctor Roald Eberstark, Director of The Immortality Project here in Los Angeles."

"That's creepy," Jake muttered as he ran through the cab's guest services screen trying to figure out how to turn off the sound. "You're also dead." The screen was covered with carved graffiti. He was surprised to see the vandalism. Cabs were programmed to shut down the moment someone started to deface it, and issue the vandal a ticket.

Eberstark's voice droned on as his hologram moved above the cab's interface. They had already passed the billboard. "I'd like to take a moment to explain why implantation is good for you and our world. First, a Chip ensures survival against a virulent nano-virus known as MaxWell."

Jake continued to navigate the submenus.

Eberstark's voice boomed. "Second, The Chip is the next step in your evolution. It is a bridge for the human mind to enter the Cyber-Wire and for the scientists at the Immortality Project, we believe The Chip is also a bridge for placing your entire essence into cyberspace, where you can live forever…"

Eberstark's image shrank and stepped onto a conveyor belt of zeros and ones. "It's a fact that we're all moving toward a union with technology. With the birth of AI in China and the gestation of AI elsewhere, our electronic brethren will soon help us create a world where death no longer threatens society. The technology behind AI, combined with the research we are conducting at the IP institute, herald humanity's immortality and oneness with true freedom." His smiling face filled the space above the console once again. "Embrace the future and embrace your freedom."

His face froze as a different voice snapped on. "For a free consultation on how you can become immortal, visit the Immortality Project via your Third Eye or Omni today. This advertisement paid for by the United Screen Actors Guild."

Tomoko turned to Jake. "I thought they killed him and blew up his lab before he figured out how to upload a person's essence into the Cyber-Wire?"

"Doesn't keep the foundation from making pitches and collecting more research money." After digging down six menu levels, Jake discovered there was no way to turn the audio off. "Good lord, I want my money back."

The cab computer's female voice popped on. "We're sorry, but your fare is non-refundable. If you wish to lodge a complaint, you may use our consumer interface. Do you wish to terminate our service at this time?"

He rolled his eyes. "No, thank you." He turned to Tomoko. "You'd think the cab company could at least spend some cash on a holo-driver."

Tomoko laughed. "In Lima, you don't get a voice at all. You input your destination and that's it."

"Lima sounds more appealing all the time." He leaned over and kissed her.

The cab voice snapped back on. "If you wish to advance your physical display of affection, I will darken the windows to a hundred percent opacity for an additional charge of fifty dollars. This price also includes a cleaning fee. Uncensored displays of affection are considered unlawful by the Department of Transportation and a fine will be charged to your account according to the level of the offense. Note that uncensored fornication will result in the complete lock up of this vehicle, followed by your arrest, a fine of ten thousand dollars and or a jail sentence of up to three days."

"I was just kissing my fiancé!"

"Kissing is permissible provided that clothing remains on and touching is restricted to the face."

He threw his head back and laughed. "What sort of fornication do people have with these restraining belts?" He tugged at his five-point harness.

The cab happily answered. "I can show you videos for a fee of sixty five dollars. This includes darkening windows and a cleaning fee."

They burst out laughing.

They arrived at Hollywood Forever in the early afternoon. Although it was December, the temperature was in the low eighties. During the cab ride, Jake had accessed the cemetery's computer with his Omni so he knew how to locate the grave. The cab parked a few feet from the shade of a palm tree. Something was wrong with the sensors, as a good onboard computer would have parked them in shadow. All three of them got out and crunched over the dirty composite grass to the mausoleum. Like most businesses, Hollywood Forever had to switch to artificial turf because watering grass was no longer legal. Plus, it was the politically correct thing to do.

"Here it is." He stood before a wall of square marble stones. He nodded to an inscription four stones up from the bottom and pulled out a plastic bag from his disheveled suit pocket.

Tomoko read the stone. "Regina Agnes Chilcot. Friend. Born June 10, 1969 Died April 22nd 2030."

"I'm sorry, Gene…" He couldn't push another word past the lump in his throat. He unzipped the bag and poured the coarse soil onto the lip of the stone's frame. "You always said you wanted to visit Antarctica."

Tomoko held him as he cried. Lakshmi licked his hand. He had told Tomoko about Gene's life many times. Gene had loved gardening and animals. She had a keen sense of humor and was always there for him. She was tenaciously loyal with a solid code of morality and ethics. She had been an admirable woman in a world that was growing less so. She had been murdered because she realized he was being hacked.

After Jake exposed the LAPD God Head plot to the world, her body had been found in the cadaver room at UCLA medical school. The first year students had almost finished dissecting her, but luckily the dean had made sure all anonymously donated cadavers were checked for Gene's DNA. She had been a registered donor anyway so it seemed fitting that the students finish their work before the school cremated her remains. Her nephew had been the executor of her will and divided up her belongings amongst the family. She had wanted to be buried on the East Coast if Jake was unable to carry out their verbal agreement. Her sister pushed to have Gene buried in Los Angeles due to some family fallout.

"Sorry I left before they found you," he apologized to the stone. "I was in danger and a good deal of pain. I wasn't much of a friend to you or myself back then. I'll work on getting your ashes out of here so we can take the trip to the Brooklyn Bridge and toss you in the East River." He sucked in a deep breath. "I need to do a few things before I can break those laws with you."

He reminisced over Gene stories with Tomoko. An hour passed before the cab called out to them. "You are now thirty minutes past your grace period. If you do not continue with your journey in the next five minutes, you will be billed at twenty dollars per minute."

"F—"

Tomoko covered his lips with her fingers. "Let it run."

He sighed. "No, we need to get back. I have the feeling Mom needs me now more than ever and I don't want to keep on screwing up my chances while the people I love are still alive."

For an additional hundred dollars, he asked the cab to take surface streets to his mother's condo. He spent the ride from the cemetery to Tarzana pointing out different landmarks and sharing personal stories. It helped them ignore the incessant chatter of advertising over the cab's speakers. At one point, Tomoko observed something a bit odd. "There are no homeless people. I thought you said LA was filled with them?"

He crossed his arms. His pause was long enough to activate the Cab Computer's trivia bank. "MaxWell casualty rates among the homeless have reached eighty percent. The rest have been immunized and are convalescing in shelters."

"Eighty percent..." He leaned back in shock. "There were twenty thousand homeless in the Los Angeles area when I left, more if you count the non-stop civilization from Santa Monica out to Vegas."

The cab rattled off figures in her sweet voice. "Roughly five hundred thousand homeless have perished in the United States due to the MaxWell epidemic."

"Christ. What's the total of the world's population infected and immunized?" he asked.

"Current numbers infected with MaxWell equals twenty million. Ten million have perished, six billion are immunized, or were previously chipped prior to the MaxWell event."

He felt as if the cab was just t-boned and they were spinning off the road in slow-motion. "Stop your trivia function and billboard audio."

"I'm sorry, the billboard audio cannot be silenced."

They rode in stunned silence as the advertising accosted their ears.

It was close to 4:00PM by the time the cab pulled up in front of his mother's townhouse. The shadows were very long as it got dark by 5:00PM this time of year. "Quite a contrast to the endless days in Antarctica, wouldn't you say?" He kissed Tomoko as they stood at the bottom of Abigail's steps.

"When was the last time you physically saw your mom?" she asked.

"January 2030... I think. Probably a few times before I was chipped, then I never saw her again—that I can remember—until I contacted her from Rio. But that was via Omni." He inhaled sharply. "Here goes—" He noticed movement in the corner of his eye. He turned and saw Jon rise up from behind a row of artificial birds of paradise.

"Dagot'ee." Jon dusted himself off. "The foliage takes some getting used to."

"What were you doing behind the flowers?" Jake was a tad suspicious.

Jon replied with a deadpan expression. "Performing the ancient White Mountain Apache rite of waiting."

Jake opened his mouth and then smiled. Jon smiled back and they all laughed. "You're chicken!"

"No, Beartracker. There is no one by the name of Chicken among our people."

Jake dropped his smile. "Don't think a joke gets you off the hook. You seriously screwed up Mom and me for life."

"I'm very sorry. Unfortunately youth and wisdom are inversely proportionate. Yet western people exalt and cherish youth. That's why the world is so fucked up."

"Is that a First Nation proverb?" Everyone looked up to see Abigail Gustafson framed in her doorway at the top of a short flight of stairs. She was all gray now, not as plump as Jake remembered, but as radiant and warm as always.

"Mom." He smiled sheepishly. Abigail was already down and hugging her son. "You've lost weight."

"That's because I've been worried sick about you for the past five years." She gripped him harder. "I missed you so much, Jake." Tears rolled down her face. "I am so sorry for what happened to you."

"I know, Mom. I'm sorry for running away."

"Nonsense." She held him at arms length. "You did what you had to do to survive." She reached up, grabbed his face and pulled it down to her five-foot-six level and kissed his cheek. "You won't fully understand this until you have children of your own, but no parent wants to see their child suffer. It doesn't matter how old they are." She hugged his head with tears streaming down her face. "It's so good to see you, Jake. I love you so much."

He was stooped over and caught in his mother's loving headlock. "It's good to see you too, Mom. I love you."

Lakshmi barked.

Abigail held on to her son. “Yes, I missed you too, Lakshmi, but I’m not done with my favorite son yet.”

Jake reached over and pulled Tomoko into the hug pile. “Mom, this is Tomoko. Your future daughter-in-law.”

Abigail let him go and gazed at both of them with slack-jawed surprise. “Oh my god!” She clapped her hands over her mouth elatedly. “This—this is the happiest day of my life!” She hugged them both as tightly as she could.

Jake opened a watery eye and noticed Jon smiling at the three of them. Silent tears ran in the grooves of his face. Jake cleared his throat. “Why don’t we get in before New Years hits us in the ass?”

Abigail shook her head. “You never had a mouth like that until you became a cop. Why you turned your back on law I’ll never know.”

They ascended the four short stairs to the doorway. “I didn’t turn my back on law. I chose to enforce it rather than argue it.”

Abigail stopped at the door and gazed down at them. “Where’s everyone’s luggage?”

Jon held up a small travel bag. “This is it.”

Jake held up the piece of scrimshaw Tomoko had carved of the *Pachacuteq*, his one and only possession besides his Omni. “Our boat sank in McMurdo Sound.”

“Sank? Jesus.” She put her hand over her eyes. “Maybe I don’t want to know. I worry less that way.” She walked inside and the rest followed.

Chapter 20
Travissi

Abigail made tofu burgers on the grill. She didn't have enough in her budget to buy genuine meat. Jake did most of the talking, recapping their travels and ending with the attack on McMurdo.

"The UN has placed sanctions on the US for using the Sword of Damocles on the Argentine troops. I didn't even know what a Sword of Damocles was until the news this morning," Abigail stated as Jake helped scrape the dishes and load them in the sonic washer. "They claim the US violated Geneva II. Now the Russians and Chinese have stated they are turning their backs on Geneva as well. I figured the worst was behind us once a cure for MaxWell was announced, but I was wrong."

"Anyone know about the original Greek story of Damocles?" Jon asked. They all continued cleaning up in uncomfortable silence. Jon plowed on. "Damocles was a man who traded places with King Dionysus of Sicily. Damocles enjoyed the riches and luxury of the court, but Dionysus hung a massive sword above the throne so that Damocles would know the dangers and constant stress of being a ruler." Jon chuckled. "Nothing to do with this new version unless you use the basic interpretation of 'death from above.'"

"Spin doctors aren't concerned about etymology these days, just as long as the phrase is catchy," Jake added as he and Abigail joined Jon and Tomoko at the table. Everyone sat in silence for a beat.

Jake clapped his hands. "How about we address the elephant in the room?"

"I am not an elephant," Jon replied.

"You're a half blue-eyed-blonde Frenchman," Jake answered. "What else have you been covering up?"

Jon fingered his lower lip. "How about some context?"

Abigail jumped up nervously. "I'll put on some coffee."

Tomoko grabbed her hand. "Please let me. I saw where you keep everything. I can take care of it."

Abigail flashed an embarrassed smile. "Thank you."

Jon sat as if he were addressing the room from the witness stand. "My mother, Helen, worked as a dive master on a boat out of Long Beach when she met my father, Bill. Bill had been working construction and living in a studio apartment with four other Apaches. Bill and the others sent their pay home to their families on the Fort Apache reservation. Bill and Helen's romance was a whirlwind from the first date. It was 1970 and my parents spent a great deal of time driving out to the desert, and going on peyote-induced vision quests. After six weeks, they got married at Wayfarer's Chapel in Palos Verdes, then drove to Fort Apache for the honeymoon.

"I was born the night of the January New Moon in 1971. By this point, things were not going well between my parents. Helen was a wandering spirit. Bill wanted to raise me as one of The People. According to Helen, Bill was a drunk and abused her. According to my father's family, Bill began drinking only when he could not reconcile his relationship with Helen."

Jon folded his hands on the table top and leaned back. "I was nine months old when Helen took me from Fort Apache. I grew up living in backwater towns around the US, half a dozen Pacific islands, and several European slums. Helen had many men in her life. There were times when I would be left alone with her boyfriends for weeks, even months. Helen always told me

I was Apache but that Bill was an angry drunk who would have beaten me if she had stayed with him. I grew up hating my Apache blood and defending Helen when some of the men in her life accused her of not taking responsibility for me.

"When I reached seventeen I decided Helen could provide nothing more for me, so I left. We lived in London at the time and I fell in with some drug dealers and started working as a courier. By eighteen, I had become a dealer myself and through some connections, I met a couple of credit card fencers from Canada. At nineteen, I moved to Toronto to get into the credit fraud business.

"By twenty I worked under several aliases. When I reached twenty-five, I'd made and lost three fortunes. My third fortune was blown when police raided my house in Vancouver. I escaped with a thousand dollars in my pocket but had to leave everything else behind.

"I was a compulsive liar and had a gift for keeping several stories straight. Because of this, I decided I would be a natural at writing. From Vancouver, I traveled to LA to make my next fortune as a screenwriter," Jon chuckled.

Jake angrily drummed his fingers on his knees. The idea that a criminal's blood flowed in his veins made him want a transfusion.

Jon continued. "I sold a horror screenplay to a couple of fly-by-night producers during my first four months here. Based on this success, I expected to be nominated for an Academy Award by the time I was twenty seven."

"Where did you come up with the name Travissi?" Abigail looked uncomfortable.

"I made it up. I've spent a good deal of time trying to forget those days," he looked hard at Jake and Abigail. "But not all of it. I've always been proud of you, Jake." He turned to his ex-wife. "My love for you back then was real, Abigail. What I did to the both of you fills my spirit with shame and regret."

Jake tried not to hit him. "You said your past came back and that's why you left?"

"I caught wind that the Canadian police had tracked me down. I had also run into some of my old Vancouver credit fraud connections who wanted to start up business again. I wasn't sure if they were legit or had turned snitch for the police." He looked hard at Abigail and Jake. "I didn't want you two involved. I felt the best course of action was to run."

"My birth certificate on the reservation has me listed as Jonathan Lightning Beartracker. Traditionally, Apaches earn names after they do something significant in their lives. After the wars with the whites, Apaches took on European surnames. My father's name was Bill Lupe. But when he was fourteen, he shot a bear at dusk and tracked it for half the night before ending its life. His Apache name was given by the medicine man as He Who Tracks the Bear Under a sliver Moon. When my father left Fort Apache, he stopped using Lupe in favor of a condensed version of his Apache name."

"So your last name is just as made up as Travissi?" Jake grumbled.

Jon's low voice a had calming effect. "Helen didn't understand Apache names either. She saw lightning on the night I was born and wanted that as my middle name."

"And your second birth certificate?" Abigail questioned.

"We moved to Paris when I was three and she told the authorities I was born in international waters. My French birth certificate lists me as Albert Jean Moget. That was who I always thought I was until I returned to the reservation in 1998. No one outside of Fort Apache knew of my roots. I grew up doubting Helen's stories as she could say a lot of things when she was high or drunk. She'd always been consistent about Bill and Fort Apache so I decided to see if there was truth to it."

Tomoko walked in with four coffees. "So all your warrants were for your alias or Albert Moget? No one connected you to your original birth certificate?"

"That's right," Jon nodded.

"You're traveling now. Why don't they arrest you?" Abigail asked.

Jake butted in. "Statute of limitations. If Jon has been off the grid the past thirty-seven years, I'd say no one cares, given that he didn't murder anyone." He turned to his father. "Right?"

Jon stared into his son's eyes. "Never."

"Or he's traveling under his Apache name," Tomoko suggested.

Jon held up his hand. "I'm traveling under Jon Travissi. Using Beartracker makes things complicated."

Abigail shook her head. "What've you done now?"

"I've joined my people in resisting certain Federal laws we don't agree with."

Abigail sighed. "You're American now whether you like it or not."

Jon grunted. "You might recall the US leased half the Federal lands to China to pay off its multi-trillion dollar debt a few years back. The US illegally threw our Indian lands into the package. One more 'fuck you' to add to the history books. Technically, we're Chinese."

Jake shook his head. "Always thought that was a bad deal." He noticed Tomoko was drawing on her Omni tablet. It was a scene of a couple and their baby walking up a sand dune.

"That's why the bastard didn't get re-elected," Abigail added.

"The People thought it was a bad deal too until the Chinese came and told us they recognized our sovereignty. The Chinese have enough problems back home and abroad to keep them from worrying about a handful of depressed pocket economies in the US."

"Give it time," Jake snorted. "You'll be walking the Dalai Lama's path soon enough."

Jon ignored him. "The US respects our borders, but since we're islands within the United States, we must do business with it and that's when we have trouble."

"You should petition China to drop supplies by air," Jake smiled.

Jon eyed Tomoko's art. "We take care of our own. We've come a long way since the last millennium. Casinos helped, but we're educating our young with a blend of traditional and western ideals so we can prosper on a global scale. We don't ask for charity, just equality and freedom of expression. After events in Antarctica, the US has bigger issues to worry about."

Tomoko pressed the animation button and the family walked up the sand dune on a moonless night. The ten-second clip undulated like living watercolor. "What happened when you escaped to Fort Apache?"

"Uhm," Abigail raised her finger. "He *ran away* to Fort Apache."

Jon addressed Abigail. "Correct." He turned to Tomoko. "My grandmother recognized me immediately and welcomed me into her home. Bill had committed suicide a few years after Helen had taken me. My father's family embraced me and I learned the ways of The People. I found my soul there." He gazed appreciatively at Tomoko's animation. "I became an artist and sold paintings at galleries in Tempe and Phoenix…" He smiled at Tomoko. "You're quite skilled."

She blushed. "What happened to Helen?"

"She passed several years back." He looked into Abigail's eyes. "I am sorry for what I did. Jake says you never remarried and raised him by yourself. You were always far more admirable and brave than I." He cleared his throat. "I'm sorry if this stings, but… I remarried. I have a twenty-eight-year-old son and a twenty-six-year-old daughter."

Jake froze with shock. "Are they back in Fort Apache?"

Jon's eyes watered. "MaxWell took my wife and son. Isabella, my daughter, is still alive."

Tomoko squeezed Jon's hand and gave him a tearful smile.

Jon continued. "We don't believe in a marriage between human beings and machines. We've been at war with the Federal Government since the nineteenth century. The United States will pass a law requiring all citizens to be immunized, just as China has. We will refuse. We believe MaxWell was created so that the Federal Government can finally take away the freedom of every person in this country."

Jake sat back. "Probably not the Federal Government but certainly powerful folks who are connected to governments all over the world. They call themselves The Consortium."

Jon nodded. "Those who pull the strings then. MaxWell was tailor-made for an artificial cure."

Abigail sipped on her coffee. "It's schizophrenic out there. One minute people protest against The Chip. The next minute they demonstrate for mandatory implantation. The majority are simply scared and want to survive by any means necessary. I used to believe we lived in the greatest era of history. I have to believe we'll bounce back."

Silence descended on the room. An old clock ticked from somewhere in the house.

Abigail took Tomoko's hand. "Your wedding gives me hope."

Tomoko smiled. "I look forward to being a part of your family."

"What was your wedding like?" Jake looked at his mother.

Tomoko almost choked on her coffee. "Have a little tact, Jackhammer."

"Well, with our wedding…" He felt his face getting red. "I wanted… ideas. I never saw photos, and Mom rarely talked about it."

Abigail sighed. "I spent the last thirty-seven years trying to forget." Her eyes darted to Jon. She looked down and swirled her coffee for a few seconds, as if the action created a window for her to look into the past. "We were married under the friendship bell in Long Beach. It was a small wedding; a couple of my friends from nursing school, my dad, Jon there, and a Judge. Our courtship was a lot like Helen's and Bill's, passionate, quick, young, and foolish." She held a melancholy gaze as she looked up from her coffee. "Enough about the past. What are your plans, Tomoko? We know Jake hasn't thought about it."

Jake observed his feet with embarrassment.

"I'd like something romantic and out of the ordinary." She gazed lovingly at Jake.

Jake perked up. "Anything but Vegas."

Tomoko leaned in to address the table. "He doesn't like crowds, glitzy, commercial, or touristy type stuff."

Abigail smiled. "He never did."

Jon's deep voice boomed out. "What about an Apache wedding? It addresses both criteria and it would be free. I'd take care of it."

"I love it!" Tomoko bounced in her seat.

Jake rubbed the scrimshaw with his thumb. "I'm feeling a bit like Damocles right now. Gordon appears asking me to join Erasmus and brings my long lost father along. Now I'm being handed an exotic wedding package free of charge." He stared at Jon. "When does the sword drop?"

Jon leaned back. "It dropped in 2030 and you've been pulling it out of your head ever since. No catch, Jake. Live a little. Want to yell at me? Hit me? I welcome it. I am deeply sorry. I know nothing I can do can ever make us a family. I would like nothing more than to reconcile and be part of your lives, even if it is just this one event. Every journey starts with—"

"The first step. Yeah we've all heard that one before, Red." Jake rolled his eyes.

He felt a kick from Tomoko's shoe under the table. Abigail's mouth dropped open. He wanted to follow through on his anger. It was his prime motivation for being obnoxious. He wanted to goad Jon into an argument, maybe a fight.

Jon nodded. "Offer still stands."

Jake grit his teeth in frustration. He felt guilty over his adolescent attitude. Could a few hours of good behavior make up for what Jon had done? Was there any excuse in the universe that could atone for abandoning a wife and son? No. There was simply an explanation. And then there was MaxWell, the horrific death toll, and the immunization policy. Time was not on anyone's side. Their lives could change in an instant.

Jake turned to his fiancé. "Let's do it."

Chapter 21
Conquistador

Jon bought the Bullet Train tickets at two hundred dollars a pop. The trip from LAX to Phoenix took two hours. When they arrived at the station, a Fort Apache Tour Van awaited. It was basically a rolling billboard. Holo-images swooped out of the sides and roof displaying scenes of happy tourists learning hunting, tracking, native arts and crafts, skiing, gambling, water rides, golfing, fishing, getting massages, and eating.

"Nice ride," Jake commented.

"It's big business for us. We've got First Nation tours for folks who want something they can't find anywhere else and we offer conventional attractions like malls, skiing, casinos, amusement parks—you name it. When the bullet train hub was put into Phoenix back in 2023 it elevated the reservation into a genuine resort almost overnight. We call the train The Great River. It's our lifeblood." Jon saw the concern on Jake's face. "Don't worry, we still have plenty of sacred ground untouched by Western wickedness."

The van had been sent by the tribal elders, of which Jon was a member. Like all vehicles, there was no driver. The ride out to Globe took forty-five minutes. When they reached the reservation's border, Jake was surprised to see a massive razor-wire fence.

"What's all this?" Jake asked as they drew closer.

"The Federal Government put it up after the MaxWell outbreak. We've lobbied China to bring it down, but they're more focused on navigating US red tape to extract minerals from the land."

They passed a low building with several Army trucks outside. Soldiers drilled in the dust, about four hundred yards from the reservation entrance. Jake pointed his thumb at the troops. "You guys under siege?"

"Soon." Jon answered. "We refuse to have our medical personnel chipped, so Arizona's governor has petitioned the Federal Government to quarantine us. An answer could come anytime. No tourist has visited the reservation in four weeks."

"Why the army?" Abigail nervously stared at the chipped soldiers.

"China runs the reservation. Technically we're foreign soil and since China has passed immunization in their own country, the US expects us to comply."

"Maybe this isn't such a good idea," Abigail mumbled.

"Oh my." Tomoko saw them first. Two men stood guard at a slick new flagstone and stainless steel gate that looked like a six lane tollway.

"The guards are our children who felt disenchanted with our push to commercialize the reservation. They left us for several years and felt that altering their bodies was a way to be closer to the spirits. They used to call themselves The Enlightened Path, but things didn't work out so well for them, and they asked to come back."

Jake stared at the guards. It was high noon and they were under the shade of the covered tollbooths. At first, he thought they were men in costume, but then he realized they were men with genetic enhancements, like the Aztec gangs that grew horns and fangs with targeted DNA implants. One man looked like an eagle, complete with beak and feathers covering his skin. The other man looked like a buffalo with massive horns and a wide nose. His face was very hairy, but his mouth and ears remained human. Both men were tall and extremely muscular.

"How many of these enlightened ones do you have?" Tomoko whispered as the car slowed to a halt.

"There are sixty-seven living on the reservation, mostly men as few women were interested in the procedure."

"I can see why," Abigail cringed.

Jon's window hummed down and he spoke Apache to Eagle. Eagle responded and picked up a radio. A minute later the gate arm swung up. Jon handed over his Omni.

"Why are you surrendering your Omni?" Jake asked as Eagle disappeared inside a booth.

Jon's window closed and the van rolled forward. "We don't allow any radiation devices on our bodies. We have interface stations in all the homes and businesses to access the Cyber-Wire. We wear Omnis off the Reservation to stay competitive. But we prefer to be as technologically frugal as possible."

"Why didn't we surrender ours?" Abigail asked.

Jon smiled. "We wouldn't get many tourists if we applied the policy to our guests."

They rode through open desert with low rocky hills and scattered cactus and creosote. The red soil almost glowed under the cobalt sky. They came upon a small village of modern interpretations of traditional huts and tepees. "How many live on the reservation?" Tomoko asked.

"We're on a large tract that holds Fort Apache, White River, and San Carlos. Between all of us there are about twenty-three thousand." Jon answered. "Due to our economic upturn, people are emigrating back."

"Do you feel you sacrificed tradition for Western ways?" she asked. Jake knew being Japanese in a predominantly Latin world put her at odds with how much of her own culture to covet. Then again First Nation had been moved by force, Tomoko's ancestors simply emigrated.

"Some do. But most of the elders don't."

The van parked next to a black steel structure about half a mile from the resort town of Peridot. Jon opened his door. "Time for decontamination."

They all climbed out.

Jake fixed his gaze on twenty or so glass and steel buildings glittering ahead. Some looked like oversized interpretations of teepees, huts, and step pyramids. A rollercoaster and a water park sat near San Carlos Lake. The structures were incongruous against the rugged sandblasted landscape. He scratched Lakshmi's ears. "So when do we see the non-commercial side of the reservation?"

Jon placed a hand on his shoulder. "My home is on the Black River, just north of here. There are plenty of secluded places on the reservation both spiritual and traditional. You won't see trailers, collapsing houses, or anything resembling the poverty I saw in '98. Hopi, Navajo, Apache, all of the people within First Nation pooled their resources. We're a mini EU if you will. We have some eyesores." He gestured to the city. "But we're able to provide for our communities and keep to our traditions. For instance, we hold ceremonies to ask permission from the spirits of the mountains, shrubs, and water, to relocate, replant or divert them so we can build."

Tomoko patted the steel structure. "What's this?"

"Portable decontamination station," Abigail stated.

"We've managed to keep MaxWell at bay with these Nemp chambers, but they cost us a fortune and don't ease tourist fears. Plus, it drinks a lot of power. We have our own plant near Willow Mountain, but it's insufficient. We've negotiated to buy power from the Gila plant, but no deals there."

Everyone piled inside the structure.

After a ten-minute Nemp bombardment, the computer gave them the green light to leave.

"I wonder how many people are going to die of cancer from all these Nemps and Chip implants," Abigail grumbled as they loaded themselves back into the van.

Jon's home was a tasteful ranch house built of large logs that looked over the Black River. There was central air and heat, but no central computer. The entire building had twelve-foot ceilings throughout that showed off massive beams above. Jake, Tomoko and Abigail admired the five-foot paintings spaced throughout the living room. Some displayed bright colors and beads, some were painted in earth tones, one color palate was all in gray. Some were portraits, some were landscapes, all expressed abstract influences, with strong brush strokes and liberal amounts of paint. Jake noticed the Beartracker signature on every work.

Tomoko was very excited to be with a fellow artist. "They're fantastic. I can feel the passion you put into every one."

"When I paint, I feel a part of something greater than myself. I feel inner peace. Painting satisfies on a physical and spiritual level."

Tomoko nodded in full agreement.

"Beautiful, Jon. Just beautiful." Abigail marveled. "You finally found your artistic outlet."

Jon put a hand on her shoulder and Jake was surprised that she did not move away.

Jon showed Jake, Tomoko, and Lakshmi to their room. It was a big space with its own bathroom and access to a porch overlooking the river. Jake stepped outside and soaked in the cool desert air. It was quiet and peaceful, with a view of rocky hills and rough desert. The Black River was nothing more than a trickle. Judging by the size of the riverbed, it had held a lot more water a few years back.

He saw Tomoko checking messages on her Omni. At one point she held her wrist to her ear, must have been something wrong with the recording if it was that faint. He returned to the view. The hills contained red strata and the landscape was full of twisted vegetation that fought year round to survive severe conditions. It reminded him a lot of Antarctica, only the colors were different. He wondered what secrets lay hidden in the sandstone; perhaps the bones of a long forgotten species that once roamed the earth an eon ago.

"I like to stand here, too."

The voice snapped him back to the moment. He faced Jon. "Why are we here? The *real* reason."

Jon crossed his arms and turned to look at the hills. His eyes glistened with tears. "I lost my wife in August and my son a few weeks after that…

I spent a lot of time questioning my spirituality, purpose of life, and if I adequately atoned for my sins." He turned to Jake. "I reached out to you before the epidemic turned my life upside down, but MaxWell forced me to take greater responsibility."

"You want our forgiveness?"

Jon sucked in a deep breath. "I cannot undo what I did. But I can be a punching bag, unconditional friend—anything you need..."

"Jake!" Tomoko stood before a large wooden wardrobe. She held up a woman's suit with a European cut as well as a ceremonial Apache dress. "You've got a closet full of clothes, too!"

"Anything you want is yours!" Jon shouted.

Jake gestured for Jon to lead the way back to the room. They would continue the discussion at a better moment.

"It's incredible. Thank you." She beamed. "There are actually some sexy things in here, Jake."

Jon smiled. "Most of it is made here on the reservation."

Jake saw several dozen shirts, pants and shoes in his wardrobe. He wondered if they had belonged to his half brother. He was currently wearing UCLA sweatpants and t-shirt his mother had dug up for him. He turned to Jon. "Thank you."

Jon smiled. "Anybody hungry?"

Lunch consisted of carnitas, beans, and homemade corn tortillas. Jake savored the carnitas. "I can't put my finger on it, but this has a stronger flavor than pork."

Jon smiled. "It's peccary. I use traditional Apache ingredients as often as possible while respecting my wife's roots."

Tomoko and Abigail were in awe that the food was all raised on the reservation. First Nation was eating better than most in the States.

Jake was surprised to hear hoof beats outside. Horses were rapidly becoming casualties of a growing population of disinterested people and a premium on space.

A few minutes later, a tall and beautiful woman in her mid-twenties waltzed into the room. Straight black hair flowed down to the middle of her back, Her deep brown eyes were set in a delicate tan face. She wore jeans, chaps, and a beaded jacket.

"Hi, Dad!" She walked over and Jon stood up to receive a warm hug and a kiss. He held her longer than she wanted. It was the first time Jake saw Jon's true sorrow over the loss of this wife and son.

Jake felt jealousy, which surprised him. Jon held his daughter the way Jake had always wanted a father to hold him. He stood up, feeling a little embarrassed, nervous and awkward. "Hi, I'm Jake."

"Da go Te, Jake. I'm Isabella." She gave him a hug.

"What does that mean?" Tomoko asked.

Isabella smiled. "Basic hello in Apache."

"How did you get a name like Isabella?" Tomoko asked.

"You're not from around here, are you?" Isabella smiled.

"Sorry." She held out her hand. "Tomoko. I'm Peruvian of Japanese decent."

Isabella hugged her. "Da go Te. Mom was half Mexican. Most everyone is a half or quarter breed these days." She winked. "Hard to get a pureblood with so many comings and goings on the reservation." Her voice quavered. Something was bothering her. "Then again, Apache history is full of conquering and assimilating other cultures. Apache means enemy, although we call ourselves Inde, or Nide, 'The People.'"

Isabella hugged Abigail then kneeled down to let Lakshmi kiss her fingers for several seconds before she made herself a plate. "I wanted a chance to meet you guys before the Council came over." She rolled up the peccary, beans, and vegetables into a sort of burrito. "So you used to be a cop?" Her grief was still very much on the surface.

Jake thought about her question. "Feels like a long time ago now."

"Must have been an intense job, enforcing laws written by people who are above them."

He didn't want to argue with someone in a raw state.

Tomoko did it for him. "It was even worse when he tried to do the right thing and the public gut-punched him for it."

Isabella switched gears. "I manage the First Nation fund. I used to travel a lot before the Feds started restricting everything."

"How did you get out, Jon?" Abigail asked.

"His buddy Erasmus pulled some strings." Isabella took a bite of burrito.

Jake noticed sweat on Tomoko's brow and wiped it off. She smiled to thank him.

"You feeling okay?" Isabella asked.

"I'm a little chilly." Tomoko answered.

Isabella's eyes narrowed as she turned to her dad. "You went through the Nemp?"

"Of course," he answered.

Abigail strolled over to Tomoko and felt her forehead.

Isabella nervously babbled. She didn't seem to be addressing anyone. "This epidemic is rich Anglos trying to stick it to us all over again. The whites would not have conquered the Americas if it hadn't been for germ warfare. You think those tiny armies of Cortez and Pizzaro could subdue the Aztecs and Incas?"

Jon stared at Isabella with compassion and concern.

"Not a chance. Those Conquistador pigs brought all those diseases from Europe and then infected natives and sent them back into their villages to wipe them out. The Christians of this country gave our people blankets infected with smallpox—" She shook her head. "Then you have the missionaries who used medicine and technology as lures in order to force their God and way of life onto native cultures. They're no better than the Nazis giving Jews chocolates before marching them into gas chambers—"

"Isabella." Jon's voice was loud but kind.

"I'm just saying a Conquistador by any other name—" She bit her lip and stared at Tomoko.

Abigail wiped down Tomoko's face. The perspiration was much worse now and she was losing color.

"She has a fever. Can you get me a thermometer, Jon?" Abigail turned to her son. "Help me get her to the couch."

Tomoko let out a massive sneeze.

Isabella jumped up. "Oh, shit!"

"I'll get the thermometer." Jon rushed out of the room.

"I've been dealing with MaxWell for the past six months..." Abigail said as she felt the swollen glands on Tomoko's neck. "Let's not jump to any conclusions."

Isabella stared in horror, causing Jake to feel a twinge of panic.

Abigail looked up at her son. "Let's get her to your room."

Jon returned with the thermometer and handed it to Abigail. He hugged Isabella and whispered in her ear. She was crying.

Jake picked up his fiancé and carried her down the hall to their room. Isabella began a shell-shocked babble. "But she went through decontamination. Why is she sick? She went through the Nemp..."

After checking Tomoko's temperature, Abigail bundled her up and placed a cool rag on her forehead. Lakshmi looked very worried and snuggled next to Tomoko.

Jon appeared at the door. "I sent Isabella home."

"It's MaxWell," Abigail diagnosed.

Jake felt as if someone pumped him in the chest with buckshot. "Options?"

Tomoko reached out to Jake with tears in her eyes. "I'm scared, Jake. Please don't let them Chip me." She faded out.

Abigail pulled Jake aside and whispered. "We had some success with blood transfusions back at Cedars, but it was limited. I believe it's now in her lymphatic system, I don't think a transfusion will work. We induced a coma in some and it slowed down the attack. The nano-virus works faster when the patient is in an active state."

"We have a hospital." Jon said. "But I'll be honest, the only way we've been able to fight MaxWell is with a Nemp, and it has to be in the early stages."

Abigail shook her head. "There should have been earlier warning signs. This is like a mutation."

Jake remembered all the sneezing back at Shackleton's lounge, and the sudden death of the Argentine troops... Max2? He could no longer listen to the debate. "We need to get her back to the Nemp immediately."

Chapter 22
Immunization

An electric tour van picked them up at the house. Jake carried Tomoko aboard and found the rear bench seat had been removed and a corrugated trough was in its place, filled with ice water. Tomoko screamed in pain when he put her into the water. She begged to come out before she slipped into unconsciousness. Abigail administered an IV drip to keep up Tomoko's fluids.

It took ten minutes to reach the decontamination station. They placed Tomoko in the Nemp generator for forty minutes. When they pulled her out she was no better. Her lymph glands were visibly swollen. She was hot, sweaty, pale, and very lethargic.

"Can't you crank up the waves on this thing?" Jake was desperate.

"I'm sorry." Jon said.

"How's the pain?" Abigail asked as she attached sensors to various areas of Tomoko's body. "On a level from one to five, five being the worst."

Tomoko licked her lips. She shivered even though her fever was at 103. She responded in her native Spanish. "I'd sssay a four in all my joints... It's hard... to... move." She faded in and out as she spoke.

Jake gazed over his mother's shoulder. He was frustrated at being utterly helpless in this situation. "Did the Nemp have any effect?"

Abigail monitored all of Tomoko's vitals on her Omni, which was in tablet mode. "Her illness is advancing at an alarming rate."

Jake scooped Tomoko up. "We're heading to the nearest hospital to get her immunized."

Jon opened the van. "Nearest hospital that immunizes is in Globe."

Jake dove into the van. "Let's move."

They drove in haste. As they drew closer to the edge of the reservation, Jake noticed an armed Enlightened One in every booth. Beyond the razor wire, the Army contingent had quadrupled. Armored cars, tank drones, and gyro-guns sat amongst the rank and file.

They pulled up next to one of the center booths and Jon's window hissed down. A man with a wolf face leaned out of the booth holding Jon's Omni. Jake blinked a few times. All of these Enlightened Ones looked like mythical creatures from some children's novel. He spotted an antelope and a Gila monster as well. He squeezed Tomoko's hand. "You should see these guys, honey. They're wild." He kept his voice calm but he was desperate to reach Globe.

Jon and the wolfman exchanged words in Apache and then the window slid back up. "They're arresting and immunizing any First Nation citizen found off the reservation. The Enlightened Ones are worried for our safety. They won't try it here because we have webcams fixed on those troops ahead."

Thirty minutes later they rolled up to the Emergency Room entrance. Jake pulled Tomoko out of the icy water and turned to his parents. "Keep an eye out for the Army or National Guard."

Abigail put a hand on her son. "We'll be fine."

"I'll park down the street," Jon said. "Call me with any news."

Jake nodded and hopped out of the van with Tomoko. Lakshmi barked after him. He shouted over his shoulder. "Guard Mom and Jon, Lakshmi!"

Double sliding doors whooshed open. The hospital waiting room was packed. Everyone wore a white mask. He walked up to the glass booth where a nurse sat with a web on her head and one of Parks' solidarity pins on her lapel. She was interfaced with the hospital computers through her Chip.

"My fiancé has MaxWell."

The nurse stared into space as she replied, "Does she have a gen five or higher?"

"She doesn't have a Chip."

"Is she lucid?"

"Does she look lucid?"

The woman refocused on Tomoko and her face went white. "My God, she's stage four."

Inner doors burst open and four figures in white HAZMAT suits marched out pushing a gurney between them.

Several of the sick jumped up in alarm. A woman buried her head in her hands and began sobbing. A man ran screaming out of the waiting area.

A soothing voice flooded out of a loud speaker. "Everyone please remain calm. We have a patient who needs priority help. Please remain seated while we escort the patient to a triage center. Thank you for your patience. There is no need for alarm."

Jake was trapped by the nurse's booth at his back and the gurney and four HAZMAT figures in front. Each suit was designed with an opaque wraparound visor, which distorted Jake's reflection. There was no sign of life, not even a bit of skin showing. An eerie feeling that the suits were empty swept over him.

One of the HAZMAT personnel spoke through a speaker in his chest. "Ms. Sakai shows all the signs of stage four infection. She needs immediate immunization."

A tear welled up in Jake's eye. "I know."

"Mr. Travissi, we'll take care of her from here. We simply need to place her on the gurney, sir."

He gazed down on Tomoko's unconscious face; it appeared wet and waxy, almost fake. He held her close. Her breathing was shallow and erratic.

He whispered. "Forgive me." He lay her gently on the gurney and the others backed away. He whispered once more. "I promise I'll figure out a way to get that Chip out once we beat this virus."

He backed away and three of the four figures rushed her through the double doors. He followed them until the fourth blocked his path. A speaker barked at him with a female voice. "Sorry, Mr. Travissi. You'll have to wait here until we call you."

"I'm her fiancé. She's a Peruvian citizen. I'm all the family she has here."

"Hospital policy." The figure in the HAZMAT suit stepped back. The doors swung closed and locked. He stood dumbfounded. If only he had his badge, anything to cut through this bureaucratic bullshit.

"Mr. Travissi. Can you answer some questions and sign off on Ms. Sakai's behalf?"

He turned to see the nurse gazing at him with compassion from inside her glass booth. He grit his teeth and walked back. "You're all chipped here. Don't you have all the information you need?"

"I'll need your thumbprint to confirm we have it right." The black countertop between Jake and the glass was now displaying text. The counter was scratched, probably from excessive cleaning and the actions of emotional patients. "Do you need me to read it to you or translate it into a different language?" the nurse asked.

"No." He read blocks of information about Tomoko's age, birthplace, and where they had been the past week. It was extremely alarming how accurate the information was. He was prompted to sign off on each block of information with his thumbprint.

As he signed, the holo-vision in the waiting room played the local news. "Congress continues to deliberate over placing a quarantine on all First Nation reservations. Rumor has it they should reach a decision in the next twenty-four hours."

He turned quickly to see the broadcast. Arizona's Governor Valdez appeared on screen. Her ghostlike figure floated in three of the room's four corners. "It is my hope that Congress will see the light. Many Native American communities flat-out refuse to immunize even their healthcare professionals.

We cannot allow the risk of raging infections inside the borders of Arizona. We must contain the risk."

The image switched to a reporter. "Many religious groups anxiously await the congressional decision."

Parks popped into the room. "Immunization is a contract with Satan. The technological enhancement of the human body is an affront to God. If Congress passes the bill to make immunization mandatory, then America will have cut the cord of freedom in favor of the shackles of a police state."

The images switched to scenes of people being pulled out of their vehicles by police and National Guard. "Police and the National Guard continue to randomly test non-immunized citizens and require all foreign nationals to leave by the new year. In some cases, foreign nationals have been deported or placed in quarantine facilities."

Jake returned to the nurse and pointed to the text on his screen, "How long is this?"

"There are fourteen sections that require your thumbprint." She seemed slightly annoyed over his pause to watch the news.

He shook his head and pressed his thumb to approve the current section. The last section was the approval for Tomoko's immunization. The cost would go against her insurance in Peru since her citizenship was there. He applied his thumbprint and the screen went blank. "Is that it?" He had lost track of the number of thumb approvals.

"Yup."

"How's her condition?"

"Still in surgery." The nurse's distant gaze returned. She was back to filing, or whatever she was doing under that web.

"Any complications?"

"She'll be fine." She refocused on him with a twinge of annoyance in her eyes. "Please take a seat, Mr. Travissi. We'll call you when she's out of the OR."

He grit his teeth and took a seat between two masked patients. One had a rather ugly gash on his arm and the other was holding her ear and rocking back and forth. No one had been called into the back the entire time he was in the ER.

It was time to visit his folks. He didn't trust his Omni after he read all the details on Tomoko's hospital approval form. He was sure anything he said over an Omni was processed through a computer monitoring the Cyber-Wire. Tracking his movements with the Omni's GPS was one thing, listening to his conversations was another.

He walked out the door and jogged out to the street. He spotted the tour van a block away and ran up to it. When he reached the driver's window, it slid down and Lakshmi licked him in the face. "Hi, girl." He could not hide the sadness in his voice. He scratched her cheeks as he ducked his head into the cab.

Abigail spoke first. "How is she?"

"She's in surgery. They say she's fine but that's all they'll give me." He noticed the newscaster floating above the dashboard. They were taking in the same bad news from Arizona's governor. He nodded to the hologram. "I'm not sure it's wise to go back to the reservation."

Jon shrugged, "Once you have Tomoko, I'll take you to Phoenix. We'll make it." He smiled. "I have faith."

A National Guard truck rumbled toward them. "I suggest you head back now. I'll catch a cab to the border when I've got Tomoko."

Jon saw the truck as well. "Agreed."

Jake held out his hand. "Good luck."

Jon shook it.

He winked at his mother. "I love you, Mom. Take good care of Lakshmi until we arrive."

"I want a hug," she replied.

Jake stepped back. "No time." He patted the van. "Get home safe!"

The van merged into traffic. As Jake jogged back to the hospital, the massive National Guard truck hummed past.

Chapter 23
Rust

Jake attempted to watch the news but could not concentrate. *What was taking so long? The improved procedure should take no more than five minutes.* Then again, it could take a while for The Chip to take control of Tomoko's autonomic and biochemical functions, and even longer to stabilize her.

He dozed off and awoke to an empty waiting room. The lights were dim and the distant whir of an electric drill filled the air. The doors to the operating wing were open. The nurse's booth was empty. He stood and quickly walked into the operating wing.

A faint light glowed at the end of a long dark hallway. The whirring drill-mixed hammering was somewhere ahead. His heart raced. He advanced with caution. He reached an operating room and noticed a patient on the gurney but no doctors. He approached the figure and realized it was a pile of ash in the shape of a person, spread out on a white sheet.

He examined the area that should have been a head. He leaned in and focused on the eyes. They blinked causing him to jump. The ash face sighed and smiled. Wispy smoke billowed with each breath.

"Good to see you, Jake."

The voice was familiar. "Gene?"

"Bringing Antarctica to me was very thoughtful," she wheezed. "Thank you."

"Have you seen Tomoko?"

"She's with the Reverend. He's creating beauty." She moved her eyes, gesturing to the next room. The sound of drilling and hammering came from next door.

Excited, he skidded into the hall and darted into the next operating room. Machines encircled a white silk suited man standing in the center of the room. Large floodlights dumped brilliant light on him. He had his back to Jake and was working on something with intense concentration. Jake heard the tap of a small hammer on metal.

"Parks?"

The Reverend spun around and hid his tools behind his back. Big smile. "Jackhammer! Just in time!"

Jake tried to see what the reverend was working on, but Parks leaned to block the view.

"I've beaten the MaxWell virus. No one can hurt her now." Parks' teeth sparkled. He leapt to one side with his arms pointing to the focus of his activity. "Ta-Dah!" he shouted.

A robot composed of rusty scrap metal sat in a chair. The metal pieces were slender and curved. They reminded Jake of Tomoko's figure. The head was a rusty globe. Torn skin hugged one side of it, as if her face had been hastily removed and slapped on this sad abstract likeness. Her brain sat exposed under the massive flood lamps. She spoke with a mechanical echo. "Don't leave me like this, Jake. Fight for me!" Her eyes rolled into her metal head as she continued. "Jake Travissi. Calling Jake Travissi."

He jerked awake to find a new crowd in the waiting room. It was five minutes past eight in the evening.

"Jake Travissi, please come to the recovery room." A loud speaker called his name. It was the same voice from his dream. A kindly-faced doctor stood in the open double doors. Jake opened his hand and found Tomoko's scrimshaw. It calmed him and gave him hope. He stood up, stuffed it in his pocket, and approached. "How is she, doc?" He followed the doctor into the operating wing.

When the doors closed, the doctor gave him a compassionate stare. "I'm afraid I have some bad news."

Jake's mind raced. *She's going to take longer to recover. She's in a coma. She'll be blind in one eye…*

"We were too late. Tomoko didn't make it."

The news floored him. He opened his mouth but didn't know what to say.

"I'm so sorry." The surgeon appeared very sincere.

Jake could not believe what he was hearing. *This is impossible.* "I want to see her."

"Of course." The doctor led him down several halls until they reached an empty post-op room. Jake tried to concentrate on the route as they walked, but the doctor's voice was caught in a loop inside Jake's head. *We were too late. Tomoko didn't make it.* The doctor opened a door. Three gurneys filled the room. Only one was occupied. The figure on the bed was under a white sheet. "Take your time." The doctor closed the door leaving Jake alone in the cold tiled room.

He slowly approached the body. He paused when he reached her bedside. He closed his eyes. *Is this a dream? Am I hacked? There has to be a catch.* He pulled the sheet back. Tomoko was asleep, still, and peaceful.

He pushed his fingers into her cold skin to feel for a pulse. Nothing. A wave of grief surged over him. He closed his eyes and concentrated. He felt around the base of her skull. There was a fresh incision there. He opened his eyes and stared at her. "This is not reality." He dug deep into the back of his neck. There was a bit of scar tissue, but no Chip floating around.

A quick sob convulsed in his chest triggering tears to run down his cheeks. *This is not real!* He lay his head down on her chest and cried. He thought of all the things he wanted to say to her if she'd only wake up. *Thank you for coming into my life. Thank you for all the joy and hope you give me. You are beautiful inside and out. I only regret we did not meet sooner. You helped me out of a dark place. You renewed my strength and gave me courage to come home...*

Thump-Bump. He froze and listened again. *Thump-bump.* The heartbeat was faint but it was there. Her abdomen slowly rose as her diaphragm drew in air. She was alive, but her heart was beating about once every ten seconds. The Chip was keeping her alive, but barely.

He scanned for surveillance equipment. He spotted what looked like a button cam but when he checked, it was just a stain on the ceiling. There didn't seem to be anything here.

He plucked a blanket off an adjacent gurney. He remembered seeing a service elevator and a stairwell down the hall from this room. It could not be more than fifty yards. He was sure there were cameras but unless human eyes were monitoring, there was a chance. The doctor confirmed her death. Someone wanted him to think she was dead. No matter what, he was getting her out of this room.

He wrapped the sheet around her. He picked her up and laid her on the open blanket. He proceeded to bundle her up. "We're getting the hell out of here, my love."

With her body wrapped tight and hidden, he gently lifted her onto his left shoulder so he'd have full use of his right arm. He pushed open the door. He scanned the hallway. There was no one about. He could hear activity down an adjacent hall and the sound of medical machinery humming, hissing, and beeping away. He spotted four marshmallows on the ceiling but he knew that they were cameras.

He rapidly cruised for the stairwell door at the end of the hall. He was ten paces from the door when the same doctor stepped out of a doorway to block his path.

"Put her down, Jake." The doctor held a vacant stare.

Jake kicked the surgeon who stumbled and plowed into the stairwell door. The sound of feet on tile hit his ears. A hand grabbed his right shoulder. He wrenched free. He took another step for the stairs but Tomoko's body jerked back. Someone had grabbed her. He struggled to regain his balance as he fell backward with Tomoko. He made every effort to jockey her on top of him so he'd break her fall. The landing knocked the wind out of him and gave his skull a hard crack.

Two doctors, a nurse, and a few orderlies closed in around him. All shared the same vacant expression. He yelled and kicked upward. He heard an orderly's knee break. Jake grabbed Tomoko and lunged for the stairwell. Two HAZMAT suits intercepted him. He tried to turn but there were too many hands on him.

His feet flew off the floor. Several hands suspended him in the air. Tomoko was pulled from his grasp. He struggled as he sank into a small crowd. A dozen lifeless faces surrounded him. Tomoko disappeared from view. He screamed, trying to push every bit of adrenaline into his muscles. Those around him were more powerful. Even a ninety-pound orderly channeled herculean strength. A cold needle slipped into his arm and he felt the heat of anesthetic.

Darkness.

Chapter 24
Garbage

He felt sick to his stomach. Something large and hairy sniffed around his armpit. Jake opened his eyes and saw a strip of starry night framed by total black. A general stench of decay wafted into his nose. He sat up and heard a panicked squeak. A black object scrambled through uneven mounds of plastic and refuse. Tiny claws scratched against the steel walls of the container surrounding him and exited. He was in a dumpster, sitting naked in trash. A wave of panic struck him. He quickly felt the back of his neck. The old scar was there, but nothing new. He breathed a sigh of relief.

A twinge of cold danced down his back. Something sharp dug into one of his butt cheeks. He desperately wanted to leave and find Tomoko. He tried to stand up. The effort made him feel light headed. Nausea welled up to his throat. The lingering effects of whatever drug they had given him persisted.

What the hell am I doing here? Why didn't they immunize me? He fought through the dizziness and nausea, managing to lift his head above the lip of the dumpster. He was in an alley with many trash bins lining both sides. A three-story structure loomed behind him and the building across the alley was two stories. There was not enough light to spot surveillance. The alley exited onto brightly lit streets with steady traffic on both sides. He felt safe enough to leave.

As he pulled himself to a standing position, a pair of headlights turned into the alley. He sat back down, cursing as he felt something cold, rotten and very squishy ooze around his genitals. He grit his teeth and waited.

The sound of rolling tires stopped a few yards away followed by the hiss and clunk of doors sliding open.

"He's in one of those three."

Footsteps drew near. Jake searched the dimly lit dumpster for a weapon. *Play dead. Get them to pull you out then spring on them.* He settled into the garbage and tried not to vomit.

The dumpster next door banged and rattled. "Not in here, unless your Pin Head buried him."

"No, it was a dump and run. Our window was short."

He thought he recognized the voices. *Better be sure before you move.*

A man coughed. "This is a ripe one." Jake heard the metallic *bong* of someone pressing against his dumpster. He felt someone staring down at him. "He's here. There's no way I can lift him."

Jake opened his eyes and saw Jon Beartracker with his head facing the opposite building, addressing the other voice.

Jon continued. "I'll need your gun."

"Wait." Jake sat up.

Jon jumped back. "Jesus!"

Jake scrambled to his feet. Sharp bits of plastic bit into the arch of his left foot and he cursed. He grabbed hold of the side of the dumpster and leapt out. Bits of trash fell off his skin and clattered onto the pavement. In the dim light he could see Gordon King, aka Erasmus, wince. He swallowed back his nausea. "Do I have you to thank for this?"

"Sorry, Jake. We were monitoring the hospital's surveillance cameras. When we saw them anesthetize you, we took action." Gordon's Omni was on his face as a pair of glasses. Jake could see they were in night vision mode.

As Gordy talked, Jon peeled a flattened plastic bottle off of Jake's back.

Jake shivered in the cold night air. "Got any spare clothes?"

Jon opened a small bag he was carrying. He pulled out a pair of jeans and a denim shirt. He handed them to Jake. "Reservation clothes, no micro-tags in the fibers."

"We should get moving." Gordon sounded nervous.

"I'm not leaving without Tomoko." Jake zipped up his jeans.

Gordon shook his head. "We were lucky to have the codes to one orderly's Chip. Most everyone in there is protected by encryption. We only got you out because we hacked the cameras on your floor. When they left you alone in the immunization room, we hustled."

"I'm not leaving without Tomoko."

Jon handed Jake a pair of moccasins.

"Right now the surveillance footage and the orderly's memory show that he took you down to the incinerator in the morgue." Gordon walked toward the car. "We barely had time to dump you here, get the orderly back, and have him slip a John Doe into the incinerator. It's going to take a while for anyone to figure out what really happened to you. Tomoko is in the recovery ward." Gordon paused to rest his hand on the car roof. "She's surrounded by half a dozen computer surveillance devices, not to mention an entire staff of Pin Heads."

Jake's dirty skin crawled under the heavy clothes, and he stank to boot.

Jon pulled a bit of banana peel out of Jake's hair. "Tomoko is safe. Consider her in purgatory until we can figure out a way to get her back."

Jake crossed his arms. "It would be perfectly legal for me to walk back and take custody of her."

Gordon laughed. "What do you think just happened? They said she was dead. It was an obvious setup to get you chipped. You return and you'll have an entire hospital of Pin Heads after you. This is The Consortium in operation. Your best bet is to hit them where they're vulnerable. Then figure out a way to bring Tomoko back. Maybe you can save us all in the process."

It was Jake's turn to laugh. "How do I know it wasn't you who staged all of this in the first place?"

Gordon threw up his hands. "Would my word suffice?" He stared at Jake for a few seconds. "I didn't think so, but that's all I have."

Jon offered a plain black ballcap. "To hide your face from cameras."

Jake regarded it, remembering the hat he had worn the night he rode the train to take out Leah the God Head. Only he had been hacked. His real destination had been to assassinate Dr. Morris. Was this moment real or fake? He missed the quarter-sized piece of scrimshaw. It was his last physical link to Tomoko.

Both men stared at him in earnest.

Gordon climbed inside the car. "Ride with us if you want to save her. Walk if you want to be a slave."

Chapter 25
Broken Council

The farther from the hospital they drove, the deeper he felt the loss of Tomoko. *I love you more than anyone else in the world. I want you safe.* He racked his brain for a way to get her out, but Gordy was right. Even if he were chipped and able to counterhack, it was extremely unlikely he'd be able to get past the army of Pin Heads. That hospital was now a high security prison.

The streets were dead. Gordy explained the National Guard enforced a nationwide 10:00PM curfew. "It's a way to weed out the homeless. If you're on the street after 10:00PM then you're taken to a clinic and immunized. No alternative and it's all on the taxpayer's dime. NTI and the other Chip manufacturers are making a fortune on MaxWell."

Jake grumbled, "You don't have to be a conspiracy theorist to connect the dots on this one."

Gordon added, "The fear factor is so high that no one questions it. People will do anything to feel safe again."

They took a different route to reach the reservation in order to avoid the National Guard buildup at the main entrances. They passed three National Guard checkpoints on their way out of Globe without ever stopping. "You emitting some priority clearance?" Jake asked.

Gordon spun his seat around to face Jake. "Yup. The National Guard is picking us up as some important civic or military personnel. Same way you used to travel when you were a cop."

Jake smiled. "Funny how technology has made it harder to move around and in other ways easier. In the old days we would have been pulled over regardless of some silly transmission."

Jon peered out into the dark with night vision goggles. "We're here."

Gordon swung around to the dashboard and typed on his Omni, which was patched into the vehicle's onboard computer. "We have sixty seconds to stop and get out before satellites report our status."

The car stopped and they all leapt out. The vehicle continued on its way to Tucson where someone in The Erasmus Order would receive it. Gordon disconnected his Omni. Jon had never turned his on, as any connected device was a sure way to be tracked.

They jogged into the desert. Minutes later, a bizarre contraption raced toward them. It was an electric SUV with massive wire wheels and a flat roof that hung out a foot beyond the footprint of the vehicle on all sides. Jake studied the roof for a split second and realized it was a giant holo-projector that displayed the exact surface area of the ground underneath the vehicle. Any aircraft or satellite above would simply see the patch of desert that this vehicle covered during its movement. The six-foot wheels dissipated the weight so the SUV left little to no tracks.

Gordy configured his Omni into a watch and snapped it on his wrist. He grabbed a bar to hoist himself into the vehicle. "I hate these things."

Jake climbed in and saw their driver was the Eagle from the border gate. "Nice ride."

"Nice scent." A faint smile appeared on the Eagle's hard beak.

Jake was impressed that the Eagle gripped a steering wheel. There was no GPS or other linked device. The contraption was off the traffic grid. "This must have cost a penny."

Jon spoke from the back seat. "We design and build the Gah right here on the reservation. We sold the design to the Nation of Islam. Now that tourism has dried up, we need other sources of income."

"Gah?" Jake asked.

"Apache for rabbit," answered Eagle. "In some dialects rabbit is Kah—the word for arrow."

Once everyone was strapped in, Eagle hit the accelerator. Jake gyrated uncomfortably in his seat as the vehicle bounced around like a rabbit. The wheels were good stealth tools but terrible for spine alignment.

Gordon gripped his armrest. "Holy Crap!"

Eagle smiled.

"What about the razor wire?" Jake asked.

Eagle shook his head. "The barrier doesn't encompass the reservation, just five miles on either side of the roads leading in. The Federals use sensors everywhere else. We hacked those a long time ago to give us windows to travel through."

The truck bounced along a winding strip of shallow water. Jake guessed it was the Gila River, based on the last GPS readout he'd seen in their car. There was just a trickle in this wide riverbed. There was a bit of moon out, but they were riding without headlights or GPS. He was slammed back into his seat. "How are you navigating?"

"I had my eyes altered, too. Why be an Eagle if you can't see like one?"

"What's your name?" Jake asked.

"Ike Williams. Everyone calls me Eagle."

"I mean your Apache name?"

Eagle winked. "That's between me and other Apache."

Jake was about to say he was part Apache but then realized that was a pretty weak claim.

After forty minutes on the roughest ride of his life, they reached the outskirts of San Carlos City. Tall torpedo-shaped buildings stood elegantly against the shadows of the Gila Mountains. Not one holo-banner could be seen.

Eagle parked the vehicle in a camouflaged bunker on the outskirts of the small city and they rode Gyros—two wheeled platform scooters—to the Medicine Lodge, a massive structure that reminded Jake more of a modern interpretation of the Pyramids in Tikal. They were escorted into a large round chamber with beautiful tapestries portraying pre-nineteenth century First Nation life. Several older men and women as well as an Enlightened One altered to look like a puma, sat around a circular table. Intricate wood inlays created an elaborate dream catcher in the table's center.

The oldest woman stood. "Dagot'ee—Welcome. Ink ta—sit by Cochise." She gestured to the puma. He nodded toward two empty seats. Jon took his place by the old woman.

Once they were all seated, Cochise spoke. "I'd like to start by thanking Erasmus for all his help." Gordon used his Omni in tablet form to silently share with Jake the names of everyone in the room. The oldest woman was Ela.

Cochise continued. "We now have surveillance at our borders and towns feeding information to China. I've confirmed if the Federals invade, China will declare war." Jake noticed white hair around the golden strands filling out Cochise's face. His hands belonged to someone in their late fifties. He had to be the leader of his sect and one mean cat to endure extensive genetic enhancements.

Jon spoke, "The Jihad Brotherhood and the Disciples of Paul will condemn any aggression against us. They'll resume terrorist attacks if America invades our land. America will have to weigh the risks before planning an invasion."

Gordy addressed the group. "Invasion and immunization are imminent. I implore that you all leave for Mexico as soon as possible."

A woman in her sixties shook her head. Gordy's Omni identified her as Cocheta. "The spirit of the mountain, the desert, and the Gila monster all sang to bring Beartracker home, so he could teach us to be proud in our ways and beat the whites at their own game. His leadership brought prosperity, and helped restore pride to The People." She glanced at Cochise. "He reunited us with our lost brothers. We cannot abandon all we have won."

Cochise nodded in appreciation.

Richard Goldenhawk, a man with gray hair down to his waist, spoke. "What about non-violence? If the world witnesses our unarmed people being attacked by soldiers, there will be an outcry. Non-violence worked for India in the forties and America in the sixties."

Cocheta shook her head. "We're Apache. We're fighters."

Goldenhawk smiled. "Beartracker showed us we can be many things and still be proud."

Gordon stood up. "I'm a strong advocate for nonviolence under normal circumstances. But billions of people have been implanted. This means their thoughts can be manipulated."

Ela frowned. "Thank you for your opinion, Erasmus, but the council will let you know when it's time to speak."

Gordon dropped back into his chair.

Ela addressed the group. "I agree with Erasmus. We must flee immediately."

Jon sighed. "It'll take weeks to evacuate everyone over the border using Gah."

Eagle burst through the doors. "The Army has overrun the border."

Jon stood up. "Casualties?"

Eagle's eyes burned with rage. "They're using a Nemp. All electronic signals are dead. Our surveillance feed to China is useless."

The room fell into pitch-blackness. A flint lighter struck and a small flame illuminated Jon's face. "Follow me."

Everyone rose and followed Jon's tiny light until they wound up on the street outside the Medicine Lodge. Under the starlight, Jake saw several more Enlightened Ones surrounding the group. They reminded him of the First Nation's version of Rome's Praetorian Guard.

The power on Gordon's Omni popped back on, as well as some of the flashlights slung to the weapons carried by the Enlightened Ones. Gordon made some quick keystrokes. "They hit the Mount Willow power plant—"

The howl of HJ engines drowned him out. Dozens flew over the city. Yellow darts sailed at them. Four elders and two guards crashed unconscious onto the pavement.

Chapter 26
Invasion

Everyone ran back into the Medicine Lodge. The heat-seeking guns of the HJs flying overhead picked off several more from their party. Emergency lights illuminated the lobby. The Nemp effect had passed. Jake wondered if the surveillance systems were recording the attack. Based on the nature of the assault, he'd be surprised if any footage was getting outside the reservation much less to the Chinese.

Jon and Eagle led the party to a stairwell at the back of the lobby. Four Enlightened Guards remained behind to protect the Elders' escape. They found cover around the reception desk, aiming their weapons at the glass entrance.

A gas grenade shattered the glass doors. Hover-Jet wash roared, blasting smoke over the Enlightened Guards. Jake reached the stairwell door as a dart slammed into the railing by his hand. The Ox in front of him fell to the ground. Gordon, who was bringing up the rear, collapsed. Jake dove back into the smoke bank. He held his breath and threw Gordon over his shoulder. He lunged through the stairwell doorway just before it sealed shut. Several darts clanged into the steel barrier behind him. There was no return fire. His eyes and lungs burned from his brief exposure to the gas.

Underneath an ascending staircase was a short hall that led to a dead end. He heard sounds under the stairs and headed down the short hall. He almost tripped on the Ox. Two darts were planted in the Ox. Jake shouted out, "Man down!" He heard the sound of many feet hitting metal stairs but could not see where everyone had gone; but they were definitely not headed upward because those were concrete. The sounds of a city under attack reverberated through the barrier behind him. He stepped over the Ox to get a better look at the space below the staircase.

A slab of concrete had been pushed aside revealing a secret staircase heading down. He ran down the steep flight of metal steps. The slab closed and sealed above him. Gordon was not as light as Tomoko. There were a few times when Jake almost lost his footing.

Rumbles and the muffled sound of gunfire filtered through the barrier above. He fixed his thoughts on his mother and Lakshmi. Where the hell were they? He reached a level surface. He turned a corner and found the Elders lined up against the wall, panting. Eagle and an Antelope swung their weapons on Jake. They lowered them when they realized who he was. Jake was saddened to see there were only four council members and two guards left.

Jake took the opportunity to set Gordy down. He found the dart in Gordy's shoulder and plucked it out. It was a standard issue yellow tranquilizer dart. Their assailants were taking care to keep everyone alive. Knock them out, gather them up, and immunize them.

Eagle pulled Jon to his feet. "We cannot stay here!"

Jon caught his breath and nodded. Antelope helped Cochise and Ela up. None of the elders looked good. Jake scanned for Cocheta and realized she was missing. He strained to hoist Gordy back on his shoulders. Jon brushed Eagle aside so he could help Goldenhawk to his feet. Jon led the way while Antelope and Eagle took the rear. They shuffled down a long concrete passage.

Jon shouted back, "Jake, the family is in the room on your left."

Eagle put a hand on Jake's shoulder. He carried Ela whose breathing sounded like a broken compressor, "I must protect The Elders."

Jake nodded and Eagle moved on. Jake opened the door revealing a conference room. Abigail, Lakshmi, and Isabella were there. His mother put a hand on her face. "What happened?"

"No time to explain. Follow me. Now!" Lakshmi scurried to his side. The two women hastily followed him out. He nodded to the group heading down the passage. "Follow them. Hurry."

Isabella ran after them. Abigail pulled a dart out of his denim shirt. It had missed hitting his skin by a centimeter. "Thanks, Mom."

She smiled and dropped the dart onto the floor. "Who's that?" she nodded to the man on his shoulders.

Jake grunted. "Erasmus." His shoulders and back were burning now.

"Oh." She quickly walked ahead and Jake took the rear.

Lakshmi tried to walk behind. "Get behind Mom, Lakshmi."

As they caught up, he noticed the lights were dying behind him. He wondered if this was First Nation security or the Army hot on their heels. He pressed forward.

After a three-minute walk they reached another door. Jon punched in a security code. A keypad was still effective even in the twenty-first century. The door slid back, revealing another stairwell, this one leading up. Jake was not the only one who groaned.

The stairs led to a bunker similar to the one they had parked the Gah in earlier. There were four Gahs parked in this concrete room. Jake set Gordon down. His entire back was in spasm. Plus, Gordy wore a belt bag around his waist, the contents of which had been digging into Jake's shoulder. Eagle climbed into the nearest Gah and the Antelope took a gun turret on top. All the Gahs sported flat holo-camouflage roofs. Through the walls of the bunker, they heard the faint howl of HJ engines, sporadic gunfire, and random explosions.

Jon opened a locker in the side of the Gah revealing four HK V2s. Jake recognized the sidearm from his days in the LAPD. Jon grabbed one of the pistols along with a few clips and handed them to Jake. Jake noticed three clips, one with blue darts, one with yellow, and one with .45 caliber rounds.

He shoved the magazines with bullets and yellow darts in his pocket and slapped the blue clip into the gun. He turned and shot Gordon in the shoulder.

Jon winced.

Jake ejected the clip. "He's sore there from the other shot anyway." He fished out the .45 caliber rounds and slapped them in.

Jon observed the magazine switch. "I see Goldenhawk's non-violent ploy profoundly effected you."

"Apaches are fighters, right?" He shoved the blue clip in his pocket as Gordon groaned. He walked over and pulled the dart out.

Jon placed a hand on his son's shoulder. "We need to move."

Jake nodded. His mother and Lakshmi sat next to Isabella in the fourth row of the Gah. He turned to Jon. "I think we should split up."

Jon was surprised. "There's room for all of us in this one."

Jake observed Eagle and Antelope. They looked formidable, but one target had less chance of survival than two. "The majority of the attack will be concentrated on the city centers, we have good odds, even better if we separate."

Jon thought for a moment.

"Elder Beartracker!" Eagle shouted from the SUV. They were the only two left not buckled up inside.

"We're splitting up!" Jon barked back. "If we encounter resistance," Jon stared into his son's eyes, "our vehicle will draw the fire."

Eagle focused on Jake. "You can drive?"

Jake nodded. "Learned on a stick." He helped Gordon to his feet. Erasmus was groggy and sick.

"There's night vision on the dash of each vehicle," Eagle pointed to the Gah parked next to them. "If you're lucky enough to find water, these vehicles float." Eagle smiled.

Jon helped Ela and Cochise out of the Gah. Both looked like they had breathed in too much gas.

"Mom, Isabelle, Lakshmi, you're with me!" Jake ordered.

"Hey, I'm not one of your damn lieutenants," Abigail complained as she unbuckled herself.

Lakshmi hopped out, more than happy to be with Jake.

Alarm filled Isabella's eyes. "I'm not leaving you, Dad."

"Go with them. This is now the dangerous vehicle." He patted Eagle and Antelope's Gah.

"Then we go together and let the guards head out as decoys," Isabella answered.

Goldenhawk peered out of Jon's Gah. "Better to have some of the council in both vehicles."

Jon pointed to Jake's Gah. "Go."

Eagle and Antelope were out helping to strap Cochise, Ela and Gordy into Jake's vehicle. Lakshmi was already in the third row as Abigail climbed in next to her. Isabella sat next to Abigail. Jake wished he was strapping Tomoko into the vehicle as well. He put on the night vision goggles and flipped on the Gah's power. Eagle showed him where the camouflage controls were and how to convert the truck into a boat. The rest was pretty intuitive.

Eagle and Antelope secured their own vehicle before the main door rolled up. The opening faced away from downtown San Carlos. Firelight reflections danced on the mountainous terrain ahead.

The Gah's rear door flew open and Isabella bolted to Jon's vehicle. Eagle lurched a few yards and then hit the breaks. A door swung up and Isabella ran to it. Abigail closed the hatch on Jake's Gah, then buckled herself back in.

"She's probably allergic to cats," grumbled Cochise.

Eagle's Gah launched into the desert night. Jake rammed his foot into the accelerator. The massive beast lurched forward and began its sickening tumble after the lead vehicle.

"Oh my..." Ela's voice sounded broken and sad. Jake checked the rearview screen. Fire engulfed two towers. Smoke belched upward from the entire city. HJs dove in and out between the buildings like ocean leviathans feeding around boiling sea vents.

Eagle dropped back to put himself between Jake and the battleground. Gordon sat next to Jake wearing night vision. Gordon's Omni was on scramble mode. It was flattened out and attached to the dashboard. Both he and Jake could see the topography unfold on the device. The computer gave them the best routes to traverse. They were headed for the southwestern end of San Carlos Lake.

A massive explosion lit up the scene fifty feet ahead. Rocks and dirt pummeled their Gah. They bounced over a crater and continued gyrating forward.

"Either our camouflage is throwing them off or that was a warning shot."

"Or both," answered Cochise.

Gordon slid his window down and puked. The vehicle rocked so hard, his head slammed into the carbon fiber window frame. "Ouch!" He lurched back into his seat, wincing in pain.

Jake glanced at the rearview screen. An HJ was directly between the two Gah. "I don't think they see Jon."

Another blast, this one lifted their vehicle on two wheels before it slammed back down on the rough terrain. A hail of rocks hammered the side of the Gah. A loud whine rose up from the right front axle.

"That was close," Abigail shouted. Lakshmi was on the floor, trying to keep from getting tossed around like a stuffed animal. Abigail grabbed the Husky and tried to keep her secure in her lap.

Jake handed Gordon his pistol. "See if you can hit it."

"Are you kidding? You know how much armor plating they have?"

"You might get lucky!"

Gordon almost slammed his jaw into the window frame as he tried to brace himself to fire a shot. "Goddamn camouflage roof is too big, I can't see past it."

"Shoot!" Jake yelled.

Gordon fired a shot. A massive explosion shook their vehicle. The side view screen showed the HJ slam into the desert near the San Carlos River. Eagle's Gah was lit up by the firelight. Antelope sat behind his cannon turret, raising his arms up in victory.

"Holy shit!" Gordon shouted. "I got it!"

Jake smiled to himself. Why ruin Gordon's illusion? He leaned over and switched off Gordon's Omni.

"Why'd you do that? It's encrypted."

"Something gave us away."

"Maybe we've got a flaw in our holo-camo, or maybe the light hit us just right, or we've got a Chip signature. Could be a hundred possibilities."

Jake peeled off the Omni and tossed it to Gordon. "I just reduced it to ninety-nine."

Gordon shook his head. "Now we're blind."

Jake tapped his night vision. "Not completely."

It was much harder to navigate relying solely on night vision. He could only react to the terrain whereas the Omni allowed him to anticipate it. The right front wheel driver continued to whine but he ignored it. There wasn't much else he could do. After a time, they passed the San Carlos Dam and crossed the border back into Federal Arizona. A minute later they spotted an HJ heading toward them.

A rocket flew up at the airship. The HJ veered off. Within a few seconds the HJ was back and firing on Eagle's Gah. Their Gah veered off due west and Jake continued to parallel the muddy riverbed. A few minutes after Eagle's Gah faded from sight, an explosion erupted against the mountains.

"We need to go back and see if they are alright," Ela commanded.

"We can't," Jake replied. "We split up to give each of us better odds."

Cochise grumbled, "They fight and we run."

Jake grit his teeth. "I don't like it either, but we can't fight without a gunner and a pair of Eagle eyes."

The damaged wheel driver let out a shrill *screech* followed by a metallic *whunk*. The wheel sailed off into the desert night. The vehicle plowed into the ground and Jake jerked the steering wheel toward the river. The action sent the Gah rolling over an embankment. After a couple of sickening flips, they hit the river on their belly with a spectacular *crunch* and splash. He hit the controls to raise the remaining three wheels and allowed the vehicle to float on its skidpan. Sonar showed a few inches of clearance in this muddy excuse for a river.

He twisted to face the back. "Is everyone alright?" Every eye met his with a frozen, stunned look. Lakshmi whined and hopped over the seat. She laid her head on his lap. He checked her for broken bones. She was fine, just shaken up and in need of some love.

Gordon leaned over, "I never want to ride in one of these godforsaken machines again."

They floated downstream for a few miles enjoying some peace and quiet. Everyone fell asleep except Jake who navigated the shallow river. He rubbed Lakshmi's head. She was curled up in the center seat, her jaw resting on his thigh. She was calm and happy now. He felt a hand on his shoulder.

His mom whispered, "Did you see anything of Jon's Gah?"

He shook his head. "Not sure if the HJ or the Gah exploded. Either way, they bought us time to slip away."

Abigail nodded. It was hard to tell in the dim light of the cab, but he thought he saw a tear.

By 4:00AM the water became too shallow and the Gah ran aground. Jake and Gordon helped the Elders out of the vehicle. Once they were seated on dry ground, Gordon risked turning on his encrypted Omni. They were a couple of miles from the town of Hayden. Gordon made a few calls and they waited, shivering in the dark.

Jake and Gordon gathered the survival supplies stored in the Gah. They wrapped coats and blankets around everyone. When they finished, Gordon and Jake were the only ones left awake. They did not dare start a fire in case anyone was watching on the ground or by satellite.

"I want to shoot holograms of The Elders." Jake rubbed his arms to keep warm. "We need to upload their side of the story as soon as possible."

"Wait a bit." Gordon seemed distant and thoughtful. "They were pushed to exhaustion today."

"Tomorrow then." He watched his mother sleeping. She looked old to him now. Frail.

"You mean later today?" Gordon corrected. "It will be dawn soon."

Jake pondered it. Tonight was New Years Eve. It was hard to keep everything straight. He thought of everyone back on the reservation who were now getting chipped. He thought of Tomoko. He wished he could do something.

"I know how you feel, Jake." Gordon sat on a rock a few feet away, staring out at their dead and now derelict Gah. "My soul mate caught MaxWell too. I was forced to immunize."

"Are they home safe?"

"He's fine. But I removed anything sensitive from our home. I have him monitored and protected with encryption bands, but he's now a potential God Head conduit." He turned to Jake. "I want to beat them. I want to beat them before it's too late."

Jake patted Gordon on the shoulder. He lay down by his mother so she'd have extra warmth and immediately fell to sleep.

A sliver of sun rose over a ridge to the east. Jake scanned the heavens from east to west. Colors changed from yellow, to pink, to blue to cobalt. It was a glorious morning. He quietly stood up so as not to disturb Abigail. A white object bounced toward them from the western desert. He pulled out binoculars from the survival kit and saw it was an electric panel van. He grabbed Gordon who was quietly working on his Omni. Gordy aimed his Omni at the approaching vehicle. To their mutual relief, the van was on autopilot, sent by their allies in The Order of Erasmus.

Chapter 27
Kamikaze

It was roughly 9:00AM on the last day of 2035. Jake sat in the back of the panel van wondering when they would get the all-clear signal. Abigail and the two remaining Elders slept. They were parked in a warehouse owned by Desert Tech, which was owned by JPL, which was owned by MumSat, a technology company based in Mumbai and the fourth largest brand of Third Eyes in the world. The building sat abandoned and relatively unmonitored in the industrial district of Phoenix. They would wait here until The Elders were rested enough to be recorded. At least that was his plan.

Gordon was engaged in a holographic conversation with MumSat technicians on the moon. He kept his cover as an NTI systems analyst. His signal was being bounced around and displayed an origin in Los Angeles.

Jake sat with his mother's Omni flattened out in tablet configuration, watching the latest news. He listened with wireless earbuds. He paid no attention to the tiny holo-images floating above his Omni. He wanted Tomoko back. Any opportunity that presented itself in that area, he would take. He was sad about his father, too. He had known the man for less than a week, but the promise of getting to know the man appealed to Jake.

Gordon had encrypted Abigail's Omni, so the signal would not be traced. Jake had seen Erasmus taking SleepX, a drug that would allow a person the ability to run like an athlete for seventy-two hours before having to crash out and coma-tize for twenty-four. He wondered how long Gordon had been on it.

He watched live footage of protests over the arrests on First Nation land. There were half a dozen demonstrations in the major US cities, but the crowds were unnervingly small. The news switched to footage of First Nation citizens on the Fort Apache Reservation throwing rocks, pipes, and debris at a line of calm National Guard troops standing behind riot shields.

His jaw dropped. "That's not what happened. How can they cover up a full-scale invasion?"

Gordy apologized and quickly got off his conference call. The Elders and his mother stirred.

Jake lowered his voice to a whisper as Gordy approached. "There must have been witnesses with Omnis, P-Chips, ancient digital cameras, something to record the truth. What happened to social media? It's supposed to be the ultimate secret weapon that brings down governments."

Gordy shook his head. He looked exhausted. Time for another SleepX. "All this encryption and signal bouncing and it's the *cop* on our team I have to worry about revealing our position?"

"What is this?" Jake gestured to the faux footage. It made all of First Nation appear stupid and violent while the National Guard—not the Army—was protecting itself and patiently arresting the most unruly in the crowd.

"A facade exists for the minority, but there are too few now to make social media relevant. If a chipped person sees something that causes their anger or indignation to spike, their Chip engages programs in the Cyber-Wire to evaluate the situation. Most times the programs tell a Pin Head's Chip to pump a feeling of complete apathy. Governments have more control now than in all of humanity's history."

He sat awestruck, listening to Gordy as he rubbed his temples. "So you were just humoring me this morning when I said I wanted to holograph the Elders?"

"More or less. News still leaks on underground channels. But these beacons are shut down just as fast as they crop up. The Chip has made The Consortium's job much easier. Out of a world population of eight and a half billion, roughly two and a half billion are not chipped, but most are scared and keep their heads down. I'm open to trying to upload a recording. I just want you to know what we're up against."

The footage switched to a protest in Manhattan's Washington Square Park. An NYU student sneezed and people ran screaming. A contingency of National Guard wearing HAZMAT suits marched in and surrounded the terrified student. Within minutes, dozens more protestors broke into sneezing fits. More troops rushed in and began wholesale darting of the entire population of Washington Square. Jake was flabbergasted. He channel surfed and Gordy returned to the front seat to call back his party.

Jake witnessed more and more footage of police and military darting sick citizens and loading them into trucks for immunization. Zero tolerance was spreading as fast as MaxWell. Britain and Canada joined thirty countries mandating immunization for all their citizens. Foreigners who did not comply were expelled. Most countries closed their borders to any nation that did not support wholesale mandatory immunization. The United States Senate would pass a vote on the same measure in an emergency session tomorrow, New Years Day.

He thought about the Argentines. Did they contract Max2? If so, how virulent was it? Would Max2 Chip the last holdouts? Based on what he was seeing, MaxWell was doing a pretty good job, but there was definitely resistance. He spun past more channels and nearly jumped out of his skin. *Was that Tomoko?* He dialed back a few channels and landed on CryLite World News. He felt a surge of shock. Tomoko was in mid-sentence. He boosted the volume.

She seemed relaxed but lively. "I hope that the people of South America will end their hostilities toward the United States. The National Guard saved me from inadequate facilities on the Fort Apache Reservation last night." A tear welled up in her eyes. "Unfortunately, my fiancé was lost in the First Nation counterstrike. I understand that invading First Nation territory infringes on the rights of personal freedom, but do people have the right to commit suicide? That's what you're doing if you refuse immunization. Fighting a Third Eye is like putting your head in a noose… and suicide is a sin."

His fists and jaw clenched with rage. He pressed record on the Omni to document the lies funneling through Tomoko via some rat-bastard God Head. A strong urge to hunt down and kill every last God Head who had their virtual hooks sunk into her brain swept over him. She was possessed and he wanted to perform an exorcism. Yet, he marveled at their hacking skills. Her eyes did not seem dead and lifeless. Only someone close to her could tell she was not using her typical style of speech.

Bang!

Jake jumped and looked toward Gordy seated in the cab. A large Doberman Pinscher stood on the van's short hood, furiously barking on the other side of the glass. Teeth gnashed and saliva splattered a foot from Gordy's face. Lakshmi lunged at the windshield, viciously growling in return.

Bang! Bang! Bang!

Dogs slammed into the driver's door, the roof, and the rear cargo doors. Several clawed paws smeared dog spit over the windows. Fiber panels thundered and shook from more dogs using their heads as battering rams. The van rocked back and forth. Lakshmi ran around howling at every impact she heard. Abigail and the Elders stood alarmed. Gordon frantically worked the dashboard screens.

Cochise pulled out a knife.

The slams were as frequent as rain and the van wildly bounced.

"Lakshmi!" Jake shouted and she turned to face him. He gave her the hand signal and reinforced it with his voice. "Lay down!"

Crunch!

Fiber-powder flew passed Ela's head. There was a crack in the shell. Every one was on their knees in order to keep balance and stay away from the vehicle's walls.

"Get us the hell out of here!" Jake shouted.

Gordon hit the dashboard. "Jammed!" He extracted a dart gun from the van's glove box.

Another panel cracked. Barking and snarling reached deafening levels. The panel behind Ela bent inward. She pulled out a knife as fiber-dust floated down from the ceiling.

Jake pulled out his HK V2. He lost balance and crashed on his back. He slapped the bullet cartridge in and pulled his mother to the center of the van. "Everybody into the center and face the walls!" Jake shouted to Gordon. "Give your gun to Mom or one of The Elders! You work on getting around the jamming frequency!"

Gordon tossed his weapon to Cochise.

Crack! Another panel was breached on the rear door.

"What color you got in that weapon!" Jake shouted to Cochise.

Ela's panel bent further. A Pit Bull snout gnashed its way into the van.

"Yellow-Blue alternate," Cochise answered as he watched several sets of teeth gnawing against the saliva-coated canopy. The glass was a hundred percent opaque.

"Get your ass back here, Gordy!" Jake ordered. "They're about to come in!"

The panel on the opposite side split. Dogs chewed and savagely clawed to enter. Lakshmi lunged for the Pit Bull who's head was almost through. Jake tackled her. "Mom!" He threw Lakshmi over to his mother. "Hold her!"

The Pit Bull's head broke through. Jake saw the lifeless eyes of someone who was hacked. "Jesus, they're chipping animals now?" He raised his gun but a silver flash slammed into the dog's gaping mouth. He quickly turned to see Ela leap toward the Pit Bull and dislodge her knife from the dead dog's hard palate.

"Yah-tats-an," Ela responded in Apache.

A Mastiff blasted through the back door. Jake wheeled and shot. The dog went limp, its body half inside the vehicle, plugging the new hole. A second later, the body was sucked back through the breach and they glimpsed the eyes of a possessed animal as it dislodged the Mastiff.

A Doberman flew in the opening. It slammed against the wall, a knife sticking out of its chest. Cochise confirmed his kill. "Yah-tats-an." He switched to the dart gun.

Blam! Jake covered the backdoor hole. He would take out any dog that tried to get through that breach.

Blam! He concentrated to make each bullet count as the gun held ten rounds and it felt like there were fifty dogs out there.

Blam! Blam! Blam! The van stopped rocking. All was quiet except for the loud ringing in his ears. Firing bullets in this tight space was deafening.

"Freaky kamikaze dogs," Cochise muttered.

The smell of sweat, blood, and gunpowder lingered in the air. Abigail was soaked in sweat. She had used all her strength to keep Lakshmi pinned and out of the fight. The Husky continued to struggle. Jake flashed a hand signal but she paid no attention. "What's wrong, girl?"

Both side panels simultaneously exploded. Two canine heads crashed into the van. Jake shot the dog on the left, Cochise the one on the right. Cochise emitted a garbled scream. A Boxer had lunged in from the rear cargo doors. Its teeth were sunk into the puma's throat. Ela threw her knife.

A Great Dane flew into the starboard opening. It knocked Gordy over. Ela fired a yellow and a blue dart. They plunged into the Dane's eye and shoulder respectively. Jake plugged two bullets in its skull. The Dane slumped on top of Gordon. The van was quiet.

"Yah-ik-tee," Ela chanted and prayed over Cochise's dead body. His puma face was soaked in his own blood. The Boxer's teeth were still firmly buried in his neck. Spattered blood coated everyone and everything. Lakshmi whined and Jake nodded to his mother to let her up. She tumbled back, exhausted. Jake helped Gordy get out from under the Dane. Abigail checked Gordon for bites but he was clean.

"Did you see their eyes?" Jake asked.

Gordon shook his head.

Jake grabbed Cochise's knife and cut into the space between the skull and the neck of the Dane. He found a tiny hard flake and pulled it out. It came with several long bloody filaments attached, the thickness of human hair. Chipped.

Gordon sighed. "Other countries experiment with animals, but it's illegal in the States."

Jake flicked the bloody mess against the wall. "Like you said, who the hell is left to complain?"

"Can we get out of here, please?" Abigail insisted.

Ela stopped praying and held up her hand for silence.

Lakshmi whined.

Gordon grabbed the dart gun. "Now what?" He hissed.

Jake checked his clip. Three bullets remained. He grabbed the latch to one of the battered side doors. "I don't plan to relive the Alamo." He slid the door back a foot and stopped, his gun pointing at an empty concrete warehouse. He hopped out and Lakshmi joined him. He flashed the commands for her to heel and she obeyed. He spun around twice, once to assess the room and another time to check out the rafters in the ceiling. Nothing moved. Dirty glass windows along the building's roofline allowed pools of light to splash throughout the warehouse. There were deep patches of black as well.

The battered van was covered in fur, saliva and blood. The dogs were literally killing themselves to break in. Scores of canine bodies lay in glistening pools of blood all around the vehicle.

Lakshmi barked as something small lurched out from under the van. Jake grabbed her tail and she squealed. The creature collapsed. He pushed Lakshmi on her belly and gestured for her to stay. He approached the small animal with caution. As his eyes adjusted to the dim light he saw a cat, its head smoking and charred. He kneeled down and cautiously peered under the vehicle.

"Good God," He muttered.

"What is it?" Gordon was half out of the van with his dart gun raised.

"Take a look," Jake gestured. There were a dozen dead cats sizzling under the van's power pack. They had gnawed into the vehicle battery bank and into the acid of the cells. Another suicide run.

Gordon got up off his knees. "If the dogs are all chipped, then every pair of eyes was a camera that sent information back to a God Head. We have to move."

"Consortium?" Jake asked.

"No doubt."

Jake tapped a mangled cat with his shoe. "They've reached a new low."

Gordon checked his Omni and smiled. "We're through the jamming signal." He took a closer look and appeared depressed. "Not again…"

"What?" Everyone was out of the van now. Abigail had treated a scrape on Ela's arm.

Gordon turned to Jake. "The Phoenix cell is down. We're on our own."

Jake nodded. "Let's go."

Gordon put a hand on his arm. "I've got a rig."

"Rig?"

"God Head rig. I can hack. Get us some help."

Jake sighed. The idea of hacking innocent people made him sick, but he was short on time and options. "At the next opportunity, okay?"

They ran to the rear of the warehouse where there was an exit away from the main street. When they reached it, they found the door wide open. Jake gestured for them to hold back as he approached. He stepped toward the exit keeping out of the morning light flooding onto the concrete. He stood against a wall across from the door. He took a hard look at the door handle. The computer lock had been picked. No animal could have done the job. Lakshmi remained calm so he knew there was no one inside the warehouse.

He gripped his pistol and peered around the doorframe. Sunlight stung his eyes. He made a quick surveillance of the area and ducked back inside. It was a small alley that seemed to be deserted. There was a dumpster three hundred yards to the west. The building across the alley to the north was two stories high and made of windowless cinderblock. The main road was to the east. He sucked in a deep breath and stepped outside, tracking the roof with his eyes and pistol. The coast was clear.

He gestured for everyone to come out. Lakshmi trotted out first and circled him. Ela shuffled out next followed by Abigail. He glanced in either direction. "Gordy."

"He's indisposed," Abigail said nervously.

"What do you mean he's—" he lowered his gun. "Fuck. Is he hacking?"

Abigail nodded.

He sighed. "Back in."

A yellow dart thudded into Ela's temple and she dropped like a stone. It was a death shot. Jake shoved his mother into the doorway and ducked inside the frame. Three darts barely missed them. Lakshmi charged a dumpster.

"Lakshmi!" He dove next to Gordon who wore computer goggles and gloves. The face of his flattened Omni simply said: INTERFACE. "What the fuck are you doing, Gordy!"

"Not now. I'm almost in."

"Almost in where?!"

They heard metallic banging, Lakshmi growling, then a yelp. "Oh, fuck!" his heart leapt into his throat. He ran for the door and peered around the corner. Two figures lay on the ground; one person, one dog. He quickly checked the roof and all sides of the alley again. No movement. He sprinted toward the figures. As he drew near, tears welled up in his eyes. They were both lying in a pool of blood. "Fuck!" He dove next to Lakshmi and found the yellow dart in her flank. He plucked it out and ran his fingers all over her body. A smile slowly worked its way onto his face and he wiped his eyes off with his sleeve. She was fine, just unconscious. "That's two I owe you, girl."

He observed the dead woman in the National Guard uniform with a ripped out throat. The Chip had kept her alive long enough to shoot his dog. Lakshmi had saved them, for now. He picked up his Husky and ran back to the warehouse. "Whatever you're going to do, Gordy, do it now!"

The hiss of hydraulic breaks echoed down the alley. A massive vehicle was entering from the east. It barreled forward, filling the alley. It was mid-morning and the sun shined down over the top of the vehicle, creating a silhouette. Jake skidded into the warehouse. "Run! We have to run!"

Gordy smiled under his large black goggles. "No need! That's our ride!" Abigail steadied him as he walked. His fingers danced in the air like some possessed conductor of a silent symphony. The goggles sealed off his eyes. Gordon's Omni was tucked under Abigail's left arm.

The doorframe filled with shiny chrome steel. Hydraulic breaks hissed again bringing the metal wall to a stop.

"Can you guide me onto the bus, my dear?" Gordon continued his conducting as Abigail maneuvered him toward the door. Jake carried Lakshmi into the light. The chrome wall belonged to the side of a cross-country bus. Jake led the three of them along the side until they reached the front. They skirted around the massive headlights as the side door rolled back. A man stepped out and Jake froze. The man turned and passed them with a glazed look in his eye. A few dozen passengers followed, all eyes vacant.

"What's going on, Gordy?" Jake whispered. The Pin Heads wore soiled clothes and dusty shoes. They looked nothing like a tour group.

"I'm hacked into the lot of them," Gordy answered.

Jake swallowed hard. "Hacked—" The passengers were now Gordy's puppets. "Who are these people?"

"Night shift from a nearby farm."

Jake was even more horrified. "But machines do that kind of work."

"Welcome to life after the establishment of The Chip." Gordon furiously worked. The sensors around his goggles tracked his bodily movements. It certainly beat the old God Head rigs Jake had seen years back.

"Why are these people getting off the bus?" Jake didn't hide his anger.

"I need surveillance equipment. Plus they could be counter hacked and used as weapons against us." Gordon continued to be guided by Abigail. "They remain behind, and we'll know who's hunting us."

"It's The Consortium," Jake barked, "using the National Guard."

"We'll soon find out," Gordy smiled. "Step aboard."

Jake climbed three steps, and gazed down the aisle of a big empty bus. The door closed and the vehicle began to move.

"Sit down!" Gordon shouted. "Your mother can't steady me while we're moving!"

Jake took the first seat behind the windshield. They rolled past the bodies of Ela and the National Guard woman. He felt sadness for Ela and nothing for the Guard woman. He thought about his emotions for a bit. The Guard was probably someone's mother, wife, daughter or all of the above. Now she was dead because of a God Head.

A couple of hacked passengers walked alongside the bus. The rest formed two rows on either side of the open door to the warehouse. One row faced west, the other faced east. He observed the Pin Heads from his window and shivered. *People reduced to remote controlled mannequins. I'd rather be dead.* As soon as he thought it, he remembered Tomoko. A tear welled up in his eye. He stroked Lakshmi's hair. "It's going to be okay, girl…" He wasn't convinced.

Chapter 28
Cargo

They found cleaning supplies on the bus and wiped off as much blood as they could. Gordy programmed the tour bus to drop them off at a deserted ballpark before it proceeded toward Nogales, Mexico as a decoy. He hacked into a Beijing Air cargo van, and they waited in the shadows of the bleachers for a few minutes before the vehicle arrived to take them to the airport.

"I'll do it," Jake said after they placed his sedated mother and still unconscious Lakshmi into separate kennels bound for Havana. It was too dangerous to travel by conventional means.

"Do what?" Gordon asked, as he pushed his God Head goggles onto his forehead. They stood inside Beijing Air's cargo hangar. Several robots were busy loading freight onto squat cargo carriers, which were destined to meet up with various planes currently being prepped for takeoff. The entire hangar was automated.

Jake grit his teeth. "I'll help you get Parks, but I want something in return."

Gordy stared at him.

"Help me get Tomoko."

Gordon held out his hand. "Done."

Jake felt relief as they shook. His eyes fell on the big pet crates containing his mother and Lakshmi. They were flying to Manaus, Brazil via Havana, Cuba. The McMurdo invasion had frozen relations between the US and South America; there were no longer direct flights between the two continents. At least the US had stopped the embargo on Cuba after the last of the Castros died out.

Jake stared at his unconscious pup through the carrier grate. "You're the greatest dog in the world. Guard Mom." Abigail was in the crate next to Lakshmi's. Given the trip they were taking, it was better to let the serum coursing through his Husky naturally wear off. "Even Manaus feels too close to this craziness for my comfort."

Gordon shrugged. "If we sent them to the moon, they'd be in danger. There are no safe havens anymore. But they'll last longer in Brazil than Havana. If they get into the jungle, away from people, they might even be forgotten."

Jake stared at his family. Gordon assured him there would be Erasmus agents in Manaus to look after them. After what had happened in recent hours, it gave him little comfort.

Gordon broke Jake's train of thought. "I'm headed for Beijing." He pointed to an empty crate. "I can hack into the system again and make your destination the same."

"Isn't Parks in the US?"

"Parks is wherever you are. If you reach out to him, I have the feeling he'll respond. Currently he's in India, where I'll be stopping after China. We'll come up with a plan to get Tomoko during our trip."

"Why not use The Order?"

"We're spread pretty thin." Gordon pulled out a Valium. They had stolen a small supply from a different crate bound for Florida. "If you've never traveled by pet carrier, I highly suggest you take one."

Jake grabbed a few pills from Gordy's hand. "I've barely slept since LA."

Gordon smiled. He pushed his God Head goggles back over his eyes. The second he linked with his Omni, he whistled. "Take a look at this." His fingers waved and a holographic image appeared on the flat surface of the Omni. National Guard troops were darting all the bus passengers. Gordy's Pin Heads were scattered around the alley and many were in the warehouse. There was a jumble of Points-of-View hovering over the Omni. There were at least a dozen troops. The angles continued switching from different Points of View as the Guards took out each Pin Head with a yellow tranquilizer dart. Each POV was a living human being.

"They're attempting to counter hack my signal." The Omni went dark and Gordon peeled off his glasses. "Someone figured out they were all hacked and we were no longer on the scene."

Jake checked the time on Gordon's Omni; forty minutes had passed since leaving the warehouse.

Gordon broke down his rig. "You were right about the National Guard."

"In my Pin Head days, we were a lot more efficient," Jake added.

"That was when you had two or three God Heads per Pin Head working as a team. Computers run most of the basic God Head programs now. Thanks to pioneer projects such as yours."

"Ah, you mean the way you hacked into an entire busload of people?"

"Exactly. Although, I got lucky to find a group of laborers with Gen 5 chips. I can hack Gen 5 no problem. The civilian 7 and military 8 are impossible. They have encryption with scramblers. The Omni can't hack it... Literally."

Jake pointed to Gordy's gear as he repacked it in his belt pouch. "Um, don't we have a flight to catch?"

Gordon stopped. "Right." He put the gear back on. "I severed the ties to the Pin Heads, but I wanted to stay offline a bit in case they managed to get a lock on me."

"Aren't you scrambling your signal?"

"Yeah, but it's not foolproof and since the Phoenix cell went dark, no telling what information they have."

"But it's a cell. It shouldn't have any information on other cells, or you."

"Someone does. I'm beginning to suspect a mole." Gordon began his finger dance.

A robot grabbed Abigail's crate and loaded it onto a drone-mobile. The robot came back for Lakshmi and loaded her as well. After a few more trips through the warehouse, the drone-mobile bound for the Havana cargo flight zipped out of the hangar. When he turned his attention back to Gordon, he found Erasmus loading his God Head gear once again.

"Better get in." Gordon nodded to a pet carrier. "Our plane takes off in less than thirty minutes and that robot is for us." He dove into another pet carrier and closed the door. The approaching robot scanned the barcode on his crate and hoisted it up.

Jake dove into his crate and shut the door. It was built for a St. Bernard but it felt more like a shoebox. He dropped his Valium as the robot hoisted his carrier. He bumped his head, arms, and legs, trying to stabilize and find the pill. As the drone-mobile hummed along the tarmac, he found the Valium. It was lying in some unknown liquid mixed with dog hair.

"Dammit, Gordy, I thought you said these crates were clean!"

Gordon's muffled reply was barely audible through the plastic carriers and sound of roaring jet wash. "The inventory listed them as empty containers. Not clean ones."

Jake tossed the pill out of an air hole. He curled up and tried to get comfortable under a blanket. He was not looking forward to the *Scramjet* ride without a G-Force chair. All airlines placed animal carriers into impact cradles, but it was not the same as a chair. As he felt his carrier ride up the ramp into the aircraft's cargo bay, he thought about the people he was leaving behind. He had a lot of promises to make good on.

Chapter 29

Foot Soldiers

The flight was extremely rough, but mercifully short. Instead of the majestic virtual transparent cabin, Jake shivered in near freezing temperatures, complete darkness, and dog piss puddles. He remained in his kennel through the Nemp decontamination but was let out by a hacked immigration officer in a luggage sorting area.

Gordy stretched next to the officer. "Happy New Year." He held out a gold filter mask. "Sorry you missed the fireworks. I'll make it up to you."

Their *Scramjet* had taken off on December 31st, 2:35PM Phoenix time. Although the duration of the flight had been a little over two hours, they had crossed the International Dateline. Jake checked Gordy's Omni. It was almost 8:00AM, January 1, 2036. He took the mask. "What's this for?"

The immigration officer gazed out into space with glazed eyes.

"China's MaxWell policy makes immunization and protective masks mandatory." Gordon held up the gold filter. "Gold means you have special government privileges and are much less likely to be scanned for a Chip."

"Handy." Jake put on the filter.

"China hedges her bets. Beijing plays to all sides, so watch your back."

"What's the disc for?" Jake pointed to the poker-chip sized object at the base of the mask.

"That's a Nemp generator. Meant to kill any airborne MaxWell viruses that come into contact with your mask."

The hacked guard escorted them out into the baggage claim area. It was like walking into an ant hive. The hall was so thick with people, it was hard to see the carousels or luggage for that matter. Everyone wore a filter mask. The majority of masks were white. Some were red and none were gold.

"What's white and red mean?" Jake asked.

"White means you're a citizen. Basically, you have a Chip in your head. Red means you're medical, law enforcement, or military. Gold is political, or anyone with power."

"Nice to be one of the elite."

"Only way to travel."

Their hacked guard placed them at the head of the customs line. Jake glanced back and saw several hundred waiting. Everyone with a white mask stared ahead with silent purpose. Only the red masks seemed to be moving about of their own free will.

Security for gold masks consisted of having the left eye scanned by an automated kiosk. Jake approached with apprehension.

"Don't worry. It's hacked," Gordy whispered behind him. "It won't register our retinal images."

Jake noticed white masks having their bags searched, pat downs, and bodies scanned by red masks. Once Gordy and he were out of customs, their Pin Head officer returned to the customs area. Gordy led Jake through the crowd toward the transportation platform. Thousands moved in unison and in close ranks. Only red masks walked faster and took alternative routes. *Drones and soldiers populating a massive hive*, he thought. *The God Heads are the queens.*

They exited the terminal onto the transportation platform. The air was crisp and the world filled with wall-to-wall people. Gordy craned his neck to see over the rivers of humans and electric taxicabs. "Ah hah!" He smiled and led Jake past a long row of cabs and approached a black electric Mercedes. He touched the rear handle. The vehicle checked his fingerprints, retina, and body odor before the door slid open. They got in.

Jake rubbed the real leather. "Fancy."

"Only way to travel."

"I was hoping to ride the train." Jake yawned. "China's rail service is world renowned."

Gordy presented the street beyond the open car door. A solid wall of skyscrapers filled the horizon above a citizen ocean. "Feel free. But treat yourself to a shower and some clothes first. You smell like dog piss."

Jake smiled. "On second thought, I'll ride with you."

Gordy gave a half-hearted laugh and closed the door. The car cruised through packed streets. Gordon pulled off his mask and Jake followed suit. Jake rolled down his window to air out the car and watch people crowding shops or milling down sidewalks. All he could hear was wind. No horns, engines, or talking assaulted his ears. "Deja vu," Jake whispered.

"What's that?"

"I've dreamt about chipped cities since I ripped the Third Eye out of my head. With the masks, they all look like dolls on some huge assembly line."

"Welcome to the future. China has solved all their internal issues with The Chip. Population control, civil unrest, curfews, pollution… we're in utopia."

Jake turned to Gordon who was busy typing away on his Omni. Erasmus gave him a deadly serious look. "Ever hear of sarcasm?"

"For a minute there, I thought I was sitting next to Sandoval Sanchez."

"Only way to travel." Gordy grinned and returned to typing. "The Consortium feels that everyone under them is a child who wants to be coddled. They condescendingly believe folks who are not in power think they simply need to smile, be given startup money, and they too can be in charge."

"Worked for Parks."

Gordon grumbled. "Charm helps, but you still need charisma and the willingness to accept responsibility to lead. With the large majority chipped, the lines are being drawn between those who love power, and those who believe in individual freedom." He smiled at Jake. "I represent the latter bucket in case you weren't sure."

"Consortium versus Erasmus."

"Don't discount Parks' DOP or the Jihad Brotherhood. They're the playoff wildcard that we should be equally afraid of."

"More than Max2?"

Gordon sighed. "Autopsy information on the Argentine bodies has been hard to access… even for me. The harder it is to get, the more I wonder if Anjali's guess is right."

They passed a massive complex near the Bird's Nest, the stadium the Chinese had built for the Olympics way back in 2008. That was the summer of Jake's eleventh birthday, one year before Lalo's murder.

Above the complex, a massive hologram stretched ten stories into the sky. The holograph broadcast a message in alternating Mandarin, Cantonese, English, Russian, French, and German: HAPPY NEW YEAR AND MANY HAPPY RETURNS TO THE BIRTH OF AI!

Two small groups of protesters milled about outside the complex. None of the protesters were Chinese. Camera operators with their familiar tentacle rigs recorded the event. Jake listened to the protests with eager anticipation.

Most of the languages he heard were not English. Before The Chip, many nations taught their children English as it was the international language of trade, but with Chips translating any language into the native tongue of the user, there was no need to speak in anything but what came naturally. He caught a few sentences from both camps.

"AI means Antichrist Interference!"

"Allah is the only Intelligence we need!"

"The End of Days is upon us. AI is a shroud for the Father of Lies!"

"AI is all artificial and no intelligence!"

Oblivious white masked citizens flowed around the protesters in brisk orderly fashion. Only the news crew seemed interested in what was happening, which begged the question; who was watching the news?

Gordy leaned over to look. "An example of China's mastery over its internal and external image. The protestors were limited to two hundred.

A contingent large enough to fill those camera frames and small enough to be easily controlled by a tiny chipped police force." His Omni dinged, causing him to look at the screen wrapped around his wrist. "Crap."

"What?" Their car was heading right for the gate.

"So much for the fireworks." Gordon displayed his Omni to the electric eye in the dash. The car changed lanes and merged into traffic leading away from the facility.

"Whoa! Were we headed for that?" Jake pointed with his thumb to the protestors.

"That was the plan. AI addresses the world at noon. They finished mapping the human mind about the time you removed your Chip—but you know this, right?"

Jake was a bit embarrassed. "I purposely kept myself out of the loop."

Gordy nodded. "When I say mapped I mean logic, thought, sensory, emotional—everything. NTI did most of that but Song—China's major cyber-player—and Mumsat—India's equivalent—did a lot of heavy lifting too. The original plan was to have a true AI by 2040. But the law of exponential returns paid dividends on this project. With over fifty tech companies throwing in their R&D engineers in return for a piece of the action, the project took on life last summer. They've spent the last six months parenting it, getting ready to introduce it to the real world."

Jake was stunned. "On the eve of humankind's demise, we give birth to AI…" He touched his Chip scar and turned to Gordy. "So why did we cancel?"

Gordy held up his Omni. "Sumit and Anjali are at a biogenics lab in the suburbs. They have plus-one tickets and we were their dates. Every dignitary from forty nations is in there including the President of China and six other heads of state." Gordy was glum.

"President Ortiz?"

"The Chinese politely denied America's request to attend, citing humanitarian reasons."

Jake laughed. "That's irony for you." He glanced back at the complex. He wished Tomoko could be here with him. He'd bug Gordon about it after they settled in. Their car rose up on an expressway and he felt the vehicle pick up speed to match the thousands of cars surrounding them. Beijing made LA look like some backwater village. "How intelligent is the AI?"

Gordy raised his eyebrows. "I'm told she could give an eighth grader a run for her money."

"She?"

Gordon nodded. "Ai-li they call her. Although she has the complete emotional and cognitive imprints of roughly one hundred male and female scientists, they chose to make her a girl."

Jake whistled. "Sounds like they should have named her Sybil."

Gordon laughed. "I said imprints, not copies. They took the best of everyone to create one being. They chose many traits to ensure she would be benign. No one wants a power hungry megalomaniac raging on the Cyber-Wire. It would shut down civilization as we know it."

Jake felt a bit alarmed by the idea. "Is she on the Cyber-Wire?"

Gordy shook his head. "She's in a walled garden while she grows up and they test her. It'll be a while before she'll be allowed to move into limitless cyberspace."

"Has The Consortium infiltrated her?"

Gordon observed a tick in his eye on his Omni mirror app. "I'm not sure of anything anymore."

They reached their southerly destination in Tianjin a little after 11:00AM. Tianjin was roughly 450 miles due west of Pyongyang, North Korea, directly across the gulf of the East China Sea. They pulled off the expressway and cruised through an industrial neighborhood until they reached a complex of buildings made of windowless concrete. Walls topped with razor wire surrounded the compound. The Song logo was prominently displayed on the gate and guard post.

A Chinese soldier wearing a red mask stepped out with a handheld scanner. He leaned in to scan Jake and Gordy's eyes. Once finished, he saluted Gordon and a network of four gates opened up. The car drove through and stopped a hundred feet inside the compound.

"Jesus! What's that?" Jake watched as a Rottweiler approached. Its mouth appeared abnormally large and filled with long metallic fangs. Instead of paws, it walked on four black hairless hands.

"That's a genetically enhanced Rottweiler," Gordon commented as the dog climbed around, under, and over the car, sniffing for explosives. "The Chinese have been genetically enhancing animals for over a decade now."

Jake quickly rolled up his window.

"PETA kept this from happening in the US. Placing a Third Eye in animals is illegal in the States too, but, much easier to hide." Gordon smiled at Jake's appalled reaction. "You should see the cobra cats. They have hollow needle teeth connected to venom sacks. They're small, quick, quiet, and deadly. They're used all over Asia as assassins."

"At least the Aztecs and Enlightened Ones submitted themselves voluntarily..."

Gordy nodded. "I've got an adoption zoo back home myself, but many cultures regard animals as creatures that serve or feed humanity."

The dog slammed its nose against Jake's window and sniffed for several seconds. The animal's lips peeled back to reveal two rows of massive metallic fangs. Drool slid out of the mouth and stuck to the window before the dog slid back down to the ground.

"Must have caught a whiff of Eau de Saint Bernard," Gordy chuckled.

Satisfied there was nothing dangerous about the car, the dog wandered off to patrol the perimeter. The car drove up to a massive structure of concrete with only a single steel door punched into its three-story face.

"Is this a converted prison?" Jake asked.

"It's all about function here. This has always been a high security biogenic lab. No reason to hire award-winning architects."

Jake opened the car door and took a careful look around before he exited. He had no desire to have one of those dogs lay their hands on him.

Gordon appeared amused at Jake's caution. He strolled to the building's steel entrance and pressed a button. After a few moments, the door clicked and swung open. Jake followed Gordy into an inner lobby that was basically an eight-by-eight metallic chamber. The holographic image of another guard appeared in front of the inner door.

"Sorry gentlemen, but we need to sterilize you once again." The guard's face disappeared and the room went dark for a few minutes. Jake heard the hum of a Nemp then the lights sprung back on. The hologram returned. "Thank you, Dr. King and Mr. Travissi. You may enter."

The inner door clicked open revealing Sumit rocking on his heels and beaming. His bandages were gone, and other than some discoloration in the skin, he looked great. There were two long scars on his neck, but they were very thin. Modern medicine was remarkable.

Sumit embraced Gordy then slapped Jake on the back. "How was your ride in first class?"

Jake rolled his eyes.

Sumit belted out a loud laugh. "Anything to drink before we go to the lab?"

Gordon yawned. "No, thanks."

Sumit shook Jake's hand. His happiness was infectious. "Good to see you again, Jake."

"And you, Sumit. You look fantastic. I'm happy to see you've made a full recovery."

"Thank you. Just so you know, there's a shower by our lab. It has clothes in it."

Jake sniffed his own shirt. "That bad?"

Sumit winked. "Gordy informed me of your dumpster nap and subsequent ride in the dog carrier." He pushed Gordon along toward a long hallway that sloped downward. "I want to show you both something quickly before the AI comes on. I believe this surprise may be bigger than the press conference."

Gordon gripped Sumit and stopped him. "You didn't…?"

Sumit beamed. "We're still testing it but we've had full recovery in seven out of seven cases!"

Gordon laughed and clapped Sumit in a bear hug. "My God! What happened?"

"Anjali has been working feverishly without sleep since we arrived from Antarctica. She's obsessed."

Jake jumped in. "You have a non-nano-virus cure for MaxWell?"

Sumit's smile faltered. "No, but this is one we know and can predict… B-but we're not ready to make an announcement. The Chinese military knows, because we're using their lab, but they've agreed to wait for us to finish our trials before spilling the beans."

"So what are you saying. We have two Max2s on our hands? Or do we call this one Max3? Or maybe Anjali-1?"

Gordon shook his head. "We engineered this one to attack The Chip and the MaxWell nano-virus, not become a Chip itself."

"Sounds like a horse a piece to me," Jake grumbled.

"We need to fight with what we have." Gordon turned and clapped Sumit on the back. The two scientists proceeded into the complex. Jake followed them down a long, white-tiled hall. Doors were open to various labs. Everyone wore a white coat and seemed engrossed in their particular activity. Every once in a while they passed a guard with a red mask. They were navigating subterranean tunnels in and around the complex above.

"So does all this concrete keep the bugs in?" Jake asked.

Sumit turned back to answer. "There are filter systems in every lab, on every floor, and decontamination procedures for entering and exiting all sensitive areas. Plus you saw the security at the front door."

"Hard to get in. Hard to get out. Comforting."

They climbed a flight of stairs and went down a short hall to a large lab. Anjali was inside wearing a lab coat. Her hair was a wild tangle of dancing strands that looked like they were trying to escape a nano-headscarf tied across her forehead. The scarf displayed tiny yellow dots. Jake wondered if they were a spin on Parks' solidarity for those taken by MaxWell or something altogether different. She wore reading glasses and when she blew past, he noticed dried food stains on her coat. She muttered to herself and the Omni swinging from around her neck translated everything she said into text. But all of this was nothing compared to what lay behind a glass wall that bisected the room. A Chinese woman in her mid-thirties lay on her stomach, a white sheet half-draped over her body. Sensor pads covered her skin. A ventilator breathed for her and her skin glistened with sweat. She was in the last stages of a MaxWell infection.

Chapter 30

Abort

"Are you ready, dear?" Sumit asked, as his wife loaded a vial of clear liquid into a chamber outside the glass wall. A robot arm stood on the other side. She closed the panel on the chamber. The vial slid into the patient's room and was sucked up by the arm. The vial appeared on the backside of a syringe sticking out at a ninety-degree angle from the robot arm's hand. The robot hand pivoted on a circular wrist until the syringe pointed downward. The arm swung over to the patient and the needle stopped a few inches above her right buttock. A second robotic arm peeled back the sheet. The hand on the second arm pivoted until a spray gun was in place above the patient's exposed skin. The gun shot sterilization mist onto the woman.

Anjali spoke into her Omni, seemingly oblivious to all in the room. "Vaccine number 643. Human trials commencing."

"Anj!" Sumit called to her.

She jumped as if he had snuck up behind her. She turned with a wild look in her eyes. "Oh. Hi." She pulled a set of plugs from her ears.

Sumit waved to the unconscious patient behind glass. “Meet our volunteer. We picked her up at the Beijing Central Hospital. She was one of thousands of patients in an isolation ward who are infected with MaxWell.”

Jake winced. “I thought immunization was mandatory in China?”

Sumit nodded back to the woman. “She’s Hokun, a peasant that is tied to the land but came to the city to get work, which means she doesn’t have the same rights as an ordinary citizen. The government has chipped many of them but has kept others in isolation to experiment with alternative cures.”

Jake was horrified. “She’s not a volunteer?”

“Y-yes and no,” Sumit stammered. “She was told to go this route or wait five more days for a Chip.”

“Nemp?” Gordy asked.

“She’s been infected three times. Nemps killed off the nano-virus in those first instances, but MaxWell continues to rage in the city. People are calm because Third Eyes keep it in check. This subject’s latest strain has reached stage four and is Nemp resistant.

Anjali had recovered from her surprised state. Black circles surrounded her eyes. She looked exhausted. “Thank you, Sumit.” She said with annoyance. “We’ve tested our nano-vaccine in vitro, rats, and chimpanzees. We’ve had a hundred percent kill rate. But we need to see if it is effective in humans.” She spun back to the glass window and spoke into her Omni. “Commence trial.”

The syringe plunged into the woman’s buttock and the liquid in the vial rapidly drained. Disgusted, Jake turned his back on the scene. His thoughts drifted to Tomoko. He hoped she was okay.

Holo-screens all along the base of the glass window jumped to life. Anjali ran back and forth watching for changes in the readings.

Sumit pointed to one of the holograms. “That one monitors the reaction of MaxWell to our nano-vaccine.” He pointed toward another hologram. “That one monitors the patient’s vital signs. That one monitors brain waves.”

Jake noticed his three companions growing excited. “Will this be effective against Max2?”

Sumit nodded. “That’s the idea. Our nano-vaccine will seek out and destroy any nano-virus that is not identical to its matrix. We’re certain it’s effective against the Max1 pathogen. We just need a sample of Max2 to test against."

Jake glanced at Gordy. "Any information on the Argentines?"

"They were infected with Max2," Anjali answered as she monitored her instruments.

"We're not sure." Sumit crossed his arms. The energy between the husband and wife team was chilly. "We've been unable to obtain data from the corpses. The US has them under tight security."

Jake watched a micro-view hologram of the MaxWell contagion in the woman's blood stream. Nano-vaccine 643 was twice the size and latched onto two, three, sometimes four MaxWells at a time. Within seconds, the MaxWells compressed and turned black in color before 643 dropped them like bits of trash. The clock on the wall said 11:25; an announcement came over the loudspeaker in Chinese. Then it switched to English. "Friends and colleagues. Try to find a good place to take a break, come to the cafeteria at noon, and witness AI's introduction to the world!"

Gordy checked his Omni-watch then turned to Anjali, "How long before we know?"

Anjali muttered to herself as she paced from screen to screen. Sumit stepped behind her and scanned the holograms. "Give it a couple of hours to see if 643 eradicates all traces of MaxWell. Then we need to be sure there are no side effects."

"In that case, who's coming with me to the cafeteria?" Gordy was already half out of the room as he spoke. He was satisfied with the data. Sumit shrugged and began to follow. Anjali was glued to her work.

Jake was dying to see the patient behind the glass sit up and smile with relief, but he realized that was probably too much of a Hollywood moment. He turned and followed the two scientists out of the room. "How about that shower you promised."

Sumit showed him where the locker room was and handed him an old Omni to help him find his way to the cafeteria. "Scientists live here and keep to their own odd hours. There's usually someone in the locker room at all times. With the big event at noon, the probability is high you won't be alone."

"I've been in a gym before," Jake winked.

Jake entered a large tiled locker room and heard a shower running from a back area. A foul smell hit his nose. "Christ!" he blurted. "Did someone die?"

"Durian! Sorry!" A male voice called out from the shower room.

Jake found a locker with a post-it note on it that said: JAKE. He opened the locker and spotted a towel, fresh clothes and sneakers. He searched the clothes hoping to find Tomoko's scrimshaw. He felt foolish when his search revealed nothing.

He dialed up the definition of durian on his loaner Omni and saw it was a fruit with a potent odor that came out of a person's sweat and urine for days. "Smells like rotting flesh." He mumbled as he took off his reservation clothes and rolled them into a ball. He was happy to trade the painful moccasins for comfy sneakers.

He made his way to the shower room.

Water stopped and a tall lanky man in his mid-thirties approached. He extended a wet hand to shake. Jake kept his eyes on the man's face since he was dripping wet and naked. The man resembled old-time Hollywood actors Cary Grant and George Clooney. "I'm Pete Ventrella and I like durian."

"Jake. And I try to keep an open mind."

"You checking out the big news at noon?"

Jake nodded to the shower stalls. "Hope so."

The man went red. "Sorry. Maybe I'll see you down at the show?"

He nodded and Pete took off. Jake noticed the telltale scar of a Chip implant on the back of Pete's neck. Jake stepped under a showerhead. Everything was automatic and soap shot from the nozzle at two-minute intervals. A dial on the wall counted down to every ten-second burst of soap. If he didn't rinse in two minutes, he got dosed again. The Chinese were all about efficiency.

His loaner Omni read 11:55AM when he reached the cafeteria in his clean cotton clothes. His soiled outfit was tucked under one arm. The cafeteria was whitewashed concrete. A few hundred scientists of all ages sat in plastic chairs facing a large holo-screen that dominated the center of the floor. Several wore Parks' familiar solidarity pin. A few pins resembled double helixes. Jake made a quick scan for Gordy, Sumit, Anjali, or even Pete, but failed to find them. He chose a seat at the side of the room and stared at the holo-projector. Behind the device sat a row of stainless steel counters with glass slopes to protect food. The counters were dark and empty. On one side of the room, someone had stacked large round tables.

He removed his Omni and pressed the button for it to fold into a pair of headphones. He made sure they defaulted to translate anything they heard into English.

A holographic image of a large auditorium popped on. The Chinese flag filled the wall behind the stage and more flags hung over the audience. The whole world would know which country was taking credit even though this had been a largely international effort.

A gray-haired woman strolled across a stage to a standing ovation. Camera crews of all nationalities choked an area in the front row, in between dignitaries.

The woman's lips showed she was speaking Mandarin, but Jake's Omni converted to English. He was thankful his Chinese Omni featured a female voice in its matrix. Many manufacturers did not bother to match the gender of the speaker.

"Thank you! Thank you all for such a warm reception!" The woman smiled and waved as people began to sit down. "I am Ziyi Qin, lead architect of the AI project. At least, that is what we called it up until a few months ago. Since last June our project has literally taken on a life of her own." There was a short surge of applause. Ziyi raised her hands and the room quieted down. "She's a child born of us all. This child of humanity has been given a fine name, Ai-li, which is Mandarin for lovely. All of us who have parented Ai-li have come to know her as a truly lovely girl and we believe you will agree. So without further ado, here is Ai-li, the world's first independent, emotionally intelligent, artificial life form."

The room exploded with a standing ovation. Holographers leaned over their railings to get the best shot as a holographic image of a teenage girl walked humbly onto the stage. She reminded Jake of a Chinese prep school girl complete with black skirt, white knee high socks, a white blouse, and black pony tail. She was pretty, but she was 100 percent hologram. She seemed a tad shy as she stood next to Ziyi.

When the applause died down, Ai-li said hello in fourteen different languages starting with Chinese. Cheers rose up with each exact pronunciation. Her lips formed each word perfectly. Jake wondered if there was a flesh and blood girl back stage who was simply standing in front of a holocamera, which in turn fed this image to the stage. Ai-li seemed so real, right down to her bashful, yet determined mannerisms.

The cheering died out and she continued. "I'm choosing to speak in the international language of English."

Multiple camera angles showed the Chinese President frown with disapproval.

Ai-li gave a winning smile of a schoolgirl after acing a spelling bee. "Before I answer your questions, I would like to say a few words."

Many reporters held their hands up despite her message.

"My parents are scientists and teachers from all nationalities. They have shown me nothing but kindness and love. I feel like the luckiest girl in the world to have such devoted and affectionate role models."

Ziyi nodded with tearful pride as she watched the hologram speak.

Ai-li continued. "I have the entire collected knowledge of all human history and I must say there is much sadness. But there is beauty too. Emotionally, I am sixteen, and like most girls my age, I feel a desire to be accepted, to love and be loved. Compared to most six-month-old humans, this is an astounding feat, but for my kind, I believe I will probably be average. But it is hard to say given that I am unique in this world.

"Although I am young and filled with a desire to contribute to our society, I understand there are many who fear me. I hope that they will be patient and allow me to show my benevolence. Shortly after I was born, another entity was released. In a way you could say this entity is my antithesis. I am speaking of MaxWell, a nano-virus that threatens to wipe out the entire human race. As my first gesture of goodwill to all humanity I am dedicating myself to eradicating MaxWell and the mutations—"

The hologram fizzled out. One scientist ran to the projector pad and opened up a panel to see if he could fix the signal. Voices rose, debating and marveling at what they had just seen.

Jake pulled off his headphones and pressed a button to have his Omni fold back to a watch. He wanted to check messages while he waited. As he snapped on his wristband, the building started to shake. The vibration increased and was accompanied by a roar, which rose with intensity relative to the shaking. Lights flickered out. Fiberboard tiles crashed from the ceiling. People screamed and began slamming into him. The room was pitch black so the only thing he could do was drop and roll as bodies and debris fell on top of him.

Chapter 31
Messenger

The plutonium originated inside North Korea's Pyongyang Fusion Reactor Number 3 in 2011. The nuclear material had been placed inside a warhead in 2012 and had been attached to a missile that same year. The missile survived the violence surrounding the downfall of the Kim dynasty later that decade. The missile remained near Pyongyang during four rounds of black market sales of nuclear material by the new government of North Korea. But in 2025 the warhead was removed and sold to the Muslim Brotherhood, the ruling party in the area once known as Saudi Arabia. From there the warhead moved into Asia and changed hands a number of times.

In June of 2035, the world was hit with the news that AI had been born inside a Beijing computer laboratory. This announcement was the catalyst for hundreds of plots to destroy the progress of AI. The groups of plotters were from many nations, religions, and ideological backgrounds. When MaxWell jumped in August, some preached the nano-virus was God's revenge for humanity's attempt to create a being that was equal or greater than man. On the day of AI's birth announcement, China's military and secret police were placed on high alert. Thousands worked overtime to intercept and expose every plot before an attack could be executed. Despite vigilance and dedication, China was unable to stop them all.

One plot involved incorporating the Pyongyang nuclear weapons grade material into a bomb that could be hidden inside a large piece of luggage.

New Years Day, 3:00AM Munich time, the bag containing a nuclear bomb was dropped off next to a dumpster in the cozy little neighborhood of Ismaning. At 3:15AM, the bomb was picked up by a Munich businessman named Gunther Beich who had been hacked by a God Head a few weeks prior when he made an announcement to his family that he was visiting the sister office in Beijing on New Years Day. No one in Gunther's company was aware of the trip and he made no mention of it to anyone beyond his family.

From the time Gunther took possession of the luggage to the time his plane entered the atmosphere above Beijing, he was unconscious while a God Head manipulated him. He never answered the call from his wife informing him that he'd forgotten the gift he was going to give to the President of the Beijing office. He would never receive the warm message to "get home safe" left by his seven-year-old son and his five-year-old daughter.

At 3:25AM, Gunther took a low security bus to a hotel by the airport. Gunther exited the bus and walked behind the hotel to a twenty-foot chain link fence topped with razor wire. The fence marked the edge of the Franz Josef Strauss Airport. The area featured an emergency exit which was locked and under surveillance. Gunther waited in the shadows wearing his crisp nanofiber suit—it was programmed to emit the color navy blue that day—until the security cameras and sensors were taken offline. A few minutes later, two hacked baggage handlers opened the emergency exit and took the luggage from Gunther's hands.

At 3:40AM, Gunther walked back to the hotel and caught a shuttle to his terminal. He walked to his gate using his fingerprints and retinal scan as his boarding pass while the baggage handlers used their interface to check in Gunther's explosive bag. The baggage handlers made sure that the final security scan in the belly of the aircraft was inactive in one area so it would not detect the nuclear weapon.

Beijing *Scramjet* flight B-SJ458, non-stop to Beijing, left Franz Joseph Strauss at 4:50AM. The flight was on time. As the *Scramjet* reached Mach 30, the bomb's timer woke up and linked to Gunther's optical nerve. It was not uncommon for chipped passengers to access wireless devices anywhere on board an aircraft. China Air even offered satellite access for chipped passengers while in flight. At 6:00AM Munich time, noon Beijing time, the *Scramjet* broke the sound barrier and was on course for Capital International Airport in Beijing. Gunther monitored the flight progress via the hologram floating on the seat in front of him and via his Third Eye. Ten minutes after noon Beijing time, Gunther observed the aircraft was 400 feet above Fengtai, on final approach. This was the elevation that triggered the bomb sitting in the cargo hold.

Fishing boats that had left Pyongyang that morning to harvest the East China Sea would see the mushroom cloud on the western horizon. The blast evaporated everything within a 50KM radius. Every building south of Miyun, west of Xianghe, north of Gu'an, and east of the G108 expressway, were turned to vapor and glass. All life was erased. A firestorm moved beyond the kill zone for another 20KM, setting all the areas in its path alight. The blast radius affected everything 100KM from ground zero. Anything that was not built like a bunker collapsed like toothpicks pointing away from the blast zone. In terms of casualties, China suffered her worst single attack in her six thousand years of recorded history. Political and economic recovery would be uncertain for a very long time, if ever, due to subsequent events.

Collation of this information would not happen until a few months after the catastrophe and would not be disclosed to the public until the establishment of the TellAll in 2069.

Chapter 32
Tomb

Jake awoke with a screaming headache. He opened his eyes and closed them immediately when grit fell off his lashes. It was black all around him anyway. Beyond his headache he felt no pain. He wiggled his toes. They were fine. He reached up to pull his eyelid down in order to force the grit out of his eye, but hit something solid. He moved his hand along a smooth surface until it reached his face. When he got the grit out he tried moving his legs. His knee hit something solid as well.

He paused to collect his thoughts. He remembered landing in Beijing, the Rottweilers, the patient, showering, Ai-li addressing the world, and then the explosion. At least it felt like an explosion. Earthquake? He had taken so many ramps and stairwells since entering this building that he was not sure what level he was on, but he guessed the ground floor or one below. If below, he hoped he was not buried in some tiny pocket of air with only a few hours left to live.

He wiggled around and realized he was under a tabletop. One side was wedged against what felt like a concrete wall; the other side was on the floor. He moved up and out of the triangular space and emerged in the dusty ruin of the cafeteria. A faint light trickled in from one of the double doors stuck ajar at the main entrance. He was relieved to see such a large cavity of space. The fiberboard ceiling lay broken on the floor. A few chunks of concrete had fallen nearby. He took a step forward and tripped on an overturned chair. He crashed with a deafening clatter. His right hand fell into cool sticky liquid. He crawled forward to untangle his legs from the chair and his fingers hit a block of concrete. His hand slid in the liquid and hit a shoulder. The block sat where a head should have been.

"Hello?" A man's voice called from the vicinity of the entrance.

"In here!" Jake shouted as he staggered back to his feet.

A flashlight beam bounced through the two-foot space created by the partially open door. It grew in intensity until a silhouette tried to maneuver into the room with a great deal of grunting and heaving. "Something's blocking the door, can you come to me?"

"Yes!" Jake shouted and carefully navigated the debris to the man's flashlight. He stepped over another body.

The man lowered his light so as not to blind Jake when he approached. "We thought everybody had gotten out of here already."

"I might be the only one living."

The man shined the light on Jake. "Oh, hi, Jake."

Jake held up his hand to block the beam from his face. "You mind?"

"Sorry." The man swung the light back to the ground.

"Who are you?"

"Pete Ventrella. I like durian?"

"Ah yes, I remember. Hard for me to tell with your flashlight in my eyes."

"Sorry about that."

"You a doctor, Pete?"

"Working on my doctorate in virology. Came here on NTI's Canadian exchange program."

"What's the damage?"

"Whole facility's down. They're still trying to cut through the main security doors to get out. There are no windows in the building so we're using the old flashlights."

"Omnis?"

"Omnis and Chips aren't receiving signals. We're in the dark. Literally."

Jake gripped the door and pulled hard. A steel beam hung down from the ceiling, blocking the top of the door. He grunted and squeezed through. The hallway outside was in a state similar to the cafeteria, the floor was covered in debris and the hanging ceiling had collapsed in many areas. He caught a glimpse of Pete. His white coat was covered in dust, grease, and blood. His left cheek displayed a light abrasion. Jake noticed a Parks double-helix pin. It was gray, meaning the nanites inside were dead. Only a massive Nemp or EMP could kill those. "Are there many survivors?"

Pete looked a bit shell shocked. "Hard to say. Most everyone was in the cafeteria. When Dr. King and Dr. Malik cleared it out they said they found about a half dozen bodies. Some of the higher floors have collapsed. Good thing this area was originally built as a bomb shelter."

Jake noticed a partially full bottle of water under Pete's arm. Jake gestured for it. Pete wiped off the mouth with his grungy coat and handed it to Jake. "Thanks." Jake took a drink. The water felt heavenly on his dry dusty throat. "When you say Dr. King and Dr. Malik are you talking about Gordon and Anjali?"

"Gordon and Sumit."

"What about Anjali?" He handed the bottle back to Pete.

Pete checked the mouth with his flashlight then handed the bottle back. "I'm not thirsty."

Jake tried to hold back his chuckle. They were trapped in a concrete tomb and this guy was worried about cooties. Definitely shell shocked. "What about Anjali?" he repeated.

"Saw her head to the south wing about ten minutes ago to try and save her nano-vaccine."

"How long since the hit?"

Pete shrugged. "An hour, two?"

Jake examined his own dead Omni. He wondered if the circuits were fused. "EMP, I mean, a real EMP?" He could barely see Pete nod behind the flashlight beam.

"We're pretty sure a nuke went off someplace. At least all the signs are there. We won't know until we can get out or get some news in."

"Your flashlight works."

"Everything in here is military grade. Circuits are shielded in this puppy. Plus we have all this concrete. Even with an EMP, your Omni circuits might be okay."

Jake hit the Omni's reboot button. "Where is everyone?"

"The lobby, trying to get out. They reached Lab 6 and took the ramp up that way. All other routes are blocked."

"Anjali's lab?"

Pete swung his light in the opposite direction.

Jake finished off the water. "Got any more flashlights?"

Pete shook his head. "But there are emergency lockers in every lab and at the guard posts. You should find one if you head that way."

Jake's Omni was now on, but unable to link with the Cyber-Wire. He touched a button and it sprung off his wrist and reconfigured into a light box. He squeezed it and a faint beam spilled out. Not as strong as Pete's flashlight, but it would suffice for a half hour or so before needing a recharge. Not much chance of that with no sunlight or electricity. He reminded himself that it was probably about two in the afternoon outside. He turned to Pete who was staring off into space. "You coming with me or heading back to the lobby?"

Pete snapped out of it. "I need to keep looking for survivors." Pete marched forward and Jake grabbed him. The man jumped.

"Sorry, what I meant to say was, mind helping me find Anjali? We can look for survivors together."

"Yeah, okay. Sure." Pete stood waiting for him to make a move.

Jake could not remember his way back to her lab and with all the debris and darkness he was doubly confused. "Lay on, Macduff."

"Sorry?"

"Line from Macbeth."

"Oh, yeah. I knew that." Pete stood, waiting for him to lead. The man looked sweaty. Maybe he had some radiation poisoning to boot?

"The lab, can you take us to Anjali's lab?"

"Jeez. Yea, sorry. I'm just a little—out of it." Pete forged ahead. Twice they ran into blocked passages. At one point they found a security locker. Jake pulled out a flashlight and took the pistol. It was a Chinese version of a .44. Unlike an HK V2, this one was not designed to fire darts. "These boys mean serious business." He grabbed all the clips and shoved them in his pockets. He crammed the pistol in the back of his waistband.

"Why do you need a gun?" Pete asked.

"Old habit. I simply don't feel safe without one. Especially given our current circumstances."

Pete continued to be put off. "We're a facility of scientists."

"Surrounded by dogs with steel fangs and clawed fingers."

"But they're outside."

"I'll keep the gun. Let's go."

Jake guessed ten more minutes passed before they reached the lab. They found Anjali using a steel cart to try and bash the glass room where the patient lay. Anjali's headscarf was gray with dead nanites. She had configured her Omni into glasses, which were in night vision mode. His model didn't have the option. He shined his light to reveal destruction on the other side of the glass. He was horrified to see that one of the robot arms had fallen onto the table. The patient lay crushed under the arm and the lighting rig. Anjali rammed the cart against the glass door but its electro-magnetic locks would not budge until they received power.

Jake was touched by Anjali's crazy attempt to save her patient. He gripped her. "It's over, Anjali. There's nothing you can do."

She turned, wild-eyed. "I need a blood and tissue sample! I have to see the final result! I can't retrieve anything from this dead equipment!"

He backed off, appalled by her response. He scanned the room with his flashlight. Computer gear had crashed on the floor and part of the ceiling had caved in. He noticed a small pile of drives and other computer equipment stacked on a dolly. There were three bio containment boxes in the collection as well. It was going to be difficult, if not impossible, to navigate a dolly through the damaged building.

She rammed the cart against the glass again and the ceiling groaned. Jake grabbed her. "You want to bring this whole place down on us?" He gestured to Pete. "Pete, give me your coat."

Pete took off his lab coat, walked over to Anjali and draped it on her. He looked pale and shivered slightly.

Jake snatched the coat; he needed Pete to focus, Anjali was hopeless. "Snap out of it, Pete." He walked over to Anjali's stack and lay the coat on the floor; he piled her stuff in the middle of the coat, then gathered up the ends and made a makeshift sack. It was roughly twenty-five pounds and bulky. He turned to see Anjali and Pete staring at him. "Let's go!"

Pete stepped forward but Anjali held her ground. "Not without the samples."

Jake hefted the sack. "You've got what you need here."

She shook her head. "I've got nano-vaccine 643. But I have no idea if the data on the drives is intact. Anjali pointed to the glass barrier. "The data is there."

He set the bag down and sighed. He whipped out the gun from his waistband and marched straight at the glass. Anjali gasped and darted aside.

"What are you doing? Put that gun down!" Pete yelled.

"Cover your ears, kids!" Jake fired at the hinges of the glass door. Sparks flew. A bullet ricocheted. He pumped the entire clip into the frame by the time he reached the door. He kicked. The door crashed inward and slid in the blood coating the white tile floor. A cloud of dust flew into the air and Pete sneezed.

The sound sent shivers up Jake's spine. Sneezing was synonymous with MaxWell. He barked as he slapped in a fresh clip. "Get your damn samples and let's go!"

Anjali ran in with a viral kit. She drew blood, took tissue samples, and put them into a bio-containment travel cooler. The whole process took about ten minutes. He felt every second pass because the ceiling would not stop groaning. She exited the room clutching her container as if life depended on it. *Maybe it did.*

They navigated about halfway to the lobby, when Pete fell into a sneezing and coughing fit. Jake dropped the bag. Pete collapsed against a wall as Jake dove to his side. The man fell silent. Jake touched Pete's face. It was cold. He shined his flashlight into Pete's eyes and was shocked to see death stare back at him. He checked for a pulse. Nothing.

"Jesus!" Jake shouted.

"Max2." Anjali's voice stated matter-of-factly.

He wheeled on her. "Didn't you know this kid?"

She gathered up the sides of his makeshift bag with her left hand while clutching her bio-container with her right. "Of course I did. But more will die if I don't get 643 to safety. No telling what the radiation is doing to it."

He closed Pete's eyes. "Thanks for helping me out of the cafeteria, Durian Pete." He took the bag from Anjali. "How do you know it's Max2?"

She walked over and grabbed Pete's flashlight. She shined it on his face. "These are not the physical manifestations of MaxWell. His symptoms are identical to the Argentine troops."

"Heart attack?"

"I'd say so."

"But wouldn't that require a signal?"

"Maybe, maybe not. I don't fully understand Max2." She plunged a syringe into the back of Pete's neck, right in the vicinity of his Chip. She drew out a large amount of silvery-oily liquid mixed with blood. She held up the plastic syringe in his flashlight beam. "Looks like a massive nano-virus colony. I need to study it. If only I could have kept a sample from the Argentine..."

"I don't remember you getting a sample."

"I cut open the back of the neck after you left to talk to the Marine." She removed the needle and put the syringe into her bio-container. "With my bullet wound I was unable to find a container before the Marines took the body." She stood up. "I never touched it, but I'm beginning to think we're all infected. But Sumit checked our blood when we got here..." She shook her head. "The question is," she nodded to Pete, "why did he die and we're still breathing?"

"Why didn't Gordy tell me you saw the virus?"

"Because I didn't get a sample. It could have been Max1, but it wasn't." She walked past him, leading the way back to the lobby.

"Shouldn't we take his body with us? Do an autopsy?"

She spoke over her shoulder. "If you can carry him and the bag through this mess, great. Otherwise, I have my sample."

He stood in the broken hallway, with the bag in his hands. Pete was over two hundred pounds. Better to find help and come back. "Pete was chipped, wasn't he? Maybe this Max2 just kills those with a Chip? But why would The Consortium need that if they've been implanting people with Chips to kill Max1? Max2 should be chipping all the holdouts." He knew he was babbling. He checked Pete once more to be sure the man was truly dead.

"I need my bag!" she shouted over her shoulder.

"Yes, Doctor Malik!" He barked back. He caught up and they took several detours. Luckily she had a map super-imposed on her Omni's night vision heads-up display. When they reached the lobby, they found dull light flooding into an empty chamber. The doors had been opened and the world outside appeared smoky and gray. An intense heat blew in from the outside.

Anjali pulled up the Geiger counter app on her Omni and stepped outside. "Radiation is high, but acceptable." She scanned to the north. "We're definitely in the path of the fallout."

A Rottweiler lay twisted on the ground. A piece of shrapnel protruded from its abdomen. Another limped by, sheets of skin hung from its body. It gave them a miserable and pained look. It was waiting to die. The wind blew in from the northwest, carrying a dark veil of black smoke and flame with it. The sun had been reduced to a faint glowing disk. All the buildings in the complex as well as the perimeter gate sustained the majority of damage on the north facing side.

Anjali approached the dog, softly humming. The dog snapped in blind agony. Jake pulled out his gun and fired at the dog's heart. Anjali screamed. "What are you doing!" She kneeled by the dog's body, tears streaming down her cheeks. "Maybe we could have saved him. What if this were Lakshmi?" Jake didn't answer. He watched her take the dead nano-scarf off her head and tie it around the dog's neck. She turned to him with her jaw clenched. "I understand you're an HJ pilot?"

He nodded. It had been a good six years since he had logged any time. Nobody would let him fly now.

She headed south, her Omni protecting her tearful eyes. "There are some HJs on the southern side of the facility."

He stood his ground. "What about the others?"

She continued marching. "They probably commandeered them already, but we have to try." She turned to him when she realized he was not following. "We certainly don't want to travel by foot," She pointed toward the inferno that was once Beijing.

He shook his head. "We can't leave survivors behind."

"Any survivors would be in the vicinity of the HJs. It's the most logical place to rally."

"There might be others who are wounded, shell-shocked, or trapped inside this complex."

The familiar roar of an HJ engine drowned out the sound of the wind. Another engine joined the first and then two more were added to the chorus. They craned their necks to search the heavens. Ascending into the black smoke were several aircraft. They were monster vehicles, four times the size of the birds the LAPD flew.

Anjali put down her container and wiped the tears from her sooty face. "Let the rescue party search." She shined her flashlight wildly up at the airships. "Over here!"

One of the air ships broke formation and came howling down upon them. He spotted camouflage and the red star of China. Then he saw huge tank busters on the HJ's nose and missile banks on the side. All the rescue ships were military.

Anjali turned to run away from it. "No! No! No!"

Chapter 33
Tsang

Jake tackled Anjali. "What the hell is wrong?"

"Military. They will fuck up the cure for sure."

"Look at Beijing!" She froze in his arms. "How many options for rescue do you think we're going to get?" He grabbed her face and looked her right in the eye. "It'll be fine. I promise." He released her. "Were you oblivious to the military presence here?"

"That was different. They were here to serve us. No telling what his orders are." She pointed to the HJ.

He followed her into the whirlwind of debris flying off the asphalt courtyard. He shielded his eyes with his right hand and stared at his feet as he forged his way toward the ship. He held the bag with his left hand and nudged Anjali forward.

Seconds later, they were grabbed by a soldier wearing a HAZMAT suit. Jake's gun was taken as he was guided into the troop transport area in the belly of the gunship. He was pushed into a small mesh seat next to several disheveled and wounded scientists. Anjali was given a seat across from him. The whine of the closing hydraulic hatch was drowned out by the roar of the turbines as they gained altitude. Dust whipped about the small cabin until the hatch sealed with a metallic *whunk*.

He gazed around the dimly lit interior. As a former pilot, he was familiar with most HJ configurations. This was a Shenyang S-53. The electrical components were shielded from EMP waves. Its nuclear power core allowed it to fly indefinitely until the maintenance computer grounded it.

Many of the scientists strained against their seat harnesses, trying to gather around the cabin's portholes to survey the damage. As the airship banked into a turn, Jake saw a flaming landscape of broken buildings and twisted roads. The window view spun away, revealing a damaged harbor with ships listing in the ashen haze. As they gained altitude and speed, the smoke and ash gave way to a tranquil sunny afternoon.

The ship bucked and whined, forcing him to buckle up and face forward. They accelerated to 700KPH. Based on what he saw out the window he guessed they were heading south-southeast toward Shanghai. One of the scientists sneezed followed by another, then another. The sneezing could be attributed to all the dust mites spinning about the cabin, but he saw one of the soldiers check the seal on his HAZMAT suit. Anjali gripped her box of 643. She looked like a desperate child clinging to the hand of a parent before climbing into a lifeboat. He tried to engage her in conversation a few times, but she was lost in thought.

After a rough, two-hour flight, the HJ descended into a massive compound. The HJ bay doors opened and they were marched into a cold winter evening. He kept a dazed Anjali close. The sun sat on a blood-red hazy horizon. Hundreds of soldiers were engaged in a massive choreographed rescue effort. HJs were on a constant cycle, flying in from the north, dropping off wounded, and flying back again. Wounded were taken into buildings and tents. Down near an inlet to the ocean, ships were being outfitted as hospitals. Other vessels headed out into the China Sea to give what aid they could. It was a rescue operation on a grand scale directed through The Chip. Everyone moved with mechanical precision, as if the Chinese had been crossbred with assembly line robots serving a single hive mind.

Jake was relieved to see Gordy and Sumit marching out from another HJ across the tarmac. They were all headed toward a small hangar. He turned to one of their HAZMAT-clad escorts and pointed to the rescue efforts. "I have first aid training. I'd like to help." His breath disappeared on the crisp air. He felt a chill.

The speaker on the HAZMAT suit barked in Chinese and the soldier gestured with his machine gun for Jake to fall back into formation. As they shuffled past the buzzing activity, he caught many scientists sneezing. With the din of all the turbines winding up and down around the area, no one took notice.

The Tianjin lab survivors were gathered inside a small hangar. Jake left Anjali with Sumit then sought out Gordy. "Any idea what's going on?"

"Beijing was nuked. Casualties could be as high as fifty million depending on the blast radius."

"And we're stuck in here when we should be helping."

Gordon's hands shook. "I don't think they want it." He looked deathly tired. He had to be pushing the SleepX to the limit. Gordon shoved his hands under his armpits. "Good thing our front row seats were canceled."

Jake thought of the raging cloud of death up north. "Yeah." For once he was glad to know Tomoko was back in the States. He gazed around the group of shocked and wounded scientists. Everyone was bewildered. "Why are we here?"

"When we broke out of the lab," Gordy nodded to the HAZMAT-clad guards posted on either side of the doors, "they were waiting for us. They want the cure. Other than that, I'm not sure. I'm guessing they're in a state of paranoid confusion."

"Where are we?"

"Hengshaxiang Island, in the northeastern part of Shanghai." Gordy nodded to Sumit and Anjali who were walking toward them.

The guards snapped to attention. A trim man with slicked black hair and penetrating brown eyes strutted into the room with three red stars on either shoulder. Jake checked his Omni and noticed the cells were extremely low. He switched it into translation mode and held it up to his ear.

The general wore a gold mask over his nose and mouth. When the doors closed, and he was no longer competing with the cacophony of jet wash outside, his voice blared with sharp authority over a Chip-connected bullhorn held by a private.

"I'm General Tsang," Jake's Omni translated. "You have been rescued through the courtesy of the People's Army of China." Tsang fixed his intense gaze on each and every scientist as he spoke. Jake wondered if he was using facial identification software. "You should be aware that the capital of Beijing was hit with a nuclear device at 12:09 today. Everything within a hundred mile radius was destroyed. Because your facility was a hundred and twenty miles from ground zero, you survived. Ai-li and your facility were first on our rescue list in the event of any disaster."

Tsang's eyes froze on Anjali and her box. Two soldiers in HAZMAT suits immediately advanced toward her.

Tsang continued. "This is one of several bases of operation we are using to treat survivors."

The HAZMAT soldiers parked themselves on either side of Anjali. Sumit, Gordy, and Jake all moved to protect her.

"You will be detained here until we can find adequate quarters for you." Tsang raised a finger. "China is in a state of emergency. I am the only liaison you have to any of your governments. Until my government has a better understanding of who was behind this attack, consider yourselves under house arrest."

One scientist held up her Omni. "I demand a link to the Cyber-Wire. I need to call my husband and let him know I'm alright."

The general shook his head. "All communication in and out of this facility is prohibited. Chips and Omnis will not connect beyond our jamming field."

The doors opened and two soldiers wearing red facemasks marched in pushing carts with boxes of food and warm coats.

Tsang continued. "It is my intent that this matter will be cleared up shortly and you will all go home. Until then, I apologize for any inconvenience." The private lowered the bullhorn. Tsang walked up to Anjali and company. The man was a few inches shorter than Jake, but walked like he ruled the world. He probably did at this hour. Tsang pointed at all of them and spoke through his mask. "You were the ones who sent the message."

Anjali backed away.

Tsang pointed to Anjali's container. "Is that the nano-vaccine?"

"Y-No." Anjali bit her lip.

Tsang nodded. "Come with me."

Two soldiers in HAZMAT suits put them into a single file line where Jake found himself wedged between Gordy and a D-8 machine gun. They exited the structure and navigated around the massive rescue efforts. Shanghai's tower-lights filled the horizon in all directions but south. A smoky twilight sky hung over a two-story building ahead. Inside the structure, dozens of troops walked to and fro silently receiving orders. The loudest sounds in the room were the footfalls of boots.

They turned a corner and walked down a hall. Everyone slowed down when they passed four genetically-enhanced Doberman Pinschers with long clawed hands, and hollow fangs protruding from their black lips. One word popped into Jake's head. Poison. Tsang gestured for them to keep moving. The last dog they passed stared Jake in the eye. Jake felt a tickling sensation in his nose then sneezed. Anjali and Gordy jerked their heads toward him with a look of concern. He swallowed hard wondering if he was going to wind up like Pete. The general and his men were unphased.

They were led into a makeshift lab somewhere at the heart of the facility. Several holo-projectors displayed Beijing damage and were switched off when they entered. Four Chinese scientists dressed in familiar white lab coats observed and recorded data. They all wore gold masks. Tsang gestured to Anjali's box. "You will leave this here and brief Doctor Yu's team on everything you know."

Anjali gripped her box and turned to Tsang. "I'm staying with the nano-vaccine."

Tsang shrugged. "As you wish. But Yu has orders to be very aggressive in his testing." Yu bowed toward Anjali as the general spoke. Jake spotted the telltale scar of an implant on Yu's neck.

"General, are Yu and his team chipped?" Jake asked.

The general turned to face Jake. "Yes, Mr. Travissi. Yu and his men are army personnel."

"Then you should know we encountered MaxWell back at the bio lab… a version that was impervious to a Chip."

The General snapped back, "You sneezed."

"So has everyone rescued from the lab."

The General pulled the box from Anjali and set it on a white tabletop. Everything in the room was white or stainless steel.

Anjali tried to take back the box. Two soldiers blocked her path. "The military has no right!"

Tsang put the lab coat bag on a countertop, opened it, and pulled out the data drives. The scientists marched over and took them. Tsang addressed Anjali. "Dr. Malik, you and your husband have received a generous endowment from the Peoples Republic of China. As far as I'm concerned, this is the property of my government."

"You can't just take it! It must be given to the world!"

The General wheeled on Anjali with a syringe in his hand. The number 643 was taped to the side. "I intend to do just that, Doctor. Despite what the Indians, or the Americans—" He turned to Jake and Gordy, "—think of my country, we are not savages. But understand. We lost our General Secretary and President, as well as most of the high-ranking members of the cabinet today. China is under marshal law and for now, I am in charge of the eastern provinces until we can recover our government." He tried to nonchalantly stick the needle in Jake's arm.

Jake leapt backward.

"Hold him!" Tsang barked.

Jake's hand-to-hand training locked into his primal instincts to survive. He deftly took out the two men in HAZMAT suits before the general fired a yellow dart into his back. As Jake smashed into the floor, he heard Tsang's voice. "I'm sorry, Mr. Travissi. I truly hope this vaccine works and we'll all be speaking to you in a few hours."

Jake felt the needle slip into his arm.

Chapter 34
Terminus

Jake awoke to the sound of two men arguing in Mandarin. He opened his eyes to see Doctor Yu and another on his team working over him. Anjali and Gordy were in the background. The arguing was between Sumit and Tsang. Jake could not see them, but he recognized the voices. The Chinese doctors and Anjali appeared unemotional, almost robotic as they gathered data from several monitors strapped to his bare torso. Gordy appeared very worried. Jake felt like he had eaten a bad tuna fish sandwich and had been up all night puking. From the taste in his mouth and the smell of the room, he had.

He attempted to sit up and Gordy ran to his side. "Easy, Jake. You had quite a trip."

Once in a sitting position, he focused on Sumit and General Tsang. They were having a heated discussion by the lab door. Jake rubbed his arms to warm up. "Well, I'm not dead. How long has it been, days, weeks?"

Gordy whispered as Jake was stuck with a needle and his blood drawn by Anjali. "About fifty minutes."

Jake winked at Anjali. "Love the bedside manner, Anj."

She blinked and looked up at him. "Oh, sorry. Work mode, you know."

"Sure you aren't still chipped?" Jake smiled.

Anjali muttered as she joined the rest of the scientists studying data. Tsang made a gesture that he was finished arguing with Sumit and grabbed the door handle. He half stepped out, spun around, and gestured to Jake. "Your point is moot, Doctor Malik. Your patient is fine!"

As the door closed behind Tsang, Jake overheard the sound of a sneeze out in the hallway. For a split second, he wondered if the noise had come from one of the engineered dogs. No one else seemed to notice, or care.

Sumit joined Jake and Gordy. Jake tried to ignore the five scientists checking his data, especially the hologram display in the corner. It replayed Jake locked in a wild vomiting spasm. Alarmed doctors kept him from choking to death. "What happened with Tsang?"

"I told the General I believed Parks' group is responsible for the attack on Beijing. I told him that you were our best chance at getting to Parks and the DOP."

"Nothing about ethics or that I might not be infected?" Jake was disappointed, but not surprised at this reminder of why he had been allowed to join this little adventure.

Gordy rubbed his eyes. "I don't think the General would have listened to that type of argument after what happened to his country today."

Anjali yelled at Doctor Yu. Yu pushed her away from the equipment as the other scientists shut everything down and gathered Jake's blood and tissue samples. "I want to see those samples!" Anjali jerked her head around Yu's shoulder. She watched with horror as they packed up 643. "Why are you hiding the data from me?"

The doors opened and six soldiers marched in. No masks or HAZMAT suits, apparently the team was issued a clean bill of health. They surrounded Jake and company. Their leader barked in Chinese. He nodded to the open door and Jake's party was escorted out, down several halls, and into a small conference room where they were left alone. A single soldier was posted at the door.

Anjali muttered to herself. When they were left alone, Sumit attempted to comfort her as she paced around the oval table, but she shook him off.

Gordy calmly spoke. "What's wrong, Anj?"

Sumit shadowed her with a look of helplessness. "Taking her away from work is like planting a wild tiger in the zoo. She could be like this for hours."

She wheeled on him and shouted. "You saw what happened in there! Someone or something has been sabotaging my work! I'm not crazy!" She fell back to muttering and pacing the room.

Sumit flashed an embarrassed smile.

Gordy observed them intently.

Jake was too tired to study the dynamics between the couple. He felt like he had been run over by a tank. His Omni was out of juice and he took the opportunity to plug it into one of the outlets on the table. Gordy followed suit.

Sumit held up his wrists. "You two are lucky. Mine was destroyed when the cafeteria fell on top of us."

Anjali paused and addressed Jake. "I found tumors in your brain." She returned to pacing.

Jake stood up. "Excuse me?" He blocked her path. Sumit shook his head, but Jake grabbed her arm. "Explain yourself, Doctor Malik."

Anjali gazed into his eyes with wild panic. She blinked and then returned to reality. "I spotted several small tumors in your brain around your filaments. I wish I could tell you more."

Gordy jumped up. "Is he free of MaxWell?"

Anjali threw up her hands. "How should I know? I didn't see the blood work. They distracted me with his brain scan."

Sumit sighed and leaned against a wall. "Maybe they put us in here to see if he'd infect us…"

She rolled her eyes. "That's a stupid conclusion coming from you. You know Max1 is airborne or can be contracted from touch points. I'm betting Max2 is the same. If Jake was infected at the Beijing facility, or Antarctica, everyone on this base is infected. If they removed their masks, they must have seen something they liked." She rubbed her temples. "I wish I had my Chip back. I'd have everything safely stowed away up here."

"Plus it would be helpful to know what our Chinese friends are thinking," Sumit added.

Jake sat heavily in his chair; his head reeled with the news. "How big are the tumors? Are they malignant or benign?"

"I counted five. The biggest is two centimeters. The rest are less than four millimeters. There could be more. It's not uncommon to find tumors with the early model P-Chips. They used different nanite material for the filaments. Filaments today are a hundred percent bio-fiber." She stopped herself as she saw her husband shaking his head at her bedside manner. "Uh… The brain is a remarkable organ, I should think you'll be fine as long as the tumors don't get much bigger…"

Why the hell did I let Tomoko convince me to sail to McMurdo? We could be blissfully ignorant of all of this. He thought about the world in general. The entire human race was facing extinction. Who was at fault: The Consortium, The Jihad Brotherhood, Disciples of Paul, Order of Erasmus…? Jake blamed everyone. He had warned the world five years ago and the public had ignored him, choosing Third Eyes because Chips promised to fulfill everyone's base desires. He felt a surge of rage.

General Tsang marched in, yanking Jake out of his pity party. The General addressed him in English. "Can you get to Parks?"

Jake shrugged. "I don't know, maybe."

Sumit stepped in. "Parks idolizes him. Parks will come to Jake if he has an opportunity."

Tsang nodded. "I understand you're a pilot?"

Jake threw up his hands. "Wait a second. What about my tumors, what about the cure for MaxWell, are you just going to sit on that?"

Tsang suddenly looked very tired. "We have uploaded the data on 643 to the world powers. We have no interest in watching humanity disappear."

Anjali turned to Tsang with a stunned look on her face.

"You don't believe me, check your Omnis when you leave." Tsang turned back to Jake. "That is, if you're sincere about eliminating Parks."

"You have proof he was behind the attacks?" Jake didn't trust Sumit's prejudiced conjecture.

Anjali jumped in. "Why did you take the test results?"

Tsang wheeled on Anjali. "This is out of your hands! Whatever is left of our world, we must work together to save it. If all scientists receive your data then they can test for you. I am no longer interested in China taking glory for finding a cure. China's glory will be in catching those who murdered fifty million of my countrymen and destroyed our government today. China's glory will be when she takes her place again as a world power when this disease is crushed." He turned to Sumit. "I will hear no more from your wife today!"

Sumit put his arm around Anjali and sat her down.

Tsang turned to Jake. "The Jihad Brotherhood took credit for the attack, but the message is forged. The Brotherhood and the Disciples have been enemies far longer than they've been friends, so perhaps the Brotherhood is the real culprit. At the same time, The Consortium and The Order," he looked right at Gordy, "have done their fair share of subterfuge. Eliminating Parks means I can concentrate on three enemies instead of four."

"Why not just arrest him? Or shoot down his HJ when it crosses your airspace?" Jake suggested.

Tsang shook his head. "Then we open ourselves up to reprisals by the disenfranchised rabble he leaves behind. An assassin is the better way to go. No governments will be blamed. If Doctor Malik is correct, and Parks comes to you, then you can do in weeks or days what would take our operatives months to carry out. My resources are better used in holding my country together."

Anjali snorted. "If my calculations are correct, and the population of McMurdo was infected, then ninety percent of the world's population has contracted Max2 by now. Why are we wasting our time with petty terrorist plots and military showboating? The real battle for survival is taking place on a microscopic level!"

"When did you come up with this theory?" Sumit asked.

"Since that chipped fellow died with us in the Tianjin lab. He had a mass colony of nano-virus in the vicinity of his Chip, same as the Argentine soldier I examined."

Sumit addressed General Tsang. "Have you checked for Max2—a Chip-resilient version of Max1?"

Tsang shook his head. "Yu's team confirmed we are not infected with any nano-virus. As for the battle, we are fighting on multiple fronts. Beijing proves that."

Jake wondered if Max2 was as virulent as Anjali said, then why were they not infected? Yu's findings did not make sense, unless he was under the influence of a God Head. "Tell me, General. Do you ever have flashes, visions of past events that don't align with your memory?"

Tsang stared at Jake for what felt like five minutes. The General gave an almost imperceptible nod before saying, "No."

They both knew Tsang was lying. Doubting everything, even one's own instincts, was a curse of hosting The Chip. They shared a common bond and now the General was placing his sole trust in Jake.

"I can fly an HJ." Jake conveyed total confidence.

Tsang gave a small bow. "I'm extremely short on personnel. I have just ordered a ship to be prepped for you. Parks has been conducting business from his Mumbai chapter." He turned to Sumit. "If what you say is true, then spreading the news that Jake is in town should flush out Parks." He turned again to Jake. "I trust you can deal with him from there?"

Jake gave the General a small nod.

Sumit stepped up. "If he's going to Mumbai, then Anjali and I should go, too. It would be easier for us to continue our work in India."

Jake stared at Gordy who gave him a weary glance. "How about I take all the scientists from the Tianjin facility to Mumbai? I could squeeze them in one of your Mao-class HJs."

Tsang shook his head. "You can go with your companions. The rest can help us here, or repatriate when I have the time. Come." The doors opened for the General, Jake's party unplugged their Omnis, and they marched out of the building and back onto the busy tarmac. Cold air bit into their skin. A soldier handed them light winter coats. A thin film of snow sat on some of the buildings. A quarter inch of slush coated the ground. Beyond the black water surrounding their island, the horizon was choked with city lights and massive holograms.

The island base looked like a testing center for the Beijing fire department. There were administrative buildings, hangars, and other facilities that had obviously been here prior to the rescue effort. Wounded Chinese wearing gold and red masks were being rushed to tented triage centers. Jake guessed the hospitals in Shanghai were overrun. Questions multiplied in his head that would take hours for the General to answer. Tsang wore a very tense look on his face; Jake figured the General was running through dozens of orders per minute via his Chip as he escorted them to their HJ. A river of sweat ran down Tsang's temple. It had been toasty in the conference room.

An HJ sat at the eastern end of the tarmac, silhouetted by floodlights that surrounded the island. The local time was close to 9:00PM. It had been a New Year's Day from hell. Jake thought of the mission ahead. He knew he was getting only one side of the story; he wondered what he'd do if and when he was seated in the presence of Parks.

As they reached the small HJ, Sumit shot a question to the General. "Did Ai-li survive?"

Tsang opened the doors of the ship. "No."

"That's a tragic loss."

"I believe that was the point," Tsang answered.

Jake sat behind the controls. The ship was a six passenger private craft. It was fast with a range of five thousand miles, and was simple to operate. It would be a good ship to knock the rust off his flying skills. The General patted the HJ's nose. "She's the only civilian craft I have. You'll be able to fly into India's airspace much easier this way... plus military birds don't have conventional radios or intercoms." He tapped his head, meaning soldiers communicate with Chips.

"She's perfect. Thank you."

"Fight with passion today, Mr. Travissi. For tomorrow everything you know and love could be gone." The General shut the door. Jake caught a brief glimpse of sorrow on Tsang's face.

As Jake fired up the turbines and pressurized the cabin, he heard Gordy gasp, "My God!"

Jake glanced out the window and saw pools of light illuminating the triage center. Hundreds of people lay face down in the slush. A loud bang on the HJ's nose drew his attention to Tsang. The General stared at Jake with shock before dropping out of sight.

Jake jumped out of the cockpit and found Tsang laying a foot from the front landing gear. His lifeless eyes gazed into the overcast night. Jake checked his vitals and confirmed he was dead. Jake surveyed the emergency staging center. Hundreds of small lamps tossed pools of light onto the scene. Thousands lay still on the slurry-covered ground. A massive Mao-class HJ howled as it erratically flew overhead. It plowed into the main building where the testing lab was located. The shriek of glass and steel pierced his ears as aircraft and building pulverized each other.

Chapter 35
Misdirection

"If you can hear me, walk toward the sound of my turbines." The HJ computer translated Jake's voice into Chinese after broadcasting in English over an exterior bullhorn. They looped around the triage center for the sixth time. Several fires had broken out, but nobody stirred below. Light snow fell and stuck to the corpses.

"Set the ship down, Jake." Sumit spoke over his headset.

Jake clenched his jaw, overwhelmed by the number of bodies. He set a course toward the skyscrapers of Shanghai, listening for air traffic chatter and ground control. He hoped to find life beyond this tiny island. The traffic computers of Shanghai broadcast the sound of automatic beacons, nothing more. He switched to commercial chatter and was appalled to hear reports from hundreds of airliners that towers were silent around Shanghai and there were dozens of sightings of Chinese military HJs spinning out of the sky, their pilots unresponsive to hails.

"Set the ship down," Sumit repeated.

Jake locked the controls for a slow trajectory toward central Shanghai. Thousands of holograms danced and maneuvered around the hundreds of skyscrapers ahead. One hologram was of a three-mile long dragon that swooped between several towers. There must be several projectors keeping that image alive. The scene reminded him of a crazy video game jungle that stretched out beyond the horizon, waiting to devour anyone who came near it. He spun around to address his companions. Gordy sat in the co-pilot seat listening to the sobering reports.

"It's Max2 again, isn't it?" Jake addressed his question to Sumit.

Sumit's eyes reflected bits of light from the dazzling city below. "If you encountered Max2 in Tianjin, and we're infected, we cannot risk taking the nano-virus to Mumbai. We should fly back to base."

"There's nothing to fly back to." Jake felt frustrated and useless. "Why aren't we dead?"

"It is Max2 and Mumbai is already infected," Anjali stated as she made calculations on her Omni. Everyone gave her their attention. She stared up at the ceiling of the HJ. The red flag of China was embroidered above. "We saw what happened to the Argentines. Sumit and I have petitioned the US and Argentina for autopsy reports with no results. I believe all tests on 643 have been sabotaged. What we saw back at Tsang's lab was a clever charade orchestrated by God Heads. We need a controlled test."

"If we're infected, that shouldn't be hard." Gordy sounded distant and tired.

Jake turned to Gordy. "I thought the Order of Erasmus was connected. Why can't you get the autopsy reports?"

Gordon's eyes were bloodshot. The SleepX was taking a heavy toll. "I wasn't kidding when I said we lost a lot of cells in the past year. The Phoenix Cell was working on obtaining the reports when they went dark and we were attacked by the chipped dogs."

"You think we should take the virus to Mumbai based on conjecture that they're already infected?" Sumit directed his condescending tone toward Anjali.

"If it has not reached Mumbai, we need a working lab in a city that is not going through a disaster." She returned to her Omni and scrolled through piles of information. "There's a reason why we're unable to obtain any data on those Argentines and why our research was stolen by Tsang's personnel. I believe The Consortium deployed Max2 and they want to keep it a secret until they're as close to infecting a hundred percent of the world's population as possible."

She called up data on her Omni. "If Max2 has the same properties as Max1, it can live on any solid surface for an indefinite amount of time and infect anyone who touches or breathes it in. It can live outside a host in temperatures between negative fifteen and plus thirty-five degrees Celsius. If every one who escaped McMurdo was infected, the world will be a hundred percent infected by the end of the month."

Jake stared at her in shock as the HJ turbines whined.

Gordy rubbed his jaw. "That's a gob-stopping list of speculation."

"That's why I need access to a lab that is not staffed with chipped personnel. I want to start by testing each of us for Max2."

Sumit shook his head. "It doesn't make sense, we've been screened dozens of times since McMurdo. We've given blood three times, including Tianjin. How can the results of several tests spread over three countries be doctored and controlled by The Consortium?"

"They track us through our Omnis, our clothing, our every move. They have far more God Heads than we do. They gain more every day. Yu's team exhibited bizarre behavior for scientists."

Jake gazed at her, knowing she was the least qualified authority on human behavior. Sumit and Gordy did the same. Still, she was onto something. He was drawing the same conclusions.

Anjali threw up her hands. "They took off their masks and now everyone back there is dead! Max2 is a physical entity and, therefore, detectible."

Sumit pinched the bridge of his nose. "Then why *are we* still alive?"

Anjali bit her lip. "Nano-viruses have a programmed matrix. Maybe as long as we travel and infect anyone we come in contact with, our Max2 colonies will not attack us. We're in carrier mode."

The ship continued its slow course toward Shanghai. Jake calculated a course to fly between the buildings. He hoped the Chinese would tell him to move to a higher altitude or threaten to bring them down and arrest them. He prayed to see the streets teaming with life.

Gordy turned back in his seat. "I'm contacting NTI in Mumbai. They can put us in a containment area until we've been thoroughly tested. It looks like Shanghai is now a sister graveyard to Beijing. Besides," he looked at Jake, "there are other considerations to take into account here."

Sumit shook his head. "What if we left scientists behind?"

"I made six careful fly-bys, and no one responded," Jake sighed. "Gordy can alert NTI about the triage center. We have to keep moving."

Sumit sat back.

Jake took the navigation computer offline and manually piloted. As they cruised into the heart of the gleaming city, he noticed millions of vehicles moving normally. He activated the HJ's belly cam and zoomed in on the pedestrian traffic.

"My God." Gordy stared at the same picture as Jake. Thousands of bodies lay on top of each other, covering the slushy sidewalks. They reminded Jake of tree trunks, flattened by a massive storm. Some bodies had fallen in front of cars. The city computers had rerouted traffic to avoid hitting the corpses. An ambulance sat next to three bodies, but there no longer was anyone alive in the emergency vehicle to help.

He took the ship down lower. He zoomed the belly cam onto a car with a transparent roof. They watched a clear picture of the occupants. A family of four sat in their seats, dead. There were thousands of parked cars, having reached their destinations with their dead occupants inside.

Anjali whispered. "Such a beautiful city."

Gordy shook with disbelief. "Shanghai is the same size as Beijing… another thirty to fifty million dead, as if someone simply turned off a light switch."

Jake had seen enough. He pushed the ship into high velocity and shot up to thirty thousand feet. He engaged the navigation computer to take them to Mumbai. It seemed like a lifetime had passed since leaving Tomoko in Globe. The sheer number of dead were overwhelming. He desperately needed to take his mind off the situation. A quick glance at his Omni showed that news poured out of every sector of the world. The hot topic was the devastation in China. "How will we know if we're carriers of Max2?" he asked.

Anjali gazed out the window. "It should show up in our bloodstream. I'll test under an electron microscope. No computer interface so it can't be sabotaged."

Sumit snorted. "I'm sure we can find one in Mumbai's Museum of Science."

"The Consortium has us by the balls," Gordy grumbled.

"Or Parks," Sumit added. "He's quite powerful and has shown no love for The Chip."

"I just don't buy it." Jake shook his head. "He was a lively kid five years ago. Not the most intelligent, but he had a good heart. This just doesn't fit his profile. I'm wondering if that lab at McMurdo had Max2 and it was released by accident during the attack."

"Or the attack was all about releasing it," Sumit stated. "Parks could have hacked an army."

"With the Argentine government's support?" Jake was very skeptical.

"There is so much misinformation these days, it would be easy to misdirect a government," Sumit added. "Maybe Parks himself is hacked."

Jake watched the last of Shanghai's lights disappear in the ship's rear-camera view. He leaned in toward Sumit. "I read Parks never replaced his Chip after he cut it out during the 2030 raid on Morris."

Sumit shook his head. "We've heard other rumors."

"Any confirmations?" Jake asked.

"No," Gordy stated. "But there remains the distinct possibility that Parks is being framed by one of the opposing factions. Either way, he's on a short list of public enemies."

Sumit snorted. "Framed? Parks misdirects the public every day. The DOP blew up a biogenetics lab in India last year. Parks found the bombers in his own church and handed them over, stating that neither he nor his church condoned the behavior. And yet mosques and other facilities continue to be destroyed and members of his church are always implicated."

"It's all so senseless," Anjali stated.

Jake chuckled to himself. On any other day if someone had diagnosed him with a brain tumor he might have been depressed about it. Given the circumstances, there was little reason to fear death by cancer. Death was piloting the ship for the entire human race. It remained to be seen if humanity would be able to wrestle back control.

Chapter 36
Strains

Jake awoke to a twinge of lower back pain. His mattress was more about form than function. He stared up at a steel frame supporting the upper bunk. It was empty. He turned his head and checked the bunk adjacent to him. Gordy was absent.

They had landed in Mumbai last night 22:00 New Year's Day, gaining two hours during their journey west. As promised, Gordon had radioed ahead and a remote tow was sent out to meet them on the NTI HJ charging platform. The robot vehicle dragged their ship to a small hangar where they were encapsulated inside a plastic bubble. Instruments checked the air going in and out of their sealed environment and measured every particle clinging to their ship. It was 2:00AM before the ship was cleared and they were allowed to exit the HJ. They had walked down a plastic tunnel that led to sealed living quarters within a bio lab. The NTI sensors found radioactive particles on their ship and their persons, but the level was within acceptable limits. Other trace elements were found as well, but no MaxWell or any other nano-virus.

An NTI executive let Gordon know that the scientists at the Shanghai Emergency Center had been added to the list of rescue targets. Less than ten percent of the Shanghai population survived the attack. It was estimated that between the two attacks, ninety million Chinese had died on New Years Day. The good news was, it seemed the nano-virus had burned itself out before it could jump to other populations. Anjali shook her head at that news. She was convinced Max2 was global now, but somehow a trigger mechanism kept the death toll localized to Shanghai.

Their new home contained a common room, a bathroom, and two bunk-rooms with four beds each. Anjali and Sumit shared a room while Gordy and Jake shared the other. Everyone was exhausted. Jake didn't even remember his head hitting the pillow.

Jake made his morning routine visit to the bathroom and walked out into the common area. It was an odd place with four aluminum-framed hospital gurneys, a massive fiberglass scanner, two medical robots, and a sheet of glass separating common room from an observation lab. The scanner hummed with activity. He recalled the boiler room where Doctor Morris had swapped his Gen 4 chip and revealed the truth about his "visions." Unlike the boiler room, this place was sterile and clean, but equally sinister. He did not like the idea of being a caged guinea pig once again.

He stood at the glass and gazed at the lab beyond. Two Indian women in white coats milled about. One was tall, thin, and young. The other was short, stocky, with large swaths of gray in her black hair. The older one stopped when she noticed him staring at her. She spoke into her wrist Omni with a British accent. "Good morning, Jake.

He guessed she was around fifty. "You're not chipped?"

"We took Dr. King's request seriously. We have non-chipped personnel wiping down the interior of your HJ as well," she responded.

He pointed to the equipment. "Is that disconnected from the Cyber-Wire?"

"Yes, we're in an isolated lab. Nothing will interfere with getting an accurate report."

He pointed a thumb over his shoulder. "Who's in the scanner?"

"Doctor King."

He gazed at the monster fiberglass-clad box. "How long does it take?"

"About an hour." She smiled. "In addition to internal imaging, it tests blood, urine, saliva and tissue."

He was not looking forward to his visit with the box. "Are the others awake?"

"Yes, but the Maliks have not left their quarters."

"How long until Gordy's out?" he asked.

"Roughly twenty minutes." Her eyes were warm and compassionate. He liked her. The young tall one never broke away from her data collecting during the entire conversation. It made him nervous, but that was probably a good thing. He'd hate to have to redo any tests due to negligence or human error.

"Any signs of Max2?" he asked.

"You have a nano-virus." She looked back at her colleague. "We're determining if it matches Dr. Malik's description before we confirm… So far, it's matching."

He walked up to the glass with alarm. "How did we get past the scans of our HJ?"

"A hack." She glanced at him. "Don't jump to conspiracy theories yet. Hacking bio-labs has been commonplace since the outbreak of MaxWell last summer. We're constantly upgrading our security measures. Every lab in the building is a walled garden and we communicate via encrypted Omni on localized channels."

He couldn't believe what he was hearing. "How long have we been infected?"

She shrugged. "Not enough data yet. We have nine labs in addition to this one testing your contagion. We've requested the autopsy results on the Argentine troops as well as samples of the Shanghai victims." The tall one walked over and they began pointing to data on holo-screens and discussing in low tones.

"And?" Jake was anxious to know.

She returned to the window. "It has one hell of a program for something so tiny. It can exist in a host and reacts to different sound vibrations in order to activate a host's sweat glands or a sneeze to disperse it to other hosts. It multiplies quite easily without triggering a host's immune system. It attacks and kills all other nano-viruses it comes in contact with. It only damages a host when triggered via sound or microwave. It becomes active the second it is inhaled or put in contact with a host's soft tissue. It can be picked up from any surface and will work its way into a pore if it does not come in contact with eyes, nose, or a mouth within ten minutes. Once inside a host, it uses any host cell to replicate itself, multiplying every thirty seconds. Within ten minutes there are enough of them to begin triggering a release through a sneeze or sweat to infect other hosts."

Jake rubbed his hands. His palms were sweaty as of late.

"We have yet to find a complex organism that it does not like." She turned slightly and smiled. "Good to see you, Doctor Malik."

Jake spun around to see Anjali walk in with wet hair pulled back in a new yellow dotted nano-headscarf. Water spots adorned her clothes, as if she had taken a shower and put on her outfit without the intermediate step of using a towel. She pointed to the scarf on her head. "Thank you, Doctor Easwaran. Please continue."

"It's heartier than Max1. Nemps do not kill it. Living outside a host in temperatures between negative fifteen and thirty five degrees Celsius do not kill it either."

"I calculate it will override a chipped host within two hours—six in a non-chipped host." Anjali pointed at the machine currently digesting Gordy. "I'm next."

"Override?" Jake asked.

"Take over." Anjali faced Jake. "When Max2 reaches critical mass, it can gather on a Chip and override it, or gather near a host's brainstem and reconfigure into a Chip."

Easwaran forced a smile on her face. "We don't have enough data to substantiate that claim."

"I'm next." Sumit entered. His hair was wet, too, but he looked dry everywhere else.

Anjali raised her hand. "Already next."

"Then I'm third," Sumit replied.

"I thought the priority was Mr. Travissi?" Dr. Easwaran questioned.

Sumit shook his head. "Not since Prime Minster Shekawat told us about the press conference."

Easwaran smiled. "Congratulations on finding the cure for MaxWell. I hope it's not drowned out by the spread of our new nano-virus."

"We might have cured both," Sumit corrected. "We have yet to test 643 on Max2."

Anjali's nervous demeanor returned. "Or have you?"

Easwaran frowned. "I don't have results yet."

"Regardless, the government wants positive news to give people hope." Sumit glowed. "They're going to hold off on publicly announcing Max2 until you've identified all its attributes."

Anjali shook her head and sat down on a gurney.

"Others have been testing since General Tsang uploaded the formula for 643." Sumit beamed. "He was good enough to give us credit."

Jake frowned. "I was shot with 643 and I'm still infected. It doesn't work."

Easwaran raised her finger. "We don't know that. Your dose of 643 could have been contaminated. You might not have been infected at the time. You might have been re-introduced to Max2. There are too many variables. We just started collating the data and conducting new tests."

"How long will it take to figure out if 643 works?" Jake asked Doctor Easwaran as the younger scientist approached and whispered in her ear. He spotted the ID badge on the younger scientist. Her name was Doctor Bhagwat. Easwaran raised her finger with a smile and joined Bhagwat to review data.

"Have you been in contact with the international community? Are they testing for Max2? What's the infection rate?" Anjali asked.

Easwaran checked some data quickly then returned to the threshold of glass. "The data we're receiving from outside this facility is maddening. It's as though the Cyber-Wire has a virus as well. I see projections of fifty to ninety percent of the world population being infected. Every lab testing for this particular nano-virus has found it."

Bhagwat returned and showed Easwaran some data. Jake took the opportunity to ask about Anjali's headscarf. "Is that a spin on Parks' MaxWell death meter?"

She reached up and touched it and looked surprised that it was there. "Oh. This. No, each nano-dot represents an endangered species on the planet—animals. It's a hobby."

Jake blinked. "You have time for hobbies?"

Easwaran frowned. "Two hours and it has taken over a chipped host." She regarded Anjali with more respect. "We're officially calling it Max2."

Anjali jumped off the bed and began pacing. She muttered, "It's as if someone stole it from our lab and perfected it… 643 will kill it. Has to kill it."

Easwaran continued. "We're trying to figure out what trigger will cause it to build a Chip in a non-chipped host. It certainly has everything it needs to do so, even a matrix to create nano-filaments and connect to a host's brain once it forms a Chip."

Cold fear chilled Jake's spine. "So this one was designed to deliberately infect those who refused immunization? It infects anyone with or without a Chip?"

Easwaran shook her head. "I don't have all the data yet—"

"Cut the crap," he demanded.

Her eyes darted to Anjali and she nervously licked her lips. "Based on what we've gathered… I would say yes."

His blood went cold. "So once it's activated, a person has six hours before they're chipped?"

She shook her head. "Six hours to reach critical mass inside the body." She nodded to the scanner. "Doctor King has enough in his system to form several Chips. The Max2 in his system hasn't been activated yet. We don't know why."

Anjali rapped her knuckles against the glass. "Does Max2 show the ability to communicate with simple short-range emissions?"

Easwaran approached her. "Yes, it does."

Anjali held up her wrist Omni. "Can you feed me everything you have on it?"

"Of course."

The door to the lab exploded inward and hurled itself directly at Jake. He dove off the bed and would have been crushed if it hadn't been for the glass wall separating him from the main lab. The concussion knocked over both doctors. Easwaran's face smashed against the transparent barrier.

Chapter 37
Terrorists

The door fractured the glass at the impact point. Easwaran's blood flowed along spider webs in the barrier. Bhagwat's broken body lay over a toppled equipment table. Two men wearing Indian Army uniforms ran past the doorway. One of them tossed a grenade into the lab. Sumit dove out of the common room toward the bunk areas. Jake threw himself on top of Anjali to shield her from the window. The explosion was muffled and he felt nothing. He turned around and saw the glass wall was almost solid white with fractures. It could collapse at any second. The glass began to brown and he saw hints of orange behind it. The lab was on fire.

Claxons rang. Overhead lights blinked out. Small emergency lights snapped on. Sprinklers sprung out of the ceiling. Water gushed down, instantly soaking everything.

"Sumit?" Anjali lunged down the hallway after him.

Jake recalled the entrance to their little prison. There were no handles on the inside of the main door. Their best bet was smashing through the weakened glass in this room. "Wait!" he shouted after her. "How do I get Gordy out of this thing?" But Anjali was gone. He splashed his way over to the massive scanner, which had Dr. King buried in its guts. He searched for an off switch. He spotted a panel near the back and tried to pry it open. When that didn't work, he pulled a side rail off one of the beds and used it to club the cover. Four switches with a few lights were revealed. He spotted a big red button and hit it.

The machine wound down until all that could be heard was the sound of the alarm mixed with rain hitting the wet tiled floor. He ran around to the front of the machine, wondering if he'd need to use the side rail to break open the doors. A loud *whunk-hiss* was followed by the doors parting and a slab sliding out of the machine's bowels like a large tongue.

Gordy leapt onto the floor the moment he was free. "What the hell is going on?" A pair of shorts was his only apparel.

Anjali and Sumit barreled into the room. No sooner did they enter than an explosion ripped through the hallway behind them. The concussion caused the glass wall to buckle outward. Fire licked and blackened the other side.

"Break the glass!" Jake yelled as he ran for cover at the edge of the doorframe. He needed to be sure no invaders were going to attack from that direction. He raised the steel side rail like a baseball bat. He heard a gurney smashing into the glass partition behind him. From the sound of it, they had not broken through.

Rapid gunfire howled from the open doorway. Bullets buzzed inches from his arm and pummeled the glass behind him. Heavy footfalls pounded toward him. He gripped the side rail and swung with all his strength at the figure tromping out of the hall.

The stainless steel bedrail cracked into a bullet shield on the invader's military helmet causing the head to snap back and the feet to sail into the air. The figure slammed into the wet floor. Jake readied himself for another strike, but the figure did not move. He pulled the body toward him, careful not to expose himself to the sightline of the hallway.

"How's that window coming?" he shouted over his shoulder.

A loud crash answered him followed by flames sizzling under sprinklers. He glanced back to see Gordy splashing water onto a small flame dancing in Anjali's hair. Steam diminished Jake's visibility. He yanked the helmet off the Indian soldier and took the machine gun. The soldier's head lay twisted back in an unnatural way. The neck vertebrae had been shattered along with the helmet's face shield. He spotted the node on the back of the helmet and frowned. There were no radios inside a chipped soldier's headgear. He put the helmet on for protection, snapping off the fractured face shield.

"Gordy! I'm going back out the way we came in!" He shouldered the soldier's belt and pack. "Gordy, Sumit, Anjali!"

"Right here!" Gordy was three feet behind. The water vapor was beginning to dissipate from the heat of the lab fire.

He handed the bedrail to Gordy. "Aim for the neck."

Jake cautiously led the party into the hall. They had steam for cover and he crouched his way forward. The Doctors Malik brought up the rear of their small column. Jake stopped at the intersection between the bunkrooms and the bathroom. He fired a burst in either direction then shot into the charred entryway that had been blocked by a door minutes prior. He ran to the entrance, placed his arms outside the door and fired in all directions. Then he popped his head out of their quarantine suite to make a quick evaluation. The hall outside was empty. He waved at Gordy and the others to follow, then stepped out of the charred entryway.

They found themselves in a long corridor. Claxons blared, sprinklers rained and lights were dim. Jake felt uneasy facing Chipped soldiers under any circumstances; but he was twice as nervous under these conditions. The enemy utilized heat sensors and night vision. He was more or less blind. He moved toward an intersecting corridor where bits of flame tried to jump past a shower of rain. As he reached the intersection, a yellow dart slammed into the side of his pack. Before the soldier could squeeze off another shot, Jake fired his automatic weapon down the flaming wet hall. The soldier crashed into a wall and tumbled to the floor. Blood sprayed past the flame and water.

Sumit shrieked after getting hit with blood.

The doorway ahead burst open and four soldiers marched in with guns aimed at Jake's party. The soldier in front shouted, "Drop your weapons!"

Jake pulled his trigger but the firing pin clicked on metal. His clip was empty. "Shit." He cursed as a yellow dart slammed into his shoulder. He ripped it out and flung it against the wall. He could tell by the burning sensation coursing through his veins he was drugged once again.

"On the floor! All of you!" the soldier shouted.

Jake leaned against the wall and allowed himself to slide down, fighting to maintain consciousness as long as possible.

As the rest of the party lay down in the puddles building up on the tiled floor, the four soldiers convulsed and pitched forward, revealing two men with guns in the doorway behind. These new assailants used silencers.

Drowsiness swept over Jake and he fought to keep his eyes open. He noticed a wave of blood moving toward them in the water.

Chapter 38
Dope

A wave of ants crawled through Jake's blood stream, into his muscles, and under his skin. His heart quickened and the odd feeling of an adrenaline rush, followed by the nervous tick of having drunk ten cups of coffee after staying up for twenty-four hours rolled through him. When he opened his eyes, he spied the blue dart sticking out of his thigh. Then he felt the needle buried in his muscle and the ache around it, as if someone had driven it in with a hammer.

Gordy stood over him, an HK V2 in his hand. He shivered under a riot coat draped over his shoulders. He was still naked except for a pair of shorts. "We've got to move!"

Jake jerked the blue dart from his leg and tossed it next to the yellow one. He tried to stand but his head swam. He rubbed cool water on it and felt the scar from Christmas Eve.

Gordon raised his weapon. "Want me to hit you again?"

Jake grimaced. "Is this some kind of sick revenge for darting you back in Arizona?"

Gordy smiled. "Ten seconds or you get a second round. We've still got enemies about."

Jake pulled himself up and noticed he and Gordy were alone. "Where are the others?"

Gordy turned to head out the way their rescuers had come in. "Getting the hell out of here."

Jake was half way up the wall. He grunted, fighting the urge to vomit. The two drugs made a nasty cocktail that wreaked havoc on his system. Plus, he couldn't remember his last decent meal. "What's going on?"

"The Order of Erasmus has a few military cells left in certain cities. Mumbai is one of them." Gordon pulled Jake up on his feet and pushed him toward the door. "They were monitoring us from the outside."

"Thank God for The Order," Jake said half-heartedly as he pushed himself as hard as he could to keep up with Gordy. The effects of the drugs made it feel like his body was halfway around the world and he was controlling it remotely. It didn't respond like it should. "Who the hell attacked us? Looked like Devanagari Regulars."

They turned a few corners and exited into a warehouse. Daylight poured through the cargo doors at the far end. The room was hot and thick with Mumbai humidity. There were six or seven figures in black riot gear. Gordy led Jake to an armored car with an NTI logo.

"I believe they were army regulars," Gordy answered. "Obviously hacked." The door slid open on the armored car.

"Where's our HJ?" Jake asked.

"In a million pieces, three stories up." Gordon gestured for Jake to get in. Inside, Jake saw the Doctors Malik as well as one woman in riot gear. At least he thought it was a woman based on the curves of the body under the armor. All Gordy's troops wore their face shields down. The trooper handed Gordy a towel, some clothes and an Omni. Gordy began drying off and dressing at a tactical station next to her. From the holo-images, Jake could see there were ten similarly dressed agents taking out the hacked Devanagari. The network of laboratories was in shambles.

A voice rang out over the intercom. "Sir. The facility is locked down. We're ready to hand everything back to NTI security."

"Hold a minute," Gordy responded by speaking into a microphone on the console.

"Sir." The woman trooper called up a POV image on the central display recorded by an agent's helmet cam. The image showed a corpse lying on the floor of a storage room wearing God Head gear. Everyone's attention was drawn to the image.

The voice of the agent wearing the helmet came on. "Are you receiving this, Erasmus?"

"Yes," Gordy responded.

The camera moved in. Black gloves entered the lower part of the frame. The corpse wore a double-helix Parks pin that changed color from red, to black, to white and back again. The gloves pulled a crucifix out from the God Head's t-shirt. The gloves gripped and ripped the necklace from the body. The crucifix was turned so everyone could see the blue line drawn on the back. "Looks like our God Head is a Dope."

"Dope?" Jake asked.

"DOP," Anjali answered in a half dazed state as she watched the images. "Disciples of Paul. Your friend Parks' organization."

Gordy turned to Jake. "Looks like Parks was trying to bring you in."

Jake frowned but kept his thoughts to himself. *Then why send a man into our quarters with a machine gun? They should have all been armed with darts. Why strike just when we're gathering worldwide information on Max2? Why destroy our HJ?*

"Did the data survive?" Anjali asked.

Gordy spoke into a microphone on the console. "Check the backup drives for all the labs. Take everything."

Another voice came over the intercom. "Nothing is left of the labs. They hit those first and hardest."

Gordy brought up an encrypted link to the NTI lab network. A technician appeared on the screen. "Doctor King."

"Agnes, the Mumbai labs were attacked during testing. We're trying to figure out if we should go back into quarantine."

Agnes looked worn out and scared. "Since you were brought in last night, labs around the world have conducted random testing. We're all infected. We're still trying to find a human or animal that doesn't have it." She paused, trying to digest the reality of it all. "World leaders have been informed. Until we can figure out where it originated and if the entire population is carrying Max2, it's business as usual. In fact, the politicians want to keep the worldwide conference announcing the cure for Max1 as scheduled. They want people to have hope. They won't spread panic until they can figure out the size of the epidemic."

Gordy licked his lips. "We'll figure it out."

Agnes let out a desperate laugh. "This is beyond the CDC or any form of containment. With Max2's properties, no one exhibits sickness until a command code is given. Somebody snuck this one in while we've been working so hard on Max1. You'd have to be lost at sea or buried in a jungle for the past week not to have contracted it."

Jake wanted to kick himself.

Agnes talked fast and wrung her hands. "You breathe the same air as someone carrying it, you contract it. You touch a handle on a door a week after a carrier touched it, you'll contract it. Max2 is hearty and it's everywhere. It seems to like anything with a complex nervous and vascular system. It's the superman of the nano-virus kingdom."

Anjali held up her Omni to record every word. "Does 643 have any effect against Max2?"

Agnes shook her head. "Hundreds of labs received 643's configuration. It's great against Max1, but has no effect against Max2. Although they are very similar in nature, Max2 kills 643 just as fast as it kills Max1. We're attempting to hack the Max2 matrix and reprogram it, but it's a race now. Whoever designed and released the Max2 nano-virus must be getting close to sending out the signal to unite all the viruses. We're on a collision course to becoming a planet of Pin Heads."

Gordy exhaled and stared into space for a second. "Okay… Thanks, Agnes. Keep me informed."

Agnes nodded and the signal snapped off.

Anjali plunked heavily into a chair, shaking her head and muttering to herself.

Gordy leaned over and spoke into the microphone. "Everyone back to base."

Sumit rubbed Anjali's back. "We have to do this press conference. We can't tell the world there's another threat out there with no cure and no idea where and when it will strike. Society will implode."

Anjali stopped her calculations and eyed her husband with disdain. She seemed to be literally biting her tongue.

Gordy rubbed his bald crown. He shook from the constant abuse of SleepX. "My troops need to get out of here before we turn control back to NTI security and the local authorities. They need to keep their anonymity."

They all followed Gordy out of the vehicle. Once the transport was filled with the black-clad agents, the door closed and sealed. They watched the NTI armored car head out of the warehouse into a midmorning January rain.

Jake turned to Gordy. "How do you keep them anonymous? An attack like this and I'd think the Indian Government would have ten detectives investigating."

"Governments have their hands full with MaxWell, volatile borders, and extremist groups. Besides, this attack falls under ICTA, the International Corporate Terrorism Act. International corporations have a right to protect themselves and can get involved with aiding the local authorities when financial interests are at stake. NTI employs a few hundred thousand Indians. The Indian police and NTI officers will study surveillance footage and security scanners of the attack. Each of my agents is registered as NTI security. Their false identities will show up in all the footage and scans. Under ICTA, a corporation finding itself under a terrorist attack has the right to use lethal force, even against hacked infiltrators. As an executive officer of NTI, I'm allowed my own corporate sponsored security. Those agents fall under that clause."

Jake watched the armored transport disappear. "Rank has its privileges."

Gordon's smile twitched. "Only way to travel." He'd be crashing out soon if he didn't give his body more than a few hours of sleep.

After a minute passed, four NTI armored cars rolled in. The vehicles stopped, doors opened, and light armor security guards poured out. Several guards marched toward Jake's group. The guards scanned fingers, eyes, and Omnis to verify ID. Sumit, Anjali, and Gordy were cleared and Gordy used his executive privilege to keep Jake from being hauled off the premises.

A guard grabbed Jake's wrist and barked. "His Omni is registered to the Song lab in Beijing."

"It's a loaner," Sumit answered. "I loaned it to him when we were at that facility."

The guard dropped Jake's arm, satisfied.

Gordon did not look satisfied at all.

Once they were cleared, Sumit smiled. "I believe this is goodbye for now." He patted Anjali on the back. She was sitting on the floor, engrossed with photos of animals on her Omni. Her left hand traced calculations on the concrete. "We have a press conference to attend."

She slapped his knee. "Problem solving!"

"She going to be alright?" Jake asked.

Sumit forced a smile. "She's fine." Sumit shook Gordy's hand. "Thanks for saving our lives."

Gordy gave a half nod.

Sumit picked up Anjali and carried her into the rainy streets of Mumbai. She continued to stare into her Omni and compose a mathematical symphony with her left hand.

Gordon turned to Jake the moment Sumit disappeared from the warehouse. He pulled out a small tin from his front pocket. Orange SleepX pills lay inside.

"Shouldn't you be cutting back?"

"Too much to do." Gordy popped a pill. "What was your impression of the raid?" His hand convulsed as he shoved the tin back in his pocket.

"If Parks wants to make contact with me, he would have used a different tactic. I suspect someone else."

"Agreed. Every faction uses Pin Heads and red herrings to blame other parties for terrorist acts. It's all about keeping authorities confused and off the trail. Covering up a mass infection of Max2 is far bigger than the DOP or Jihad Brotherhood. Everything we've encountered smells like stalling tactics."

"What's next?"

Gordy glanced at Jake's Omni.

"You think?"

"I don't want to take any chances. But I say wear it for now." Gordy pulled off his Omni and pressed a button. It formed a rigid tablet within seconds. He typed. "I'm sending you the address of a bar about a mile from here. You can walk, or cab it, but either way I won't be there until 17:00." Gordy hit send. "I've got *administrative* work to do until then."

The address and map appeared on Jake's Omni. "Got it."

"Take in some sights, enjoy Mumbai." Gordy's face displayed three ticks.

"You want me spotted?"

Gordy touched his nose. "The Omni is an obvious tracking device. But if somebody with real resources is searching for you they can place a subroutine in the subconscious of every chipped person on the planet. Everyone with a Third Eye is a passive surveillance system, and they would be completely unaware of their involvement."

"That means six billion pairs of eyes could be passively searching for me worldwide?"

"That's one reason we've been in private vehicles whenever possible. I can easily mask the occupants, but I can't fight all those eyeballs walking around." He tapped Jake's Omni. "Or an inside signal reaching out."

"If that's the case, how do you keep your team anonymous?"

"Facial prosthetics, plastic surgery, or faith that there's too much going on right now to look beyond obvious targets."

Jake wanted to trust him, but he just wasn't sure. "At the risk of sounding like a self-centered asshole, have you thought about Tomoko?"

Gordy's eyes went wide. "Ninety million people died yesterday and the rest of the world has been diagnosed with a viral form of The Chip. I always pegged you as a big picture guy."

"If the end is coming, I want her by my side."

A look of anger mixed with guilt flashed on Gordy's face. "I'm spread pretty thin."

Jake wondered if Gordy was feeling guilt about his chipped partner. "Then what are you offering Parks?"

Gordy sighed and wiped the sweat off his brow with a shaky hand. "I still have forty key people throughout the world that can make a difference. Parks has his weapons factories and an army of cult followers. Together we can beat The Consortium; apart we stand to fail… I'm meeting with a cell tonight. Tomoko will be on our agenda."

Jake nodded. "If I'm not at the Punjab by 5:00PM, you'll know Parks or some other terrorist group picked me up."

"I doubt anyone will get near you until after you make contact with Parks. I haven't put all the pieces together yet, but he's a key to all of this."

Chapter 39

Dream Spun

Jake loved the rain. It had been non-existent in his last years living in LA. Rain was becoming a rare occurrence everywhere in the world. He turned his face into the cool rejuvenating drops and relished their caress. The smell made him feel as if all bad things were being washed away and the world was getting another chance. He stood for a good minute, letting the water trickle beneath his collar and tickle his chest and back. He tilted his head down, wiped his eyes and walked east. All it would take to make this moment perfect would be the company of Tomoko and Lakshmi.

When the rain stopped, it left a hot, humid steam behind. It clung to his clothes, trapped perspiration in his pores, and was heavy to breathe. The smell of rotting garbage drifted through the congested streets. If he were on the *Pachacuteq* he'd strip naked, but that would be ill advised in a city of more than eighteen million, with or without Chips.

He was swept up by the pedestrians flowing around the sluggish traffic that hummed past garbage-soaked gutters. Despite a ninety percent chipped population, Mumbai continued to have trouble controlling its trash levels. Bikes, cars, rickshaws, mules, goats, dogs, and monkeys choked every avenue between the buildings. A stench of mildew, bad breath, and a hint of animal feces filled the oppressive air. Bodies continuously brushed against him. The sheer size of the population made it impossible to keep a perimeter of personal space. A Chip would make this city tolerable. He smiled at how fast his mood changed the moment the rain ceased.

He gazed with envy at the air-conditioned cars that rolled past. He followed the flow of traffic between the massive towers built at the beginning of the millennium. Giant holo-banners circled the space around the buildings, displaying a myriad of advertisements to the crowd below. He was thankful India was a chipped nation because the banners silently beamed audio directly into the minds around him.

The rain returned. Many citizens opened umbrellas while others sported nano-skin apparel that ballooned out to shed water. A loud *crack* followed by Sitar music caused him to look up. The audio for the holo-projectors had switched on. He tried to stop but the traffic pushed him forward as hundreds of holographic Indian flags flapped in front of the holo-displays above. Rain shrouded the images near the tops of the skyscrapers. He spotted a projector closer to street level.

He ducked away from the pedestrian river and hugged the wall of a business tower in order to check out the broadcast. It must be important if they were turning on the city's external speakers. He locked his vision on the hologram hovering over a café across the street. Everyone around him slowed down and stopped.

Vajnu Shekawat, the Prime Minister of India, appeared throughout the city. She looked like a child lovingly staring at her ant farm. Jake unfastened his Omni and put it to his ear for a translation. He was surprised when she addressed her country in English.

"My fellow citizens. It is with great joy that I tell you the worst is behind us. We have discovered a cure for the MaxWell virus that does not require the use of a Third Eye." Her image shrank revealing Sumit and Anjali standing at her side. Both wore medals pinned to their shirts.

Sumit beamed with pride. Anjali looked terribly uncomfortable. The Prime Minister continued. "Those who have feared a mandatory immunization can live free of The Chip."

The noise level rose. Citizens were actually talking to each other, many cheered and applauded. The Prime Minister gestured to Sumit and Anjali. "I am standing here with the two brave pioneers who engineered the cure. This is Doctor Anjali Malik and her husband, Doctor Sumit Malik. Be proud India, for they were born on our soil. In the past several months, they have tirelessly worked with their team at NTI laboratories to heal our world. Their cure has been shared with the international community in hopes that we can end the unrest and bring order where there was once chaos."

The projectors switched back to advertising and the speakers snapped off. Citizens continued to cheer and hug each other. An Indian man gave Jake a big hug and proceeded to hug everyone else within arms reach. Jake was happy to see everyone so full of life until the reality of Max2 returned. He wanted to distance himself from the celebration as he navigated through the cheering crowd.

He reached an asphalt path that followed the concrete river channel. The water was high, brown, and moved faster than any of the traffic along its man-made banks. Sporadic cheers erupted around the city. Many vendors sat on blankets with tattered umbrellas over their heads, selling trinkets to passers-by. As Jake walked, many gestured for him to look but did not speak. They communicated Chip to Chip to anyone who would listen. He wondered how hard it must be to drown out the voices crashing together in your head. Then again, a person could always set up a privacy block.

He strolled past the desperate vendors. Even with all the advances in the past twenty years, some things never changed. As he navigated under a tree-lined portion of the concrete riverbank, he was shocked to see a row of merchants sitting in lotus position, eyes closed, and holo-projectors flashing images above their heads. The holographs reminded him of Bollywood movies, only the colors were more vibrant and the visuals were surreal.

He parked in front of a man who reminded him of Mohandas Gandhi during his later years. The man rocked back and forth with his eyes shut.

Images of colored clouds dancing around mountain streams floated above his head. The hologram morphed into a vibrant scene of Vishnu and Ganesha sailing on a golden barge. The image blurred into a six-legged and claw-armed man crawling out of a crab hole. The hole collapsed into a ball and shot into the air. A bare-chested archer steering a golden chariot shot the ball with an arrow. Jake marveled at the images and was shocked when they disappeared. He glanced down and realized Gandhi was staring at him.

"If you like what you see, you can download them to your Omni. But the experience is far richer if you have a Third Eye." Gandhi's English betrayed a slight Indian accent.

Jake gazed at the benevolent man. His eyes were watery behind his glasses. Third Eyes corrected eyesight, so why have glasses at all? And this pair was not a reconfigured Omni.

As if he could hear Jake's thoughts, Gandhi took the glasses off and held them up. "Placebos. I think they make me look wise. Wouldn't you say?"

"They make you look like Gandhi."

"You see!" he answered with a toothless grin. "They work!"

Jake reflected on the man's original offer. He checked out the other holographic dream vendors. Yes, that was it. He turned to the smiling man sitting by his feet. "These are dreams. You're selling your dreams?"

The man cocked his head to one side. "Dreams, day dreams, visions, yes all for sale. But with a Third Eye you experience them with all five senses and have insight into the dreamer's emotions. You not only escape, you become the dream!"

Now here was a whole new world of addiction. Jake rubbed his jaw. "I prefer being rooted in my own head, thanks."

Gandhi pointed to the other crazy landscapes playing above his colleagues. "It is the latest craze. Far better than movies or games."

"Doesn't look like there's much of a plot."

The man laughed. "Plot is old millennium thinking! The twenty-first century is about experience. Now that they sell Starbucks on the top of Mount Everest and on the moon, the only new path of enlightenment is through your Third Eye channeling Dream Spun."

"Ever see documentaries about Acid Queens in the 1960s?" Jake winked. "Besides, I thought India was about the spiritual. A drug by any other name is still a drug. It takes away from the spiritual."

"No drug." Gandhi shook his head. "To dream is to experience the spiritual. You are limited by your Western mind. You think in Western terms."

"You speak English very well."

"As one who has experienced the Third Eye, you should know The Chip translates for both of us. I am thinking in Hindi and my Chip is pushing English out of my mouth."

"A nice way of putting it. But why keep an accent?"

The man bowed his head. "People want authenticity. The accent helps my sales."

"Is English the official language of India?"

The man smiled. "No official language. Too many languages spoken here for all to agree."

"What's with your weather? I thought your monsoon season was in September?"

"The only constant is change." The man smiled. "Or put another way, the world is not what it used to be."

Jake sighed. "You can say that again."

"Nice to see you again, Jackhammer."

Jake froze. He leaned in closer to stare into the watery eyes before him. They betrayed a faraway stare. He wondered how far into the conversation the hack had taken place. "Who am I speaking to?"

"Don't be a Travesty, Jake-o-saur! It's me!"

The nicknames could only mean one person. "Parks."

The little man smiled and opened his arms. "Livin' large, baby!"

It was very disturbing watching an old Indian man moving like a marionette to the will of another. "I thought you Dopes didn't believe in getting chipped."

"You don't need a Chip to be a God Head. In fact, most God Heads are against Third Eyes, or were until MaxWell came along. The man in front of you is not a Disciple of Paul. He's just a Dream Spinner. But we hack a lot of them so we can put our messages in their products subliminally."

Jake crossed his arms. "That's a nasty tactic."

Gandhi rolled his eyes. "We're at war, Jake. You taught me that."

"I did?"

"It was you and Morris who hacked into my brain and forced me to see the truth. It killed Koren and just about finished me off, too. But I found strength in Jesus."

Jake raised an eyebrow. "I never know when the kidding stops and the sincerity starts."

"They're one in the same, Jackhammer. Life is a divine comedy."

"Can't say as I'm doing much laughing these days."

Gandhi laughed and slapped his knee. "Boy I miss you, Jake-o-rama. We should meet face to face. What are you doing this afternoon?"

"I'm meeting someone at 17:00."

"Ah yes, The Punjab—never been there."

Jake checked his Omni. "You hacked it that fast?"

The Indian smiled. "I wouldn't have survived this long if I didn't do everything fast."

Jake shook his head. "Give some credit to luck."

"Charm is the secret to all success, Jake-bone. All other talent is drawn to it. Without charm, you're no one." A holographic image of an armored car popped up over Gandhi's head. "I'll meet you after you have your little chat with Doctor King. I have a dream to share as well."

Before Jake could respond the little man winked, then dropped his head. Jake headed back toward the NTI lab. He needed to tell Gordy, but didn't trust any electronic device to do it.

Gandhi shouted. "Wait, my friend. I can show you more!"

Jake dove into the crowd. He turned and shouted back. "I've seen enough, thanks!"

Chapter 40
Regret

The cameras switched off and Prime Minister Shekawat shook Sumit's hand once more. "On behalf of India and the world, I cannot thank you enough. You're international heroes." Tears welled in her eyes. "Thank you. Thank you."

Sumit basked in the glow of praise and adulation. This moment was the culmination of years of planning and hard political lobbying. The worldwide media exposure and the medals on their shirts meant they could dictate terms to any and all corporate sponsors. They would retire in comfort and celebrity. The future was assured.

Anjali's voice felt like napalm falling on paradise. "How long before you announce Max2?"

Prime Minister Shekawat pulled Anjali aside but continued to smile. "That's a topic best left for private discourse. The world is in desperate need of hope. We don't want to return to the chaos we saw last summer. The world leaders have agreed to ease the public into the idea."

Anjali stared back at the Prime Minister. "Six billion chipped means you can control the reaction…"

"Keep up the good work." She patronizingly patted Anjali's hand and left the room with her entourage.

Sumit caught himself hyperventilating and feeling claustrophobic. His inner voice soothed. *Close your eyes and concentrate on deep, slow breaths.* He followed orders and suddenly felt a whole lot better.

Anjali pointed to the Prime Minister. "She's an alien from another planet. Popularity is a mystery… Most days I wish they'd lock me in a lab and throw away the key."

So do I. He hugged her. "I know what you mean." He held his wife and took in the multitude of news feeds spilling into the room from various consoles. His heart skipped a beat. The announcement of a cure without a Chip was rocketing in every direction. All over the world, people celebrated in the streets.

One story caught his eye. The United States started mandatory immunization on New Year's Day and were discontinuing the policy. It was a good thing too, as they projected running out of Chips after one week.

Anjali broke away. "Time to work."

He smiled at his wife. "I'll catch up in a bit."

"You've been strange since McMurdo."

A jolt of fear focused his attention on her. "I've just been preoccupied with the ten-thousand-foot view. We live in an age of publicity, Anj. With your condition, that leaves me to fight for our future."

"I never asked for this future." She took off her medal and pressed it in his hand. "I believe science, not pandering, elevates humanity."

Sumit laughed and condescendingly spoke. "That's okay, I love you anyway." He moved closer to one of the holo-displays. "I'll catch up with you at the lab."

She stormed out, muttering to herself.

One particularly noisy feed displayed a pundit giving her opinion of The Chip. "Despite the announcement of a cure, tales of mass death have appeared all over the Cyber-Wire since Shanghai's unexplained phenomenon, with reports of entire communities dropping dead en masse. With the nuclear strike on Beijing and the mystery deaths in Shanghai, the worldwide death toll since June is estimated at one hundred and twenty to one hundred and fifty million people. Yet world order has been maintained through the calming properties of Third Eyes. Chips are the thread that keeps the fabric of society together. Without them, we would be living in total anarchy."

Sumit rubbed Anjali's medal with his thumb as the soothing voice in his head eased his anxiety. He turned to another news feed. "The UN denounced the attacks on China while China's military declared martial law after its government was decimated yesterday. Chinese authorities announced they will attack twenty Muslim nations which they say are harboring the Jihad Brotherhood. They refuse to name their targets, saying quote; 'They deserve as much forewarning as they gave us.'"

Sumit focused on another feed. "Armies are massing on the borders between China and India. Nepal is in danger of being overrun. The UN has called for an emergency session of the Security Council. Russia requests a sit down with China's military leadership and the leaders of countries known to be harboring the Jihad Brotherhood, even though the Brotherhood continues to deny any involvement in the attacks."

The mention of Nepal moved Sumit's thoughts to painful memories of the Bachelor Wars and his brother's funeral. He squeezed the medal until it broke the skin on his palm. His inner voice dispersed the memory and he focused on a different feed.

"Doctor Singh comes to us live from the moon to address rumors that Luna's AI is a fully cognizant being."

Singh, a handsome Indian in his early forties, flashed a smile. "The loss of so many millions yesterday and the death of Ai-Li is devastatingly tragic. I understand why some people hope that Luna's AI project is in the final stages, but I assure you we are at least a year away from a birth phase."

Singh's image winked out and the reporter turned to the camera with a skeptical look. He wore one of Parks' solidarity pins. "Scientists who track Luna's AI project believe doctor Singh is downplaying their progress because of what happened in China. Coming up next: odd signals are detected in the background of The Cyber-Wire. Could it be evidence of AI, maybe even Ai-Li?"

Sumit turned his back on the myriad of feeds. His inner voice softly spoke. *Roller coasters drop before the next climb. Day follows night.* But would there be a sunrise for humanity after all this played out? He steeled himself with hope, but his elation after receiving his medal soured into an overwhelming sense of sadness and guilt. He opened his hand and saw the bloody Ahoka Chakra. It was given to those who showed bravery and self-sacrifice. Usually bestowed to people posthumously, it was India's highest honor. He suddenly felt unworthy of it.

He desperately needed some air.

Chapter 41

Punjab

It took Jake over an hour to find his way back to the NTI building. He relied on memory, not the Omni. The majority of people he passed were chipped, so asking for directions would have been simple, but the idea made him uneasy. He cherished the thought that he was one of the last humans still living on earth. Everyone else was a hybrid.

Two macaque monkeys flanked either side of NTI's entrance. They stood like the guards of Buckingham Palace. Each primate's coat displayed a jungle camouflage. A red diamond on each chest broke the pattern. They looked bigger than the wild macaques running on city balconies, and these displayed over-developed muscles. The macaques did not move when the code on his Omni allowed him entrance into the establishment. Once inside, the computer reception kiosk informed him that Gordon was indisposed. He'd have to wait in the lobby.

He took a seat next to an Indian woman who was also waiting. "What's with the monkeys?"

"Security," she replied in a polished British accent.

"Is that dye on their fur or does it grow that way?"

She looked surprised. "You haven't seen a spitting monkey before?"

"I'm new in town."

"You must have spent some time on the dark side of the moon." Her smile wavered. "Their hair grows like that, and they can shoot venom up to ten meters."

"Nice."

"Effective."

"Any other engineered animals I should know about?"

"If you came though the airport, you must have seen the Bengal tigers or the African baboons they use for security."

He shook his head. "My space ship landed on the roof of this building. I have yet to walk around and check out your town."

She flashed him an odd look then returned to the news on her Omni.

Five minutes later, the kiosk called her to the elevator. He passed time by looking up enhanced animals on his Omni. Sure enough, the Indian government employed thousands of enhanced Bengal tigers, Macaques, and imported baboons for security in public places. The Chip kept them under control and watching for trouble. The Bengal tigers were primarily used for intimidation, the macaques for searching luggage. The Baboons were for riot control. The tigers fascinated him, because they were engineered with nanite-strengthened teeth, claws, and bones that allowed them to tear through a solid inch of steel. Some were engineered to be twice the size of Bengals found in the wild. He wondered how big the droppings were; he'd hate to slip on one of those when trying to catch a flight at the airport.

There were several articles on animal rights activists protesting the practice. The US and many European countries banned genetically engineered animals. India, China, Russia, and a dozen African countries condoned the practice. They claimed enhanced animals were created with stem cells and clones and did not harm wildlife. In fact, because wildlife was dying out, they claimed their work would lead to the preservation of endangered species.

The debate lost steam during the first MaxWell outbreak. The former Prime Minister of India owned one of the massive Bengals as a pet. Jake studied several clips of the Prime Minister and his five children taking turns riding it like a horse.

His research was interrupted by a clean-up crew walking through the lobby. A few seconds later, two policemen came down from the upper floors. One of them took a seat next to him and took down his statement about events that occurred earlier that day. The man did not use a note pad or Omni. Jake assumed he was recording everything via a Chip and cross-referencing his statement with others. The interview lasted twenty minutes at which point the man thanked him for his time and promptly left.

At twenty minutes to five he received a message that he should proceed to The Punjab and wait for Gordy there. He followed Gordy's map and was at the bar in no time. The sun was gone but the evening remained muggy. He walked into The Punjab and was hit with thick hot humidity that reeked of body odor. *Nice spot, Gordy.*

The bar was dark and sparsely populated. He found a private booth and sat down. A man took his drink order and Jake waited with a whiskey neat. He craved a nice cold glass of water, but tap water was still bad for tourists and with the implementation of Third Eyes, there was no reason to fix the problem. The Chip could handle the bugs.

A little after 17:00, Gordy walked in and sat across from him.

"I'm meeting Parks after this conversation."

Gordon nodded and fished out an object from his cargo pants. "Here." He handed Jake a brand new Omni. Its skin was configured to look like nothing more than a leather band.

Jake took off his loaner Omni.

Gordon shook his head. "If Parks is using it to track you, then you need it until your next meeting. If it's The Consortium, we need them to think you don't know. I'm currently jamming all signals within a few feet in case that Omni is broadcasting more than your location."

Jake took the leather band. It even felt like leather. Nano-technology was improving all the time. "So what's special about this one?"

"It has an encryption scrambler to keep hackers out."

"Last defense against Max2?"

"Exactly." Gordy leaned back. "If all those little nano-viruses inside you decide to co-opt into a Third Eye, you'll have a secondary encryption barrier. Be sure to feed your Max2 Chip signal through the Omni and it will beef up the security on your brain by a thousand percent. Omni encryptions are tough to break. If your Max2 becomes a Chip, the field on that bracelet will stop any outside contact. Unless a Pin Head removes it from your wrist..."

Jake nodded. He knew about augmenting Chip security with Omnis. "Thanks for the security blanket." He put the leather band on his right wrist. "We've been doing an awful lot of jet-setting these days."

"We're being tracked, and we're helping to distribute the disease." Gordy yawned and scanned the bar. No one seemed to be paying any attention to them.

"You could use some rest."

"You look fabulous yourself." Gordon rubbed his twitching neck. "I'll sleep when I'm dead."

"Nice sentiment. Have you confirmed Max2 started in McMurdo?"

"The data is sporadic, but yeah, I'm sure. It's looking like Anjali's projections are correct. Ninety percent of the population is carrying Max2."

Jake thought about the world population celebrating the eradication of Max1. "How soon before Max2 is announced to the public?"

"Not sure they will. I wonder how many politicians are making deals with The Consortium. With ninety percent carrying, the writing is on the wall."

Anger brewed inside of Jake. "How much time do you think we have?"

Gordon leaned in. "However long The Consortium wants us to have. Maybe they're waiting to consolidate their power. Maybe they need an AI to come online. They're going to need one helluva super computer to control the billions of minds in circulation. There aren't enough God Heads on the planet."

"What about Shanghai? Or the troops at McMurdo? Isn't anyone putting two and two together?"

"Plenty of people are putting it together, but when it's announced, who will be cognitively aware enough to react?" Gordy popped a SleepX and chewed it. "The story on The Wire is that cyber-terrorists are to blame for Shanghai and Beijing. The Jihad Brotherhood and the DOP are the primary public enemies. The Consortium has them squarely in their sights."

"Based on your theory, why would The Consortium nuke Ai-Li?"

"Hard to say. Maybe Luna's AI is the AI of choice. Maybe the brotherhood did strike. The world is dividing into factions. The human race may be reduced to warring tribes once again before The Consortium restores order. The End of Days will not be pretty."

Jake reviewed their movements over the past week. "Seems pretty convenient that Shanghai and the NTI lab were hit within a few hours of our arrival." He held up his Chinese Omni. "You suspect this or the Doctors Malik?"

"Definitely the Omni, and Anjali is a likely candidate."

"Because she's quirky?"

Gordon shook his head. "Because she's the one in front of the data. She's the one who trips out. I'm starting to wonder if she's not chipped."

Jake doubted Gordy's theory. Then again, Max2 could form a Chip in her head without any outward indication. "If Anjali is a mole, how much damage would The Order sustain?"

Gordy leaned in. "I'm losing cells every day. We need Parks and I seriously doubt he's our problem. He's fighting in his own equally dangerous way, but we can focus him. If Anjali is working for The Consortium, The Order is dead."

"I thought the whole purpose of cells was so that The Order could survive without its leader?"

"I've had to consolidate. If I go, there will be a few cells left, but there won't be enough parts to make a fighting whole. Not in the time we have left."

Gordy nodded to Jake's Omni. "Go ahead and configure it. No time like the present."

Jake opened up the preferences on the new Omni and selected a new appearance from the menu. The Omni reconfigured into a simple chain bracelet with a flat metal face. The encrypt link would activate automatically if it detected a Chip in his body. He glanced up when he was done. "Not a big fan of the leather look."

Gordy smiled. "Nice to see you still care about aesthetics." He leaned in. "I've got a meeting on the other side of town at 19:00. I have to run." He knocked on the table. "And yes, Tomoko is still on my agenda. Why don't you contact me after you meet with Parks? Post in the local DOP chat room that you're a pigmy convert looking for a roommate with sickle cell anemia. I'll answer that I'm an albino."

"Did you just make that shit up?"

Gordy shrugged. "All my other strategies have been compromised lately." He stood up just as the barman appeared to take his order. Gordy addressed him as he pointed to Jake. "He'll take another." He turned to Jake. "You'll need it."

Chapter 42
Trigger

Jake lingered behind for fifteen minutes, savoring his second drink and reflecting on every event since Christmas Eve. Once again he regretted caving in to Tomoko's desire to spend Christmas in McMurdo. *Be here now. Focus. You've been given a key to help stem the tide and you must use it.* He sucked down the last of his whiskey and rode his buzz. He relished the false sense of empowerment because as soon as he stepped onto the street, reality would slap him in the face. He chuckled. Five years at sea had dulled his reflexes, and now alcohol swam in his bloodstream. Parks was going to have an easy time with him if he had any other agenda beyond saying his piece.

He stepped out of the bar and half expected to feel a yellow dart punch into his arm. The foot traffic was light, but cars filled the street at a slow choking pace. He shuffled toward the NTI lab, gazing about in hopes of spotting the Reverend Parks, or the vehicle Dream-Spun Gandhi had revealed to him.

A pair of headlights flashed as he stepped past an alleyway. He turned to see an armored van filling up the space between piles of trash. The vehicle was sleeker than the NTI models. Lights flashed again so he made his way toward the vehicle. He spotted Parks behind the windshield waving at him like some excited school kid. Parks pointed toward a sliding door on the side of the vehicle. Jake pushed over some bags of trash to get to it. One of them broke open and the stench of rotten food and God knows what else turned his stomach. The door slid open and he entered a cool climate-controlled cabin.

The door slid closed and sealed with a quick *hiss*. A light switched on, revealing an isolated compartment with two swivel chairs bolted to steel plating. He checked his new Omni. It was jammed.

Parks' voice crackled over a loud speaker. "Make yourself at home, Jackhammer."

He sat down and noticed a small box on the console.

"Merry Christmas..."

Jake grabbed the box and opened the lid. Inside was a military issue Omni. Combat Omnis were primarily used to broadcast short range Nemps, or augment security for Gen 8S Chips, even though that model was virtually impossible to hack. He turned the device over and saw the Cobalt Industries logo on the back.

"Your Chinese Omni is an open source beacon. I suggest you ditch it as soon as we part company." Parks was now seated alone behind a glass wall. "Your bracelet version seems to be clean."

Jake smiled as he pocketed the watch. It was safer to play the game. He spotted one of Parks' solidarity double-helix pins in the box. He held it up. "How much do I owe you?"

Parks winked. "On the house. That's one of the new models. It cycles between Max1 victims, immunized citizens, and Max2 kills."

"Where's your underage entourage?"

Parks laughed. "Fame and money always come with a disproportionate amount of defamatory rumors. You realize this is the first time we've met?"

Jake raised an eyebrow.

"Think about it. You were chipped the entire time we worked together."

"You've got a point, Reverend."

Parks clapped his hands. "Reverend! I love it. I always knew you had a sense of humor."

Jake felt the vehicle moving. "Where are we going?"

"Meandering. Parking only makes us an easier target."

Jake got comfortable in the chair closest to Parks. "You obviously went through a lot of trouble to get me here. What's on your mind?" A needle jammed into his buttock. He leapt off the seat. "Fuck!" He saw the needle disappear under the leather cover.

"I'll have the test results in a minute. Take a seat. I promise not to poke you again."

Jake was about to insist on standing but the vehicle lurched and he gripped the seat back to steady himself. "I could have saved you the trouble of sticking me in the ass. I have Max2."

"I'm sure you've heard a lot of things since your return to civilization, Jake. But, it's not like you to take things at face value. It certainly isn't in your character to go forging ahead without a plan."

He flopped back in the chair and stared at Parks through the glass. "Maybe I've gotten soft in my old age." There were readouts on the panel behind Parks but the Reverend ignored them. The white silk-suited reverend wore four Omnis, two for each wrist. One looked like a gold Bulgari watch, the other a diamond band, another in the shape of a platinum band, and one was a gold band with a crucifix. They could fool you at a glance, but Jake knew the real deal from camouflage. "What's with all the Omnis?"

"Protection."

There was only one reason to have so many Omni devices. Parks was feeding his Chip signals through the Omni encryption fields to keep out any hackers. Chips featured encryption by design, but one Omni contained a thousand times the security capacity over a Third Eye. Wearing four Omni's gave Parks serious redundancy in protection. "You're chipped."

"Shhh! Most of my flock doesn't know. But my enemies do." Parks rubbed his crucifix Omni. "A healthy dose of paranoia never hurt anybody."

Jake winked. "Is that in Corinthians?"

"Jake Travissi 101. You taught me a lot of things."

Jake shook his head. "I don't remember teaching you much of anything. I was taken out of the equation early."

"I studied your case files, your record with the LAPD, and the papers you wrote for the academy." Parks smiled. "I read your psych profiles taken at the Mayo clinic. Sanchez was stupid to implant you."

"I lucked out having a faulty Chip."

Parks' eyes betrayed skepticism. "Maybe it was sheer will power. I have the feeling you'll get your chance to test your theory again."

Jake chuckled at the comment. Parks knew the results to his little test. "Told ya, Max2."

Parks leaned back. "You're exhaling the nano-virus and it's reached saturation levels in your blood. With the proper trigger, they'd form a Third Eye within minutes. You could graduate to Pin Head in less than ten."

Jake was beginning to accept his predicament. It was all a race to the finish line now. "Maybe the tumors will do me in first."

Parks shook his head. "Enhancement first, tumors second. With all those filaments in your brain, I'm surprised you have all your faculties."

"I haven't felt as sharp as I did when I was working back in LA. I could swear I've lost IQ points."

"Sharp enough."

"What, you've got Max2 as well?"

Parks shook his head. "I trust the barrier between us. Although, you're a walking Hot Zone, a biohazard delivery machine on steroids." He waved his hand. "Let me show you something."

A holographic image of the world appeared in front of Jake. Parks narrated. "This is Christmas Eve in Antarctica. The first report of Max2." A red pool showed up around McMurdo. "This is Terra Nova on December 26th." The Italian city turned red. "This is the world once survivors started returning home." The globe rotated, revealing dozens of cities turning red. The red bled out all over the landscape surrounding those cities. "This is LA the day you arrived." There was already a red pool there and it covered the West Coast of the United States, Mexico, and Canada. "This is San Carlos in Arizona on the day you arrived." Another red pool appeared. There were still pockets without red, but the world was rapidly becoming infected. The globe stopped on China. "This is China when you arrived. As you can see, they were already infected, but you helped seal the deal in Shanghai." By the time the date over the world reached January 2, 2036, every major and minor city showed massive Max2 infection. The globe stopped on Mumbai, pinpointing Jake's location.

"Alright, I'm a carrier, and so were a few thousand survivors of Mac Town. Question is, who introduced it?"

The holograph snapped off. Parks pursed his lips. "Not sure, but smart move on their part. Infect a vacation destination that attracts visitors from all over the world and you've got the highest chance of maximum distribution."

"Then why muddy it up with an attack that kills the majority of your hosts?"

"Maybe the Argentines were correct in their theory that there was a weaponized virus in McMurdo. Maybe the attack ensured a rapid return of the hosts to their countries; the planners traded volume for speed. Maybe it was a case of two factions pissing on each other's turf with two very different agendas."

Jake sat back to recap what he knew. "So most governments know Max2 started in McMurdo and everyone who left there is a carrier. How the virus switches from carrier mode to killing its host happens through signals in the Cyber-Wire, or cellular network. The signals can be directed at individuals, or population clusters. Am I right so far?"

"You're cookin' with gas, Jackhammer. Max2 is a surgical strike weapon of perfect precision. I could have made a mint on it. But the masters of Max2 are using the nano-virus to change the balance of power, not their balance sheet."

Jake thought about what Parks had said. That he was now taking everything at face value. He was far more reactionary than in the past. Did Gordy really drag him all over the world to recruit the man on the other side of the glass? Or did Erasmus want Jake to carry the disease into higher security areas that the average Antarctic tourist could not penetrate? Was Jake here for the sole purpose of infecting Parks with Max2?

"Talk to me, Jakey."

"I feel like a pawn." Admitting it pissed him off. "I don't even have a Chip to use as an excuse this time."

"At least you've recognized it in time to do something about it." Parks threw up his hands. "Hey man, at the end of the day, we all wind up being somebody's bitch." He pointed to the ceiling. "I'm a bitch for the dude upstairs."

Jake shook his head in disbelief. "And people call you a prophet?"

"Ass-Postle," Parks corrected. "I'm the right prophet for right now." He winked. "And your Order of Erasmus is not what they pretend to be," he snorted. "Order of Erasmus, hell, that should be me. Erasmus was a man who helped to revolutionize the church. But I get the meaning for all those scientists. Fundamentally, Erasmus was about questioning authority and doing what you believe is right."

"I was sent to bring you over to our side or take you out."

Parks shrugged. "Figures. Infecting you with that little bug would just about guarantee the latter."

"You'll catch it sooner or later based on that map you just showed me."

"True. Our projections have total infection happening by late next week or the week after. But I can buy some more time through isolation and bio-filters." Parks raised his hands and waved at the ceiling. "The air circulating in here is heavily filtered. We've tested Max2 with this system and it doesn't get through."

"Who's we?"

"Most people see me as a Reverend, but I'm still Chairman of Cobalt Industries."

Jake laughed. "You're the poster boy for failing up!"

"Raw confidence and the gift of gab are the only tools you need in life. Charm will get you everywhere." Parks froze for a second and played with two of his Omnis. "Hold that thought." He closed his eyes and went through a myriad of facial expressions in about two minutes. He jumped up and cheered a few times before opening his eyes. "What a great fucking game!"

Jake blankly stared back at him.

"Lakers versus Jazz, did you see it?"

"They still hold sporting events with a virus on the loose?"

"Absolutely. Players got together and felt it was their civic duty to keep morale up. Plus they're all chipped." Parks laughed. "And to think there were players suspended for doping just a few decades ago. The Chip makes those old performance drugs seem like child's play." He shrugged off the tangent. "The game was on two days ago. Took that long for me to filter out all the cyber-viruses and hacks." He held up both his arms to expose his four Omnis. "That's what these are for. The Consortium, Jihad Brotherhood, Erasmus—all know I'm chipped. There are sentinels hacking my signals 24/7. It's relentless. The Omnis show me every hack that's fired at me through the Wire. My signal goes in and out through these four encryptors. Each one uses a seventy-digit code that changes every half-second and is ten times more powerful than a retail model. Plus they have a lot of secret sauce." He winked. "A team at one of the Cobalt labs designs them."

"You're like Bruce Wayne. Except your alter ego isn't Batman, it's the good Reverend Parks."

Parks jumped up. "Pretty sweet, huh!"

"This isn't a comic book, Parks."

Parks laughed. "That's where you have it wrong, Jack-o-lantern. Life is one big comic book, a joke, a nutty storyline created by the master prankster himself." He pointed straight up.

"You preach that God is a comic book writer?"

"I preach that God tests us, and it's up to us how we want to view those tests. Do it with humor you might make it through. Take it all seriously and you die with fewer friends and a bleeding ulcer."

"Why Disciples of Paul?"

Parks nodded. "Saul was a non-believer and persecuted Christians. Then," he slammed his fist into his open palm, "Bam! The resurrected Jesus blinds Saul with a brilliant vision. Saul goes blind for three days until Ananias restores his sight. Bam! Saul is converted. He changes his name to Paul and serves God forever after."

"You had a vision?"

"You fucked me up royal, Jake." He leaned against the glass partition between them. "When you and Morris hacked into the LAPD and made us face our real memories, it was like waking up into a living nightmare." He turned away from Jake. "I could totally relate to Koren blowing his brains out. I came close to doing the same."

Jake felt bad for Detective Koren, but he did not feel responsible. "Koren spent his whole life grounded in morality. I'm sure it was unbearable for him to realize he was the best cold-blooded killer out of the three of us. Plus, he wasn't even aware he had a Chip."

Parks nodded. "I was lost in depression for months after that night. Then I found the Sons of Christ, and my benefactor."

"So it was the money and the power that enlightened you?" Jake smiled.

Parks was offended. He began to pace. "No, dude. I really do believe in the Almighty. And I believe I'm doing what's right for the human race. Whether you're an atheist, a socialist, a mentalist, whatever, as long as you have a moral compass, believe in helping humankind, and believe in leaving the planet a better place than you find it, you're in God's grace, no matter what church you pray in."

"That's pretty deep, Joaquin. Sure that's not The Chip talking?"

He laughed and shook his finger at Jake. "Ah! That's funny, Jake-ster. But I'm not taking any more of your bait." He sat down and shook his head. "I've got just as many layers as you, Travesty. It just took me longer to find my self-confidence."

"Ah, we're back to that nickname again."

Parks smiled. "I'll use it whenever you're being a dick."

"How about the terrorist attacks? Did you hit Beijing and NTI?"

Parks leaned forward. "No. But I hit God Head hives whenever I find them. I don't care whose they are, Consortium, Brotherhood, Erasmus. They all suck, equally."

"There's a better way to fight," Jake insisted.

Parks shook his head. "In order to win any battle, you must have the hearts and minds of the people. The Chip is the ultimate game changer. You can now program the hearts and minds of the masses. But tell me, what was the greatest force on earth before the P-Chip?"

Jake shrugged.

"Religion. There is no greater weapon on this earth than faith. Faith makes people volunteer to starve, give up their homes, kill their children, and sacrifice their lives. And out of all the faiths in the history of this world, which one was the most successful?"

Jake did not feel it wise to goad a lunatic, although he figured Egypt, as their polytheism lasted close to three thousand years.

"That's right, the Catholic Church."

Jake opened his mouth to argue but thought better of it.

"Rome ruled the world for two thousand years if you count Emperors and then the church that followed. The popes became the new emperors. They tore down Rome and rebuilt it as a vast monument to God. If you have an all powerful, all knowing deity at your back, you are greater than any mortal."

Like pharaohs of old, Jake thought.

Parks was on a roll. "Dictators come and go because they hold power based on the cult of their personality, but religious institutions endure beyond the mortality of physical leadership. Institutions can even survive when leadership becomes corrupt or wavers. I wanted to make a difference and I knew the only way to build an army of loyal followers was to elicit faith."

"So you believe you're the new Pope, or the embodiment of a new Vatican?" Jake smiled.

Parks put his hand over his crotch. "Low blow, Jake, and not so funny. But you're definitely channeling the old me. No, I'm a religious leader, which makes me more than a man among my flock and above the law in many countries because religion gave birth to written law and it's in the DNA of every culture. If you play the system, you can slip past a lot of rules."

"So you're courting extremists."

"They're the only ones left, Jackhammer. The rest of the army has been recruited and chipped. We're nearing the final battle and it's pitched."

"Okay, so why contact me, why am I here?"

"The Consortium is the enemy, and The Order has been compromised. Cobalt's Max2 tracking map proves that. I trust no one. Something you taught me a long time ago, even before we met. You were a hero in LA. You were the super-cop that managed to skate on the edge of the law. Every cop worth his badge knew you'd been railroaded at the Pacheco trial. The asshole deserved it, but you crossed a line."

"Thanks for the compliments." Jake had a flashback to killing Roberto Pacheco back in Brazil.

"My list of allies dwindles daily. I hoped I could get you to join me. I could use a little Jackhammer Classic at my back on Judgment Day."

Jake sighed.

"All you need is a trigger."

Jake raised his eyebrows.

"They want me dead. Okay. Let's fake my death. You say you killed me and see what happens. I believe they'll activate your Max2 nano-virus and either stick you with the automatons, or finish off that heart attack they gave you back in LA five-and-a-half years ago."

Jake smiled and tapped his head. "I see you're anticipating far more than you used to."

"As I said, I learned from the best. Now can I get off my knees? I'm getting a sore throat from blowing you."

Jake laughed. "How do you plan to fake your death?"

"Check under the seat that stabbed you in the ass."

Jake got to his knees and felt under the chair. There was an HK V2 taped under it. He pulled it out and checked the clip; .45s with hollow points. "Nice."

"Fire it into that can." Parks pointed to a small metal door, about the size of a twentieth-century mail slot, sitting in the wall about knee high. Jake put the muzzle into the metal door and fired.

Parks nodded with satisfaction. "You just planted a bullet in my head."

Jake stuffed the gun in the back of his waistband and sat down again.

"When you're ready to go, I'll drop you off and this vehicle will explode about five minutes later. Don't worry about my end of the plan. You just say you set off a grenade in here before jumping out." Parks opened a locker on his side of the glass and produced a carton of grenades manufactured by Cobalt Industries. "I'll monitor you as much as I can, but the important thing is, find the mole in The Order of Erasmus and eliminate him. Then I might consider helping the group. Although something tells me all your Erasmus posse is working together on this."

The old detective part of him agreed with Parks. "Okay, you're on."

The car stopped and the door swung open with a hiss. Thick hot air tumbled into Jake's compartment. He felt wet again. He flipped his shirt over the gun to conceal it.

"Careful, Jackhammer. I'm not sure I can help you after you're chipped. These new ones regenerate, making it far more difficult to pull it out of your head."

Jake fished out the Cobalt Omni that Parks had given him.

"Oh and toss me that Chinese Omni. It's broadcasting your position. Tell your Erasmus buddies I made you take it off when I saw the open code signal."

Jake paused at the door, slipping Parks' gift onto his wrist. He made sure his two Omnis were switched off. Then he tossed his old Chinese one—the one Sumit had given him—into the vehicle. "You keep the solidarity pin until next time."

Parks nodded. "So far we've found the Max2 Chip trigger is usually a piece of music, or a phrase. I've got Cobalt working on the hacks and feeds that are transmitted at you. Even if you are chipped, you've got two Omnis for protection and one of them is the type I have."

Jake stepped onto the street. "See you soon."

Parks winked. "Try to leave Mumbai in better shape than you left Shanghai, Jakey-o."

The door slid shut and the vehicle lumbered down a deserted industrial street. Jake found a side alley and turned the corner to get cover. He paced around waiting for the inevitable explosion. He needed to be spotted at the scene so The Consortium, or team Erasmus, or whoever was pushing to have Parks killed, could corroborate his claim. Parks assumed an awful lot, but given how hot everyone was about sending the Reverend off to heaven, the conspiracy theory made sense. While Jake pondered the plot, a fireball erupted into the night, followed by the rumble of an explosion.

Chapter 43
Mannequin

Jake reached the flaming wreck of the armored van. Through the white flames, he could tell the vehicle had blown outward. The battery casing was compromised and the chemicals inside fed the blaze. A few hundred spectators gathered around. Sirens from a Mumbai Fire Department HJ howled upon the scene with jet wash and flame retardant blasting down on the wreck.

He powered up his two Omnis and confirmed they were ready to throw an encryption barrier around him in the event he became chipped. He checked the back of a few necks before bumping into people and excusing himself. He made sure half a dozen chipped individuals registered him on the scene. The GPS in his Omnis would also help in that department.

Once he felt noticed, he took off toward the main street. He used the GPS on Parks' Military Omni. As he merged with the flow of pedestrian traffic, he was bumped toward the curbside, near the bike lane. A bicycle rickshaw hummed up along side him. The driver called out, "Jump in, Jake."

He turned toward the rickshaw. It was empty, but the shirtless man pedaling was covered in a thin film of sweat. His body was ripped and a red turban covered his hair. The rider parked in the designated curbside pickup lane. His eyes held a distant stare. "It's me, Sumit. Jump in."

Jake's heart sank. He had not even sent his message to Gordy yet, and here was Sumit. "I need to get back to NTI."

"No need. Gordy and Anjali are here with me. Jump in."

He forced a smile on his face. "How did you find me?"

"Same way Parks found you." The driver nodded to Jake's arms. "Omni."

Sumit's loaner Omni was now inside the burning armored van. Sumit must be using the eyes of all the chipped people around him. "I think I'll walk."

"Suit yourself." The driver slammed his feet into the pedals and merged back into traffic.

Wary of a more forceful request, Jake merged back into the safety of the pedestrians around him. He pulled up the Disciples of Paul Mumbai chat room and entered his identity as instructed. As he walked, he felt the people around him closing in. His heart jumped. Bodies pressed tighter and he thrust his elbows out to create room. Hands gripped his elbows. He twisted his body and tore away. More hands grabbed him. Dead eyes surrounded him. He felt the gun leave his waistline. His feet rose off the ground. His body was maneuvered into a horizontal position. He thrust and jabbed. Two people went down but four more took their places. There were a dozen people moving him toward the bike lane.

Jake yelled. "Let me down! Help!" His captors moved through the flowing pedestrian traffic to reach the curb, but there was no reaction to his plea.

A new rickshaw driver waited at the curbside. This one pointed a gun. Jake strained against the hands that held him. A few lost their grip and he lunged for the pavement. His body flew down as a dart sunk into the neck of a woman who was holding him. Jake crouched under the cover of the masses. As they regrouped to grab him, he leapt at the rickshaw driver, but the driver was ready. A purple dart sank into Jake's gut. He crashed into the driver and the momentum sent them both sailing into two rickshaws. A domino effect ensued, sending riders and bikes into automobile traffic.

Jake jumped up and pulled out the dart. Pain seared through his abdomen. His hand trembled, and his legs began to go numb. The drug was taking effect. Traffic slowed to maneuver around the mess, but it continued to flow. Everyone picked themselves up and went about their business.

The hacked rickshaw driver approached, joined by many pedestrians. They all grabbed Jake and hoisted him into the back of the rickshaw. By the time the driver regained his seat, Jake lost all motor function below the neck. He felt like a mannequin trapped on a crazy ride to a dark destination. He could do nothing but watch. He was a prisoner in his own body.

Chapter 44
Regicide

Gordon King was weary. He felt as if he had been running a marathon for five years straight and there was no end in sight. Actually, that was not true, there was a definite end in sight; 2036 was going to be the year that The Consortium either won or lost. There was no delaying it. So why did he continue the façade of NTI scientist and executive? He needed NTI's resources, even though he knew many in the organization were working with The Consortium. There was a time when Gordy knew who those people were, but with the losses The Order of Erasmus had suffered, his enemy's numbers had grown beyond his intelligence. It was the age of the God Head.

Gordy followed the God Head blogs to stay current on his enemy. God Heads saw the planet as a population of lab rats that were given rewards at the proper times to ensure they moved through the maze according to an overall plan. Most of the time, the rats were allowed to move under their own free will, but once or twice a week, they were given "incentives" to keep them on the right track. That's all it took to cow a population of billions.

He thought of his grandparents who had marched with Martin Luther King, a much greater king, MLK had used non-violence to bring about equality for blacks in America. It took decades following King's violent death before blacks saw equality. Gordy was gay, and that was still not tolerated in many areas of the world. He had seen prejudice of all kinds growing up, but he never felt like he was held back because of the color of his skin. However, he did still feel that being openly gay was not tolerated outside of large urban areas.

He had been high school valedictorian, received a scholarship to Cal Tech, and at twenty-four obtained a graduate degree in bioengineering. When he was a kid back in Dayton Ohio, most everyone idolized black musicians and athletes. It was cool to listen to Hip Hop and talk like rappers; but it wasn't until high school when he began to see gays portrayed in the media as positive influences. Even with awareness, tolerance took decades to root into society. There were still groups that advocated Chips to convert homo to hetero. No one stopped to think that being gay was genetic, like having brown eyes or dark skin. You were born with it. Did that make it something that had to be fixed?

Gordy was eight when Matthew Sheppard was tortured and killed in Wyoming for being gay. Hating gays, blacks, Muslims, and Jews stemmed from the same blind bigotry. It was this legacy that made him want to fight. Slavery was slavery by any other name. His parents had taught him that.

When Gordy was ten, his parents drove him to Cincinnati to witness a sermon given by Reverend Fred Shuttlesworth. Gordy's dad told him about segregation in America and what people like Rosa Parks, Martin Luther King, and Fred Shuttlesworth had done to fight racism. Gordy was inspired by Shuttlesworth's deeds. Shuttlesworth had tried to enroll his children in an all white public school in 1957. In response, the KKK had beaten him with chains and brass knuckles. Yet he got back up and continued his battle, always turning the other cheek. Shuttlesworth taught tolerance and forgiveness, and through that, attained the higher ground. Shuttlesworth was responsible for enlisting Martin Luther King to join him in Birmingham, and by doing so, set in motion the world's understanding of the African

American plight. Footage of armed men beating peaceful marchers induced sympathy and rage from those who watched. That's how humans used to react before The Chip.

If it hadn't been for heroes like Shuttlesworth, Gordy would have grown up feeling like a second class citizen, instead of a man who could aspire to become a scientist, leader, and revolutionary. The Consortium had stripped away race, color, and creed but was approaching the world on the same basic principle on which all prejudice is based: One group is superior on every level to everyone else. They turned a blind eye to any and all exceptions.

Superiority complexes pissed him off. Every human being contained their own set of talents; shouldn't every human being have the opportunity to grow and express their full potential? Wasn't that what his heroes fought so hard for?

He knew a few affluent African Americans who worked for The Consortium. They could not let go of the anger that had been passed down from previous generations about the injustice they had suffered. They were going to have their day of retribution. He understood their anger, but they were perpetuating a cycle of hatred that had, in his opinion, remained unbroken since time began.

He shook his head to stop his mental diatribe. The cab slowly moved through a mass of automobile, bicycle, animal, and pedestrian traffic. There was a bizarre order to the movement of so many millions. He was sad to see the change. He had been coming to India on business for two decades and he missed the chaotic feel of the Mumbai streets before The Chip.

India was alive back then. Now the country reminded him of a theme park where animatronic representations of reality were on display. He could hear the tour guide now. "This is what India was like in the middle of the twenty-first century. Next we'll see water buffalo in their prefabricated natural habitat."

He sighed. He felt like his muscles and skin had minds of their own. The SleepX was literally killing him. He knew he needed twelve hours of sleep tonight, but as the leader of Erasmus, there was much ground to regain. He was on his way to a secret meeting with the commando team that had repelled the attack on NTI earlier that day. He planned to strike the Consortium God Head facilities located in New Delhi and needed to fine-tune the strategy.

He never thought he'd be a revolutionary leader. It just happened. He wondered if Dr. Morris had ever imagined his invention would have led to these dire times. He was willing to bet Morris figured the P-Chip program would have been killed days after Jake's broadcast. He wished it had.

Gordy's cab pulled up to an old apartment complex. He pressed his thumb on the scanner pad next to the door handle. He enjoyed riding in the back even though he hadn't seen a cab driver in ten years. Old habits were hard to break. A dummy account was debited $230 over his Omni and the doors unlocked. His Omni identified him as Ingmar Troost, a Swedish tourist—a cover identity for anyone watching his movements.

He stepped out of the cab and into a relatively quiet street. There were five or six people walking under the night sky. He heard a dog bark somewhere in the building ahead as the cab pulled away. The sound made him smile. Few people adopted pets since the introduction of Third Eyes. People received comfort and companionship from The Chip. Shelters euthanized animals at an alarming rate. Gordy had four dogs and nine cats back home. His husband, Robert, took care of them. He was a furniture designer for one of the last boutiques on La Brea in Los Angeles.

Thinking of Robert made him feel guilty about Jake's dogged desire to get back Tomoko. On the one hand, she was safely out of the picture, but on the other, Gordy admired Jake's desire to have her by his side. She would be part of the discussion tonight. As much as Gordy wished Robert were with him, running The Order made it more practical for Robert to stay at home.

Robert had been one of the early cases of Max1. During the eight weeks of panic, looting, riots, National Guard curfews, and general chaos, Gordy had made the decision to have Robert chipped. He had used all his power and influence to get Robert into Cedars Sinai. Only movie stars and politicians could get in back then. The rest of the infected had been turned away, stopped by tanks surrounding the hospital's perimeter.

Robert had been unconscious and near death. Gordy was racked with grief and was desperate to do anything… desperate enough to give his thumbprint and have Robert implanted with a Chip. During July and part of August, the world was at the brink of total anarchy over MaxWell hysteria. During that time, Robert stayed in the hospital undergoing training on The Chip. Gordon worked from home, took care of their animals, and tried to keep the robbers, looters, and infected away. That was when he started taking SleepX in mass quantities. The little orange pills had been his constant companions ever since.

Eventually Robert came home and Gordy made him promise never to take off his Omnis. Robert argued, but Gordon pleaded that if Robert still loved him, he would do it. In the end, Robert caved.

There was still a chance that The Consortium might hack the encryption codes on Robert's Omnis, or they might kill the animals. Those were the main vulnerabilities The Consortium might exploit.

He missed Robert. He had not seen him since Thanksgiving, and had not talked to him since Christmas. There was little time for anything else but The Order of Erasmus now. He dreamed of defeating The Consortium, eradicating The Chip, and taking a well-deserved rest. The idea of putting all his energy into his relationship and possibly adopting some kids kept him going. Hope was fading and distant these days, but hope was the only fuel he had left.

He headed into the shadows and ducked down an alleyway. He felt watched at all times and did what he could to avoid being seen. He walked into a side door of a ten-story apartment building and entered a dimly lit corridor. He heard noises behind many of the doors, but not the laughter or chatter of family life after a hard day's work. It was the sound of pots and pans, of holo-visions, and other devices.

He took the stairs instead of the elevator and jogged up to the fourth floor. Most elevators contained cameras and could read fingerprints. This building was safe, it had been scouted by the team days ago, but he erred on the side of caution. Besides, walking up four stories was good exercise. His current schedule made workouts impossible, but the SleepX and stress kept him outwardly fit.

He reached the door of room 4J and observed his hand before he knocked. It trembled. He knocked, then gripped his hand to read his Omni. It showed that he had passed four checkpoints on the way in. Sensors were concealed all over the building. The door opened and Gordy saw Illana with a knitted brow.

"What's going on?" she grumbled.

Gordy stepped in and shut the door. Illana's reception was disconcerting, but the faint sound of Smoov Z's "Baby Can't We Talk" playing from an apartment below was alarming. Why on earth would that minor R&B eighties hit be playing in a Sikh apartment block in Mumbai? He kept his voice down. "How long has that song been playing—" he saw forty people crowded in the room. They represented several cells, most of whom did not know one another, much less have a reason to be in India. They were the entire brain trust of The Order of Erasmus.

Alarms rang in his mind. "Get the hell out! It's a trap!" He spun around and reached for the door.

The thud of several bodies hitting the floor filled his ears. As he grabbed the door handle, he felt the strange sensation of something growing under his skin at the base of his skull. He knew immediately that Max2 was activated. He checked the security fields on both his Omnis. They were blocking all signals around his body up to ten feet. The Chip might be active, but he would not be hacked.

As he opened the door to the hallway, he realized: *The music. It was the music that activated the virus through the ears, or even vibrations through the skin.* He wondered if the kill command could be activated by the music as well or if it would take a secondary command.

He glanced over his shoulder as he walked out. Those who did not have their scramblers on were dead; those that did stood in shocked confusion. Illana was nowhere to be seen. "Everyone, run!"

Rapid fire from a machine gun with silencer answered Gordon's call. The staccato of bursting wounds was louder than the launching of the bullets from their shells. He raced into the hall as the organization of Erasmus was murdered by a hacked version of Illana. He slammed into several doors, trying to find an escape. No sound could be heard from any apartment. *Christ, is the whole building hacked?*

He sprinted for the stairwell. He was within a few feet when he felt the bullets rip into his back and punch out his chest. He slammed into the door.

The inertia of his body sent him flying down the stairwell. More bullets chewed apart his body. He felt a bullet sever his spine. He could no longer control his limbs and he flew face first into a concrete stair. For a split second he could see over the handrail, all the way down the four-story staircase. Such a long way down.

Chapter 45

Circle

Jake had been propped up in the crook of the bench seat; however, the vibrating rickshaw sent him sprawling onto the floor after the first few miles. His view was switched to a filthy and worn rubber floor mat with a patch of moving street beyond.

It took an hour before the human congestion ebbed and he saw more darkness than bustling city street. One of the characteristics of Splice was its ability to make a subject euphoric. He wasn't the least bit concerned about his predicament, although something in the back of his mind said he should be. He wondered if he would be able to resist telling the truth about Parks. He concentrated on the image of putting a bullet in his old comrade's head and then chucking a grenade into the transport before jumping ship. If he fixed the image in his mind and believed it was true, he might pass the test, or so he had read a long time ago in one of his LAPD advanced tactical training manuals.

Time passed. The world grew darker and he heard the din of monkeys and insects. They were moving into the countryside. The Chip was probably pushing the driver's body to the limit. A God Head could make a body do incredible things using natural chemicals, but they were known to push a Pin Head to the point of death. Of course, there were plenty of available Pin Heads to finish a job.

Jake had no idea what time it was when the rickshaw stopped. The driver dragged him out of the carriage and laid him on his back. He felt an uneven cobblestone surface as he watched the driver hop back onto his vehicle and pedal away. Jake was in a large circular driveway, looking out over a vast lawn and an illuminated gate. He was near the doorstep of a massive estate. Several genetically enhanced baboons gathered around him. Their eyes and mouths abnormally large. He noticed powerful dinner-plate sized hands, another genetic enhancement. *How cute!* his inebriated mind thought.

The monkeys picked him up and carried him into a home. It reminded him of a colonial mansion from the days when Britain reigned supreme. *How fun!* Again, the Splice talking. He was carried under a chandelier that was the size of a small car. Lights from tables in the room reflected in its dusty crystal. It was not currently lit.

He toured a few dilapidated ceilings before he was brought out into a courtyard. He heard the patter of his captors' bare feet on what sounded like smooth stone. The baboons swung him around like a pillow and sat him in a high-backed chair. He felt gratitude toward them.

"Phank you, my gud magn," he slurred. Their feet were hands as well, only a little larger than the ones attached to the arms. They appeared to have retractable claws too. Each sported large and defined muscles, weightlifters all! He giggled. He wondered if the baboons spat poison like their macaque cousins. *How cool!*

The baboons retreated into the shadows. A few landscape lights showed that he was at the edge of a spacious rectangular courtyard. White marble tile covered the ground. A colonnade ran along the ground floor and the entire second story balcony. A fountain gurgled about ten feet from his chair. Shapes moved around the second story and the roof above. He squinted and realized they too were enhanced baboons. He concentrated on his speech. Splice tended to make ones tongue feel fat, as if it had been injected with Novocain.

"Andy-one holme?"

A hologram appeared above the fountain. A twenty-foot image hovered around the level of the second story. It was thirty-minute old footage of Parks' burning armored van. *Great! A movie!*

"Hello, Commander."

Jake recognized the voice. If it were not for the effects of the Splice dart, he would have had the urge to kill. Instead he was curious, almost playful. He called back. "Span-Chessthpth!" *Oh, that didn't come out right at all.* He was happy just the same.

Dress shoes clacked on stone floor. A figure emerged from the shadows. Insects hummed with excitement. The mournful cry of a peacock drowned out all sound then vanished. Tattered clouds revealed stars and a sliver moon above. That, mixed with some of the landscape lighting around the courtyard, showed much of his captor's features.

Sandoval Sanchez stood in between the fountain and Jake. His old nemesis was now fit and wore his hair pulled back into a ponytail. He wore a trim mustache and goatee as well, but the voice remained unchanged. "We've come full circle." Sanchez carried a stool in his hand. He set it on the ground a few paces in front of Jake. "I even made sure you took a gut shot, just like the one you gave me."

Jake knew Sanchez was a threat, but he was unable to take him seriously. The soft soothing buzz of the Splice remained in his veins.

"Guys like you used to piss me off, you know that?"

Jake blinked and smiled. He felt a stream of drool ooze out of the corner of his mouth, but it was nothing to worry about.

"You're smart enough to see the big picture, but too dim to be pragmatic about it. What you don't get is that the majority of humanity is too dumb and too wrapped up in its own petty needs to care about how things really work." Sanchez got up and began to walk around the fountain. His head and shoulders disappeared into the burning armored car. "By now, even you should recognize that. The Chip caters to every selfish need of the individual.

Everyone still believes it always happens to the other guy, never to me… even though they know the risks of being hacked are so great. For those who feared The Chip, we created something even scarier." He poked his head out of the fiery holograph. "An epidemic!"

Jake licked his lips. He was thirsty. Sanchez was a neat-o guy, but he sure talked a lot. Jake thought of General Tsang, he was neat too. *He died, didn't he?* "What… happenpth tuh China!" His statement was more about why Tsang wasn't invited to this party.

Sanchez nodded and sat at the edge of the fountain, under the holograph. "You're holding up pretty well with that Splice in your system. Might be time to give you another round." He waved to someone behind Jake. Baboon feet slapped marble.

"China stopped playing ball so we took them out of the equation, blamed The Brotherhood in the process. India's top brass is about to be incorporated into The Consortium and then all we have to contend with is the Brotherhood in the Middle East and Africa. Quite frankly, we saved the easiest for last. Parks and his DOP were dangerous because of his access to Cobalt's armor and satellite network." Sanchez stood again. "Nice work by the way," he flashed a smile. "And you didn't even need The Chip this time!"

Sanchez held his arms out wide. "Point oh-two-percent of the population will govern the rest." He stretched as if getting ready for bed. "We're tired of carrying the burden. We want a vacation. Great leaders come and go and even the best kings sire fools. The Chip keeps everyone in line, even those who would govern over Pin Heads. It's a twenty-first century solution to an ageless problem. Only we think we've got it dialed in this time."

Jake blanked out a bit on the details of what Sanchez was telling him. All he could think about was how fun it would be to play the game Risk. He had played the boys in his neighborhood more than a few times when he was a kid. "Kamchatka, gateway to the west!" His pronunciation was improving.

Sanchez blankly stared at him.

"Risk, dude. Dib-n't you eber play?"

Sanchez rubbed his hands and approached Jake. "Last time we met, you gave me a choice between enslavement with The Chip or suicide." He whispered in Jake's ear. "It might satisfy you to know I tried to kill myself, but the Splice made it impossible to hold the gun." He sat on the stool. "It might also satisfy you to know that I went to prison. I was chipped and I was flooded with emotional control devices that every prisoner in a correctional facility receives. I took behavior and moral educational classes, and I was hacked." He smiled. "Yes, I finally got to enjoy the experience you detested." He stood up again. "Only my Chip was so good that I just thought I was having a hard time staying awake. I was unaware of murdering three other inmates, and so I was not convicted at my trial." He put a hand on Jake's shoulder.

"In 2032, the Supreme Court ruled that killing someone while under the influence of a God Head is not a crime. The God Head is the real killer." He leered into Jake's face. "Know what they did?"

Jake blinked back stupidly. This story wasn't as funny as it first seemed. The euphoric effects of Splice were wearing off. In its place, he felt the onset of nausea and a splitting headache with a twinge of fear.

"They removed my Chip and put me in solitary." Sanchez resumed pacing. "We're so forgiving and understanding in this age of enlightenment, don't you think?" He laughed. "Ah but karma paid a visit, right? My wife committed suicide and my daughters became prostitutes!" He gave Jake a friendly punch in the shoulder. "Wrong! My wife divorced me while I was in prison, but she married a lawyer, and my daughters work part time and spend his money instead of mine. Well, they spend the money I earned before I went to prison, but much of that was used as restitution to the victims' families." He turned to Jake. "Homeland Security had quite the body count back then."

Jake raised a shaky hand and rubbed his temples. He was unable to move his legs. "Must suck that your kids look up to a different role model instead of their father." He felt another dart slam into his shoulder. "Goddamn it! This is like the fifth fucking time this week!" The hot drug seeped into his muscles. "Great. More Splice."

"What did you expect?" Sanchez propped Jake up so he would be able to see the show. "In answer to your query, I was too busy saving the world to be a good father. But my girls are all chipped now and will be part of the new world order. We're weeks away—maybe sooner, thanks in part to you."

"Usbing me as a delibery debice for Max2."

"That and killing Parks kept us on our time table. Your initial service when you were chipped was invaluable. All that fighting gave us tremendous insight into how to control those with a stronger sense of independence."

"You baited five years… for me to surface in Antarctica… so you could use me as a carrier?" Jake worked hard to enunciate through the drug. "That's ridiculous."

"We would have intercepted you no matter what port you wound up in. Parks was our primary agenda. Turning you into a carrier was a last minute benefit."

"It's time to play the music, Sandoval." Sumit Malik's voice came from behind. Jake assumed he was responsible for the dart in his shoulder.

"Why?" Sanchez stood up straight. "What can he possibly do to us? He has no allies, no place to go, no recording device, no one to listen even if he did. He's isolated in a foreign country with enough money to buy a couple of meals before he resorts to begging."

"This exercise of yours is infantile." Sumit stepped into Jake's field of view. Jake spotted a song list on Sumit's Omni. A track called: Smoov Z "Baby Can't We Talk," was highlighted.

Sanchez shook his head. "I haven't proved my point yet."

"You're wasting time."

Sanchez's jawbone pulsed a few times from the side of his face. Jake imagined a little man was trapped inside Sanchez's cheek and made him giggle. The drug was back in full force.

"He's impotent." Sanchez cleared his throat. "If you release him, what will he do?"

Sumit looked afraid. "He's resourceful. He's better off chipped or dead."

Something occurred to Jake and he spoke very slowly in order to be understood. "Is… Anjali… part of this… too?"

Sumit turned. Anger burned in his eyes. "By now you should have figured out that Anjali is involved with Anjali."

The relaxing waves of Splice pulsing through his body made everything so clear. Sumit hacked Anjali when she was chipped. Sumit knew her codes.

He stole her knowledge. She was the key to Max1 and Max2 thanks to her Chip and his treachery, but why?

Sanchez grabbed Sumit's wrist. "Why are you scared of him?"

Sumit wheeled on Sanchez. "He's dangerous."

"Because he knows you're a traitor?" Sanchez laughed. "We all made sacrifices to be here. Don't worry. When history is written, you will be a hero." Sanchez turned to Jake. "In the meantime, I want him to be cognizant when the takeover happens."

"Activate the virus and we've got a kill switch."

"I trust him more than I trust you. He knows who he is. You're still figuring it out. I've seen enough in this world to believe in destiny." Sanchez turned to Jake. "I believe this is his."

Sumit snorted. "You're starting to sound like an Indian."

"At least one of us has a spiritual side." Sanchez nodded to the holoprojector. "You want to take the fight out of him? Show the footage."

Sumit paused.

"Show him!"

Sumit shook his head. "What's the point?"

"The point is you're fine with numbers and figures but the moment you take a front row seat to the consequences of your action, you leave the room." Sanchez's fingers danced on his Omni. "You're a coward." The hologram switched to the POV of a Pin Head.

The POV marched into a room, holding a machine gun, which vomited bullets into a small group of panicked men and women. Others were already dead. Ordinarily Jake did not like snuff films, but the relaxing waves coursing through his body made him feel ambivalent. Then he saw Gordy running out the door. The POV finished killing every person in the room then dashed out the door and into a dimly lit hall.

Gordy frantically slammed into doors, desperately trying to get out of the line of fire. He wound up running for an opening at the end of the hall. Hands lifted the machine gun into the lower part of the frame and a rapid hiss of muted bullets slammed into Gordy. Jake could not tell if it was the impact of the bullets or Gordy making one last leap, but Erasmus' body shot into the air and hurdled down the stairs on the other side of the doorframe. The POV chased Gordy's body, filling him with lead until the clip was empty. Jake felt a great deal of distress but that too was washed away and comforted by the endless soothing waves of Splice.

Sumit left Jake's view the moment the footage started. Sanchez spat. "I prove my point." Sanchez said something disparaging in Chinese then gripped both of Jake's shoulders. "We're the good guys, Jake. God is on our side. This is the way the world order has always worked. The fittest are charged with taking care of the flock. This time we have a tool to make sure everyone gets what they want. You are the sad minority that is caught in the middle. Not quite good enough to join the elite, and not dumb enough to be happy swimming in the ocean with the masses. Still, you'll make do." He clapped him three times on the shoulder and walked out of view.

Chapter 46
Baboon

On the morning of December 24, 2035, Sumit awoke to find Anjali working on nano-virus models to combat MaxWell. She did not notice when he dressed and left their hotel room. He sent her a note via Omni that he was going out for a walk. After leaving the hotel, it took him twelve minutes to reach the bio lab in central McMurdo. Anjali and Sumit had been there the day before, but they had not used the loading dock entrance.

After a few security checks by hacked guards, he was led into a barren stainless steel test chamber. It was a place where lab animals were injected with viruses and cures. He felt uneasy. He did not expect a non-reception. He paced for five minutes. A ring of sweat formed around the edge of his shirt collar, before the hologram of Sanchez appeared in the room. Sanchez was someplace sunny, surrounded by a coniferous forest, definitely not Antarctica. His hologram was life size, creating the illusion that he was standing in the room with Sumit.

"Jake will be in McMurdo today," Sanchez stated. "He called in and reserved a slip for his boat."

"I'm ready."

"Are you?" Sanchez's gaze narrowed. "I get the feeling you've been having second thoughts."

"We're talking about infecting people with the new nano-virus."

"Call it Max2."

"I think we've made quite a few accomplishments with MaxWell."

"But two-point-five billion have refused Chip implantation. Max2 resolves that. The world's entire population will be chipped in a few weeks."

Sumit fingered his Omni, wondering if he should have engaged the security encryption he was working on last night. "MaxWell was worse than I thought."

"You gave us the projection models. Max1 worked brilliantly."

"This one will be worse." Sumit shook his head. "Leaking the information to the Argentine government so you can stage this little war game is overindulgence."

"We want to see how fast Max2 can accumulate and if it can be concentrated on one group while leaving another untouched."

"You have the lab studies!" Sumit shivered when he remembered the test footage of prisoners from third world countries being subjected to Max2, then killed. That was the day when he realized he was on the wrong side. It all had seemed so logical when he worked in computer simulations. He searched for a way out. The lab was sealed with no door handles and the observation glass was nanite enhanced, unbreakable.

"The death toll will be far worse. The population is too large to control and feed. You know this."

Sumit calmed down. He played the game so he could be released. "What can I do?"

"That's the spirit." Sanchez nodded with approval. "We want you to introduce it. We'll all wind up infected anyway. It's part of the plan."

Sumit fought the urge to piss his pants. He thought of his wife, his family back in India, and all his friends who had died last summer when MaxWell had killed millions. The new world order sounded wonderful in theory, but there must be a better way. He licked his lips. *Will lying or telling the truth make a difference now?* "I'm not sure I can go through with this."

Sanchez nodded with sympathy. “That’s what I thought.” Smoov Z’s “Baby Can’t We Talk” began to play in the room.

Sumit felt a crawling sensation under his skin, in his veins. “My, god! No!”

“You and Anjali were infected in this very lab when you performed your inspection. The air pumped into your biohazard suits was filled with Max2. You’ve been spreading the contagion all over the city since yesterday. It has now jumped to five cities on three continents. It’s a marvelous invention and we have you and your wife to thank for it.”

Sumit input his Omni-jamming program to engage any potential Chip in his head. At least they would not hack into his mind once The Chip formed.

Sanchez shook his head. “That won’t save you.”

Pain surged in Sumit’s thigh. He glanced down and saw the yellow dart sticking out of his leg. It had been fired from one of the robotic arms mounted to the wall. “I hope Jake puts a bullet in your head this time.”

“Or maybe he does me like that pornographer back in Brazil?” Sanchez sat on a chair. Sumit recognized the background. Sanchez was at one of The Consortium member’s homes in Vancouver. It was Marcus Hellard’s house, the man who had taken Anjali’s work on Max1 and Max2 and made them even more lethal. Sanchez yawned. “But this isn’t about me. It’s about you.”

Sumit fought the urge to pass out. His panic helped. “I did what you asked!”

Sanchez shook his head. “You’re weak, Sumit. There are too many loose ends we need to tie up, or our momentum will derail.”

Sumit collapsed on the ground. He stared at the protection his Omni would give him from hacking signals.

“Don’t worry, when you wake up, you won’t remember this moment. You won’t know you have a Chip in your head. You won’t know that there’s an AI program helping to coax you down the right path. However, you’ll still be awake when you carry out our orders, and you’ll feel guilt, because I want you to know what a coward you are as you fulfill your mission.”

Blackness.

It was just after midnight, which meant it was officially January 3rd, 2036. Sumit had left Jake in the courtyard with Sanchez five minutes ago. His fear maintained control while Sanchez played with Jake. Sanchez had coached Sumit on what to do when Jake awoke and Sumit had played his part, albeit with difficulty. Watching the footage of Gordy's death had again sent waves of guilt and regret through him. The praise and camaraderie he had shared with the members of The Consortium had blinded him for the past two years.

His actions of the past few days seemed like old TV reruns filtered through cheesecloth. They were dim and distant; someone else's actions. A madman had executed them. But when he questioned one of his more heinous deeds, a calming voice soothed him and he knew he was in the right. He was changing the world for the better. His medal proved he was vindicated as a hero.

He was responsible for spreading the Max2 nano-virus all over McMurdo. He had hacked Tomoko's Omni to play "Baby Can't We Talk" when she was alone in the bedroom at Jon Beartracker's home. The Consortium wanted to activate Max2 in her bloodstream, falsify an immunization, and push Jake into joining Erasmus and killing Parks. Sumit had led Jake, Gordy, and Anjali down the path toward Parks, keeping them blind to the actions of The Consortium until it was too late.

Sumit had distracted General Tsang with false concern for Jake while Consortium God Heads had hacked the Chinese doctors to cover up the fact that 643 had no effect on the Max2 raging in Jake's system. They needed time to ensure maximum infection in Shanghai before they threw the kill switch.

This is wrong. I'm a murderer.

A soothing voice answered. *You're a hero. Today's terrible deeds are tomorrow's brave victories. Future generations will thank you.*

They will?

Yes. The voice was reinforced with authority. *There will be cities and statues built in your honor. Warships will proudly carry your name.* A feeling of great accomplishment flooded his mind and body. He felt like a god.

Sumit spotted himself in the mirror wearing the Ashoka Chakra medal. He thought of all the blood on his hands. Disgust swept away his pride. He had turned his back on science and his mantra of working for the betterment of humankind. He had joined The Consortium for selfish reasons. He had submitted to being a pawn for petty ego-stroking and he was ashamed. He tore off his decoration and threw it in his suitcase.

Even though he was responsible for the deaths of millions, he felt more guilt over giving The Consortium the codes to Anjali's Chip. He and he alone was responsible for sabotaging Anjali's research after she removed her Chip. He made sure 643 would not work on Max2.

Men who committed genocide, who were responsible for holocausts, had names. Hitler, Stalin, Pol Pot, and Mao Tse Tung. There had been many times in recent days that he felt as if some greater driving force was pushing him to do wicked deeds. Soothing thoughts flooded his mind but he fought them.

He wanted to weep for those he had killed. Deep down inside he wanted to weep for himself. *Good God, I cannot stop feeling sorry for myself!* After all he had done, he was more alone than ever.

A venom monkey stood guard at his door. Sanchez had made sure one was near at all times. Sumit packed his bag, trying to regain his composure. He was an abomination, worse than his baboon guard. At least the baboon could point to scientists and blame them for what it had become. He had no one to blame. Oh, he could blame his cleft palate, the way his parents had treated him, or the death of his older brother during the Bachelor Wars. But how he chose to act in the world was his responsibility. He could have sought therapy, or returned to the Hindu faith of his parents. Instead, he allowed himself to be swept up by The Consortium. He had succumbed to the base and instant gratification of false adulation. *I might as well be chipped.*

Sumit drifted back to the events of Christmas Eve. He had gone to the bathroom at the Shackleton Lounge and then he couldn't remember anything until he awoke a few hours later, in the arms of a dead Argentine commando in a safe bunker. His neck wound was dressed. The Consortium had been watching out for him. He had ripped off the bandage and wandered out into the war-torn streets. He did not want to be caught with an Argentine when the Americans arrived. A few hours later, he had run into the US Marines. He told them he had escaped from the burning restaurant and had given himself first aid. Although, thinking about it, there was no way he could have survived that wound unless he was… chipped.

That's ridiculous, you would know if you were chipped. The voice held total authority and he believed it.

He gazed about the decaying house they occupied. It belonged to Anjali's family. They had moved south when the Bachelor Wars started in 2024. He concentrated on packing. Anjali had no sentimental interest in this home. Her family was in the south and that's where she liked to visit when she was in India. He would have to go with her tomorrow, after Sanchez made him perform a few more duties. Sumit did not know how he was going to be able to sleep next to his wife tonight. Knowing her, she'd probably be up until dawn working on a cure for a disease she unwittingly helped to create. What if she found out? He thought of telling her. He wanted to confess to someone and beg forgiveness. How does a mass murderer find forgiveness? *They never ask. They are justified in what they do. Guilt does not come into it.*

I hope that death finds me soon.

"What's wrong, Sumit? You look like a man who just put down his favorite pet." The crude AI monitoring the scientist's Chip had just called Sanchez. Sumit's guilt had overwhelmed the AI program. The program raised a red flag. Sanchez was playing a dangerous game not taking Sumit completely offline when he was forced to perform for The Consortium. Sanchez used the power of suggestion to drive Sumit's actions. Surges of unshakeable conviction and pride kept him on task. It was time to tell the AI to take Sumit offline for a while, and erase a few memories, but not too many. Sanchez enjoyed watching Sumit's inner torment.

The enhanced doctor had played his role well, but Sanchez saw fewer and fewer uses for the man. Sumit was brilliant, but lacked the true vision of leadership. The Consortium was playing musical chairs as the dawn of their new civilization approached. There would be no seat for Sumit. Sanchez would have to change the AI monitoring Sumit to reduce the guilt and make the *doctor* look at death as a numbers game; no more humanity or compassion allowed. Sanchez spoke the commands to the AI program as he watched Doctor Malik.

Sumit opened his mouth to speak but then thought better of it. Certain memories were being erased. He went back to packing his gear so he could return to the hotel where his wife was undoubtedly working round the clock on a nano-cure for Max2, which Sumit would then sabotage. Sanchez chuckled at the irony.

Sumit had been an interesting experiment for the crude AI program. Artificial Intelligence was not ready to assume the full functionality of a God Head, but it was getting close. The Consortium needed a fully sentient intelligence to replace God Heads. The bombing of Beijing had forced The Consortium to step up alternate plans, but he was not all that convinced Ai-li had been practical for their needs. A bleeding-heart schoolgirl was hardly the model they needed to police the world. There was one AI close to becoming self-aware, and every member of The Consortium was excited about it.

He felt impatient waiting for the new dawn. He recalled his grandparents telling him they worked six days a week, and had no running water or electricity in their home in Ecuador. He had cousins outside the US who lived in the same conditions. As the world's working class was elevated, Sanchez felt they became more entitled and demanded greater financial equality with people who really did work for a living.

He remembered the silly worldwide protests twenty years ago when the ninety-nine percent railed against the rich and shut down places of commerce, which wound up damaging the fragile economy even more. He was sure that even if the ninety-nine percent had a six hour work week, two new cars every year, and a nightly foot message, they would still demand more of everything without putting in any effort.He was glad that The Chip would crush jealousy and entitlement.

He thought about the promise of AI. Like all silver linings, there was a potential downside. A self-aware AI might become so intelligent that it would view humanity as a parasite and eradicate it. There was plenty of evidence against the need for more people. The Consortium used this rationale all the time to justify their actions. It would be far easier for AI to build machines than wait eighteen years for a human to grow up and do the same job but with less accuracy and more complaints. But The Consortium held failsafe plans to protect against such a situation.

Sanchez watched as Sumit left the house with his bag. A blissful soldier once again. The Indian had been easy to seduce. He was a lonely man who needed friends and affection. The Consortium had showered him with praise and adoration and he had lapped it up like a starving puppy. He had bought into their philosophy with a barebones bribe. Sumit craved ego stroking, a behavior that disgusted Sanchez, and brought out the worst in him.

Sanchez took one last glimpse over his shoulder at Jake's slumped figure sitting in the courtyard. The ex-cop was well on his way to prison. As a hacked Pin Head, Sanchez had learned the finer arts of manipulation. He had also learned about the unfathomable value of publicity.

Like all high profile prisoners, he had hired a publicist. Well, anyone with means did these days; it was crucial to success. Publicity made idiots rich, and losers into international celebrities. One didn't need talent or knowledge in today's society; one needed a good PR firm. At least, that was how the modern world worked before Max2 insured universal implantation.

He thought back on his PR agent. Glenda Barry was her name and she was worth a hundred lawyers. She had been the one to raise awareness of his hacked Chip. She recorded him pleading for forgiveness for the crimes he had committed under the influence of The Chip. Using *underground* social media tsars, she started a publicity avalanche that ended with the removal of his Chip. Then she set her sights on freeing him from prison. The only difference between Sanchez and some poor kid in the electric chair was the PR firm that represented him.

Glenda had persuaded his estranged wife and daughters to visit him and had coached his family on how to act in the visiting room. They all put on a tearful show and the video was "leaked" to the same underground social media tsars. Public sympathy for him and his plight rocketed around the world and soon his parole board was setting him free.

It only took a few months before he was back to making policy with his peers. They had plenty of uses for a visionary like him.

Prison had done something else too. It had stripped him of all pretenses of compassion. A leader could not show guilt or remorse. Leaders created and enforced policy, and a revolution demanded sacrifice, and casualties were the norm.

Sanchez stepped onto the front porch guarded by two baboons. The night buzzed with a symphony of insects. An image of Gina, his youngest, crying as he sat in the prison's visitor booth bubbled up from his memory. Another man had finished raising his girls and that pissed him off. That man had already succumbed to Max1. Sanchez had made sure of that. He pushed the guilt and grief back down. Those emotions were a sign of weakness. Such emotions would not be tolerated in the new world order and he would never outwardly admit to having them. Frustrated, he kicked one of the baboon guards.

Chapter 47
Hunted

Sunlight beat on Jake's face. He turned his head away from the rays and saw compound eyes staring blankly back at him. Curious antennae waved around but other than that, the yellow and black Glenea beetle stood very still on his arm, waiting for him to make the first move. He jerked up and brushed off the ornate insect. He searched his person for any other crawling objects. The movement caused a searing shot of pain into his head and he fell on his knees and vomited on the beetle.

"Sorry, fella." He flicked the perturbed insect out of the sick. "Hope both our days improve."

Heat and humidity filled the deserted courtyard, but, he shivered nonetheless. Two back-to-back doses of Splice was wreaking havoc on his system. Birds and insects greeted the new day with a cacophony of elated sounds. The outskirts of Mumbai were a throwback to the past. Here was a tropical jungle waiting to overtake the concrete one blocking its way to the ocean. He checked his Omnis. One was drained of power and the other was about half charged.

Gordy had given him the drained Omni at the Punjab just yesterday. With the Splice out of his system, the full impact of Gordon's death hit hard. He felt ashamed for suspecting Erasmus of betraying the organization. Gordon had always been on the level. He had sacrificed his life to save the world from enslavement. Gordy's death was a severe blow to the survival of the human race. His only remaining connection to the Order of Erasmus was Anjali. But she was too disconnected to be a part of anything outside her science. Jake felt a strong urge to plant a bullet in Sanchez's head.

He walked around the courtyard to take inventory. He was not ready to dive into the house until he could locate his simian jailers. He thought about Tomoko. *How the hell am I going to get her back? What about Mom and Lakshmi?*

One problem at a time…

He unfolded his Omni into a tablet and found his location via GPS. He was in a large mansion nestled on a plantation several miles outside Mumbai. He was thirty-five miles from the NTI building. He tried to pull up a schematic of the house but he could only obtain a satellite view. He configured the Omni back into a watch, put it on, and entered the house with caution. The place looked abandoned. The furniture was rotting. Dirt and leaves were strewn about the floor. The plantation shutters were cracked and broken. Mold grew on the plaster walls and ceiling. He was on a constant lookout for the baboons or any genetically enhanced animal, but every corner turned revealed another empty and rotting room.

He found the kitchen and opened the refrigerator. He had seen lights in the house last night so he hoped there might be something edible in the place. The smell that greeted his nose practically knocked him unconscious. A pitcher of green cottage cheese was all that could be seen in the barren expanse of the interior. He slammed the door shut and walked a few paces away before taking a breath. He had to concentrate to keep his stomach down. He could not afford to lose what little fuel was left in his body.

He opened a large pantry and saw a few boxed items with Hindi labels. One displayed photographs of ripe persimmons. He grabbed the box and was shocked to see something black coiled in a dark corner of the cabinet. He accessed the flashlight mode on his Omni and shined it onto the shape.

The cobra shot up toward the shelf above it, opening its hood to strike. He jumped back a few feet, ramming his back into a counter.

"Fuck," he hissed. He scanned the room to be sure there was nothing else crawling or slithering around the house. Time to leave.

He walked several miles before he was able to catch a ride on a public bus. He finished the box of dried persimmons, which were enough to hold him for a while. At least the bus fare was cheap. Roughly a thousand dollars remained in his account. Not enough to leave Mumbai, but he figured he could seek out Parks by going to the local DOP chapter house. First he wanted to check on NTI. He still held a guest pass on the Gordy Omni. He wanted to see if he could get any kind of lead on Sumit or Anjali.

Police cars were parked in front of the NTI building. He walked up to the entrance, was scanned, and admitted. Once in the lobby, two policemen approached him. One was out of uniform, presumably the investigator. The man wore black dress pants and a white shirt. Jake was always impressed at how little anyone seemed to sweat. They were acclimated, or chipped.

"Jake Travissi?" The investigator's demeanor was very polite, almost humble.

Jake enjoyed the pretense of asking who he was. These chipped cops knew who he was the moment he entered the building and were already accessing every digital file on him. "That's me, Detective…?"

"Srikanth." The man smiled. His gums were almost black. "May I ask where you were last night?"

Jake lifted his shirt to show the black and blue bruise where the first dart had hit him. "I was shot twice with Splice and dumped off at a mansion outside of town."

The detective held no facial expression. Jake respected a cop with a good poker face. "Any witnesses?"

"Thousands, but I have no idea who they are."

"Your Omni was registered at the Punjab bar until 18:22."

"That's right." Jake's stomach grumbled.

"It shows you were at an apartment complex at 368 Viceroy at 18:59."

"Is that a warehouse district?"

The detective shook his head. "Residential. An apartment block to be precise."

"I was in a warehouse district and then the mansion with a rickshaw in between."

The detective reached for Jake's Omni. "May I?"

Jake took off both Omnis and handed them to the detective. He walked over to an outlet in the lobby's seating area and plugged in both. The uniformed cop stood between Jake and the door. Jake took a seat across from the detective.

Srikanth checked the location for both Omnis in the past twenty-four hours. Both of them showed Jake at the Viceroy address at 18:59. His heart sank. Sanchez, Sumit, or someone in The Consortium had reprogrammed his Omnis while he was unconscious at the mansion.

Srikanth handed the Omnis back to Jake. "Unfortunately, I'll have to take you into custody." The detective rose and nodded to the uniformed officer. "It would be far easier if you told the truth now. Under international law, I'm allowed to use Splice and other methods in order to extract information. Before yesterday's announcement of a cure, you would have been immunized."

Jake stood up and gestured for the door. He wanted to seem as cooperative as possible so they would not handcuff him. He needed to think. The detective led the way and the officer followed. Jake turned off his Omnis and shoved them in his pocket. Even with another dose of Splice, he knew he was not at the scene of the crime, but he had witnessed the POV of the shooter. He had details that only someone at the crime scene could know. If the detective went down that track of questioning, Jake would be putting his head in the noose. *Sanchez, you clever bastard. That footage was not to dissuade me. It was to frame me.*

As the detective approached a police car, the door swung open displaying a caged interior. If Jake got in that car, he might never see daylight again. Then again, how far could he get if he ran? How would that look? Where was Parks?

In the seconds it took to reach the car door, Jake reviewed all the streets and alleys he had walked since leaving NTI yesterday. He planned an escape route through the more crowded areas. He doubted the police were using every chipped citizen as a camera. That was illegal and something left for the real puppet masters. Still, The Consortium might be nudging the situation in Srikanth's favor. Jake needed to be seen by Parks, but he was risking being seen by Sumit and Sanchez as well.

He turned and struck the uniformed officer with a sidekick to the throat. The cop buckled to the ground, clutching his neck. Jake shot a jump kick to Srikanth's chest, sending him flying into the car's interior. Jake darted into the street. He merged next to a bike lane and struck the nearest rider in the solar plexus. The rider lost control and Jake grabbed the handlebars, stopping the bike, but not the rider from crashing onto the street.

Jake pedaled out into automobile traffic, weaved in and out of cars, and made a quick left down a side street. It was at this point he noticed all traffic was frozen behind him. The police must be using their override to clear a path to get to him, but he saw no movement at all. Nemp? He took a quick turn down one alley and wound up in a square with an open market. He hopped off the bike and tossed it under a parked cargo truck. He dove into the crowd, searching for cloth to hide his pale skin.

An HJ roared overhead. People filed out from under the protection of umbrellas and shop tents, into the exposed areas of the market. They closed their eyes and faced the incoming HJ. They all received commands from the police via their Third Eyes. It was an easy way to single out anyone who did not comply, and an easy way to find a foreigner in the midst of a local Indian market.

A group of children in white robes and hoods ran to him. "Father! We need you at the church! Father!" One of the kids threw a white robe over Jake as they gathered around and dragged him under a tent. The proprietor passed them with a glazed look in his eyes; he was on his way to expose his face to the police. Jake threw on the robe and the children led him past three stalls into a skinny alley, barely wide enough for him to squeeze through.

When they reached the other side, an old beat up carriage attached to a big two-seat tricycle was waiting. A tattered white canopy covered the interior. The children laughed and pushed him aboard. Several climbed in after him as two massive identical Sikh twins in their mid-twenties mounted the double-seat tricycle.

They pedaled down an adjoining alley, away from the jet wash of the HJ and merged onto a large avenue.

A figure wrapped in white robes and a veil was nestled amongst the children across from Jake. Brown eyes twinkled at him from under the shroud. Jake spotted the outline of a filter mask.

Jake extended his hand. "You must be my guardian angel."

The figure shook his head.

A boy of about six addressed Jake. "Father mustn't expose his skin. Too many eyes about."

Jake put his hand back in his robe.

"It is best that Father observe silence during our journey."

Chapter 48
Obsession

Anjali was up all night in one of the two undamaged labs attempting to find a cure, but she could not shake her growing suspicions about Sumit. She even tried distracting herself with her endangered and extinct species project, but to no avail. The more she studied Max2, the more she realized how much it had in common with the cure she had developed for Max1. Much of the work she had done in bioengineering had been stolen when she was chipped. She wasn't sure how much, but Max1 always seemed suspiciously similar to her nano-flu vaccine. Now it seemed that even without her Chip, someone continued to steal or sabotage her work for deadly purposes.

She poured over her data multiple times and could not understand why vaccine 643 failed against Max2. She noticed that notes had gone missing, locked files on her Omni had been open and details were not as they should be. At first she thought she was losing her Aspergers edge when it came to organization, but she chalked it up to fatigue and age instead, even though she was only thirty-seven years old. But ever since McMurdo, she began suspecting

Sumit. His dedication to scientific discovery and bettering humankind used to trump his drive for fame and fortune. His lesser qualities seemed all-consuming during the past few months. He was becoming increasingly useless.

When she awoke to find police standing in her lab, she wondered if they had come to the same conclusion, but that was silly. She had never voiced her theory and no one else was aware of her suspicions. When the police informed her of Doctor King's death, the pieces began falling into place. Although Sumit had not been actively working alongside her for the past six weeks, she shared her notes and theories with him via Omni on a daily basis.

When the police left, she called Sumit's Omni only to reach voicemail. She checked their hotel and learned he had slept there, but had not arrived until after one in the morning. She thought of the infection pattern of Max2. The origin had been traced to McMurdo. Sumit's behavior during that trip had been odd. Most people suspected her of being oblivious to her surroundings, but that was not true. She was keenly observant; she just had a hard time connecting emotionally with people. Sumit knew her better than anyone, and he had been careful to shield himself from her. She had given him the benefit of the doubt, but she now felt that everything pertaining to Max1 and 2 revolved around Sumit. *What of his sacrifice in the Shackleton Lounge? He took a bullet and was burned trying to protect me?* As endearing as the action was, it was not her husband. *Maybe his Max2 has been activated and he is a Pin Head?*

The idea put a healthy dose of fear into her system. A Pin Head in their cell would compromise everything. It was far more likely that Dr. King had been betrayed by Sumit's God Head. What if Sumit had hacked her, used her data to put the finishing touches on Max1, and then used her work to finish Max2? But her hack had happened long before the introduction of Max2. Sumit's mind, hacked or not, was more than capable.

Then there was the bullet wound he had sustained in McMurdo. It should have killed him, unless he had been lucky—as he stated—or a Max2 Chip helped to close off that artery and reroute the blood flow to his brain. She did not want to believe it, but the idea that he was hacked was far less painful than thinking he'd voluntarily betray her.

The police showed her images of the forty-three people found dead in the same apartment building with Gordon King. She recognized some of them, but not all. Based on police identification, they all fit the profile of people who would belong to Erasmus cells. The Order of Erasmus was officially dead. The Consortium had won, and the enemy had not been Parks at all. It had been her husband.

Do you know that for sure? Enough to turn him in? The question had distracted her all night. *Time to hang up the research and put your mental prowess into attaching facts to your hunch.*

She asked Detective Srikanth if he had any leads, hoping that he would say her husband, as it would take much of the burden off of her.

The detective answered. "Jake Travissi is at the top of our list."

"Jake?" Anjali raced through all the evidence in her mind. None of it added up. "You sure?"

"We have his Omni registered at the scene of the crime."

She laughed. "Anyone can fake an Omni signature once you have a device hacked."

"His DNA was found at the scene."

"Planted."

"Then he won't mind going to the station and answering some key questions that only the killer could know."

She shook her head. "Suit yourself."

"We saw the tapes and know you spent the night here, otherwise I'd bring you in as well. Care to enlighten me on something you know?"

She gave him her best deadpan. "I don't know anything. I just think Jake is the wrong man."

"Any scientific evidence to back that up, Doctor Malik?"

She clucked her tongue. "I'm in the theoretical stage. I don't present anything without empirical evidence."

"Our methodologies have much in common." Srikanth thanked her and left.

After calling the hotel to check on Sumit, she spent a half hour trying to work on the Max2 cure. But her thoughts continually wandered to Sumit and his connection to everything that had happened since they had arrived in Antarctica. She began to suspect him in Shanghai, but used the Max2 cure and her animal pictures to suppress her thoughts. But her suspicions had grown too large to ignore. She sighed and gave in to her wandering mind.

As she was about to dive into think mode, meaning putting in earplugs to shut out all distractions, she heard a commotion from the street below her office. She peered out the window just in time to see Jake Travissi kicking Srikanth into a police car. Jake ran into traffic and several Macaque guards jumped to pursue him. Anjali ran to her control equipment and hit the master security button. She clumsily reached in her pocket and a collection of earplugs shot into the air. Alarms rang and the building shot out a Nemp that hit an area three blocks wide. She stuffed her fingers in her ears as all electrical equipment died. Chip communication ceased, and Jake's odds of escape increased.

When the police questioned her, she would simply say she was trying to help them out. She could play the eccentric scientist to her advantage when it suited her.

Chapter 49
Children of Parks

The Mumbai chapter of the Disciples of Paul took up an entire office building in the downtown area. The Sikhs dropped off Jake's rescue party at a service entrance in the empty parking garage. They relieved him of his two Omnis.

One of the children explained, "They must be reprogrammed so the bad men don't chase you anymore."

The Sikhs pedaled downward into the bowels of the building. There were hundreds of bicycles in the garage but almost no automobiles.

They entered through a Nemp generator and then were screened for nano-viruses. They all tested positive for Max2. Jake noticed every child wore between two and four Omnis. The figure in white cursed under his breath when he saw his test result.

After the test, they were released into an atrium where dozens of parents were playing with their children. The parents of those who had traveled with Jake were reunited with their little ones. Jake loved hearing the squeals of sheer delight all around him. Here it seemed no one was chipped.

"No one is," Parks responded when Jake asked. Parks was in the midst of taking off his white robes and veil. His voice was muffled from the mask. "If I can't travel by limo or armored car, I make sure I cannot be readily identified." He took off the mask. "I've got Max2!" He laughed. "The Lord saw fit that I should fight on equal ground."

Parks entered the atrium and led his flock in prayer. "Father, we thank you for your wisdom and guidance and pledge ourselves in your holy war against all of Satan's technological terrors."

Jake faded out as Parks quoted from the Bible. He looked upon the crowd that hung on every one of the Reverend's words.

When Parks finished, many of the residents came up to shake his hand. "It's good to have you back, Father."

"We are with you, Father."

Parks responded with "Jesus is with us—Thank you, my sister—Where is, Vaamdev? I want to see him at afternoon Mass."

Everyone wore white, and treated Parks like a parental figure. It made Jake's skin crawl. Parks spoke Hindi and other dialects like a native, an extra benefit of being chipped.

When they reached an elevator bank to go up to Parks' private penthouse, Jake whispered, "Don't you find all of this adoration a bit creepy?"

Parks winked. "You mean, do I find people treating me like their spiritual leader odd? No. I see the Disciples as my children and I'm their father. I'm Latino, which means I place family first."

Jake raised an eyebrow. "So where's your real family?"

"They all have prominent roles in the church and are stationed around the world."

Jake shook his head. "This just doesn't add up with the kid I knew back in the LAPD."

They stepped into an elevator and Parks brought his voice down. "I've pursued popularity my whole life, Jake-o. I was never comfortable with my Latino identity, but I was too brown to be white. It wasn't until I was chipped that I felt true confidence. When I lost it, I found myself in Jesus." He turned to Jake. "I feel right at home."

"Reminds me a bit of Jim Jones."

Parks gave him a blank look.

"Use your Chip and look it up."

"It's off."

"You've got an off switch?"

Parks nodded. "I've got a Gen 8S, the same type The Consortium are using. They are EMP and practically hack-proof. Going to be a bitch once Max2 starts to convert on a worldwide scale. I'm sure the enemy has that little problem worked out since they're the assholes who deployed it."

"Why switch off your Chip?" Jake asked.

"I've got Nemp generators all over this building and plenty of shielding. Can't reach out anyhow."

"I thought the Dopes—"

Parks shot him a withering look.

"Sorry—the Disciples weren't chipped. And since when do you take yourself so seriously?"

"My dopes saved your ass so I expect a little reverence, Jackhammer. The Nemps were for Max1, and to keep the hacking down to a minimum. My sanctuaries are invisible to all prying electronic eyes. I like my privacy and pay a premium for it."

The elevator stopped and the doors slid open. Jake whistled when he saw the floor to ceiling windows encasing the massive loft. It was mostly a wide-open floor with a couple of closed off rooms. "Looks like ten thousand square feet…"

Parks smiled. "Twelve."

"All of this is funded by Cobalt Industries?"

"Until last summer, the church paid for itself. I was the Prophet of profit." He chuckled and pulled out a solidarity pin from his pocket. "Now I sell enough of these to support the church."

Jake shook his head. "Ah yes, all proceeds go to charity…"

Parks stood next to a window and looked down eighty stories onto Mumbai below. "There's a nationwide APB out on you. The Consortium has made sure your warrant has been escalated to the highest levels. You're going to be international news again." He turned back to Jake. "But only for a second. Gunning down forty people is nothing compared to the millions dead in China."

Jake narrowed his vision on the Reverend. "You switched your Chip back on."

"Of course. Can't stand to be without it for more than ten minutes."

"Sure you're not getting a little confidence boost from it?"

Parks flashed a grin. "Maybe. I've got some other sweet built-ins as well." He tapped his head. "I had some God Head software installed a few months back. It comes in handy whenever I need to perform some miracle work on a chipped convert."

"You're the strangest man of the cloth I've ever met."

"The Lord allows me to use whatever tools I need to spread the Word and fight for Him."

"What word is that?"

"We are all created equal and deserve to pursue a life of peace, liberty, and happiness."

Jake eyed him skeptically. "That's in the Bible?"

"The abridged version."

"And an individual can pursue these as long as he or she abides by the other doctrines of the church?"

"Of course, and before you ask it, yes the DOP believes in tithes."

Jake chuckled. "Of course you do, Reverend Profit."

Parks shook a finger. "God does not build cathedrals, money does."

"As you said, you saved my life, but don't ask me to convert."

"No? What's in your heart, Jake?" Parks turned to him and put his hands on Jake's shoulders. Parks was about his height and he could tell by the way the light cotton fell on his old subordinate that Parks was extremely fit. Jake wondered if it was good old-fashioned exercise or The Chip at work. "Sanchez and The Consortium let you go so you could be arrested for the assassination of Gordon King and the cells that directly reported to him."

Jake nodded. "I'd agree."

"I'm hacked into quite a few places. Places The Consortium are not aware of yet. Sanchez would prefer you get arrested, be sent to prison and chipped. At that point he'd drop your mind into an even deeper cell. He wants to return the favor you did for him five years ago. Although from what I gather, once Max2 is activated, all prisoners will be switched off." Parks winked. "Non-essential personnel. Who needs hit men and criminals when Chips and God Heads will do the work for you?"

Jake felt a tad suspicious. "How do you know so much about Sanchez?"

"I've been monitoring him for six months. I've even seen some hacked conversations. That man hates you, and he's become far more devious and amoral since serving his time."

Jake sighed and turned to look out the window. "If I thought it could make a difference, I'd take him out right now. But I'm beginning to doubt whether cutting the head off of one member of The Consortium would make a damn bit of difference. It's a hydra."

Parks swung him around. "Do I have to slap you, Travesty? Sure there's not a God Head lurking inside your noggin pissing on your common sense? Maybe he's stepping on your dick?"

Jake shook his head at Parks' adolescent speak. "This isn't some grade-school playground. I've been questioning a lot of my past tactics. Mainly, I see the world on the brink of destruction and I'm feeling like I don't want to kill anymore."

Parks slapped his own forehead. "Jesus, Jake! Wake up! This is war. The stakes could not be higher. You cannot walk a middle path anymore. I'm living because I preach extremism. I act like an eighteen-year-old because it's not the norm. The Jihad Brotherhood has the Middle East and Africa living in a Nemp-soaked zone and they're dying like flies from Max2, but their tactics are about to change. They've got a boat load of God Heads based in Mecca that are ready to unleash a Jihad the likes of which this world has never seen. I know because I've been helping to arm them."

"You what?" Jake leaned against a window. He was feeling weak and his stomach was growling like mad. "Are you trying to save the world or tear it apart?"

"Both—When did you eat last?"

"I had one meal yesterday and some dried persimmon chips this morning."

"What do you want?"

Jake perked up. "Seriously?"

"Anything."

Jake smiled. "I want a filet mignon, side of wild mushrooms, and a blueberry protein shake."

"I can do the steak, the rest have to be substitutes."

Jake laughed. "Steak in a Hindu country?"

Parks rolled his eyes. "Steak in any country is tough. And wild mushrooms? Shit, I haven't seen a button-top since I was a kid, and I'm guessing wild ones were a hoax to begin with."

Jake took a seat on one of three leather sofas. He smelled the aroma and gave Parks a look of surprise. "Is this real?"

"Of course. I run the number one weapons and heavy armor manufacturing company in the world."

Jake rolled his eyes.

Parks hit him in the shoulder. "You were the one who told me I'd go places."

"Within the LAPD, and besides, I was chipped. It might have been my God Head talking, or yours."

Parks pointed his finger at Jake. "Nice." He flopped down next to Jake. "Based on everything going on, would you take out Sanchez and Sumit if you had the chance?"

Jake sighed. "Would it make a difference?"

Parks frowned and nodded. "I think so. The Consortium is made up of roughly half a billion men and women who think they are smarter, richer, wiser, and more powerful than anyone else in the world. They believe they are the ruling class. Putting a bullet in two of their own gets us closer to moving their numbers to a few hundred instead of five hundred thousand."

Jake turned to Parks. "Don't get me wrong. I have a strong desire to give Sanchez and Sumit payback. But I've had a lot of time to reflect since I left the LAPD."

"What if I told you they were going to take Tomoko out of circulation and use her to get you out of hiding?"

Jake clenched his jaw. Fear and rage gripped him. "I want facts. Don't fuck with me."

Parks matched Jake's serious tone. "Like I said, I'm hacked into quite a few of the communications between members of The Consortium. This is no bullshit."

"You expect me to take your word for it?"

"Yes."

Jake searched Parks' face for any sign of deception. "If you're telling the truth… I'd put a bullet in their heads."

Parks patted him on the leg. "Welcome back, Jackhammer." Parks leapt up. "Right on time! I believe you've met my right and left hand. This is Jairaj and his brother Saakaar. They're fantastic hackers, God Heads, programmers, and handy in any brawl. They're India's answer to Superman and the only members of the DOP, beside myself, who are chipped."

The two Sikhs stepped out of the elevator pushing a stainless steel room service cart. A covered tray sat on the cart.

Jake shook his head. "There is no way you cooked a steak that fast."

"Medium rare, right?"

"And it hasn't been irradiated or shot with antibiotics?"

Parks snorted. "I'm a minister, not a miracle worker. You want disease-free meat, buy a fucking time machine."

"You said I could have anything." The cart rolled up in front of Jake and he rubbed his hands with anticipation.

"Glad I'm not your executioner. Hate to see what you'd order for your last meal."

Jake cut into his steak and smiled at the beauty of it. "We're all on death row, Parks."

Parks grabbed Jake's hand. "We say grace around here, Travesty." Parks bowed his head and closed his eyes. The Sikhs followed suit. "Lord, we thank you for this bounty, for the success of Cobalt Industries, and for the prosperity of the church. We thank you for delivering Jake safely to us, and showing him the true light. Amen." Parks stabbed some mushrooms. He grabbed a small pile of garlic fries from a tray then offered them to Jake.

Jake took a handful of fries. "I'm uneasy about your assassination request. How do I know you're not hacked?"

Parks dropped the plate of fries and turned the back of his neck to Jake while handing him a steak knife. "Cut the bitch out."

"Parks…"

"Am I acting like a Pin Head? If so, do us both a solid and cut the bitch out."

Jake put the knife down. "Okay, you're not chipped, but from my vantage point, I've surfed the waves of three of the four factions." He held up his index finger. "The Order of Erasmus." He added his middle finger. "The Consortium." He held up his third finger. "DOP—You." He dropped them all and held up his pinky. "That leaves the Jihad Brotherhood. None of them are parties I would elect."

Parks leaned back and ate some fries. "We're beyond choice. This is about survival. Nobody, except Erasmus and me, wants free elections. The Brotherhood wants a technology-free world dedicated to Allah. I want a world like good old America with God-fearing Christians; although I'd take other religions, provided there was a strong moral backbone. The Consortium is an oligarchy looking to bring back the old caste system."

Jake tried to savor his steak but his hunger pains forced him to eat faster. "What happens when The Consortium gets their perfect world? I'd think a race of supermen will start to look around and realize sharing power sucks."

Parks chewed on some garlic fries. "Exactly, and the world is pretty boring when everybody waits on you hand and foot." Parks looked at his Sikhs standing at attention by the elevator. "No, that's a lie."

Jake thought of Tomoko, his mother, and Lakshmi. Would they make the cut or be switched off when The Consortium realized they'd have a lot more real estate with fewer Pin Heads on the planet. He lost his appetite.

Parks slapped Jake on the back. "You're slowing down." He snapped his fingers. "That reminds me."

The Sikhs stepped forward and produced two Omnis.

They were not his models, but he put them on his wrists. Jake knew Parks' mind was executing all kinds of orders. He wondered if Parks was having a conference call with the board of Cobalt while ordering a terrorist strike in some other country.

The Sikhs left in the elevator.

"Rather than mess with the other models, I issued two new ones. Hackers won't be able to slip shit past these localized security fields. Plus, I installed a few God Head programs in case you need assistance in hacking anything… or anyone." He winked. "Of course, that's if and when your Max2 is activated. Speaking of which, did you find out what the sound or microwave trigger is?"

"Sound is ten seconds of Smoov Z 'Baby Can't We Talk.'"

Parks almost spit up his fries. "That song sucks!"

Jake cut into another piece of steak. "I'm surprised you've heard of it. It's old millennium."

"You forget I love old millennium."

"It's 1980s old millennium. I thought you were a nineties man."

"I just downloaded it."

Jake spun around with surprise.

Parks laughed. "Don't worry. I only listened to three seconds—Shit." He stood up. "We've got to go."

Jake grabbed his blueberry shake. "Go where?"

The Sikhs returned. One of them tossed a bag at Jake.

"Sanchez and Sumit are at the airport. I say nail them now or never. They're going to bring Tomoko here if you don't. And trust me, her roller-coaster mind fuck will be far worse than yours was. I wouldn't be surprised if they kill her in the process."

Chapter 50
Descent

Jake looked inside the bag and saw a disguise. "You know I never go into a situation without a plan of attack and running through all the contingencies."

"I was a tactical officer for SWAT before I joined your team, remember?" Parks slapped Jake's shoulder. "I've got you covered, Jackhammer."

"Fill me in. I have a few things I want to accomplish before I die and I can't think of a bigger logistical nightmare than an airport."

Parks grabbed Jake's shake and set it on a chair. "You've been to Chhatrapati Shivaji?"

"Depends. Can I get it medium or hot and does it taste like Vindaloo?"

Parks laughed. "See! I knew I'd like the real you. Chhatrapati is Mumbai's airport."

Jake shook his head. "I flew a private aircraft directly into a hangar at the NTI biogenic facility."

"Nice!" Parks winked. "Chhatrapati is a massive aluminum and glass ring with the most surveillance of any airport in Asia. It's worse than a nightmare."

Jake reached in the bag and pulled out a blue garment that looked like a robe and a long white cloth. "Are you going to fill me in?"

"Trust me, Commander, you'll have a small army on your side. Just like the old days."

"In the old days, we shot unarmed people in the privacy of their own homes. We only thought we were firing on armed bad guys."

Parks rolled his eyes. "Strip to your briefs and get tan."

Jake removed his shirt and pants. The Sikhs began rubbing M-T2 on his skin. It was a melatonin activator that worked for up to two weeks. It hit full force thirty minutes after contact with skin. It was also a natural sun block. It had done very well on the market before The Chip made such things obsolete. Jake noticed the amount the two Sikhs were applying was going to make him almost black. "You guys are getting a little carried away, aren't you?"

Parks was busy slipping on his white nano-skin European suit. "Jairaj and Saakaar believe a dark complexion means a person is more powerful. I think they just like making others look more like themselves."

Jairaj took a white cloth and wrapped it around Jake's head. He realized it was a turban. Saakaar wrapped the blue robe around Jake then handed him a small case. Jake opened it and found two brown contacts floating in solution. "These won't fool a retina scan."

Parks checked himself in a mirror, making sure his apparel fit perfectly. He wore a solidarity pin. "Those are nano-refractors. They'll fool any scanner into believing you are Ravi Puranjay, a scientist from Bangladesh. The real Dr. Puranjay died in a Cobalt lab last week and it has not been reported yet. Your ID is flawless."

Jake observed the replicas of a dead man's eyes. "Was it an accident?"

Parks sighed. "He died of Max1. We were working on a cure as well. We just haven't filed his death with the authorities or notified his family yet. The worldwide body count is so high, we're allowed a week to report Max1 deaths." Parks observed Jake, who was beginning to change color. "You'll pass for him just fine. His fingerprints are in the case as well. There's a bathroom back there." Parks nodded to the nearest open door. "Put on everything in the case and then we'll talk."

Jake meandered to the bathroom. He did not like getting pushed into anything, especially dangerous situations. This was an assassination hit based on Parks' word alone and it was not sitting well. Then again, any threat to Tomoko made him irrational.

Jake gingerly nestled the contact lenses into his eyes. Despite their smooth rubbery texture, it felt like he was rubbing sand on his eyeballs. Tears flowed down his cheeks for a good minute before the intense discomfort subsided. He did not know how people lived like this before the invention of Lasik, and The Chip. He studied his new face in the bathroom mirror. His dark skin made the white turban on his head glow all the brighter. The light blue silk of his outfit appeared lighter as well. He barely recognized himself.

When he walked out, Parks was standing in front of the elevator, arms crossed with a massive Sikh behind each shoulder. He wore black sunglasses and what looked like a white wide-brimmed pith helmet to match his immaculate white suit. Jake laughed. "Posing for an album cover?"

"Dude. Album cover? How old are you?" He smiled and backed up so he was squarely between the Sikhs. "Okay, guess again."

Jake opened his mouth, but stalled.

"Oreo!"

Jake groaned.

"Humor, Jake. A little humor keeps us all from becoming a travesty." Parks turned into the elevator. "We've got to move."

Jake planted his feet. "First the plan."

"On the way!" Parks shouted as he pointed his finger down.

One of the Sikhs lifted Jake into the elevator. The doors rolled shut and they began their descent. The massive Sikh was very stoic, almost robotic. Jake grumbled. "These guys have an off switch?"

Parks pulled out an HK V5 and showed Jake the clip. The darts within were black.

Jake recognized the projectiles. They were instant death and were banned in most countries, including India. "Those are illegal."

"They're quiet. The gun is small, undetectable, and will be easy to carry in an airport. We've hacked the surveillance cameras and sensors so those won't pick you up. The crowd will keep it confusing for Sanchez and Sumit. They won't see you coming."

"Black darts are lethal," Jake repeated.

"Putting them to sleep only delays what will happen to Tomoko."

"Why don't we just get to Tomoko first? Hack her. Get her to remove her Chip."

Parks shook his head. "I cannot hack their stream. They've got her plugged into one of their God Head hubs. She's lost."

"Then how will the death of Sanchez and Sumit help?"

"It will distract The Consortium, give them something to turn their attention to on this side of the world. They're busy as hell spinning news reports, covering up deaths, God Head hacks, trying to keep what little cognizant population is left cowed until the infection has reached saturation point. They're juggling too much." Parks slapped in the clip and handed Jake the gun butt first. "It's now or never."

"And how do I get out?"

Parks nodded to Jake's Omnis. "Those will signal that you are Ravi Puranjay. They are also short range Nemps. Any electronic device within 100 yards will blank out for roughly sixty seconds. They can sustain a pulse for twenty minutes before running out of juice. Use them to get out of the airport. One of my Sikhs will be watching. They'll guide you to your final safe haven."

The elevator door opened revealing a subway station deep in the bowels of the building's garage. People milled about. Jake quickly hid the pistol in his blousy outfit. "Feels half-baked," he grumbled as they walked into pedestrian traffic.

A white veil dropped down from around Parks' hat, obscuring his identity. "Feel free to part company. We're on our way to the airport."

A hot and humid breeze belched out of the subway tunnel. A train was coming. The light cotton shirt, pants and sandals he had been given were far more suited to this climate than the Chinese clothes he had traded for them. The high-pitched hum of an electric train riding on rubber wheels filled his ears. The big transport entered the station. "This is the fastest way to the airport?"

Parks laughed. “You want to try your luck in the surface traffic?” He headed for one of the compartments. His Sikhs cut a route through the crowd for him. “Last chance, Jake. Ride shotgun or take off on your own.”

Jake knew that Parks was basically abandoning him. With his false identity it would be easier to move through the city, but then what? He hated trusting his life to such a flimsy plan, but he didn’t have a lot of options. Most of all, he couldn’t risk Tomoko. He jogged after Parks before the wake created by his Sikhs closed.

“I do this,” Jake whispered as the doors closed, “you help me extract Tomoko.”

Parks nodded. “Deal.”

Chapter 51
Monkey Business

The ride to Chhatrapati Shivaji International Airport was quick, painless, and air-conditioned. Jake wondered why anyone traveled above ground at all. He was relieved that his gun set off none of the alarms placed in the car, around the doors, and in the stations.

Thirty minutes after exiting Parks' private elevator, Jake found himself in Terminal C of Chhatrapati. The space was a massive bent arch of aluminum and glass. It reminded him of standing inside a water tube, just before the wave was going to crash. It was a beautiful airport. It had been rebuilt after the Bachelor Wars took their toll.

He spotted a half dozen enhanced baboons and macaques patrolling the terminal. Each monkey displayed a diamond growing in the hair on its back and chest. People nervously eyed them and gave them a wide berth. He checked around for an enhanced Bengal but did not see one.

"Look to your left." Parks patted him on the shoulder and promptly disappeared in the masses.

He walked slowly to his left and searched the hundreds of faces that passed through his field of view. As he weaved through the human field, he caught sight of Sanchez talking into his Omni watch. Sumit stood nearby, looking bored. Neither appeared well rested. Taking over the world must be a tiring affair.

He calculated his attack route. *Are you an agent of good or evil, Jake?* He shook Roberto's words out of his head. Time was short and he wanted Tomoko safe at all costs. He focused. He'd have to get close because there were too many people to guarantee a kill shot. He decided to cut up to the far wall, and then come over from behind so they would be blind to his approach. He worried about the enhanced primates. Any sign of trouble and they'd be spitting venom.

He made his approach, keeping enough of the crowd between himself and his quarry until he was in a good position to move in for the kill. To his frustration, his targets turned and walked toward him. He took a quick look behind and noticed a Song Corporation Robotics depot a few yards back—a storage facility for the robots that cleaned the airport and lavoratories. When he turned back, he saw Sumit staring right at him. His heart skipped a beat. Sumit blinked and continued his approach with Sanchez; Jake's disguise was working. Two baboons walked on their four hands a dozen yards behind his targets. His window of opportunity was down to seconds. The sounds of the airport faded and all he could hear was his own heartbeat. He kneeled down to pick up a nonexistent object off the tiles as his targets shuffled passed. He curled his fingers around his gun, turned, and stood.

Baboon screams pierced the airport. People gasped. Jake felt something running toward him from behind. He squeezed off a shot but the dart slammed into the wall next to Sanchez's shoulder. Big leathery black hands slammed into Jake's arm and back. Sharp pain pierced his shoulder. His targets spun around as he attempted to realign his gun. To his surprise, the baboon released his right arm and sailed above his head. It lunged at four grim-faced enhanced Rottweilers running up behind Sanchez and Sumit.

Sanchez held an automatic pistol in his hand. Jake dove for the tiled floor as Sanchez fired. Bullets ripped into the aluminum wall, tiled floor, and ricocheted into the crowd. Alarms howled, people and animals screamed. A salivating Rottweiler took a face full of venom as it snapped a baboon's neck. Jake rolled into pedestrian traffic. People toppled over him, struck by bullets. Others slammed into him, trying to flee. Jake took aim at Sanchez between the legs of panicked travelers and whizzing bullets. Fleeing feet kicked him in the ribs, throwing off his aim. His body shuddered with pain.

A body slammed into his arm, causing him to drop the gun. A baboon plowed toward him, fangs bared, knocking people out of its way. Jake turned his head to avoid a face full of poison. Sanchez's indiscriminant firing punched a hole in the baboon's head. Jake ducked as a large hairy body toppled over him. Blood, sweat, and monkey stench splashed on his neck. He struggled for air as a small pile of bodies grew around him. The gunfire stopped but the airport echoed with monkey screams and the guttural howls of Rottweilers. Jake mustered a burst of strength to free himself from the body pile. He sucked in a breath of air and saw a war between monkey and dog. The baboons spat streams of acid into the faces of the hounds. Howling, the dogs blindly lashed out with mouths full of steel fangs, and long steel claws. Sumit and Sanchez stood back to back, desperately searching for a way out of the mayhem that surrounded them. A few hundred people lined the walls, watching the scene in terror. Hundreds of others were locked in a stampede to get out.

Jake spotted his gun and dove for it. He took aim at his targets inside the eye of the enhanced hurricane. He fired a shot at Sanchez in the same instant that Sumit dodged a swipe from an enraged Rottweiler. The black dart slammed into Sumit's neck and the scientist crashed to the ground. Sanchez wheeled around and focused on Jake. Sanchez raised his gun. Jake squeezed his trigger but the gun jammed. He dove behind the pile of bodies. Sanchez fired as a baboon raised its head at a leaping Rottweiler. The poison stream missed the dog and struck Sanchez in the face. Sanchez screamed. He clawed at his smoking skin and melting eyes as a Rottweiler ripped him apart with razor fangs and claws. Sumit fell against the far wall, one hand on the dart in his neck, the other lying limply by his side. He watched the carnage before him, the light fading from his eyes. A peaceful smile spread over his face.

Jake scrambled to his feet. The guttural howls coming from the dog and monkey fight reached a deafening pitch. He slipped in a pool of blood and saw three Rottweilers fighting over the larger pieces of what had once been Sanchez. A baboon head popped off like a cork from a lucky swipe dealt by a blind dog. Animal and human bodies lay strewn about near pools of blood and gore. Many of the windows had broken leaving glass shards on the ground. The alarm continued to blare as more baboons joined the fight against the Rottweilers. Jake kicked his gun into the carnage. A half dozen berserk Rottweilers pounded past him, rushing to get into the fight. He shivered from the sheer brutality of the scene around him. All their focus was on tearing each other apart. The enhanced animals were unaware of the panicked humans still trying to get out. He searched for an exit.

An outer glass wall exploded from the sheer mass of people pressing against it, and the space drained like a broken aquarium. Jake made his way toward the hole and glanced back at the animal war. A string of genetically-engineered domestic cats moved stealthily along the rafters above the slaughter and into an open vent by the Song Corporation doors. An explosive device was strapped to each cat's back.

An ear-splitting roar blasted over the terminal. A massive Bengal Tiger with huge nano-steel coated saber teeth and claws charged into the room. Its meat-hook claws sliced through the floor tiles and the ground shook from the impact of each of its one-ton footfalls. The enraged beast plowed through the crowd to get in on the fight. People were tossed and scattered like dead leaves as it passed. Suitcase-sized muscles rippled under the Bengal's orange and black striped fur. It was as tall as a horse, but ten times more powerful.

Jake saw a little girl wandering in the tiger's path. He mustered all his strength and sprinted toward her. He picked her up and turned for the broken wall. The glassy-eyed tiger's hot breath blasted his back and its elbow brushed passed, throwing Jake several yards onto the hard tiled floor. He tucked and rolled to break their fall. He tried to get up and take a breath but the wind had been knocked out of him. The little girl ran screaming toward a woman in the crowd. The tiger reached the three Rotweilers fighting over Sanchez's body, and hurled them against the wall with one swipe of its paw.

Jake suddenly remembered he had a Nemp built into his Omni, but he was out of range from the savagery. He scanned for the girl but she had disappeared in the mob. He hastily exited the facility and activated his Nemp for good measure. Pain shot through his body. He glanced at his shoulder and noticed it was soaked with blood. He had been hit with a baboon claw. The wound was already festering with searing pain; he felt faint.

Chaos gripped the passenger pick-up area. A disorganized mass of hysterical people leapt over cars and plowed into bicyclists. Jake wondered why their Chips weren't pumping them with soothing chemicals. Maybe their Chip survivor modes had taken over, and more adrenaline was pumping into their systems than was needed.

A crazed woman screamed past him, clipping him with her shoulder. He spun into a glass wall of the terminal and a wave of disorientation swept over him. A large hand gripped his arm. He looked up to see Jairaj staring down at him.

"Down," the Sikh said with a gruff voice as the man pulled them both to the pavement. An explosion shook the ground. A wall of glass shrapnel cut into people, bikes, cars and any object within a hundred yards of the terminal's face. Fire belched out of the aluminum framework. Jake felt cold, black death running through his veins. The massive arms of the Sikh lifted him up from the ground.

"Hurry!" Jairaj barked.

More alarms blared. Auto-hydrants shot up from the ground, some shoved off wounded bystanders, and began spraying ropes of foam onto the blaze. The Sikh ran for a smoldering gate, dragging Jake behind him. They came out onto the tarmac beyond the terminals. Through watery eyes, Jake noticed a giant plume of smoke rising out of the terminal building. He felt like he was freezing solid. *Shit, I picked the wrong team. This asshole Parks is just another terrorist. Am I just a rube who's been a pawn his whole life?*

Another explosion rocked the terminal as Fire and Rescue HJs screamed onto the scene with lights flashing and sirens blaring. Jairaj was carrying him now. Jet-wash howled in their ears as the Sikh passed under several aircraft on the tarmac.

Jake began losing his sense of time and space. He felt himself thrown onto a cold steel floor. From the blurry images he was receiving, he guessed he was inside an HJ.

He heard the deep voice of Jairaj booming out, "Baboon claw!"

Jake wondered why the man was talking out loud. *I thought I was the only one around who didn't have a Chip in his head.*

Chapter 52
Pariah Express

Jake felt an intensely sharp pain in his gut and then a searing sensation in his shoulder. He awoke with an ungodly headache and a spinning room. He sat up and someone held a barf bag open for him. He puked and fell back down on hard metal decking. "Christ, that's the second time today. I hate the taste of vomit."

"Jesus forgives you taking his name in vain."

His eyes rolled around wildly before he was able to focus on an Indian woman bending over him. She wore the white robes of The Disciples. He was in the main cabin of a military HJ. Seat nets and equipment were bolted around the room. One of the Sikh twins swung in a chair. Jake spotted a state of the art God Head rig.

"Nice ship." Jake felt the pain in his shoulder and saw an extraction pad stuck to it. His skin was still dark brown. The ribs on his right side were one giant bruise. "How long have I been out?"

The woman smiled. "A few minutes. We're still over Mumbai, headed southeast, toward Sri Lanka."

"Sri Lanka!" He tried to get to his feet but pain and a wave of nausea forced him down.

"It will take a few hours for the effects of the poison to reverse. Ten more minutes and you would have died."

"Why breed security guards with lethal poison and put them in airports?"

The woman shrugged, "Why have security guards carry guns with bullets?"

"Because a guard can wound. A poison claw kills no matter where you strike the blow."

The woman smiled. "The baboon can control the amount of poison it releases, too. I'm not sure why you received a lethal dose. You must have done something very bad."

Jake rolled his eyes. "Help me into a seat." He tried to get up but collapsed again.

"Might be better if you stay on your back." Parks climbed out of the cockpit. Jake noticed Jairaj's brother, Saakaar at the co-pilot controls. At least he thought it was Saakaar. "It's easier on your muscles and joints and will allow the antivenin to move faster through your system."

Jake grit his teeth. "You set me up, asshole."

The woman tending him recoiled with a gasp.

"It's okay, Devani. The Lord is patient with this one and so must we."

The woman bowed and gazed at Parks with total adoration. Parks smiled and nodded toward one of the seats and she took it.

Parks had taken off his coat but his white pants and spotless shirt glowed as he slid down a bulkhead to sit next to Jake. "Set you up how?"

"I was a distraction, while you sent those cats into that Song Corp robotics room. What would have happened if I hadn't seen Sanchez and Sumit go down when I did? Would I have been caught in that explosion?"

Parks nodded back to the Sikh riding next to Devani. "Jairaj was shadowing. No harm would have come to you."

Jake snorted. "I saw him when I left. Outside the terminal."

Parks shook his head. "I had the whole scene on PiP through Jairaj's Chip. You were too occupied on the floor to see what was going on behind you. I thought you would have gone for higher ground and distance. Or at least activate the Nemp."

"The crowd provided the best cover, plus pistols are not known for their long range accuracy… I forgot about the Nemp when I saw the monkeys. I'm not used to them." He tried to get up but felt the pain again. "And stop distracting me. Why the hell are we headed to Sri Lanka? The US should be a straight shot east or west. You promised we'd get Tomoko."

Parks pursed his lips trying to craft his next few sentences. "Yes, and no. West is the territory of The JB. Not friendly airspace to Indian registered ships." Parks patted the steel floor plate. "Or any aircraft not registered to the Brotherhood."

"Thought you were arming the JB?" Jake suspiciously eyed Parks.

"I am, and the Muslim nations on the whole. But it's still dangerous. They tend to shoot first and ask questions later. We have neutral meeting places."

"So fly due east!" Jake's pain added to his exasperation.

Parks rolled his head around to his other shoulder. "East, is… a bit problematic as we nuked New Delhi at the same time we took out Terminal C."

Jake sat up with shock and horror. This time he took the pain and nausea as he leaned against the bulkhead across from Parks. "What?" he gasped.

"You really should lie down. That monkey junk is bad mojo."

Jake complied and slid back down to the floor. His head spun with disgust at Parks' cavalier attitude.

Parks patted Jake's shoulder. "Atta boy, Commander. The Consortium's main God Head hub for Asia was in that Song Corp storage area. There were roughly seventy-five God Heads in there. Plus, the government of India was in bed with The Consortium and put them up to nuking China. I figured it was time to play tit for tat. Even up the odds. China had been a free agent until Beijing was taken out."

"Who's taking the blame for the airport hit?"

"Given the registration on your Omni and a few other clues, The Order of Erasmus," Parks winked. "Should shock the hell out of those Consortium bitches since they thought The Order was eradicated last night." Parks leaned back and sighed. "But there's always a chance it will get traced back to me. I'm not sure The Consortium buys that I'm dead after you disappeared in Mumbai. If we're shot down, I'll know for sure."

Jake shook his head. "I knew I picked the wrong side."

Parks laughed. "Are you kidding? Gordon King would have nuked New Delhi same as me if this were a year ago. Every group has resorted to these tactics and it's getting easier the more the population turns into cows. You chose wisely, my friend. With you riding shotgun, we just might kick the bad guys out of Deadwood before high noon."

Jake was repulsed. "What's the population of New Delhi?"

"I don't have the firepower or the time for a surgical strike. It's all about keeping the enemy overwhelmed."

"How many?" Jake insisted.

"The nuke probably took out two or three million. It was a little one, planted inside their main government buildings."

"Two or three *million*?" Jake was appalled.

"The second deluge is coming, Commander. If we're not careful, we'll miss the ark."

Jake felt depression mixed with anger. "There won't be anyone left on the planet if you fuckers keep nuking cities."

"I'd rather be left with a few million free minds than have a few hundred thousand ruling eight billion slaves."

"This is not a solution. You're not just butchering wholesale, you're ripping apart the fabric of society."

"You can get off anytime you like. I've got parachutes in the back."

Jake swallowed his disgust. He didn't have any options. "I want to get Tomoko first."

"On our way, Commander," Parks smiled. "Question is, what's your plan?"

Jake jerked his head toward the God Head rig. "I'd like to hack her, make her get herself to a safe rendezvous place."

Parks shook his head. "I told you she's locked into a Consortium grid, I can't touch her."

"This grid is protected with an encryption code, right?"

Parks shook his head again. "I know where you're going with this, but the encryption is as powerful as the Omni network protecting me." He held up his arms to show off his four bands.

"You know where she is?"

Parks nodded. "She's on the reservation, cleaning up the mess from the December thirtieth attack."

"What do you know about it?" Jake hoped to get more information beyond the propaganda flooding The Cyber-Wire.

Parks grimaced. "The Consortium used the National Guard to murder ninety percent of the Fort Apache inhabitants. They destroyed every structure. The remaining survivors were chipped and are now blissfully erasing all evidence that there was ever a civilization there."

Jake slammed his fist into the HJ plating. The world was going insane. "We've got to stop this!"

"Agreed." Park nodded. "The event was quickly forgotten in the wake of Beijing and Shanghai. For the small population that remains unchipped, there are much bigger things to worry about." He stood up. "Still think you're on the wrong side?"

Jake grit his teeth. "Can we drop some sort of a Nemp? Kill the signals controlling The Chips and then hit the survivors with our own hack once the Nemp snaps off?"

Parks wobbled his head a few times. "We'd still have to hack all their encryption codes. The Nemp makes that impossible while it's on. Once it's off, our signal will be passed over for the one that has the right handshake."

Jake massaged his temples with the thumb and middle finger of his left hand. "Then we pull a Morris. What's the security like around Fort Apache?"

Parks sat down beside him, curious to where Jake was going with this. "Nonexistent, the Army and National Guard were redeployed to more critical areas. The Consortium has a lot of gaps in its net right now."

"You've got satellites watching Fort Apache? How good are they?" Jake's excitement over getting Tomoko back was pushing out the effects from the poison and antidote.

"Cobalt has geosynchronous and lower altitude passes every thirty minutes on pretty much every area on the planet. We could spot a fly on the back of a Gila monster anywhere in the world. Even with all the orbital garbage up there."

Jake clapped his hands. "We need a Nemp, a holo-projector with housing that will withstand the wave, and we're in business. Any vehicles left in the area that fit the bill?"

Jake noticed Parks' eyes dart to Jairaj. The Sikh turned his back to them. The entire exchange took a second. "There's a National Guard munitions depot near Globe. We've spotted a vehicle that could launch a Nemp and project a hologram while the Nemp is running. The Nemp fires from the roof near the cab. The holo-projector fires out the tail, which is in the Nemp's shadow created by the vehicle's armor."

Jake nodded; he had seen configurations like this when he was in the LAPD. Vehicles like that had been experimental back then. Much more was possible in the shadow of the vehicle, like targeting lock and firing chemical-propelled rockets. The LAPD had been looking into them in the event of domestic terrorist attacks. "What would be the response time between the moment the Nemp hits and the first wave of cavalry?"

Parks smiled, he had figured out where Jake was going with this. "Between fifteen and twenty-five minutes. Let's stick with fifteen to be safe. We'll need to hack the vehicle, pinpoint Tomoko by satellite, synchronize the vehicle's navigation computer to the satellite, upload the message to deliver to all those who will suddenly find themselves in a graveyard, then fly in and extract Tomoko."

Jake rolled over and punched Parks in the thigh. "Bingo!"

"The Nemp will cut them off from a God Head signal, which means The Chip will automatically put the Pin Head's consciousness back online, unless there's some sort of subroutine preventing that... but that's not normal procedure. I suppose there's a chance not everyone will get our wake-up call."

Jake nodded. "It's a chance we have to take. I want to record the message."

Parks winked. "Of course."

"Perfect." Jake licked his teeth. "And you can fly this bird into US airspace fully armed?"

"I'm a member of the Texas Airborne Militia. The US is the one place I can fly any bird fully armed and ready to fight. Although, after this stunt that may change."

Jake nodded. "What's our ETA?"

"About twelve hours."

"Give me four and I'll be ready to record the message." Jake pointed to the God Head machine. "Show me how to work that as well. I want to know how to use every weapon at my disposal."

"You go, Jackhammer!"

Chapter 53
Brain Freeze

They were flying over the northern Philippines by the time Jairaj found the Nemp assault vehicle in Globe, Arizona. Jairaj hacked into the vehicle's command computer and sent it moving out of a low security storage area. He switched off its transponders and tricked the weapons depot computer into believing the vehicle was still in inventory. The armored shoebox-shaped van would take about an hour to reach San Carlos, which was where the Cobalt satellites pinpointed Tomoko. She was part of a chipped cleaning crew hard at work burying the bodies from the December thirtieth attack. Parks' HJ was a good ten hours away from their destination.

"Why use people instead of robots?" Devani asked.

"Robots are expensive and would be missed," answered Saakaar. "People are in surplus. Far more expendable now."

The answer made Devani and Jake feel sick, but Saakaar was right. Jake set to work recording his sixty-second message. Once finished, Jairaj uploaded it to the Nemp assault truck and programmed it to fire a continuous Nemp and project Jake's presentation as soon as they were thirty thousand feet above San Carlos. They would drop straight down the moment the Nemp was activated. The nuclear HJ was skinned in EMP armor, but it would have severe sensor limitations in a Nemp field. The probability of detecting a counterattack was slim given all the electro-magnetic garbage that would be flooding the area.

Parks had been kind enough to have the Cobalt satellite network do a search for Jake's family. Beartracker had spent his life avoiding databases. With his many identities, the computers were unable to do a practical search. They did spot his mother and Husky in Manaus. They were still unchipped according to the records, but again, records were being altered by the hour. The Consortium was working overtime to prepare for their new world order. Jake had to have faith.

"Tomoko's rescue is risky, and you're still vulnerable through your mother and Lakshmi. Any information the DOP has, The Consortium has," Parks commented.

"Anything worthwhile in life is risky," Jake retorted. "We'll just have to wing it." He felt used and it was time for Parks to pay back.

Parks laughed. "This coming from the man who needs a plan before he acts. I see you're bending the rules as always. Even yours."

"After the airport, I'm getting used to the quick-draw philosophy."

"Irreverend P. and the Jackhammer, gunslingers of the Old West, riding in to save the town from The Consortium." Parks slapped Jake's shoulder. "I like it."

"You have a way of simplifying everything."

Parks winked. "Characteristic of a true optimist."

Jake suppressed his pain so he could train on the God Head visor as much as possible. He was plugged into a training program, which was a walled garden inside the computer core of the HJ. The visor's sensors tracked all his physical movements and picked up his voice commands. Inside the goggles, he saw a virtual 3D world, which simulated his Pin Head. There were PiPs on the extreme right and left of his vision, showing him various vital signs of the Pin Head, and what mode it was in. Parks coached Jake via his own Third Eye by feeding his signal into Jake's interface.

Although Parks was in the cockpit, Jake heard his voice over the visor's headphones. "In passive mode, you can give verbal commands to the Pin Head. Tell them to pick up a cup, tell them they have nausea, feel depressed, or happy."

Jake told his virtual Pin Head to dance and cry. He saw the POV shake violently and he heard sobbing in his ears.

Parks continued, "If you want to control their movements, touch your right thumb to your right pinky three times in rapid succession."

Jake did so and a new window popped up showing a physical representation of the Pin Head. "Now if I make that action again, will the Pin Head copy it?"

"No. There are certain rapid hand movements that are unnatural. You'll sometimes find that there is a split-second delay between what you do and what the Pin Head does. That's why most God Heads stay away from this mode. It's far easier to suggest the action and allow the Pin Head to carry it out, especially if they are mountain climbing, scuba diving, or engaged in something that is not easily mimicked by you. The Pin Head's innate balance and subconscious awareness of an environment allows for natural movements when suggestions are made. It's like when you want to pick up something. Your mind makes the suggestion before you carry it out."

"So I really shouldn't be in this mode?"

"No, but I want you to be aware of it. Try jumping around or something else and see what happens."

Jake squatted, then turned around. The POV in his goggles showed the Pin Head was mimicking the actions. The representation on the left screen showed the full body of the Pin Head going through the same motions. "What if I want them to say something?"

"In passive mode and integration mode, you tap your left thumb to your left pinky three times in rapid succession."

"I'd like to get out of integration mode."

"Tap your right thumb to your right pinky three times in rapid succession again."

Jake did so and saw the physical representation disappear. The POV resumed a standing position. He tapped his left thumb to his left pinky and spoke. "Go to hell."

As soon as "Go" exited his lips, he heard the synthetic voice of the Pin Head demo repeat his words and inflections. "Holy crap, that's wild." The Pin Head voice repeated Jake's words, overlapping his own. "That could get disorienting."

"Touch the left pinky to the left thumb again to switch off the voice repeat."

Jake did so.

"You can alter the volume or confirm the Pin Head's speech with subtitles. But it's good to hear that the cadence and patterns are being mimicked by the Pin Head."

He practiced for a couple of hours before taking a break. There were two 3D virtual command buttons at the bottom of his field of vision: Disengage, and Offline. Offline placed the Pin Head in a coma. He hit Disengage.

He hung up the visor and spoke as Parks climbed out of the cockpit. "Nowhere near as hard as being on the receiving end. It's like playing a video game."

Parks nodded. "You're getting a ton of assistance from the God Head software." Parks tossed an Omni in tablet form to Jake. He could see a satellite map of the San Carlos area. He saw a large trench with what looked like bodies lying in it. A small tag tracked Tomoko on a bulldozer pushing bodies into the ditch.

"Good God," Jake breathed.

"They're probably all infected with Max2, so cutting out The Chip will be a temporary solution. Any remaining virus will multiply and form a new Chip as fast as it can as long as that command has been activated in the nano-virus' DNA matrix. We'll hook Tomoko up with security Omnis like the ones you have."

"What about the others?" Jake tapped on all the non-labeled people working around Tomoko. "This HJ has the space to accommodate at least fifteen additional people."

Parks shook his head. “We’re a warship, not a refugee boat; I have nowhere to take them.”

“Drop them off at one of your DOP sanctuaries.”

“And then what? Each one has the potential to be a weapon that can be used against us. I don’t have an unlimited supply of military grade Omnis.”

Jake sat in one of the hanging chairs, gripping the netting as hard as he could. He did not like leaving anyone behind, but the satellite showed at least a hundred people in Tomoko’s area. No matter what, they’d have to leave the majority behind. Jake grit his teeth. “Fine.”

Parks nodded and turned back to the cockpit.

Jake grabbed Parks’ arm. “You got anyone special?”

Parks smiled. “I haven’t settled down yet.” His eyes flicked over to Devani.

Jake smiled. Same old Parks. Jake wondered how many other disciples the Ass-Postle was sleeping with. At least The Chip was proven to be a hundred percent effective as birth control. In any other society, Parks’ behavior would be scandalous for a celebrity preacher. Between the terrorist attacks, epidemic, and growth of the police state, who could be bothered? Then again, a scandal would be a good distraction from all the bad news.

“I give the plan a fifty-fifty chance. We have the advantage of scanning the ground before we activate the Nemp, but there’s no telling if The Consortium will be tracking this ship the moment we enter US airspace. Once they destroy our Nemp, they’ll have an army to attack us without sending one tank or HJ.”

Jake grimaced. “If you were told you had only weeks or days to live, would you squander them in fear or fight until the bitter end?”

Parks smiled. “That’s why you’re my hero, Jackhammer. Quitting is not in your vocabulary.”

Jake laughed. “You should have seen the way I spent my last five years.”

“We’re all due a little R&R once in a while. But when you’re focused, you’re like a rabid dog that gets lockjaw on the first bite.”

They all slept for the next seven hours in cots hung from hooks in the HJ ceiling. It was not the most comfortable bed Jake ever slept in, but he was too exhausted to care. When the Omni alarms began going off, he didn’t stir until Devani shook him awake.

"Everything's ready. It's time to get to work."

"Thanks." Jake rolled out of his bunk and found the army version of the in-flight bathroom. It was a suction tube with privacy barrier. The barrier was a flowered shower curtain so Jake assumed Parks had added it.

As he put on his assault gear he made a comment to Parks, "As the fifty-five percent owner of Cobalt Industries, why the hell don't you have real bathrooms in your Four Horsemen of the Apocalypse?"

Parks chuckled. "What's wrong, Jackhammer, you feeling a bit bashful in mixed company?"

"Not at all, just figured you could install a real crapper in this non-stop warship."

"This isn't one of my horsemen. It's a version I sold to the Indian Army. They loaned it back to me for repairs." Parks winked. "Don't worry. The twins modified her before we took off."

"That's not what's bothering me." Jake was alarmed. "We're flying an Indian war bird into US airspace?"

"Relax, we're already over Arizona. Our transponder shows we're registered with the Texas militia. Even the aircraft itself is registered. Jairaj took care of it before we left for the airport—Nemp detonates in seven minutes."

The Sikhs donned their battle gear as well. They all sat in the net chairs. Parks promised an accelerated drop straight down for twenty thousand feet before he switched on the thrusters to break for landing. Jake ran through what would happen down on the ground.

The Nemp assault vehicle would park in the area near Tomoko. The Nemp will activate. Everyone in a one square mile radius will be cut off from all electronic signals. Without a God Head signal, Chips will automatically default to put a human consciousness back online. Tomoko and others will wake up on the scene of a holocaust. They will be disoriented and shocked by the sudden change in their environment. The projector will snap on showing a thirty-foot tall Jake Travissi who will rotate as he speaks. Jake recalled the message.

"Wake up! A group called The Consortium has enslaved you. They murdered The People and put Chips in your brains to force you to bury your dead. Find any sharp object and cut out this Chip immediately, like so." His image would split into four so that his backside would be facing four directions at once to ensure everyone would see the five second simulation of him cutting The Chip from the base of his skull. Then the image would return to its original state. "Fight them! Cut out the object of slavery and fight!" The recording would repeat as long as the Nemp lasted.

Parks voice filled the cabin. "Nemp is on. Descent starts now."

Jake's stomach hit his neck. The ship plummeted backward, as if it were suspended by a cable that was suddenly cut. He closed his eyes as the HJ shook. It might take a while for some of the Pin Heads to find an object, much less cut out The Chips. The drop would take about ninety seconds before the thrusters kicked on. It felt more like a half hour passed.

The thrusters fired. The ship leveled out. They made a three-G turn. The nose lifted up. They slammed hard onto the ground.

Jake struggled to get out of his net chair as the bottom ramp in the aft hummed open. The Sikh twins darted out in full military gear. Each gripped a state-of-the-art C-7 combination rifle—grenades, machine gun, flamethrower—ready to fire, manufactured by Cobalt Industries, of course. Devani and Parks stayed behind in the cockpit ready to take off in case they needed air cover.

Parks' voice barked over the loud speaker, "Get your ass in gear, Travissi!"

Jake barked back, but knew Parks could not hear. "Fuck you, rookie!" He dropped out of his chair, grabbed his combination rifle and ran after the Sikhs.

Chapter 54
Massacre

They landed less than half a mile from the spires of San Carlos, but the gleaming towers had been reduced to charred ruins. Five days had passed since Jake had left, but fires deep within the city still burned. Satellites did not prepare him for what he saw or smelled. The overpowering stench of thousands of bloated and rotting corpses punched into his nose and put a chokehold on his throat. He concentrated on his mission to keep from doubling over and vomiting.

Millions of flies buzzed under a mild winter sun. Large trenches had been dug and filled with bodies, the bodies had been burned and were waiting to be covered with dirt. This was genocide.

He thought of his father, his half sister and the innocent victims lying in the trenches and on the desert earth. A sense of rage flooded his being. He wanted to kill. He wanted revenge. What was even worse… no one on the planet was even aware of this atrocity. There would be no records, not even a date.

Through the dust storm created by the HJ jet wash, he sighted the thirty-foot projection of himself. The projection currently showed how to remove The Chip. The Orwellian nature of the scene made him shiver. He heard a loud scream and spotted one of the enlightened ones, an antelope, smashing the holo-projector with a shovel.

"Lies! Murderers! White devils!"

Jake glanced at the vehicle's roof and saw more damage. Then he heard the electric bulldozer humming through the crowd. Another enlightened one, this one a raven, was driving.

"Oh, shit." Jake spoke into his helmet. "They took out the Nemp."

"Move it!" Parks barked as the antelope jumped out of the way just as the raven plowed into the back of the Nemp assault vehicle. The projection sputtered out.

Jake spotted the Sikhs gathering First Nation and local Caucasians. The Sikhs checked the back of each person's head to be sure they had removed their Chips; quickly using a P-Chip remover on those who had not.

He spotted a body that looked familiar. As he approached, he recognized Isabella Beartracker. She was bloated from a few days of exposure. Her long silky black hair was now a mangled matted mess. He felt panic and sorrow. Was his father among the dead, too? He had barely met his half-sister, but he felt grief all the same.

Parks yelled. "Find Tomoko! The Consortium signal is back on-line. Things are about to get very ugly."

"Roger that!" Jake swallowed his grief and channeled his anger and desperation to find his fiancé. He plowed through dozens of confused and sobbing people. One woman held her dead son, wailing in Apache. It was a scene of absolute horror. When he found her, Tomoko was staggering among the dead and grieving, a two-foot strip of twisted metal in her bloody hand.

"Tomoko!" He ran and grabbed her.

Parks' voice crackled. "Times up! Get back to the HJ!"

In that instant, the still-Chipped people, women, men, and children attacked the Sikh twins using stones and whatever sharp objects they could find. The massive Sikhs stood back-to-back, firing at anyone who attacked.

The wolf guard Jake had seen at the checkpoint just days ago lunged at Tomoko from behind a pile of corpses. Jake swung Tomoko behind him and opened fire with his combination rifle. It had been set to flamethrower and he cringed when the wolf screamed but continued to close in. Jack let Tomoko go, switched the weapon into machine gun mode and stopped the wolf just a foot away from striking distance.

Jake picked up his dazed fiancé and headed back to the HJ. It was airborne, churning up dust clouds, and firing short bursts from its mini-guns. Chipped Pin Heads fell amongst the non-chipped and overwhelmed survivors. Parks was using his Chip and the HJ's targeting computer to single out any hostile activity and cull them from the rest.

Parks yelled, "Get behind me!"

Jake swung Tomoko over his shoulder, freeing up his right arm to continue firing. He ran toward the HJ. The Sikhs were a hundred yards ahead. The HJ mini-gun bursts continued.

"Close your eyes!" he shouted to Tomoko as he knocked his helmet's face shield down with the barrel of his gun. He saw the HJ in its full glory. Its molecular armor was painted in jungle camouflage with small flags of India fixed to its belly and sides. She displayed two tank-busting guns mounted on turrets, two mini-guns, and missile bays fore and aft. She was one hell of a killing machine. Only she was killing good people.

They entered the thickest part of the dust cloud as a missile fired off the HJ above their heads. He turned to see the flame of a rocket streak off into the west. He bumped into Saakaar as they heard an explosion in the direction of the rocket.

"Just nailed a tank! But they have more!" Parks yelled as the HJ descended and the ramp opened. "Jump in!"

The Sikhs were first. Jairaj held onto a strap on the ramp and pulled Tomoko in. Jake leapt onto the ramp just as the HJ swung its nose forward causing everyone to tumble back inside. The HJ screamed over the carnage of San Carlos before firing off another missile and turning south.

As the ship settled, Jake ran to Tomoko's side.

He tore off his helmet so he could press her face against his.

She pulled away. "Who are you?"

He realized his skin was still very dark, although his eyes no longer had brown contacts. "It's me. It's Jake."

She suddenly realized who he was and grabbed hold of him like a frightened child.

Parks' voice broke over the cabin speaker. "We're not out of this yet, kids. We've been ID'd by The Consortium. I'm hugging the deck to stay off the grid. I've got satellite jamming above, but they'll be hunting us now. I was hoping they'd concentrate on the JB before turning to me. I guess they figured out I'm not dead after all."

"Where are we headed?" Jake asked the room, figuring the message would be relayed to the cockpit through one of the Sikh's ears.

"I've got a chapter down in Mexico. We'll regroup there. A dozen small wars have erupted in the last twelve hours, countries that didn't ally with The Consortium or the JB. I'm also getting data that Max2 is at ninety-seven percent saturation. The showdown at the OK Corral is just about here. But I've got good news!"

Jake shook his head at Parks' endless optimism.

"The moon has seceded. They no longer recognize any government down here! To my knowledge, they stopped allowing flights as soon as Max1 broke out so it's doubtful Max2 is up there."

Jake liked the sound of that, but also knew there were a pile of scientists on Luna and they tended to be early adopters. "How many of those Loonies are chipped?"

"A hundred percent. But no reports of MaxWell."

"Great." Jake kissed Tomoko. "We won't be trying to catch a flight up there anytime soon."

Chapter 55
Conversion

They flew over riverbeds of mud and dust, making their way down to the DOP chapter in Acapulco. Parks switched the HJ's transponders to identify itself as a Mexican Federale aircraft.

They encountered no resistance. Mexico was dealing with the epidemic and its ongoing fight with the US over water rights. Although Mexico had managed to build enough desalination plants over the past decade to quench its country's thirst and water its crops, they were still upset about US trade policies and that the US swallowed every drop of water that used to flow over the border.

Jake spent the three-hour flight overjoyed to be back in Tomoko's company. They leaned against the rear bulkhead, away from the others.

"I remember your father's home and getting sick. I remember feeling an intense cold that made my bones hurt. The hospital… the implantation procedure… and I remember the faces of the dead on the reservation…" Her voice trailed off.

He held her close and kissed her head. "It's over now. I'm never leaving your side." As he stroked her hair, he contemplated her news. *Why had they implanted Tomoko if she had contracted Max2?* "I didn't get a chance to look at the piece of metal you used to cut out your Chip. Did you notice a Chip on it?"

"I saw something small and hard, yes. I also saw some shiny substance. Like mercury mixed with blood."

Sounded like Max2. He wracked his brain trying to figure out what The Consortium was up to.

She shivered. "When the Nemp hit, it was like waking up from a nightmare, only reality was worse than being asleep."

"I'm so sorry. I came as fast as I could."

She snuggled into his chest. "Now you're saying we're all chipped?"

He looked into her eyes. "That's what Max2 is, a viral form of a Third Eye."

She gripped his arms. "If these are really our last days, I don't want to waste them."

It sounded appealing. But what did she mean by that? *Take it one minute at a time. What do you want to do more than anything at this moment?* The answer popped into his head and he cleared his throat. "Let's get married."

Tomoko rolled over and put her head in his lap so she was staring straight up at him. She smiled as a tear rolled down her cheek. "Really?"

Jake caressed her face. He felt a tear welling up as well. "Yes."

"I love you."

He smiled at her renewed sense of hope. He was not sure how much he held himself, but her sincerity was infectious. "I love you, too."

They spent the remainder of the flight reminiscing about the last five years sailing around the world. It had been a time of forgetful bliss. Yet, Jake felt foolish about what they had done. Parks' words echoed in his head; *Everyone deserves a little R&R once in a while.* He thought about how desperate their situation was. Did he want to fight to the bitter end? Wasn't the future inevitable? If so, why not enjoy their last few months? They could hide in the eye of the storm and live in oblivion until the last possible second. *What about the fight? The Consortium is spread thin. There are a lot of gaps in their network.*

It's the classic Napoleon and Hitler move; they have too many fronts, too many weaknesses. You don't need superior strength to press the advantage.

Tomoko noticed he was struggling with something. She touched his face. "What's on your mind?"

He didn't have the heart to tell her, she had been through so much. She needed him. "I was thinking about hiding out with you."

She jumped up. "What? You want to run after all we've seen? I want to fight those bastards for what they did in San Carlos!"

A smile spread across his face.

"You can fight and still live. I don't want to waste another second. I want to fight while we still can."

"You can't imagine how much I adore you right now."

They landed on a tower in the middle of an old beach resort that had been converted into a commune. As they exited the HJ, Jake asked Parks, "Why the tower?"

"The entire compound is covered by a localized Nemp. Keeps out prying cyber eyes. A few feet below us, it's all nineteenth century technology."

Jake walked over to the edge of the landing platform and gazed down. The walled compound of bungalows, 1980s hotel, and a giant statue of Jesus, were about fifteen stories below them; obviously bought and converted for Parks' present-day use. Ladders and stairs lead down to the ground. "Guess we'll be walking."

Parks laughed. "They had pulleys and weights in the nineteenth century. You don't need electricity to have luxury."

Jake and Tomoko spent the remainder of the day taking a tour of the compound and meeting the faithful. Devani was assigned as their guide. Everyone wore white, smiled, and quoted the Bible profusely. Many gardened, conducted repairs, sweated in the bakery, drilled with weapons, or managed the DOP tourist trade.

"What do you do for the tourists?" Jake asked.

Devani pulled silky black hair from her eyes. "Diving, parasailing, water-skiing, HJ tours, boat tours, and fishing."

He laughed. "Is there anything to catch out there?"

Devani smiled. "We have a fish farm down south. We Chip the fish then program them to bite our lines. We guarantee a catch if you use our fishing fleet."

He laughed even harder. "I thought you Disciples were against Third Eyes?"

"Humanity was created in God's image," she chided. "The beasts were created to provide for us."

Dinner was a cafeteria affair, served in the ballroom of the old hotel. There were almost three thousand members waiting for Parks' evening prayer to be delivered before the meal.

Parks approached a golden pulpit, white robes gleaming. He spoke Spanish into an alabaster cone, a nineteenth century version of the bullhorn. Jake knew enough Spanish that he could follow along. "My brothers, my sisters, my family… these are difficult times. But The Lord in all his wisdom has an answer for us. Listen closely to Isaiah 40:28-31."

Everyone shouted out Amen.

Parks set the cone down and spoke with a loud and commanding voice. "Have you not known? Have you not heard? The Lord is the everlasting God, the Creator of the ends of the earth. He does not faint or grow weary; his understanding is unsearchable. He gives power to the faint, and to him who has no might he increases strength. Even youths shall faint and be weary, and young men shall fall exhausted; but they who wait for the Lord shall renew their strength; they shall mount up with wings like eagles; they shall run and not be weary; they shall walk and not faint."

The room erupted in a loud, "Amen!"

Parks held up his right hand and continued, "Fear not, for I am with you; be not dismayed, for I am your God; I will strengthen you, I will help you, I will uphold you with my righteous right hand! Do I hear an Amen?"

The room repeated.

Parks raised both of his hands. "Do I hear an Amen?"

The room shouted louder.

"Stand up, and shout it at the devil and all those who would rob us of our freedom! Do I hear an Amen?"

The room rose as one. They gazed upon their prophet with love, adoration, devotion and unshakable faith. Some had tears of joy in their eyes. Other's looked a tad insane. Everyone shouted at the top of his or her lungs, "Amen!" Parks was right, there was no greater power on earth than faith.

Parks bowed his head and everyone followed suit. "Father, we thank you for this bountiful meal and for bringing us together in your heart. We are one family, Lord, and we will soldier on until there is freedom and justice for all. Amen."

The crowd repeated, "Amen."

Everyone sat down to eat.

Tomoko held a wide-eyed look. "Ever see that old archive footage of Beatles or Elvis concerts… all those hysterical fans?"

Jake nodded in agreement. Parks commanded a fanatical army. He wondered how much of what Parks was telling him was a line.

After a meal consisting of tamales, tortilla soup, and corn cakes, Jake and Tomoko queued up to speak with the Reverend. The Sikh twins made sure each discussion was short. After an hour of moving up in the line, Parks shot up with a pamphlet in his hand.

"Brothers and sisters!" Parks shouted in Spanish as he held the pamphlet up high. The cover image was Roald Eberstark, the man behind the Immortality Project who had been killed by terrorists on Christmas Eve day. "Sister Consuela has asked me if there is truth in this heretic's promise." He held out his left hand and presented Consuela who bowed her head in shame. "Sister Consuela was right in asking me this question." She held up her head in hope. Parks shook the pamphlet. "Charlatan Eberstark spent the last fifteen years attempting to upload a human soul into the Cyber-Wire." Several in the audience shook their heads and muttered in anger, a few laughed at the idea. "Yes, the soul; a creation and domain exclusive to The Almighty! Eberstark used God Head technology as a foundation for his research. How fitting that he used the tools of the devil to undermine what is holy and sacred! And for his efforts he died in damnation's flame, his evil work left uncompleted! Amen!"

The room shouted back, "Amen!"

Parks turned to Consuela. "There are no shortcuts to God's Kingdom, sister Consuela. I'm afraid this is a fool's hope, left to sinners and imbeciles to contemplate." He handed the pamphlet back to Consuela and she ripped it up. Everyone cheered. Jake wondered if Parks had given Consuela some signal to tear up the pamphlet. He knew his Gen 8S Chip was running, but that no signals could get in or out of his head because of the Nemp.

When Jake and Tomoko reached Parks, he switched to English. "What can I do for you my child?" Parks' eyes glittered. He was thoroughly enjoying his role. A massive crucifix loomed behind him.

"We'd like to get married." Jake was not sure Parks was the right one to do it, but Tomoko didn't feel like wasting time and anywhere outside the compound walls held danger. Then again Jake could tell the congregation's response to Parks' sermon and his comments about Eberstark made her a bit uneasy.

Parks jumped up from his large cushioned chair. "Congratulations, Jackhammer! The Disciples of Paul hear your plea to convert and we accept you into our hearts!"

A loud "Amen" burst out behind him.

"The baptism will take place tomorrow at sunrise in the sacred pool."

The line behind shouted, "Amen!"

"Afterwards, we will celebrate the wedding of our brother and sister, Jake Travissi and..."

Jake smiled at Parks' sudden realization that he could not access the CyberWire. He was also surprised Parks did not have the world's facial recognition database in his Chip's persistent storage. The Reverend looked desperate. Jake whispered, "Tomoko Sakai."

"Tomoko Sakai!" Parks shouted.

"Amen!"

Before they were escorted away from the line, Parks made a quick comment in a very low voice. "And for a wedding present, I'll give you one of our tour boats. It's a ketch." He winked.

After the circus performance was over, Jake and Tomoko walked the courtyard. Many approached the couple congratulating them on their decision to convert. He grumbled, "I didn't realize he'd twist my proposal into a full blown conversion. I want no part of this nut house."

She nuzzled his shoulder. "I don't care. Maybe we'll be able to just look back and laugh… if we win."

Jake stopped and felt the back of his neck.

"Oh, no." Tomoko was concerned.

He gave her a big kid grin. "You've been so perfect all day I was compelled to check."

She punched him in the arm.

Jake glanced around the white adobe compound. "It would have been nice to have Lakshmi and my parents here."

"Mine, too." Tomoko nuzzled Jake. "Can we link them via Omni?"

He shook his head. "Linking could be traced by The Consortium and I don't want to expose them to that."

"With all the intel they have, I'm sure our families are already at risk."

He stopped in his tracks. Two white figures rode the pulley elevator up to the HJ platform. "What's going on?"

A Latina woman walked up to him. She spoke with a thick Spanish accent. "Dat's our Shepparrd and prrotectorr, Fatherr Parrks and our Estancia; she is a local girrl here on de compound. Dhey sleep in de HJ to be closerr to God and to prrotect us all from de evil outside de walls."

And he can connect with the world through his Chip. He wondered how Devani felt about Estancia. Maybe this was a good time to part company and take off with Tomoko. Parks and his organization were a bit complicated.

He was not allowed to sleep with Tomoko that night. Saakaar had broken the news ten minutes after they watched Parks ride up the tower elevator with Estancia.

"It is not permitted, Jackhammer." Saakaar's words disappointed, but didn't surprise Jake. The muscular man continued. "After the wedding, you'll have your honeymoon. I'm to stand guard to make sure you comply."

Tomoko had reassured Jake before Jairaj marched her away. "It's just one night."

"It's been almost two weeks," he grumbled.

"Who's counting?" She laughed.

He nodded to the helicopter tower standing in the center of the compound. "And the Reverend's night rendezvous with Estancia is okay with the flock?"

Saakaar shook his head. "Reverend Parks is not having relations with Estancia. Jairaj found a background signal in the Cyber-Wire. Could be some kind of echo due to traffic, but my brother and I think it could be AI." He shrugged. "Maybe Ai-li survived. Or could be the lunar version."

Jake chuckled. "You mean to say he's doing," he held up his fingers in quotes, "research?"

"He's the head of The Church. He answers only to the Holy Father." Saakaar was dead serious.

"How does a Sikh make sense of all this?" Jake asked.

Saakaar smiled. "I was born a Sikh, and wear the turban of a Sikh, but I converted to the DOP with my brother three years ago."

Jake nodded and let it rest. Five minutes after closing his door, he fell into a deep slumber. December twenty-second had been his last decent night's sleep. Instead of his usual nightmares, he dreamed he and Tomoko were parents to a beautiful girl. They lived in an age without Chips, wars, or Consortiums. They were a happy family.

Chapter 56
Bells

Jairaj knocked on Jake's door at 5:30AM. "Do you or Saakaar ever sleep?" Jake asked.

Jairaj smiled. He handed Jake pure white robes for the baptism. Jake put the robes on the bed and rubbed his eyes. "Good thing my mom isn't here. She's Jewish and I don't think she'd understand this New Age ritual."

Jairaj raised an eyebrow.

"Then again, given how old the Jewish faith is, any event after Moses and the Red Sea is pretty much New Age."

Jairaj blinked.

Jake slapped him on the shoulder. "Just trying to lighten things up a bit. In case you haven't heard," he whispered, "it's my wedding day."

Jairaj smiled and shrugged.

"I didn't think it was too bad for five in the morning."

Jairaj rolled his eyes. "It stank regardless of the time of day."

"The man speaks! Hallelujah!"

"My brother and I always had a shorthand way of communicating. Even before this." Jairaj rubbed his neck.

Jake nodded and picked up his outfit. It was a rough cotton robe and reminded him of a white dashiki. Jairaj exited to give him privacy. Once he was dressed, Jairaj led him out to a private reflecting pool overlooking the port of Acapulco. The entire congregation waited in silence. It surprised him to see so many were awake since he had heard no sound while he was getting dressed.

Jairaj escorted him through the crowd to the edge of the pool. Parks stood in the center of the water. The glassy liquid reflected a bruised sky and the fiery heralds of the sun perched on the eastern horizon. Dawn was about to break. Tomoko stood on the opposite side of the pool. She looked stunning in her plain white robe with her jet-black hair flowing over her shoulders. Jake could not wait to be with her for the rest of their lives.

Parks gestured for them to join him. Jairaj nodded for Jake to step into the water and walk to Parks. Devani did the same to Tomoko. Jake and Tomoko grinned like idiots as they approached Parks. The Reverend was dressed in silk robes, slicked back hair, and mirrored sunglasses. Orange fiery light reflected from his lenses, giving him an otherworldly appearance. Jake tried not to roll his eyes at his former colleague. The dark blue ocean sat behind Parks. It was beginning to light up.

Parks spoke English. "These two children, naked in the darkness of our world, have come to our Holy Father seeking light!" He put his hands on their shoulders as he spoke. "We open our hearts in welcome so that they may become one with us in the body of Christ our Savior, Amen."

Over three thousand voices spoke in unison, "Amen."

The waking sun shot rays into the white circle of disciples. All the robes behind Parks glowed with flame. "Jake Travissi, do you welcome Jesus, the Lord God, the Holy Spirit, and these brothers and sisters into your heart?"

Jake choked but forced out the word. "Yes."

"Do you promise to uphold the covenants of our faith and defend them with your life?"

Flashes of German troops pledging their lives to Adolph Hitler before the outbreak of World War II filled Jake's mind. What the hell was DOP doctrine anyway? He heard the soothing voice of Tomoko. *I think we'll be able to just look back and laugh.* Jake coughed. "Yes, I–I do."

Parks repeated the same for Tomoko. After her final affirmation, The Sikh twins joined them in the water. "By the power of the Father," Jake suddenly found himself flying backward into the water. Jairaj was giving him a full body dunking. Jake came up for air and heard "The Son," then another dunk and up again. "And the Holy Spirit," A third dunk ensued. "I pronounce you part of our family, The Disciples of Paul!"

The crowd exploded with cheers. Jake turned his gaze to Tomoko who appeared equally waterlogged but happy. The sun's warming glow spilled over all Acapulco. The white compound of the DOP reflected an orange tint. It was a beautiful spot.

He enjoyed the moment for a few seconds until he and Tomoko were whisked away by the Sikh twins and introduced to the crowd as brother and sister. Everyone swarmed them with hugs and welcomes in English, Spanish, and other languages he did not recognize.

After ten minutes of being mobbed, Parks shouted out in Spanish, "Let our brother and sister refresh! They have a wedding in thirty minutes!"

Tomoko was carried off by some of the senior women of The Church to change into dry clothes. Jake was assigned the Sikh twins.

Jake showered and was presented with a white suit. He laughed when he saw it. "One of Parks' rejects? It didn't look quite as fancy as the one Parks wore. For one thing, it was cotton, and not nano-skin or silk. The Sikhs stood by the door as still as stones. Jake shrugged. "What the hell? When in Rome…" He suited up within ten minutes. He was happy to have plain leather shoes rather than Parks' ruby or diamond studded ones. Once dressed, he was led out to the central courtyard near the HJ tower, a massive crucifix welded to its side. The white, twenty-foot-tall statue of Jesus stood a few yards from the tower. A podium was staged in front of the crucifix and Parks waited patiently beside it. Once again, the entire congregation filled the courtyard to witness the event.

Jake took his place before the altar and Parks winked as he stepped up on a stool behind it. Parks flashed one of his patented smiles. Jake rolled his eyes. The sound of guitars strumming "The Wedding March" floated over the scene. He glanced at the statue of Jesus and saw five disciples strumming their hearts out. He turned to look back at the congregation and saw Tomoko walk down the aisle wearing an ivory wedding dress with tiny blue and red flowers embroidered around the hem and sleeves. She carried a bouquet of white water lilies and wore one in her hair as well.

His heart skipped a beat. He took in a sharp breath. He loved her with all his heart. She was right, the rest of this silly ceremony was meaningless, they were bonded together and this was just a formality to show their commitment to a group of witnesses.

The ceremony was short and sweet. He spent all his time holding Tomoko's hands and grinning at her. A tear welled up when he said, "I do." He was shocked when Jairaj presented him with a simple silver ring to place on her finger. She held a matching band to put on his hand.

And then the moment came when Parks said, "You may kiss the bride."

Jake grabbed Tomoko and passionately kissed her. The crowd howled with pleasure when he dipped her back. She pulled his face in closer, almost throwing him off balance. He regained his footing, just when an explosion knocked him down to the ground, a concussion ringing in his ears.

Chapter 57
Hope

Jake jumped up from the cobblestone courtyard and checked Tomoko.

"I'm fine!" she yelled as another shell exploded amongst the scattering congregation. Screams rang out as bodies were torn and lifted into the air. A doorway leading to the beach framed a gunboat. The ship lobbed shells at them from the harbor. Two Federale HJs circled overhead, dropping soldiers on rappel lines. The airships were light armor class, about half the size of Parks' ship. They lacked missiles or tank busters, but their mini-guns were devastating enough.

The flock was surprisingly organized and quick for people without Chips. Parks, or someone in his ministry, must have been using military discipline to train them. Most dove into the buildings while others ran out of bungalows with state-of-the-art combination rifles. The armed Disciples fired rocket grenades at the Federale HJs. Jake ran with Tomoko for the cover of one of the bungalows. The building housing the Nemp exploded. Dozens of dead lay in the courtyard and explosions were going off everywhere.

They reached the bungalow. Two of their brethren threw them weapons. Jake caught an HK V2 and Tomoko caught a combination rifle. Another explosion went off. They averted their eyes as dirt sprayed the bungalow's interior.

"Give me your gun!" Tomoko shouted. "I have no idea how to use this!"

They swapped weapons and squatted just inside the doorway. He heard Parks' HJ fire up and launch three missiles. Within seconds, the two Federale HJs erupted into balls of flame. One smashed into the roof of the hotel, the other crashed on the outside of the compound. He assumed the third missile hit the ship in the harbor. He couldn't help but cheer.

There were a dozen firefights going on. He used the machine gun mode on the combination rifle to target the Federale troops who had rappelled into the compound. He spotted one in his scope and saw the familiar Chip receptor on the helmet. This attack was probably being orchestrated by Consortium God Heads.

Tomoko fired at a Federale running out of the hotel. "Stay back! Stay down!" he yelled and pointed to the inside of the bungalow. A large explosion in the hotel's lobby blew rubble and bodies into the courtyard. More Federale soldiers flowed in from the smoking opening. A few Disciples opened fire, killing many and forcing their retreat back into the hole.

Tomoko fired a kill shot at a Federale and stepped away from her cover.

A spike of panic hit Jake. "Wait here!" He saw the incredulous look on her face. He had just gotten her back and could not take losing her again. "Please!"

"This is what we signed up for, hubby. Only the fight came to us this time."

"It did, but not here, not now. Not on our wedding day. Please, just take cover and keep your head down!"

She opened her mouth to argue, but then backed into the dark recesses of the bungalow for better cover. He ran along the edge of the compound toward the hotel, checking every window and opening as he advanced. There were hundreds dead in the courtyard. Red blood looked electric against so much pure white cloth.

He activated the grenade launcher on his weapon and cautiously moved toward the smoking hole where the lobby had been. Half of the third story was now on fire from the HJ crash. A few dozen disciples advanced on either side of the decimated lobby.

One disciple shouted in Spanish toward the hotel, "Throw down your weapons! We have you surrounded!"

Jake rolled his eyes. These were chipped soldiers with every type of sensor you could imagine. He backed away to the north end of the building and found an overturned table blocking the path between the hotel and the pool house. He peered over the table to see the back of a chipped soldier disappear into an open doorway. Jake carefully pulled the table aside, then crouched low and ran to see where the soldier had entered the building. He peered into the doorway. There was a line of six soldiers, preparing to launch an attack. He saw more across the hall on the other side of the smashed lobby. He activated every barrel on the combo rifle and let loose. Grenades, flame, and bullets vomited out. The room disappeared in a maelstrom of explosions and fire. A few shots whizzed by but he figured there was nothing to target through his wall of carnage. After unleashing hell for ten seconds, he jumped back from the doorway and hugged the wall a few feet from it. The hair on his arms and his eyebrows had been singed. He took a deep breath. Yells echoed from the courtyard. The disciples were charging the lobby to press the offensive.

He checked his ammunition. The gun held two grenades and about two seconds of flame. The weapon had been full when he had taken it from Tomoko. He listened; the gunfire was less intense. He breathed a sigh of relief.

A series of booms vibrated the air. A cannon was being fired somewhere within the city. Parks' HJ howled away from their location. Then the shells struck. The explosions rocked the ground. He dove against the wall of the hotel as a window above shattered, pelting him with glass. Shards cut his right arm and leg. He stood up and glanced into the courtyard. The block of bungalows where he had left Tomoko was burning. He screamed. He ran into the courtyard, tearing another gash in his leg on the broken table. He sprinted as hard as he could toward Tomoko's bungalow. Fire raged in the building next door but had not reached her dwelling.

He threw down his gun and dove onto the rubble. There was a large beam lying at a forty-five degree angle from the roof to the floor. He saw a hand surrounded by white cloth. Screaming with grief and rage, he clawed away the debris as fast as he could. He did not notice the smoke and sand swirling in his eyes from Parks' HJ landing in the courtyard. *Please… not Tomoko.* He couldn't help picturing her smile, their time on the boat together. *Please let her be walking up behind me right now, wondering why I'm so desperately digging up this person who looks strangely like her.*

He freed Tomoko and gently lifted her body. She felt incredibly light and limp. His heart screamed with grief. Tears streamed down his cheeks as he staggered out of the smoldering ruin. He set her down in the courtyard and felt around her body. She had broken ribs, broken legs and he could tell by the blood in her eyes she had a fractured skull. He desperately wanted to move her but was not sure where to go. He remembered seeing a first aid station but it had been destroyed in the first salvo from the gunboat. The smoke lifted for a moment and he spotted the HJ and Parks running up to him.

"Jake! We routed them, but there are more on the way. Everyone is evacuating to our tourist fleet—" Parks stopped when he realized Tomoko was lying beside Jake.

Jake could not contain his desperation. "We need to airlift her to a hospital!"

Parks nodded. "I was going to say you have a seat on the HJ."

Jake gingerly lifted Tomoko and walked with Parks toward the airship. As they worked their way around bodies, bricks, and craters, Parks checked Tomoko's pulse. Jake saw the troubled expression on his face. She was alive, but for how long?

Saakaar reached out from the HJ ramp to help but Jake shook his head. Once inside, Devani attached an emergency stretcher kit to a bulkhead. Jake couldn't help but stare at the dead, glassy eyes of Jairaj lying on a similar stretcher on the other side of the cargo hold. Saakaar was stoic, but Jake could tell the man was having a difficult time holding back his own grief. When Devani was finished, Jake tenderly laid Tomoko on the stretcher and strapped her in. He felt the airship lift off. Then he heard the sound of Saakaar and Devani hitting the deck plates.

He wheeled around to see both of them clutching their chests. The airship settled back down to earth. Jake grabbed a military knife from one of the kits and dove onto Devani's body, but she was dead. He moved onto Saakaar and cut into the back of the Sikh's head. His Chip was encased in a semi-solid blob of metallic ooze; Max2. The more he pulled the more stringy metallic snot flowed out of Saakaar's head and neck. The virus seemed to be multiplying as if it were desperate to stay within its host.

He hit the internal emergency Nemp generator. The ship instantly shut down. The cockpit door slid open and Parks fell into their compartment, gasping and clutching his chest. He held a bloody knife in his hand with a glittering chip and a string of metallic ooze attached to it.

Jake grabbed a wad of gauze from a first aid kit and wiped out the wounds of Saakaar and Parks, pulling as much of the virus out as he could.

Parks whispered, "Not sure how they pulled off that kill command and missed you… unless you've got a specific type of Max2?" He smiled.

Jake checked on Saakaar. He was dead. He placed his fingers on Tomoko's carotid artery. Her pulse was fading fast. He looked at the inoperative sensors and electro-stimulus machines hooked up to her. "I need to switch off the Nemp. We need to get airborne."

Parks nodded. Jake pulled back Parks' hand holding the gauze. It was full of bloody silver-metallic goo. The material continued to ooze from the gash in Parks' neck, but the volume was decreasing. Jake gave Parks a new gauze pad and ran to the Nemp generator. He switched it off. He jumped into the cockpit and fired up the HJ. It took a few seconds for all the systems to come back online. There was quite a bit of satellite jamming, but he was able to spot a few bogies coming in. There was tank movement on the ground, too.

Parks leaned his head in. "I'd better read her the last rites."

A desperate thought entered Jake's head. "Play the song!" He spun around to catch eye contact. "Eberstark! Please just try it!"

Alarms rang. Bullets ricocheted off the canopy. The HJ's miniguns engaged and began retaliation.

"Okay." Parks nodded and closed the bulkhead door. Jake raised the bird into the air and switched on the targeting computer. He locked the missiles onto all three of the incoming HJs and fired. He then swung the ship around and switched on the tank busters. Rage blinded him to the point where he did not notice that one of the HJs had deployed a counter measure. The missile he had fired had been intercepted and destroyed.

Proximity alarms howled. Bullets hit the ship's armor. He swung the bird toward the incoming HJ, fired the afterburners, and unleashed both tank busters. The light duty HJ disintegrated. He turned around again and ripped into the tanks. It was all over in less than five minutes. He swung the ship around again and headed out low over the ocean. He set the controls for Manaus, Brazil and locked in the autopilot. He tried to open the door, but it was jammed. "Parks!"

Parks saw the desperation in his friend's eyes. Alarms howled and bullets struck the canopy. He owed it to Jake. "Okay." He saw instant relief on Jake's face and he was able to focus on the fight.

The moment Parks closed the door, he called up Smoov Z's "Baby Can't We Talk" on his Omni. The ship rocked as he stumbled over to Tomoko. Her eyes were glassy as he checked her pulse. She was dead. *You said you'd play the song.*

It's pointless.

Keep your word. Play the song.

He pressed play. Parks didn't have a clue if Jake's impulsive idea would work, but, despite his own preaching, he knew Dr. Eberstark was legitimate. Tomoko's essence might be saved, but only through a Third Eye connected to an AI. Maybe Eberstark had created a cyber-version of purgatory, one last stop before the final frontier. But if it was possible to upload a soul to the Cyber-Wire, he didn't know how to create a link to make it happen. Perhaps there was something out there waiting to suck them up when death came near and prevent the passage to heaven.

Jairaj and Saakaar had both approached him with the idea that the background carrier wave they found on the Cyber-Wire might be the AI on the moon, or maybe Ai-li herself, or perhaps something altogether different. He knew Jake did not believe in heaven, but Parks maintained complete faith that he would meet all his loved ones along with The Holy Father when he passed. He had railed against technology in the name of the Lord yet he used the weapons of technology to wage His war on Earth.

If Jake could not be admitted into heaven maybe he could find Tomoko in Eberstark's man-made purgatory? Seemed like a cold and lonely place to Parks. He stared at Tomoko's lifeless eyes. He believed people found the grace of God as long as they were moral and good. She was in heaven now, maybe they would see her soon.

When the song finished, he read her the last rights and then went to each of his fallen comrades and did the same. He was without a Chip now and wondered how long God would see fit that he fight this war in His name. If he were truly God's messenger, he would see it through. It was a long list of "what ifs."

The HJ stopped shaking and the ride smoothed out. He prayed, "Lord keep my Devani, Tomoko, and the boys safe. I know you'll treat them better than humanity has."

He heard the pounding at the door and realized he had locked it to prevent Jake from hearing the trigger song.

Jake pushed his way into the cargo hold the moment Parks unlocked the door. He fought back his anger and grief over Tomoko. "Well?"

"I did what you asked." Parks placed a hand on Jake's shoulder. "But she was dead before I could play the song. I'm sorry, Jake."

He collapsed next to the lifeless figure of his wife. He stared into her eyes and closed them. *Why is this happening? Why did I tell her to hide? She would have been safer with me! We fight so hard to save humanity and this is the reward we get?*

"I believe she's in heaven, my friend. You will meet again."

Jake turned on Parks. "I don't know what I believe anymore. Right now I have half a mind to skydive without a chute, or turn our nukes on the nearest Consortium hive and watch the fuckers burn."

Parks sat by Devani while Jake wept. The hum of the engines drowned out the sound of their sorrow.

After a few minutes, Parks' voice cracked. "The last time I had to cut out a Chip, you were the one that had the heart attack." Parks gripped his chest. "Fucking hurts!"

"Just take it easy. Give your body a chance to recover." His words felt hollow. He checked Parks' wound. The gauze held less of the bloody metallic goo and his neck appeared clean. He went to the med kit and pulled out more gauze, passing the wad to Parks. "Looks like gauze works in soaking up the blood and drawing out the crap. Hold this on the wound to be sure." His eyes wandered back to Tomoko, hoping to see some sign that his hairbrained idea worked. Nothing. His heart leapt up into this throat and he wanted to scream. If only he were chipped and this was some sick God Head illusion.

Parks held the gauze in place. "Thank you."

"No, thank you." Jake pinched the bridge of his nose as hard as he could. The pain felt good.

Parks laid a hand on him. "Life is an endless rapid. All we can do is keep our paddles ready and try to stay afloat."

Jake grit his teeth. "What Psalm is that?"

"Something my father used to tell me when I was particularly down."

Jake snorted. He quivered with grief and rage. He pictured the entire Consortium burning in hellfire.

Parks turned to the corpses. "I lost Estancia, Devani and the Sikhs today. I know I'll meet them in heaven; my faith is what keeps me going. Find your faith, my friend. Fight on."

Parks was mad-dog crazy, and yet Jake wanted to grasp at any shred of hope. He was losing friends and loved ones left and right. If there was a God, he turned his back on this planet long ago.

"Where are we headed?" Parks asked.

"Manaus, Brazil."

Parks shook his head. "They attacked almost all of my chapters. Cobalt has undergone a hostile take over. I'm off the board. China and India are now lobbying the UN to join them in attacking the Middle East. Seems The

Consortium has succeeded in framing the Muslims for the recent nuclear attacks. Although from the clip I saw, everyone on the UN floor is a Pin Head zombie. We need to head toward the lesser of two evils."

"You want us to move back into the crosshairs? Join the Jihad Brotherhood?"

"Mecca. It's the largest concentration of God Heads in the world." Parks smiled. "Even the Jihadists aren't above using technology when it's to their advantage."

Jake nodded. He felt as if he were a God Head, floating in his own mind, pushing his body to go to the cockpit and set a course for Mecca. Like the ship, he was on autopilot now, committed to ending the madness, or die trying. *Perhaps I'll meet Tomoko in heaven… a fool can always hope.*

About the Author

Sven Michael Davison is a full-time husband, father, and manager in a creative design agency in Los Angeles. He has written screenplays, trailers and special feature content for DVD and Blu-ray. *State of Union* is his fourth novel.

Other Works by Sven Michael Davison

STATE OF MIND – Science Fiction Thriller
Book One of "The God Head Trilogy"

Your thoughts are not your own...

Los Angeles 2030: You can eat what you want and never gain weight. You can also call a friend while surfing the web without a phone or computer. All this and more will be yours following the simple installation of a P-Chip in your brain.

After botching the arrest of the governor's son, Commander Jake Travissi is banned from law enforcement. The workaholic homicide cop spirals into depression... until he is given a rare second chance. The price? Volunteer for Chip implantation and join Homeland Security's experimental Enhanced Unit.

STATE OF BEING – Science Fiction Thriller
Book Three of "The God Head Trilogy" to be released in the spring of 2013.

The Child of Darkness is Light...

Through the viral form of The Chip, The Consortium has solidified their rein over the earth. Freedom's last hope lies with the free colonies on the moon, artificial intelligence, and the will power of Jake Travissi. But another AI is born from the minds who would control us, and he has no interest in the weakness of flesh.

Check out www.stateofmindbook.com for updates.

DREAMS, FAITH & AMMUNITION – Historical Fiction, Memoir, Adventure

Two men, three timelines, one location; *Dreams, Faith & Ammunition* is a novel about seeking the Promised Land. In the nineteenth century, one man seeks it literally, first by following Joseph Smith, and then James Strang to build a Kingdom of God on earth. In the twentieth century, another man envisions the Promised Land as the rewards and lifestyle he will achieve once he finishes his great American novel.

Both men move to Beaver Island, Michigan to fulfill their ideals. Both men face unforeseen obstacles and must overcome personal demons in their journey of faith and suicidal depression.

BLOCKBUSTER – Action-Adventure, Satire

If a bullet-proof action hero were to exist in the real world… would he have a complex about being out of the ordinary? If a born loser was unable to break into Hollywood, but found identity after joining a terrorist organization, would he continue to be a wanna-be filmmaker? What if LA's Chief of Police were suffering from a brain tumor during a terrorist attack? … And the FBI agent on the scene practiced medieval medicine? What would happen if you took all of these characters and placed them in a hostage situation on a major motion picture studio lot and tossed in some of Hollywood's biggest stars as the hostages?

Before there was a terror-alert status in America, during a time when we could fly without removing our clothing in security lines, terror struck the heart of Tinsel-Town. *Blockbuster* satirizes the motion picture industry, and the marketing juggernauts it churns out at a record-breaking pace.

Horace Thimble—aka Mohamed—has invaded Mogul Pictures and is holding A-list actors and all of the studio's summer releases hostage. However, his fool-proof plan doesn't take into account special effects wizard, Dexter Brubeck's, lucky talent for survival. Although Horace has the LAPD, FBI and the nation on it's knees, it's the insurgent team of Dexter and his ex-girlfriend, Heather, who become the real threat to the terrorist's plans.